He was a stranger, and for the first time she was in a situation in which she had no control . . . and it was all her own doing.

"You're ripe. Like a hothouse peach," he murmured.

"Nonsense," Amanda said, annoyed that his flattery had caused a faint stirring of pleasure in her. Perhaps it was the knowledge that she would never see him again after this night that excited her.

"You have a beautiful complexion, a perfectly shaped mouth—"

"It's too large," she informed him.

He stared at her lips for a long moment. When he spoke again his voice was a bit gruffer than before. "Your mouth is well suited for what I have in mind. And take down your hair . . . let me see."

"What?" His command caused her to laugh suddenly.

"Haven't you ever taken your hair down for a man before?"

Amanda had never felt this way. Her heart was beating so hard it made her dizzy.

"Are you by chance trying to seduce me?" she whispered.

By Lisa Kleypas

SCANDAL IN SPRING
DEVIL IN WINTER • IT HAPPENED ONE AUTUMN
SECRETS OF A SUMMER NIGHT
AGAIN THE MAGIC • WORTH ANY PRICE
LADY SOPHIA'S LOVER • ONLY IN YOUR ARMS
ONLY WITH YOUR LOVE • WHEN STRANGERS MARRY
SUDDENLY YOU • WHERE DREAMS BEGIN
SOMEONE TO WATCH OVER ME
STRANGER IN MY ARMS • BECAUSE YOU'RE MINE
SOMEWHERE I'LL FIND YOU
PRINCE OF DREAMS • MIDNIGHT ANGEL
DREAMING OF YOU • THEN CAME YOU

And the Anthologies

WHERE'S MY HERO?
THREE WEDDINGS AND A KISS

ATTENTION: ORGANIZATIONS AND CORPORATIONS
Most Avon Books paperbacks are available at special quantity discounts for bulk purchases for sales promotions, premiums, or fund-raising. For information, please call or write:

Special Markets Department, HarperCollins Publishers, Inc., 10 East 53rd Street, New York, New York 10022-5299.
Telephone: (212) 207-7528.   Fax: (212) 207-7222.

LISA KLEYPAS

SUDDENLY YOU

AVON BOOKS
An Imprint of HarperCollinsPublishers

This is a work of fiction. Names, characters, places, and incidents are products of the author's imagination or are used fictitiously and are not to be construed as real. Any resemblance to actual events, locales, organizations, or persons, living or dead, is entirely coincidental.

AVON BOOKS
An Imprint of HarperCollins*Publishers*
10 East 53rd Street
New York, New York 10022-5299

Copyright © 2001 by Lisa Kleypas
ISBN-13: 978-0-06-125935-7
ISBN-10: 0-06-125935-7
www.avonromance.com

First Avon Books special printing: December 2006
First Avon Books paperback printing: June 2001

Avon Trademark Reg. U.S. Pat. Off. and in Other Countries, Marca Registrada, Hecho en U.S.A.
HarperCollins® is a registered trademark of HarperCollins Publishers Inc.

Printed in the U.S.A.

10 9 8 7 6 5 4 3 2 1

To my brother, Ki,
for giving me constant love, support and understanding,
and for always being there when I need you.
I'm so lucky to be your sister.

—L.K.

Prologue

London
November 1836

"What is your preferred style, Miss Briars? Would you prefer your man to be fair-haired or dark? Average height or tall? English or foreign?" The madam was astonishingly businesslike, as if they were discussing a dish to be served at a supper-party rather than a man to be purchased for the evening.

The questions made Amanda cringe. She felt her face flame until her cheeks prickled, and she wondered if a man would feel this way the first time he visited a bordello. Fortunately, this bordello was far more discreet and tastefully furnished than she had imagined. There were no shocking paintings or vulgar engravings, and no clients or prostitutes anywhere in sight. Mrs. Bradshaw's establishment was quite attractive, the walls covered in moss-green damask, the private receiving room filled with comfortable

1

pieces of Hepplewhite furniture. A small marble-topped table was positioned neatly beside an Empire sofa adorned with golden dolphin scales.

Reaching for a little gold-painted pencil and a tiny notebook perched on the edge of the table, Gemma Bradshaw stared at her expectantly.

"I don't have a preferred style," Amanda said, mortified but determined. "I will trust your judgment. Just send someone on the evening of my birthday, one week from today."

For some reason, that entertained Mrs. Bradshaw greatly. "As a gift to yourself? . . . What a delightful idea." She stared at Amanda with a lingering smile that illuminated her angular face. The madam was not beautiful, or even pretty, but she possessed a smooth complexion and rich red hair, and a tall, voluptuous body. "Miss Briars, may I ask if you are a virgin?"

"Why do you wish to know?" Amanda countered warily.

One of Mrs. Bradshaw's ruddy, perfectly plucked brows arched in amusement. "If you are indeed willing to trust my judgment, Miss Briars, I must know the particulars of your situation. It is not often that a woman like you comes to my establishment."

"Very well." Amanda took a deep breath and spoke rapidly, driven by something close to desperation rather than the good sense she had always prided herself on. "I am a spinster, Mrs. Bradshaw. In one week's time I will be thirty years old. And yes, I am still a v-virgin—" She stumbled over the word and continued resolutely. "But that does not mean that I must remain one. I have come to you because it is general knowledge that you are able to provide whatever a client asks for. I know it must be a surprise, for a woman like me to come here—"

"My dear," the madam interrupted with a soft laugh, "the time has long passed since I was capable of being surprised by anything. Now, I believe that I understand your dilemma quite well, and I will indeed provide an agreeable solution. Tell me this . . . do you have any preferences as to age and appearance? Any particular likes or dislikes?"

"I would prefer a young man, but no younger than myself. And not too old. He doesn't have to be handsome, although I would not wish for him to be unsightly. And clean," Amanda added as a thought occurred to her. "I do insist on cleanliness."

The pencil scratched busily in the notebook. "I don't foresee that will be a problem," Mrs. Bradshaw replied, with a glimmer of something in her pretty, dark eyes that looked suspiciously like laughter.

"I will also insist on discretion," Amanda said crisply. "If anyone should ever find out what I've done—"

"My dear," Mrs. Bradshaw said, arranging her body more comfortably on the sofa, "what do you think would become of my business were I to allow my clients' privacy to be violated? I'll have you know, my employees cater to some of the most highly placed members of Parliament, not to mention the wealthiest lords—and ladies—of first society. Your secret will be safe, Miss Briars."

"Thank you," Amanda said, filled with equal parts of relief and terror, and a terrible suspicion that she was making the greatest mistake of her life.

Chapter 1

Amanda knew exactly why the man on her doorstep was a prostitute. From the moment she had ushered him inside in the manner of someone harboring an escaped convict, he had stared at her in dumbfounded silence. Obviously he lacked the cranial equipment necessary to pursue a more intellectually challenging occupation. But, of course, a man didn't need brains to do what he had been hired for.

"Hurry," she whispered, tugging anxiously on his muscular arm. She slammed the door behind him. "Do you think that anyone saw you? I hadn't thought that you would simply appear at the front door. Aren't men of your profession trained to show some discretion?"

"My . . . profession," he repeated in a bemused manner.

Now that he was safely concealed from public view, Amanda allowed herself to stare at him thoroughly. Despite his apparent dullness of wit, he was remarkably good-looking. Beautiful, re-

5

ally, if one could apply such a word to an obviously masculine creature. He was big-framed and lean, with shoulders that seemed to span the width of the front door. The layers of his gleaming black hair were thick and neatly cut, and his tanned face glowed from a precise shave. He had a long, straight nose and a voluptuary's mouth.

And he had a pair of remarkable blue eyes that approximated no other shade she had ever seen. Except, perhaps, at the shop where the local chemist made batches of ink by boiling Indigofera plants and copper sulfate together for days until they formed a blue so dark and deep that it approached violet. And yet his eyes did not have the angelic quality one might usually associate with such a color. They were shrewd, seasoned, as if he had gazed far too often at an unsavory side of life that she herself had never seen.

Amanda could easily understand why women would pay for his company. The thought of hiring this masculine, opulent-eyed creature to do one's bidding was extraordinary. And tempting. Amanda was ashamed by her secret response to him, the hot and cold chills that chased through her body, the burning color that rose to the crests of her cheeks. She had resigned herself to being a dignified spinster . . . she had even convinced herself that there was great freedom in her unmarried circumstance. However, her troublesome body didn't seem to understand that a woman should no longer be bothered by desire at her age. At a time when twenty-one was considered to be old, thirty was most definitely on the shelf. She was past her prime, no longer desirable. An "ape-leader" was what people called such a woman. If only she could make herself accept her fate.

Amanda forced herself to stare directly into his extraordinary blue eyes. "I intend to be frank, Mr. . . . no, never mind, don't tell me your name, we shan't be acquainted long enough for me to require it. You see, I've had a chance to reflect on a rather hastily made decision, and the fact is . . . well, I've changed my mind. Please do not receive this as a personal affront. It has nothing to do with you or your appearance, and I will certainly make that clear to your employer, Mrs. Bradshaw. You are a fine-looking man, in fact, and very punctual, and I have no doubt that you are very good at . . . well, at what you do. The simple truth is, I have made a mistake. We all make mistakes, and I am certainly no exception. Every great once in a while, I do make a small error in judgment—"

"Wait." He lifted his large hands in a defensive gesture, his intent gaze fastened on her flushed face. "Stop talking."

No one in her adult life had ever dared to tell her to stop talking. Surprised into silence, Amanda struggled to stem the cascade of words that threatened to flow from her lips. The stranger folded his arms across his muscular chest and leaned his back against the door to stare at her. The glow from the lamp in the tiny entrance hall of her fashionable London house cast a fringe of shadows from his long lashes onto the stark, elegant planes of his cheekbones.

Amanda couldn't help thinking that Mrs. Bradshaw had excellent taste. The man she had sent was surprisingly well groomed and prosperous-looking, dressed in fashionable but solidly traditional attire, a black coat and charcoal-gray trousers, and black shoes polished to an impeccable gleam. His starched white shirt was snowy against his swarthy skin, and his gray silk cravat was arranged in a simple, perfect knot. Before this moment, had Amanda been pressed to describe her ideal man, she would have described him as blond and light-skinned and fine-boned. Now she was forced to revise her opinion entirely. No fair-haired Apollo could begin to compare with this large, robustly handsome man.

"You are Miss Amanda Briars," he said, as if requiring confirmation. "The novelist."

"Yes, I write novels," she replied with forced patience. "And you are the gentleman whom Mrs. Bradshaw sent at my request, are you not?"

"I seem to be," he said slowly.

"Well, you have my apologies, Mr. . . . no, no, don't tell me. As I explained, I have made a mistake, and therefore, you must go. Naturally I will pay for your services even though they are no longer required, as the fault is entirely mine. Just tell me what you usually charge, and we'll settle the matter immediately."

As he stared at her, a change came over his face, his bemusement giving way to fascination, the blue eyes sparkling with a devilish amusement that made her nerves twitch uncomfortably.

"Tell me what services were requested," he suggested gently, pushing away from the door. He moved closer until his body loomed over hers. "I'm afraid I never discussed the details with Mrs. Bradshaw."

"Oh, merely the basic ones." Amanda's poise eroded more rapidly with each second that passed. Her face felt terribly hot, and her heartbeat reverberated in every part of her body. "The usual thing." Blindly she turned toward the satinwood demilune table against the wall, where she had placed a wad of carefully folded pound notes.

"I always pay my debts, and I have put you and Mrs. Bradshaw to trouble for nothing, so I am more than willing to compensate—" She stopped with a strangled sound as she felt his hand close around her upper arm. It was unthinkable for a stranger to place his hand on any part of a lady's body. Of course, it was even more unthinkable that a lady should resort to hiring a male prostitute, and yet that was precisely what she had done. Miserable, she decided to hang herself before ever doing something so foolish again.

Her body went stiff at his touch, and she didn't dare move as she heard his voice right behind her head. "I don't want money." His deep voice was threaded with subtle amusement. "There is no charge for services you haven't received."

"Thank you." Both her fists clutched into one

white-knuckled ball. "Very kind of you. I will at least pay for a hack. There is no need for you to return home on foot."

"Oh, I'm not leaving yet."

Amanda's jaw dropped. She spun to face him with a horrified glance. What did he mean, he wasn't leaving? Well, he would be *made* to depart, whether he wished to or not! Rapidly she considered her options. Unfortunately, there were few at her disposal. She had given her servants—a footman, a cook, and a maid—the night off. No help from that quarter. And she certainly couldn't resort to shouting for assistance from a constable. The attendant publicity might be damaging to her career, and her writing was the sole means of support for the household. Spying an oak-handled umbrella in the porcelain stand by the door, she inched toward it as discreetly as possible.

"Are you planning to beat me away with that?" her unwanted guest inquired politely.

"If necessary."

An amused snort greeted her statement, and he touched her chin, nudging her to look up at him.

"Sir," she exclaimed. "Do you mind—"

"My name is Jack." The shadow of a smile crossed his lips. "And I'll leave soon enough, but not before we discuss a few things. I have some questions for you."

She sighed impatiently. "Mr. Jack, I have no doubt you do, but—"

"Jack is my first name."

"Very well . . . Jack." A scowl settled over her

features. "I would appreciate it if you would kindly leave without delay!"

He wandered farther into the entrance hall, seeming as relaxed as if she had invited him in for tea. Amanda was forced to reconsider her early opinion of his slow-wittedness. Now that he had recovered from the surprise of being yanked inside her house so quickly, his intelligence was showing signs of rapid improvement.

The stranger gave her house a sweeping glance of assessment, noting the classically designed pieces of furniture in her cream-and-blue parlor, and the mahogany pier table surmounted by a framed looking glass at the back of the entrance hall. If he was looking for fancy embellishment, or obvious signs of wealth, he was to be disappointed. Amanda couldn't bear pretension or impracticality, and so she had chosen furniture for function rather than for style. If she bought a chair, it must be large and comfortable. If she bought a side table, it must be sturdy enough to hold a stack of books or a big lamp. She did not like gilding and porcelain disks, nor all the carving and hieroglyphics that were currently fashionable.

As her visitor paused near the doorway of her parlor, Amanda spoke dryly. "Since it appears that you're going to do as you please regardless of my wishes, go right in and sit down. Is there something I can offer you? A glass of wine, perhaps?"

Although the invitation had been offered with

purest sarcasm, he accepted with a quick grin. "Yes, if you'll join me."

The flash of white teeth, the unexpected dazzle of his smile, caused a strange sensation to creep over her, rather like the feeling of sinking into a hot bath after a gray winter day. She was always cold. The damp, overcast climate of London seemed to sink into her bones, and in spite of her liberal use of foot warmers, lap blankets, hot baths, and brandy-laced tea, she was never far from feeling the chill.

"Perhaps I will take some wine," she heard herself say. "Please have a chair, Mr. . . . er, that is, Jack." She shot him an ironic glance. "Since you're in my parlor now, you may as well tell me your full name."

"No," he said quietly, the smile remaining in his eyes. "In view of the circumstances, I think we will remain on a first-name basis . . . Amanda."

Well, he certainly didn't lack nerve! She gestured abruptly for him to sit while she went to the sideboard. However, Jack remained standing until she had poured a glass of red wine for each of them. Only when she had lowered herself to the mahogany settee did he choose to occupy the nearby Trafalgar armchair. The light from the well-stocked fire in the white marble hearth flickered over his shining black hair and smooth, gold-tinted skin. He fairly gleamed with health and youth. In fact, Amanda began to wonder suspiciously if he wasn't a few years younger than she.

"Shall I make a toast?" her guest inquired.

"You obviously wish to," she returned crisply.

That drew a flashing grin from him, and he raised his glass to her. "To a woman of great boldness, imagination, and beauty."

Amanda did not drink. She frowned at him as he sipped from his glass. Really, it was shameful of him to force his way into her house, refuse to leave when he was asked, and then make jest of her.

She was an intelligent and honest woman who knew what she was . . . and she was no beauty. Her attractions were moderate at best, and that was only if one completely discounted the current feminine ideal. She was short, and while on some days she could be described as voluptuous, on others she was most definitely plump. Her hair was a reddish-brown, wildly chaotic mass of curls—hateful curls that successfully defied any substance or implement used to straighten them. Oh, she had nice skin with no pockmarks or blemishes, and her eyes had once been described as "fine" by some well-meaning friend of the family. But they were plain gray eyes, with no shade of green or blue to enliven them.

Without physical beauty, Amanda had chosen instead to cultivate her mind and imagination, which, as her mother had gloomily predicted, had been the final stroke of doom.

Gentlemen did not want wives with well-cultivated minds. They wanted attractive wives who never second-guessed or disagreed with them. And they certainly didn't seek women with vibrant imaginations who daydreamed about fictional characters in books. Therefore, Amanda's two prettier elder sisters had both caught husbands, and Amanda had resorted to novel-writing.

Her unwelcome guest continued to stare at her with those keen blue eyes. "Tell me why a woman with your looks should have to hire a man for her bed."

His bluntness offended her. And yet . . . there was something unexpectedly entertaining about the prospect of talking with a man without any of the usual social restraints.

"First of all," Amanda said tartly, "there's no need to patronize me by implying that I'm Helen of Troy when it's clear that I'm no beauty."

That earned her another arrested stare. "But you are," he said softly.

Amanda gave a decisive shake of her head. "Evidently you think I'm a fool who will easily succumb to flattery, or else your standards are quite low. Either way, sir, you are wrong."

A smile tugged at one side of his mouth. "You don't leave much open for discussion, do you? Are you this decided in all your opinions?"

She answered his smile with a wry one of her own. "Unfortunately, yes."

"Why is it unfortunate to be opinionated?"

"In a man, it's an admirable quality. In a woman, it is considered a defect."

"Not by me." He took a sip of wine and relaxed in his chair, studying her as he stretched out his long legs. Amanda didn't like the way he seemed to be settling in for a lengthy conversation. "I won't allow you to avoid my question, Amanda. Explain why you hired a man for the evening." His lively gaze dared her to be forthcoming.

Finding that she was gripping the stem of her wineglass too tightly, Amanda forced her fingers to unclench. "It's my birthday."

"Tonight?" Jack laughed softly. "Happy birthday."

"I thank you. Will you leave now, please?"

"Oh, no. Not if I'm your birthday present. I'm going to keep you company. You're not going to stay alone on such an important evening. Let me guess—today began your thirtieth year of life."

"How did you know my age?"

"Because women always react strangely to the thirtieth. I once knew a woman who draped all the mirrors in black cloth on that birthday, for all the world as if a death had occurred."

"She was mourning her lost youth," Amanda said shortly, and downed a large swallow of wine until it sent a flush of heat through her chest. "She was reacting to the fact that she had become middle-aged."

"You're not middle-aged. You're ripe. Like a hothouse peach."

"Nonsense," she muttered, annoyed by the fact that his flattery, empty as it was, had caused a faint stirring of pleasure in her. Perhaps it was the wine, or the knowledge that he was a stranger whom she would never see again after this evening, but she suddenly felt free enough to say anything she wanted to him. "I was ripe ten years ago. Now I'm merely preserved, and before long I'll be buried back in the orchard with the other pits."

Jack laughed and set aside his wine, then stood to remove his coat. "Pardon," he said, "but it's like a furnace in here. Do you always keep the house so hot?"

Amanda watched him warily. "It's damp outside, and I'm always cold. Most days I wear a cap and a shawl indoors."

"I could suggest other methods to keep yourself warm." Without asking for permission, he sat right beside her. Amanda huddled back against her side of the settee, clinging to the remnants of her composure.

Inwardly she was alarmed by the solid male body so easily within reach, the unfamiliar experience of sitting next to a man in his shirtsleeves. His fragrance teased her nostrils, and she drew in the alluring smell . . . male skin, linen, a light pungent note of expensive cologne. She had never realized how nice a man could smell. Neither of her sisters' husbands possessed this pleasing aroma. Unlike this fellow, they were both stodgy and respectable, one a professor at an exclusive school, the other a wealthy town merchant who had been raised to knighthood.

"How many years have you?" Amanda asked impulsively, her brows drawing together.

Jack hesitated a fraction of a second before replying. "Thirty-one. You're rather preoccupied with numbers, aren't you?"

He was a young-looking thirty-one, Amanda reflected. However, it was an unfair fact of life that men seldom showed their age as women did. "Tonight I am," she admitted. "However, tomorrow my birthday will be over, and I shan't give it another thought. I shall sail on into my remaining years, and try to enjoy them as I may."

Her pragmatic tone seemed to amuse him. "Good Lord, woman, you talk as if you're teetering on the edge of the grave! You're attractive, you're a celebrated novelist, and you're in your prime."

"I am *not* attractive," she said with a sigh.

Jack laid his forearm along the back of the settee, not seeming to care that he was occupying most of it and crowding her into the corner. His gaze swept over her with disconcerting thoroughness. "You have a beautiful complexion, a perfectly shaped mouth—"

"It's too large," she informed him.

He stared at her mouth for a long moment. When he spoke again, his voice was a bit gruffer than before. "Your mouth is well suited for what I have in mind."

"And I'm plump," Amanda said, now determined to explain all her defects.

"Perfectly so." His gaze dropped to her breasts in the most ungentlemanly inspection she had ever been subjected to.

"And my hair is wretchedly curly."

"Is it? Take it down and let me see."

"What?" His outrageous command caused her to laugh suddenly. She had never met such a presumptuous scoundrel in her life.

He glanced around the cozy room, and then his devilish blue gaze returned to hers. "No one's here to see," he said softly. "Haven't you ever taken your hair down for a man before?"

The stillness of the parlor was underlaid with the gentle snapping of the fire in the hearth and the sounds of their breathing. Amanda had never felt this way before, actually fearful of what she might do. Her heart was beating so hard that it made her dizzy. She gave a stiff little shake of her head. He was a stranger. She was alone in the house with him, and she was more or less at his mercy. For the first time in a very long while, she was in a situation in which she had no control. And it was all of her own making.

"Are you by chance trying to seduce me?" she whispered.

"There's no reason to fear me. I would never force myself on a lady."

Of course there would be no need. It seemed very likely that he had never heard the word "no" from a woman.

This was without doubt the most interesting situation that Amanda had ever found herself in. Her life had been spectacularly uneventful, in which the characters of her novels said and did all the forbidden things she herself would never have dared.

As if he could read her thoughts, her companion smiled lazily and leaned his chin on his hand. If he was indeed trying to seduce her, he was in no great hurry. "You're exactly as I imagined," he murmured. "I've read your novels . . . well, the last one, at least. Not many women write as you do."

Amanda never liked to discuss her work. She felt uncomfortable when she received effusive praise, and she was most definitely disgruntled by critics' opinions. However, she was keenly curious about *this* man's opinion of her work. "I wouldn't have expected a pr—a man of your . . . a cicisbeo," she said, "to read novels."

"Well, we have to do something in our spare hours," he said reasonably. "We can't spend all our time in bed. Incidentally, that's not how you pronounce it."

Draining the last of her wine, Amanda glanced at the sideboard, wishing for another glass.

"Not yet," Jack said, taking the empty glass from her hand and setting it on the small table just behind her. The movement brought him directly over her, and Amanda shrank back until she was nearly reclining on the upholstered arm of the settee. "I won't be able to seduce you if you have too much wine," he murmured. His warm breath touched her cheek, and although his body didn't quite meet hers, she sensed the solid, heavy weight of him poised over her.

"I w-wouldn't have thought you'd had such scruples," she said unsteadily.

"Oh, I have no scruples," he assured her cheerfully, "it's just that I like a bit of a challenge. And if you had any more wine, you would be too easy a conquest."

"You arrogant, vain—" Amanda began indignantly, until she saw from the rascally twinkle in his eyes that he was provoking her deliberately. She was both relieved and sorry when he moved away from her. A reluctant smile pulled at her lips. "Did you like my novel?" she couldn't resist asking.

"Yes, I did. At first I thought it would be typical silver-fork fare. But I liked the way your well-bred characters began to unravel. I liked the portrayal of decent people moved to deception, violence, betrayal . . . you don't seem to shrink from anything in your writing."

"Critics say my work is lacking in decency."

"That's because your underlying theme—that ordinary people are capable of extraordinary things in their private lives—makes them uncomfortable."

"You actually *have* read my work," Amanda said in surprise.

"And it made me wonder what kind of private life the proper Miss Briars might lead."

"Now you know. I'm the kind of woman who hires a cicisbeo for her own birthday."

A smothered laugh greeted her rueful statement. "*That's* not the way to pronounce it, either." His shrewd blue gaze traveled over her, and when he spoke again, his voice changed. The amusement was tempered by a note that even in her inexperience, Amanda recognized as purely sexual. "Since you haven't yet asked me to leave . . . take down your hair."

When Amanda didn't move, only stared at him with round, unblinking eyes, he asked quietly, "Afraid?"

Oh, yes. All of her life, she had feared this . . . the risk, the possible rejection and ridicule . . . she had even feared the disappointment of discovering that intimacy with a man was indeed as base and repulsive as both her sisters had assured her it was. However, she had lately come to discover that there was something she feared even more: not ever knowing about the great tantalizing mystery that everyone else in the world seemed to have experienced. She had described passion so well in her novels, the yearning and madness and ecstasy it inspired, all the feelings she herself would never experience. And why should that be so? She had lacked the good fortune of having been loved so greatly by a man that he would seek to join his life with hers. But did that mean she should forever be undesired, unwanted, unclaimed? There were perhaps twenty thousand nights in a woman's lifetime. For at least one of them, she did not want to be alone.

Her hand seemed to reach for her hairpins of its own accord. She had pinned her hair the same way for the past sixteen years. The neat topknot was made by twisting her curling locks into a heavy coil. It took exactly a half-dozen pins to secure it as tightly as she preferred. In the mornings, her hair stayed relatively smooth, but as the day progressed, tiny curls never failed to spring out all over her head, forming a fuzzy halo around her face.

One pin, two, three . . . as she drew them out, she held them in her hand until the ends dug into the soft flesh of her palm. As the last pin came out, the coil dropped heavily, her long locks falling to one shoulder.

The stranger's blue eyes contained glints of fire. He began to reach for her hair, then checked the motion. "May I?" he asked gruffly.

No man had ever asked permission to touch her before. "Yes," she said, though it took two attempts before the word came out clearly. She closed her eyes, felt him move closer, and her scalp tingled as he sifted lightly through her hair, separating the coiled curls. His broad-tipped fingers moved amid the thick strands, brushing her scalp, spreading the mantle of curls over her shoulders.

His hand drifted to hers, gently prying her fingers open, making her drop the wire pins. His thumb smoothed over the tiny red marks the pins had made on her palm, and he brought her hand to his face to kiss the little sore spots.

His voice curled hotly inside her palm. "Your hand smells like lemons."

She opened her eyes and stared at him gravely.

"I scrub my hands with lemon juice to remove the ink stains."

The information seemed to amuse him, and lights of humor mixed with the heat in his gaze. He released her hand and played with a lock of her hair, his knuckles brushing her shoulder and making her breath catch. "Tell me why you requested a man from Madam Bradshaw, instead of seducing one of your acquaintances."

"Three reasons," she said, finding it difficult to speak while his hand was stroking through her hair. A flush of warmth came over her throat and cheeks. "First, I didn't want to sleep with a man and then forever be faced with him in social situations. Second, I haven't the skills to seduce anyone."

"Those skills are easily learned, peaches."

"What a ridiculous name," she said with an unsteady laugh. "Don't call me that."

"And third . . ." he prompted, recalling her to her explanation.

"Third . . . I am not attracted to any of the gentlemen of my acquaintance. I tried to imagine what it might be like, but none of them appealed to me in that way."

"What kind of man appeals to you?"

Amanda jumped a little as she felt his warm hand slide around the back of her neck. "Well . . . not a handsome one."

"Why?"

"Because handsomeness is always accompanied by vanity."

Jack grinned suddenly. "And I suppose ugliness is accompanied by a wealth of virtues?"

"I didn't say that," she protested. "It's just that I would prefer a man's looks to be ordinary."

"And his character?"

"Pleasant, not boastful, intelligent but not conceited, and good-humored. But not foolish."

"I think, peaches, that your ideal man is a paragon of mediocrity. And I think you're lying about what you really want."

Her eyes flew open, and she frowned in annoyance. "I'll have you know that I am honest to a fault!"

"Then tell me you don't want to meet a man like one of the characters in your novels. Like the hero of the last one."

Amanda snorted derisively. "An unprincipled brute who brings himself and everyone around him to ruin? A man who behaves like a barbarian and conquers a woman with no respect for her wishes? He was not a hero, sir, and I used him to illustrate that no good can come of such behavior." She warmed to the subject, recalling indignantly, "And readers dared to complain that there was no happy ending, when it was abundantly clear that he did not deserve one!"

"Part of you liked him," Jack said, giving her an intent stare. "I could see it in your writing."

She smiled uncomfortably. "Well, in the realm of fantasy, I suppose I did. But certainly not in reality."

The hand behind her neck closed in a gentle but secure grip. "Then here is your birthday present, Amanda. A night of fantasy." He loomed over her, his head and broad shoulders obliterating the firelight as he bent to kiss her.

Chapter 2

"Wait," Amanda said in a flash of panic, turning her head as Jack's mouth approached hers. His lips pressed on her cheek, a brush of intimate heat that astonished her. "Wait," she said again, her voice wobbling. Her face was turned full toward the fire, its yellow glow dazzling her eyes as she sought to avoid the stranger's exploring kisses. His mouth moved gently over her cheek and toward her ear, tickling the tiny wisps of hair just above it.

"Have you ever been kissed, Amanda?"

"Of course I have," she said with wary pride, but there seemed no way to explain that they hadn't been anything remotely like this. A stolen kiss in a garden or a perfunctory embrace beneath the holiday mistletoe wasn't at all comparable to being held in a man's arms, breathing in his scent, feeling the heat of his skin through the linen of his shirt. "I—I suppose you're very accomplished at it," she said. "In light of your profession."

That drew a flashing grin from him. "Would you like to find out?"

"First I want to ask you something. How . . . how long have you been doing this?"

. He understood her meaning at once. "Working for Mrs. Bradshaw? Not long at all."

Amanda wondered what would drive a man like this to prostitute himself. Perhaps he had lost his job, or been dismissed for making a mistake. Perhaps he had fallen into debt, and needed extra money. With his looks and wit and good bearing, there were many occupations he was well suited for. Either he was truly desperate, or he was lazy and dissolute.

"Do you have a family?" she asked.

"None to speak of. Do you?"

Hearing the change in his tone, Amanda glanced up at him. His eyes were serious now, and his face was so austerely beautiful that the very sight of him made her chest ache with pleasure. "My parents are gone," she told him, "but I have two older sisters, both married, and too many nephews and nieces to count."

"Why aren't you married?"

"Why aren't *you?*" she parried.

"I like my independence too well to relinquish any part of it."

"That's my reason, too," she said. "Besides, anyone acquainted with me will confirm that I'm uncompromising and obstinate."

He smiled lazily. "You just require the proper handling."

"Handling," she repeated tartly. "Perhaps you'd care to explain what you mean."

"I mean that a man who knows anything about women could have you purring like a kitten."

Annoyance and laughter billowed together in her chest . . . what a rogue he was! But she would not be deceived by his facade. Although his manner was playful, there was something underneath—a quality of patient watchfulness, a sense of restrained power—that made her nerves thrill in warning. He was no callow boy, but a fully mature man. And although she was not a worldly woman, she knew from the way he looked at her that he wanted something from her, whether it was her submission, her sexual favors, or simply her money.

Holding her gaze, he reached for the gray silk cravat around his neck, tugged it loose, and unwound it slowly, as if fearing any sudden move might frighten her. While she watched with wide eyes, he undid the first three buttons of his shirt, then leaned back and studied her flushed face.

In her childhood, Amanda had occasionally glimpsed her father's grizzled upper chest as he walked through the house in his dressing robe, and of course she had seen laborers and farming men with their shirts unbuttoned. However, she could never recall having seen anything like this, a man whose chest seemed to have been sculpted from bronze, the muscles so defined and heavy that they literally gleamed. His flesh looked hard and yet so warm, the firelight dancing over the smoothness, shadows settling in the indentations of muscle and the triangular hollow at the base of his throat.

She wanted to touch him. She wanted to put her mouth on that intriguing hollow, and draw in more of his tantalizing scent.

"Come here, Amanda." His voice was a low scrape of sound.

"Oh, I can't," she said unsteadily. "I—I think you should go now."

Jack leaned forward and caught her wrist gently in his fingers. "I won't hurt you," he whispered. "I won't do anything that you don't like. But before I leave you this evening, I'm going to hold you in my arms."

Confusion and desire swirled inside her, making her feel unanchored, helpless. She let him pull her forward until her short limbs rested stiffly against his much longer ones. He ran a large palm down her back, and she could feel a trail of sensation in its wake. His skin was hot, as if a fire burned right beneath the smooth golden surface.

Her breath shortened, and she closed her eyes, shivering, luxuriating in the feeling of being warm all the way down to her bones. For the first time in her life, she let her head fall into the waiting crook of a man's arm, and stared up at his shadowed face.

As he felt the trembling of her limbs, he made a crooning sound and cuddled her closer. "Don't be afraid, *mhuirnin*. I won't hurt you."

"What did you call me?" she asked in bewilderment.

He smiled down at her. "A small endearment. Did I neglect to mention that I'm half Irish?"

That explained his accent, the neat cultured tones tempered with a sort of musical softness that must be Celtic in origin. And it also explained why he had turned to Mrs. Bradshaw for employment. Often tradesmen and mercantile institutions would hire a lesser-qualified Englishman over an Irishman, preferring to give the Celts the dirtiest and most menial work.

"Do you have a distaste for the Irish?" Jack asked, staring steadily into her eyes.

"Oh, no," she said dazedly. "I was just thinking . . . that must be why your hair is so black and your eyes so blue."

"*A chuisle mo chroi,*" he murmured, stroking the curls back from her round face.

"What does that mean?"

"Someday I'll tell you. Someday." He held her for a long time until she felt steeped in his warmth, every nerve saturated and relaxed. His fingers slid to the high-buttoned neck of her brown-and-orange-striped gown, where muslin ruffles had been stitched to form a small ruff. With great care, and no particular hurry, he unfastened the first few buttons, baring her soft, cool throat. Amanda couldn't seem to control the rhythm of her lungs as they surged in unsteady expansions, her breasts rising repeatedly. Jack's dark head moved over her, and she made an inarticulate sound as she felt his mouth press against her throat, lips gently searching.

"You taste so sweet." The whispered words sent a shiver down her spine. Somehow, whenever she had imagined this intimacy with a man, she had thought of darkness and urgency and groping. She had not expected firelight and heat and this patient courting of her body. Jack's lips wandered in a velvet path from her throat to the sensitive opening of her ear, played lightly, and then Amanda jerked in surprise as she felt the tip of his tongue stroke along a tiny inner crevice.

"Jack," she whispered. "You don't have to play the lover for me. Truly . . . you are kind to pretend that I'm desirable, and you—"

She felt him smile against her ear. "You are an innocent, *mhuirnin*, if you think that a man's body reacts this way out of kindness."

As he spoke, Amanda became aware of an intimate pressure against her hip, and she immediately went still. Her face burned crimson, and thoughts flurried through her head like snowflakes in a wind-ravaged sky. She was mortified . . . and extremely curious. With her legs entangled in his, and her skirts riding to her knees, she could feel the powerful length of his thighs and the hard shape of his erection. She had never been held against a man's aroused body before.

"This is your chance, Amanda," he murmured. "I'm yours to do with as you like."

"I don't know what to do," she said unsteadily. "That's why I hired you."

He laughed and kissed the exposed part of her throat, where her pulse thrummed in a frantic rhythm. The situation seemed fantastical to her, so completely outside of all her experiences, that she felt as if she were someone other than Amanda Briars. The spinster with her quills and paper and ink-stained fingers, and old-maid's caps and foot-warming jars, had been replaced by someone who was soft . . . vulnerable . . . able to desire and be desired.

She realized then that she had always been a little afraid of men. Some women understood the opposite sex so easily, and yet this understanding had always eluded her. All she knew was that even in the bloom of her youth, men had never teased and flirted with her. They had talked to her about serious subjects and had treated her with respect and propriety, never suspecting that she might have liked them to make an improper advance or two.

And now here was this resplendent man, unquestionably a scoundrel, who seemed more than interested in the prospect of getting under her skirts. Why shouldn't she allow him to kiss and caress her? What good did her virtue do her? Virtue was a cold bedfellow; she knew that better than anyone.

Bravely she caught at the open edges of his shirt and urged his head down to hers. He complied at once, his mouth brushing softly over hers. She felt a shock of warmth, a rush of pleasure that paralyzed her. His weight settled on her a bit more heavily; his mouth teased and pressed harder until her lips parted. His tongue stroked inside her mouth, and she would have recoiled from the strangeness of it had her head not been wedged so securely in the crook of his arm. Sensation flared in the pit of her stomach and in areas of her body that she couldn't even name. She waited for him to taste her again . . . oh, the way he explored her mouth was odd and intimate and exciting, and she couldn't seem to prevent the small moan that rose in her throat. Her body relaxed slowly, and her hands came up to his head, stroking the coarse black silk of his hair, the cropped locks that tapered to a point at the nape of his neck.

"Unbutton my shirt," Jack murmured. He continued to kiss her while she fumbled with the buttons of his waistcoat and the placket of his linen shirt. The thin fabric was warm and scented from his body, crumpled from where it had been tucked inside his trousers. The skin of his torso was smooth and golden, rows of hard silken muscles contracting at her timid touch. His body radiated heat, luring her like a cat to a patch of sunlight.

"Jack," she said breathlessly, her hands creeping beneath his shirt to the long plane of his back, "I wish to go no further than this . . . I . . . this is quite enough of a birthday present for me."

He chuckled and nuzzled the side of her throat. "All right."

She huddled against his bare chest, greedily absorbing the heat and scent of him. "Oh, this is dreadful."

"Why dreadful?" he asked, smoothing and playing with her curls, his thumb venturing to her temple and grazing the fragile spot.

"Because sometimes it's better not to know what one is missing."

"Sweet," he whispered, and stole a kiss from her lips. "Sweet . . . let me stay with you a little longer."

Before she could answer, he kissed her more deeply than before, his large hands gently gripping her head through the mass of curls that spread everywhere. She strained upward toward his mouth and body, unable to stop herself from pressing as close as possible. A deep physical agitation, like nothing she had ever felt, welled inside her, and she arched against him in an effort to soothe it. He was strong, big-boned, able to overpower her so easily if he chose, and yet he was astonishingly gentle. Somewhere in the back of her mind, she wondered why she did not fear him as she should. She had been taught since childhood that men were not to be trusted, that they were dangerous creatures who could not control their own passions. Yet she felt safe with this man. She put her hand on his chest, where his shirt gaped open, and the strong, fast beat of his heart resounded against her palm.

He took his mouth from hers and stared down at her with eyes so dark they no longer looked blue. "Amanda, do you trust me?"

"Of course not," she said. "I don't know the first thing about you."

Laughter rustled from his chest. "Sensible woman." His fingers worked at the buttons of her bodice, deftly freeing the bits of carved ivory from their moorings.

Amanda closed her eyes, while her heartbeat became at once light and violent, like the thrashing of a panicked bird's wings. I'll never see him again after tonight, she told herself. She would let herself do these forbidden things with him, and forever afterward keep the memory in some private corner of her mind. A memory for herself alone. When she was an old woman, long accustomed to the years of solitude, she would still have the knowledge that she had once spent an evening with a handsome stranger.

The brown-striped fabric slid open, revealing a chemise made of silky zephyr cotton, overlaid with a lightly boned corset that hooked up the front. Amanda wondered if she should instruct him how to unhook the corset, but it immediately became evident that Jack was familiar with the process. Clearly this was not the first corset he had ever encountered. Her ribs were compressed slightly as he brought the front edges of the garment together and detached the row of small hooks with miraculous ease. After he urged her to pull her arms free of her gown, and she lay before him with her chest covered only in thin, nearly transparent cotton, Amanda felt horribly exposed. Her hands actually shook with the effort not to snatch up the bodice of her gown and cover herself.

"Are you cold?" Jack asked in apparent concern, noting the telltale tremor, and he drew her up against his chest. He was effortlessly strong, vital, the heat of his skin seeping through his linen shirt, and Amanda began to shiver for an entirely different reason.

Jack nudged the strap of her chemise down her arm, and lowered his mouth to the white curve of her shoulder. He touched her gently, the backs of his long fingers drifting over the round shape of her breast. His hand turned over, and his hot, slightly damp palm cupped the top of the slope until her nipple ached sweetly and rose into his hand. His fingertips toyed with her, stroking through the zephyr cotton, pinching tenderly. Amanda closed her eyes and turned her head enough to press her mouth to his cheek, lured by the faintly bristly surface. Her lips tingled as she dragged them down to the place beneath his jaw where the scratchiness blended into smooth, silken skin.

She heard Jack mutter something in Gaelic, his voice blurred and urgent, and he clasped her head in his large hands. He lowered her back to the settee cushions, and his head moved over her chest. His mouth caught at her breast, and he kissed and teased her through the cotton sheath. "Help me pull down your chemise," he said hoarsely. "Please, Amanda."

She hesitated, her rapid breath mingling with his, and then she moved to release her arms from the sleeves of her dress. She felt Jack tugging at her chemise until it crumpled in a thin ring around her waist, leaving her upper torso completely bare. It seemed impossible that she was stretched out on the settee with a man she didn't know, her body half naked, her corset discarded on the floor. "I should not be doing this," she said shakily, trying in vain to cover her plump breasts with her hands. "I should never have allowed you past the front door."

"True." He threw her a crooked grin as he removed his shirt completely, revealing a torso that seemed too perfectly muscular and finely honed to be real. Unbearable tension knotted inside her, and she struggled with inhibition and modesty as he bent over her. "Shall I stop now?" he asked, cuddling her against his long body. "I don't want to frighten you."

Her cheek pressed against his shoulder, and she relished the exhilarating sensation of pressing her bare skin against his. She had never felt so vulnerable, so *willing* to be vulnerable. "I'm not afraid," she said, her voice dazed and wondering, and she withdrew her hands from between their bodies, so that her breasts pushed directly against his chest.

An aching sound came from his throat, and he buried his face against her throat, kissing her, working his way downward. His mouth covered her nipple, tongue stroking the sensitive tip, and she bit her lip at the startling pleasure of it. The tip of his tongue circled lazily, tasting, tickling, while the heat of his mouth burned like steam. He moved to her other breast, making her whimper in frustration at his slowness, his endless leisure, as if time did not exist and he were going to spend forever feasting on her body.

He lifted her skirts and settled between her thighs, so that the hard ridge behind his trousers fitted against the front of her drawers, where the fine linen had become perplexingly damp. She lay motionless, though her entire body ached to lift upward into the weight and texture of him. Bracing his elbows on either side of her head, Jack stared at her flushed face. He rocked his hips into hers, and she gasped at the intimate pressure of him, sliding exactly against the place she wanted it most. He was wicked, to have such knowledge of a woman's body. The motion drew pleasure up from between her thighs and sent it flowing through intimate channels of her body. She felt drunk, vibrantly alive, stimulated beyond bearing. Gasping, she put her arms around his back and felt the heavy flex of muscle as he moved again.

There were still layers of clothing between them, trousers and shoes and undergarments, not to mention the troublesome heap of her skirts. Suddenly she wanted to be rid of it all, to feel his entire naked body against hers, and this longing shocked her even as she struggled to press closer to him. He seemed to understand what she wanted, for he gave an unsteady laugh and caught one of her hands in his. "No, Amanda . . . tonight you're going to remain a virgin."

"Why?"

His hand covered her breast, squeezing gently, and he dragged his half-open mouth over her throat. "Because there are a few things you need to know about me first."

Now that it seemed likely that he would *not* make love to her, it became the thing Amanda wanted most. "But I'll never see you again," she said. "And it's my birthday."

Jack laughed at that, his blue eyes gleaming, and he pressed a hard kiss to her mouth, and hugged her close while he murmured endearments in her ear. No one had ever said such things to her before. People were intimidated by her self-possession and no-nonsense demeanor. No man would ever dream of calling her adorable, sweet, darling . . . and certainly no one had ever made her *feel* that way. She both craved and hated the effect he had on her, the appalling sting of tears in her eyes, the heat of passion rising in her body. Now she knew exactly why she should never have sent for this mysterious man. It was indeed better not to know about this, when she would never have it again.

"Amanda," he whispered, mistaking the reason for her unshed tears. "I'll make you feel better . . . be still for me . . . let me . . ."

His hand searched beneath her skirts until he found the tapes of her drawers, his fingers working expertly to untie them. Her head whirled, and she lay still and trembling while her arms remained wrapped around his shoulders. He touched the soft skin of her stomach, thumb brushing lightly over her navel, and then his fingers slid downward to the place where she had never imagined being touched, where she tried never to touch herself. His hand smoothed over the patch of crisp curls, and then his fingertips searched carefully, making her hips jerk and twitch.

His Irish accent was thicker, heavier than before. "Is this where it aches, *mhuirnin*?"

She gasped against his throat. His fingertips teased and rubbed, finding the most exquisitely sensitive place of all, a tiny peak of flesh that quivered to life at his touch. Heat blossomed in her loins, breasts, head. She was a willing prisoner to his gentle manipulations, all her skin flushed and prickling from her scalp to her toes. One finger pressed and intruded until it slid inside her, the small penetration burning slightly as her body clasped him with a jolt of innocent reluctance. Her head fell back, and she looked up dizzily at his face. His eyes were a color she had never seen before, except perhaps in dreams ... bright, pure blue, filled with a sexual knowledge that stunned her. His finger flexed inside her while his thumb nudged the burgeoning little point of pleasure, and he repeated the maddening stroking until she arched upward with a shaken cry, unraveling, her volatile senses finally catching fire.

She rode on a lingering swell of feeling, drifting

through the warmth, until Jack finally pulled away with a muted groan and sat up, his face turned away from her. The withdrawal of his hands and mouth, the absence of his touch, were almost painful, and Amanda felt her entire body yearning for him. She realized that the release he had given her was not something he intended to allow himself. Tentatively she reached for him, her hand settling on his trouser-clad thigh as she tried to communicate her desire to give him the same pleasure she had just experienced. Still not looking at her, he took her hand from his leg and brought it to his mouth, turning her palm upward to receive his kiss.

"Amanda," he said gruffly, "I don't trust myself with you any longer. I have to leave while I'm still able."

Amanda was stunned by the dream-swept, far-away sound of her own voice when she replied. "Stay with me. Stay all night."

Jack threw her a wry glance, and she saw the flush that lingered on his cheekbones. Continuing to cradle her hand, he stroked his thumbs over her palm as if rubbing in the kiss he had placed there. "I can't."

"Is it . . . do you have another . . . engagement?" she asked tentatively, while a horrible feeling swept through her at the thought of him going from her arms to another woman's.

He laughed shortly. "Good God, no. It's just—" He broke off and gave her a moody, contemplative glance. "You'll understand soon." Bending over her, he brushed kisses on her chin, her cheek, her closed eyelids.

"I—I won't send for you again," she said uneasily while he reached for a nearby lap blanket and draped it over her.

Amusement curled richly in his voice. "Yes, I know."

She kept her eyes closed, listening to the rustling of clothing as he dressed himself before the fire. Floating on currents of shame and pleasure, she tried to consider all that had happened to her this evening.

"Good-bye, Amanda," he murmured, and then he was gone, leaving her disheveled and half dressed in the firelight. She kept the soft cashmere blanket over her bare shoulders, her hair coiling over her body and the arm of the settee.

Senseless ideas occurred to her . . . she wanted to visit Gemma Bradshaw and ask questions about the man she had sent. She longed to know more about Jack. But what purpose would that serve? He occupied a different world from hers: a sordid, secretive world. There was no possibility of a friendship with him, and although he had not taken money from her this time, he certainly would the next. Oh, she had not expected to feel this way, so guilty and yearning, her body still throbbing with delight, her skin tingling as if silk veils were being stroked over her. She thought of his finger reaching inside her, his mouth teasing her breast, and she pulled the blanket over her face with a mortified groan.

Tomorrow she would carry on with the rest of her life, just as she had vowed. But the rest of the night she would let herself drift in fantasies of the man who, already, was becoming more of a dream-figure than a real being.

"Happy birthday," she whispered to herself.

Chapter 3

After the death of Amanda's father, the decision to move to London had not been difficult. She could easily have stayed in Windsor. It was only about twenty-five miles from town and also harbored a few notable publishers. She had always lived in Windsor, and both her older sisters' families were located nearby, and the small but comfortable Briars House had been left to her in her father's will.

After her father's funeral, however, Amanda had sold the place promptly, drawing howls of protest from her sisters, Helen and Sophia. They had all been born in that house, the sisters told her angrily, and she had no right to sell a vital part of the family history.

Amanda had received the criticism with outward patience, but she had concealed a grim smile as she reflected that she had earned the right to do as she liked with the place. Perhaps Helen and Sophia still cherished a fondness for the house, but for five years it had been a prison to her. Her sisters had married and moved into homes of their own, while Amanda had remained with her parents and nursed each through their last illnesses. It had taken her mother three years to die of consumption, a slow and messy and singularly unpleasant process. And afterward came her father's long decline, fueled by various complaints that had led him to waste away to nothing.

Amanda had borne the load entirely on her own. Her sisters had been too busy with their own families to offer any assistance, and most friends and relatives had assured themselves that Amanda was competent to handle everything unaided. She was a spinster—what else was there for her to do?

One well-meaning aunt had even told Amanda of her belief that the Lord had kept her from marrying solely to provide someone to take care of her ailing parents. Amanda would have preferred the Almighty had made other arrangements. Apparently it had not occurred to anyone that Amanda might have caught a husband, had the remaining years of her youth not been expended in caring for her mother and father.

The years had been difficult emotionally and physically. Her mother, who had always been sharp-tongued and difficult to please, had suffered the ravages of consumption with a quiet dignity that had amazed Amanda. Near the end, her mother had been more loving and gentle-natured than Amanda could ever remember, and the day of her passing had been a wrenching one.

Her father, by contrast, had changed from a cheerful man to the most exasperating patient imaginable. Amanda ran constantly to fetch things for him, to prepare meals that he never failed to criticize, to satisfy hundreds of querulous demands that kept her too busy to do anything for herself.

Rather than allow herself to be poisoned with her own frustration, however, Amanda had started to write in the late evenings and early mornings. It had begun merely as a way to entertain herself, but with each page she had hoped her novel might be worthy of publication.

With two books published and both her parents gone, Amanda was free to do as she pleased. Her last years would be spent in the busiest, largest city in the world, among the million and a half people who populated it. Using the two thousand pounds left to her in her father's will, as well as the money from the sale of the house, Amanda took a small but elegant town house on the west side of London. She brought the two family servants with her—the footman, Charles, and a housemaid, Sukey—and hired a cook, Violet, once they arrived.

London was everything she had hoped it would be, and more. Now, after six months of living in the city, Amanda still awakened each morning with a sense of pleased surprise. She loved the dirt and clutter and bewildering fast pace of London, the way each day began with the raucous cries of street vendors outside and ended with the sounds of carriages and hacks rattling across the cobblestones to convey people to their evening pursuits. She loved the fact that on any night of the week she could attend one of many supper-parties, private dramatic readings, or literary discussions.

To her surprise, she was a recognizable figure in the literary culture of London. Many publishers, poets, journalists, and other novelists seemed to know her name, and to have read her work. Back in Windsor, acquaintances had regarded her writing as frivolous. Certainly no one had approved of the kind of novels she wrote, hinting that they were too vulgar for decent folk to read.

Amanda herself couldn't understand why her writing was so different from her own personality. Her pen seemed to take on a life of its own when she sat before a sheaf of blank parchment paper. She wrote about characters unlike any people she had ever known . . . sometimes violent, brutal, always passionate; some who came to ruin and some who even triumphed in spite of their own lack of morality. Since she had no actual pattern on which to base these fictional characters, Amanda realized that their feelings, their passions, could only have come from inside herself. If she allowed herself to dwell on this notion, she could easily become alarmed.

Silver-fork novels, Jack had mentioned to her . . . she had read many of these, stories of privileged people that detailed their extravagant lifestyles, their romances, the clothes and jewels they wore. However, Amanda knew so little about the upper class that she couldn't have written a silver-fork novel if her life depended on it. Instead, she wrote about country people, workingmen and clergy, officers and rural squires. Fortunately, her stories seemed to resonate with readers, and the sales of her books were brisk.

A week after her birthday, Amanda accepted an invitation to attend a supper-party at the home of Mr. Thaddeus Talbot, a lawyer who handled negotiations and legal questions for authors. Amanda found him to be the most cheerfully self-indulgent person she had ever known. He spent, drank, and smoked to excess, gambled and went skirt-chasing, and generally seemed to have a wonderful time. His supper-parties were always heavily attended, as guests were always assured of huge platters of food, copiously flowing wine, and a jovial atmosphere.

"I'm glad yer going out this fine night, Miss Amanda," Sukey, her maid, commented as Amanda checked her appearance in the entrance-hall looking glass. The middle-aged woman, with her small, elfin build and lively nature, had served in the employ of the Briars family for years. " 'Tis a wonder ye didn't come down with the megrims after all the writing ye've done this week."

"I had to finish my novel," Amanda replied with a slight smile. "I didn't dare show my face anywhere, in case Mr. Sheffield should hear reports of my gallivanting about town while there was work to be done."

Sukey snorted in amusement at the mention of Amanda's publisher, a dour and serious-minded man who constantly worried that his small stable of writers would get caught up in London's social whirl and neglect their writing. Truth be told, it was a valid concern. With all the amusements the city offered, it would be quite easy to forget one's obligations.

Glancing at the long, narrow window by the doorway and noting the icy frost that clung to the glass panes, Amanda shivered and gazed forlornly toward her cozy parlor. Suddenly she longed to put on one of her comfortable old gowns and spend the evening reading by the fire. "It looks horribly cold outside," she commented.

Sukey hurried to fetch her mistress's black velvet evening cloak, her animated chatter filling the tiny entrance hall. "Never ye mind the cold, Miss Amanda. There's time enough for ye to spend yer days and nights before the hearth when ye're too old and frail to stand the winter breeze. These are the days when ye must make merry with yer friends. What's a bit of a chill? . . . I'll have coals in the warming pan and a glass of hot brandy-milk waiting fer ye on yer return."

"Yes, Sukey," Amanda replied dutifully, smiling at the maid.

"And, Miss Amanda," the maid dared to instruct her, "ye might try to curb yer tongue a bit when ye're around the gentlemen. Just flatter them, and smile, and mayhap look as though ye agree with all their gabbing about politics and such—"

"Sukey," Amanda interrupted wryly, "you're not still harboring hopes that I'll marry someday, are you?"

"It could happen, sure enow," the maid insisted.

"I'm not going to the supper-party for any reason other than the need for companionship and conversation," Amanda informed her. "Certainly *not* for husband-hunting!"

"Aye, but ye do look fine tonight." Sukey's approving glance swept over Amanda's black evening dress, made of shimmering crinkled silk that had been cut very low across the bosom and fitted tightly to her voluptuous shape. Rows of glittering jet beads adorned the bodice and long sleeves, while her gloves and shoes were of soft black chamois leather. It was a sophisticated ensemble, one that made the most of Amanda's looks and generously displayed her bosom. Although Amanda had never dressed in a particularly stylish way before, she had recently consulted with a reputable London dressmaker and ordered many fashionable new gowns.

With Sukey's help, Amanda shrugged into the ermine-lined cloak, slipped her arms through the silk-trimmed armholes, and fastened the gold clasp at the throat. They settled a large Parisian hat, made of black velvet and lined with pink silk, carefully over her coiffure. At Sukey's suggestion, Amanda had decided to wear her hair in a new style this evening, with several curls spilling from a loose-braided topknot.

"I vow ye'll catch a husband yet," Sukey insisted. "Mayhap ye'll even meet him tonight."

"I don't want a husband," Amanda said crisply. "I prefer my independence."

"Independence," Sukey exclaimed, raising her gaze heavenward. "Ye'd like a husband in yer bed a sight better, I 'spect."

"Sukey," Amanda remarked in disapproval, but the maid only laughed, daring to speak freely because of her age and long familiarity.

"I warrant ye'll catch a finer man than either of yer sisters, bless them both," Sukey predicted. "The best things come to those who wait, I always say."

"Who would dare to contradict you?" Amanda commented wryly, and squinted at the sudden freezing blast of air as the footman, Charles, opened the door for her.

"Carriage is ready, Miss Amanda," he said cheerfully, a lap blanket folded neatly over his arm. He escorted her to the old but well-kept family carriage, settled her inside, and draped the blanket over her.

Leaning back against the worn leather upholstery, Amanda huddled beneath the length of silk-fringed wool and smiled at the thought of the supper-party to come. Life was very good, she thought. She had friends, a comfortable home, and an occupation that was not only interesting but profitable. In spite of her good fortune, however, she had been annoyed by Sukey's insistence that she should find a husband someday.

There was no room for a man in Amanda's life. She liked being able to act and speak with no checks on her freedom. The notion of a husband whose legal and social authority completely eclipsed her own . . . intolerable. In any disputes that arose between them, the last word would be his. He could take away all her earnings if he chose. And any children they might have would be considered his property. Amanda knew that she could never willingly give another person such power over herself. It wasn't that she disliked the male sex. On the contrary, she thought them rather clever for having arranged things so clearly to their advantage.

And yet . . . how nice it would be to attend parties and lectures with a beloved companion. Someone to talk and argue and share with. Someone to share her meals, and cuddle in bed to keep the winter chill away. Yes, independence was the best path, but it wasn't always the most comfortable one. Everything came with a price, and she had bought her autonomy with a good amount of loneliness.

The memory of what had occurred only a week ago was still at the forefront of her mind, despite her best efforts to set it aside. "Jack," she whispered, one hand creeping to the center of her chest, where a wistful ache had settled. Impressions of him still lingered in her memory: the unearthly blue of his eyes, the richly frayed timbre of his voice. For some women, a romantic evening was an ordinary occurrence, but for her, it had been the most extraordinary experience of her life.

The moment of wistful reflection dissolved as her carriage rolled to a halt in front of Mr. Talbot's house, an attractive red brick structure with white columns. Its three stories were set on a perfect little garden square, and resonated with light, laughter, and social chatter. As might be expected of a successful lawyer, Talbot's home was elegant. The entrance hall was a charming oval with plastered copses on either end, and the large receiving room beyond was painted a soothing shade of light green, its elaborate plasterwork ceiling reflected on the gleaming, dark oak floors below. Pleasing smells filled the air, promising a fine repast, while the clinks of glassware provided a sparkling musical undertone to the strains of a string quartet.

The central block of rooms was crowded, and Amanda nodded in greeting as various smiling faces turned toward her. She had an awareness of being popular in the manner that a favorite great-aunt might be . . . often she was slyly teased about this gentleman or that, although no one had any real belief that she entertained any romantic interests. She was fixed far too firmly "on the shelf" for that.

"My dear Miss Briars!" a robust masculine

voice exclaimed, and she turned to see the hearty, cheerfully ruddy countenance of Mr. Talbot. "At last the evening holds true to its promise . . . it wanted only you to be complete."

Although Talbot was at least ten years her senior, he possessed an eternally boyish quality that belied his distinctive shock of long white hair. His fleshy cheeks bulged with a mischievous grin. "And how attractive you are tonight," he continued, taking her hand and pressing it between his chubby palms. "You put all the other ladies to shame."

"I am accustomed to your easy flattery, Mr. Talbot," Amanda informed him with a smile. "And I am far too sensible to fall prey. You'd do better to direct your pleasing words to some unfledged girl who will prove far more gullible."

"You are my preferred target, however," he said, and she rolled her eyes and again smiled at him.

Taking Talbot's proffered arm, Amanda accompanied him to a massive mahogany sideboard, flanked by two large silver urns, one steaming with hot rum punch and the other filled with cold water. Talbot made a great show of directing a servant to fill a goblet of punch for her.

"Now, Mr. Talbot, I insist that you attend to your other guests," Amanda said, letting the spicy aroma of the punch fill her nostrils. She relished the warmth that seeped through the glass goblet. Despite the thin covering of her gloves, her fingers were cold. "I see several people I wish to speak with, and you will hinder my progress."

Talbot laughed jovially at the mock reprimand, and took his leave of her with a deep bow. Sipping her steaming punch, Amanda surveyed the crowd. Authors, publishers, illustrators, printers, lawyers, and even a critic or two—all mingled, separated, and regathered in constantly shifting groups. Conversation rippled through the room, punctuated by frequent bursts of laughter.

"Amanda, dear!" came a light, silvery voice, and Amanda turned to greet an attractive blond widow, Mrs. Francine Newlyn. Francine was the successful author of a half-dozen "sensation" novels, stories of high drama that often involved bigamy, murder, and adultery. Although Amanda privately considered Francine's books a bit overwrought, she enjoyed them nevertheless. Slim, feline, and a lover of gossip, Francine made it a point to cultivate friendships with any writers she deemed successful enough to be worthy of her attention. Amanda always relished her conversations with the woman, who seemed to know everything about everyone, but she was also cautious not to tell Francine anything she wouldn't care to be embellished and repeated.

"Dear Amanda," Francine purred, her slender gloved fingers curved daintily around the heavy stem of a goblet, "how nice to see you here. You may be the only person of good sense to have walked through the door so far."

"I don't know that 'good sense' is all that desirable at an affair such as this," Amanda replied with a smile. "Charm and beauty are doubtless much more welcome."

Francine answered the smile with a wicked one of her own. "How fortunate, then, that you and I both possess all three qualities!"

"Isn't it," Amanda replied dryly. "Tell me, Francine, how is your latest novel progressing?"

The blonde stared at her with mock reproof. "If you must know, my novel is not progressing at all."

Amanda smiled sympathetically. "You'll come through it eventually."

"Oh, I don't like to work *sans* inspiration. I've abandoned all attempts to write until I find something—or someone—to stimulate my creativity."

Amanda couldn't help laughing at Francine's predatory expression. The widow's predilection for love affairs was well known in the publishing community. "Have you affixed your interest to a particular someone yet?"

"Not yet . . . although I do have a few candidates in mind." The widow sipped delicately from her goblet. "I wouldn't mind becoming friends with that fascinating Mr. Devlin, for example."

Although Amanda had never met the man, she had heard his name mentioned frequently. John T. Devlin was a notorious figure in London's literary culture, a man with a mysterious background who in the past five years had turned a small printing shop into the largest publishing house in the city. Apparently his rise to power had been unimpeded by any concern for morality or fair business practices.

Using charm, deception, and bribery, he had stolen the best authors from other publishers and encouraged them to write scandalous sensation novels. He placed advertisements for these novels in all the popular periodicals, and paid people to rave about them at parties and taverns. When critics complained that the books Devlin printed were destructive to the values of an impressionable public, Devlin obligingly published statements to warn potential readers that perhaps a certain novel might be especially violent or lurid; and, of course, sales skyrocketed.

Amanda had seen John T. Devlin's five-story, white stone building located at the busy intersection of Holborn and Shoe Lane, but she had not yet set foot inside the place. Behind the swinging glass doors, she had been told, there were hundreds of thousands of books stacked on shelves that went from floor to ceiling, to provide the benefits of a circulating library to an eager public. Each of its twenty thousand subscribers paid a yearly fee to Devlin for the privilege of borrowing his books. The upper galleries contained stacks of books for sale, not to mention a bindery and printing department, and, of course, Mr. Devlin's private offices.

A dozen delivery wagons were constantly coming and going from the place, carrying loads of periodicals and books to subscribers and customers. Huge frigate ships were loaded daily at the wharves with his deliveries to foreign shores. No doubt Devlin had made a fortune from his vulgar enterprise, but Amanda did not admire him for it. She had heard of the way he had driven other, smaller publishers out of business, and crushed the several circulating libraries that competed with his. She did not approve of the power he held in the literary community, not to mention his misuse of it, and she had made a pointed effort to avoid meeting him.

"I had no idea that Mr. Devlin would be here tonight," Amanda said with a frown. "Good God, I can't imagine that Mr. Talbot would be friends with him. From all I've heard, Devlin is a scoundrel."

"My dear Amanda, none of us can afford *not* to be friends with Devlin," Francine replied. "You would do best to earn his goodwill."

"So far, I've managed quite well without it. And you, Francine, would do best to steer clear of him. An affair with a man like that is the most ill-advised notion I've ever—"

She stopped abruptly as she caught a glimpse of a face in the crowd. Her heart lurched, and she blinked in a spasm of astonishment.

"Amanda?" Francine asked, clearly perplexed.

"I thought I saw . . ." Troubled and sweating, Amanda gazed at the milling crowd, while the throb of her own heartbeat muffled all other sound. She took a step forward, then back, looking from side to side with a wildly searching gaze. "Where is he?" she whispered, breathing much too fast.

"Amanda, are you ill?"

"No, I . . ." Aware that she was behaving oddly, Amanda tried to maintain her dissolving composure. "I think I saw . . . someone I wish to avoid."

Francine glanced speculatively from Amanda's tense face to the milling crowd. "Why should you wish to avoid someone? Is he a disagreeable critic, perhaps? Or some friend you've fallen out with?" A sly smile curved her lips. "Perhaps a former lover who ended the affair badly?"

Although the provocative suggestion was clearly meant to tease Amanda, it was close enough to the truth that she felt her cheeks prickling. "Don't be ridiculous," she said crisply, and scorched her tongue on a gulp of hot punch. Her eyes watered slightly at the burn.

"You'll never guess who is coming this way, Amanda," Francine commented idly. "If Mr. Devlin is the man you wish to avoid, I'm afraid it's too late."

Somehow Amanda knew, even before she looked upward.

Shocking blue eyes ensnared her with a steady gaze. The same deep voice that only a week ago had whispered endearments to her, now spoke in a tone of calm politeness. "Mrs. Newlyn, I hope you'll introduce me to your companion."

Francine responded with a throaty laugh. "I'm not certain the lady wishes it, Mr. Devlin. Unfortunately, your reputation seems to have preceded you."

Amanda could not breathe at all. He was, impossibly, her birthday visitor, "Jack," the man who had held and kissed and pleasured her in the shadowy privacy of her own parlor. He was taller, bigger, swarthier than she remembered. In an instant she recalled the way her body had strained against his heavy weight, her hands grasping the hard muscles of his shoulders . . . the sweet, dark heat of his mouth.

Amanda swayed a little, her knees locked and shaking. Yet she must not make a scene, must not draw attention. She would do whatever was necessary to conceal the humiliating secret they shared. Although it seemed impossible to speak, she managed a few unsteady words.

"You may introduce this gentleman to me, Francine." She saw from the wicked glimmer in Devlin's eyes that he had not missed the ironic emphasis she had placed on the word "gentleman."

The sleek, pretty blonde studied them both thoughtfully. "No, I don't believe I will," she stunned Amanda by saying. "It becomes apparent that the two of you have met before. Perhaps someone would care to enlighten me as to the circumstances?"

"No," Devlin told her, tempering his blunt refusal with a charming grin.

Francine's fascinated gaze flew from Devlin's

face to Amanda's. "Very well. I'll leave the two of you to decide whether you are acquainted or not." She laughed lightly. "But be forewarned, Amanda. I'll have the story out of you one way or another."

Amanda barely noticed her friend's departure. Utter confusion, outrage, betrayal . . . she was too overcome to say anything for a moment. Each breath she took seemed to scorch her lungs. John T. Devlin . . . Jack . . . stood there patiently, his gaze as intent as a tiger's.

He had the power to destroy her, she thought in panic. With just a few words, and perhaps a public confirmation from Mrs. Bradshaw, he could ruin her reputation, her career . . . her ability to provide for herself. "Mr. Devlin," she finally managed to say with stiff-backed dignity. "Perhaps you would care to explain how and why you came to my home last week, and why you have deceived me."

Despite her obvious fear and hostility, Amanda Briars looked straight into Jack's eyes, her gaze bright with challenge. She was no coward.

Jack experienced the same keen awareness he had felt the first moment he had seen her, at the doorstep of her home. She was a luxuriously made woman, with her velvety skin and curly auburn hair, and her decidedly voluptuous figure . . . and he was a man who appreciated quality when he saw it. Her features were pleasant, if not precisely beautiful, but the eyes . . . well, they were extraordinary. Penetrating gray . . . the light gray of April rain . . . intelligent, expressive eyes.

Something about her made him want to smile. He wanted to kiss her spinster-stiff mouth until it was soft and warm with passion. He wanted to charm and tease her. Most of all, he wanted to know the person who had written a novel filled with characters whose proper facades concealed such raw emotions. It was a novel that should have been written by a woman of the world, not by a country-bred spinster.

Her written words had haunted him long before he met her. Now, after their tantalizing encounter in her home, he wanted more of her. He liked the challenge of her, the surprises of her, the fact that she had done extremely well for herself. They were alike in that way.

Yet she possessed a gentility that he lacked and very much admired. Just how she could manage to be so natural and simultaneously so ladylike, two qualities that had always before struck him as being completely opposed, was an intriguing mystery.

"Amanda—" he began, and she corrected him with an offended hiss.

"Miss Briars!"

"Miss Briars," he said evenly. "Had I not taken advantage of the opportunity presented to me that evening, I would have regretted it for the rest of my life."

Her fine brows knit together in a repressive frown. "Do you plan to expose me?"

"I have no immediate plans," he said thoughtfully, but mischief sparkled in his devil-blue eyes. "Although . . ."

"Although?" she prompted warily.

"It would make an interesting bit of gossip-fodder, wouldn't it? The respectable Miss Briars, hiring a man for her pleasure. I would hate for you to be embarrassed in such a way." His teeth flashed in a grin that Amanda did not respond to. "I think we should discuss the matter further. I'd like to know what incentives you might offer to encourage me to keep my mouth closed."

"You intend to blackmail me?" Amanda asked in rising fury. "You villainous, treacherous, mean-spirited—"

"You might want to lower your voice," he advised. "In fact, Miss Briars—and I suggest this out of concern for your reputation, not mine—let us talk in private. Later."

"Never," she returned smartly. "Clearly you are no gentleman, and I will offer you no 'incentives' of any kind."

However, Devlin had the upper hand, and they both knew it. A lazy smile touched his lips, the smile of a man who knew how to get exactly what he wanted and would stoop to anything in the process. "You'll meet with me," he said with certainty. "You have no choice. You see . . . I have something of yours, and I plan to make use of it."

"You blackguard," she muttered in disgust. "Do you mean to say that you stole something from my house?"

His sudden free laugh drew a multitude of interested gazes toward them. "I have your first novel," he informed her.

"What?"

"Your first novel," Jack repeated, enjoying her expression of dawning outrage. "The title is *An Unfinished Lady*. I've just acquired it. Not a bad bit of work, although some judicious editing is required before it is ready for publication."

"You couldn't have it!" she exclaimed, choking back a flurry of scornful words as her sharp tone attracted much interest from Talbot's guests. "I sold it to Mr. Grover Steadman, years ago, for ten pounds. As soon as the money changed hands, he lost interest in the thing and locked it in a drawer, for all I know."

"Yes, well, I recently bought the novel and all the rights to it. A pretty penny Steadman charged, too. Your stock has gone up since your last novel sold so handsomely."

"He wouldn't dare sell it to you," she said heatedly.

"I'm afraid he did." Jack drew closer and added in a confidential murmur, "In fact, that was the reason I came to call on you." He was standing so close to her that he detected the faint fragrance of lemons in her hair. He sensed rather than felt the stiffness of her body. Was she remembering the blistering heat of their lovemaking? He had suffered for hours afterward, his loins aching viciously, his hands itching for the feel of her soft, silken flesh. It had not been easy to leave her that night. Yet he hadn't been able to take her innocence under false pretenses.

Someday he would be back in her arms, with no deception between them. And the next time, no power in Heaven or hell would be enough to stop him.

Her voice sounded unsteady as she snapped out a question. "How was it that you came to call at the exact time I was expecting my, er . . . other guest?"

"I seem to have been willfully misled by our mutual friend, Mrs. Bradshaw."

"How is it that you are acquainted with her?" Amanda's silvery eyes narrowed in accusation. "Are you one of her customers?"

"No, peaches," Jack murmured. "Unlike you, I've never solicited the services of a professional paramour." An irresistible grin tugged at his mouth as he saw her face turn scarlet. Oh, how he enjoyed rattling her composure! Rather than prolong her discomfort, however, he continued in a soft tone. "I'm acquainted with Mrs. Bradshaw because I've just published her first book, *The Sins of Madam B*."

"I suppose it's filthy stuff," Amanda muttered.

"Oh, yes," he said cheerfully. "A threat to morality and decency everywhere. Not to mention my best seller yet."

"I'm hardly surprised that you exhibit pride rather than shame at that fact."

He raised his brows at her prudish tone. "I'm certainly not ashamed at having the good fortune to acquire and publish a work that the public obviously likes."

"The public doesn't always know what is good for it."

He smiled lazily. "And I suppose *your* books are appropriate for the public diet?"

Amanda flushed, clearly embarrassed and incensed. "You can't put my work on the same level as the vulgar memoir of a notorious madam!"

"Of course I can't," he said at once, relenting. "Obviously Mrs. Bradshaw is no writer . . . reading her memoirs is like listening to a few hours of below-stairs gossip. You, on the other hand, have a talent that I sincerely admire."

Amanda's expressive face clearly registered her conflicting emotions. Like most writers, who shared the universal need for praise, she took reluctant pleasure in the compliment. However, she could not allow herself to believe he was sincere, and she threw him a glance of ironic suspicion. "Your flattery is unnecessary and wholly ineffective," she informed him. "Spare yourself the effort, please, and go on with the explanation."

Jack continued obligingly. "During a recent conversation with Mrs. Bradshaw, I mentioned my acquisition of *Unfinished Lady* and my plans to become acquainted with you. And then Mrs. Bradshaw surprised me by evincing a friendship with you. She suggested that I should come to call on you at the specific hour of eight o'clock on Thursday night. She seemed certain that I would be well received. And as it turned out," he couldn't resist adding, "she was correct."

Amanda shot him a discreet glare. "But what reason would she have for making such an arrangement?"

Jack shrugged, unwilling to confess that the same question had bothered him for days. "I doubt that reason had anything to do with it. Like most women, she probably makes decisions that don't conform to any pattern of logic known to man."

"Mrs. Bradshaw wanted to make sport of me," she said in a sullen tone. "Perhaps of us both."

He shook his head. "I don't think that was her intent."

"What else could it be?"

"Perhaps you should ask her."

"Oh, I will," she said grimly, making him laugh.

"Come, now," he said in a gentle tone, "it didn't turn out all that badly, did it? No one was hurt . . . and I feel compelled to point out that most men in the same circumstances wouldn't have acted with my gentlemanly restraint—"

"*Gentlemanly?*" she whispered in seething outrage. "If you had possessed any manner of integrity or honesty, you would have identified yourself as soon as you realized my misunderstanding!"

"And spoil your birthday?" He adopted an expression of mock solicitude, and grinned when he saw the way her small gloved hands clenched longingly. "Don't be angry," he coaxed. "I'm the same man I was that night, Amanda—"

"Miss Briars," she corrected him instantly.

"Miss Briars, then. I'm the same man, and you liked me well enough then. There's no reason we can't cry *pax* and be friends."

"Yes, there is. I liked you better as a prostitute than as a thieving, manipulative publisher. And I cannot be friends with a man who intends to blackmail me. Furthermore, I will never allow you to publish *Unfinished Lady*. I'd rather burn the manuscript than see it in your hands."

"I'm afraid there's nothing you can do about it. However, you're welcome to visit my offices tomorrow and discuss the plans I have for the book."

"If you think I would even entertain the notion—" she began heatedly, then clamped her mouth shut as she saw their host, Mr. Talbot, approach.

Avid curiosity was stamped all over the lawyer's face. He regarded them both with a smile of appeasement that caused his round cheeks to push up beneath his merry eyes. "I've been called forth to intercede," he said with a low chuckle. "No quarreling between my guests, if you please. Allow me to point out that the two of you are hardly well enough acquainted to regard each other with such animosity."

Amanda seemed to bristle at the attempt to make light of their brewing argument. She spoke without taking her gaze from Jack's face. "I've discovered, Mr. Talbot, that a mere five minutes' acquaintance with Mr. Devlin is sufficient to try the patience of a saint."

Jack replied softly, allowing his simmering amusement to show in his eyes. "Are you claiming to be a saint, Miss Briars?"

She colored, and her lips thinned, and just as she was ready to unleash a barrage of furious words, Mr. Talbot interceded hastily. "Ah, Miss Briars," he exclaimed with an overly hearty laugh, "I see that your good friends the Eastmans have just arrived. I beg you to act as my hostess and assist me in greeting them!" Throwing a warning glance at Jack, he began to steer Amanda away.

Before they left him, however, Jack bent to murmur close to Amanda's ear. "I'll send a carriage for you tomorrow at ten."

"I won't come," Amanda muttered, her body rigid except for the slight, luscious quiver of her breasts, encased snugly in beaded black silk. The sight gave Jack an immediate shock of awareness. Heat seemed to dance beneath his own skin, until his body began to awaken in dangerous places. Some unknown emotion surfaced in him, something like possessiveness, or excitement . . . or even tenderness. He wanted to show her whatever small scrap of goodness he might find at the bottom of his soul, to entice and tempt her.

"Yes, you will," he said, knowing somehow that she could not resist him any more than he could resist her.

The guests proceeded into the dining room, a large mahogany-paneled room filled with two long tables, each set with fourteen places. Four gloved, liveried footmen bustled quietly around the tables, assisting guests to their chairs, pouring wine, and bringing out huge silver-plated platters of oysters. Next came sherry and bowls of steaming turtle soup, followed by turbot fish dressed with tart hollandaise.

Jack found himself seated next to Mrs. Francine Newlyn. He had a feeling that Francine had designs on him, but though he considered her attractive, she was hardly worth the trouble of having an affair with. Especially if one didn't care to have one's personal life revealed in detail to a horde of gossips. Still, her hand kept sliding to his knee beneath the table. Each time he brushed the hand away, it returned to explore further territory of his leg.

"Mrs. Newlyn," he muttered, "your attentions are most flattering. But if you don't remove your hand . . ."

Francine's hand slid away, and she regarded him with a catlike smile, her eyes round with mock innocence. "Forgive me," she purred. "I had merely lost my balance and was trying to restore it." She picked up her small sherry glass and sipped delicately. The tip of her tongue retrieved a golden drop that clung to the rim. "Such a strong leg," she commented softly. "You must take exercise quite frequently."

Jack suppressed a sigh as he glanced at the other long table, where Amanda Briars had been seated. She was involved in an animated conversation with the gentleman on her left, something about whether the new serial novels published in monthly installments were truly novels. The debate was currently a popular one, as several publishers—including himself—were launching serial novels without much success so far.

Jack enjoyed watching Amanda's face in the candlelight, her expression by turns thoughtful, amused, and lively, those gray eyes gleaming more brightly than the polished silver.

Unlike the other women present, who picked at their food with appropriately feminine disinterest, Amanda displayed a healthy appetite. Apparently it was one of the privileges of spinsterhood, that a woman could eat well in public. She was so natural and straightforward, a refreshing change from the other sophisticated women he had known. He wanted to be alone with her. He envied the man seated next to her, who seemed to be having a better time than anyone else present.

Francine Newlyn persistently pressed his leg with her own. "My dear Mr. Devlin," she said silkily, "you can't seem to take your gaze from Miss Briars. But surely a man like you couldn't entertain an interest in her."

"Why not?"

A laugh came sputtering from her lips. "Because you're a young, full-blooded man in his prime, and she . . . well, it's obvious, isn't it? Oh, men *like* Miss Briars, certainly, but only in the way they would like a sister or an aunt. She's not the kind who would arouse a man's amorous instincts."

"If you say so," he replied blandly. The woman clearly considered her own attractions far superior to Amanda's, never dreaming that a man might prefer a spinster's charms to hers. But Jack had been involved with women like Francine before, and he knew what was beneath her shallow, pretty facade. Or, more to the point, what was *not* beneath it.

A footman came bearing a dish of creamed pheasant, and Jack accepted a serving with a nod, suppressing another sigh of frustration as he thought of the long night ahead. Tomorrow morning, and Amanda's visit to his offices, seemed like an eternity away.

Chapter 4

I'll send a carriage for you tomorrow at ten.

I won't come.

Yes, you will.

The remembered exchange had troubled Amanda all night, echoing in her dreams, causing her to awaken far earlier than usual the next morning. Oh, how she would love to give Mr. John T. Devlin a well-deserved set-down by refusing to step into his carriage! However, his underhanded acquisition of her novel *An Unfinished Lady* would have to be dealt with. She did not want him or anyone else to publish it.

It had been years since she had written or read the thing, and although she had done her best at the time, the novel undoubtedly contained many faults of plotting and characterization. Were *Unfinished Lady* printed now, she feared it might be harshly reviewed by the critics and reviled by readers unless many revisions were made. And she had neither the time nor the inclination to do painstaking work on a novel for which she had received only ten pounds. Therefore, she would have to retrieve the book from Devlin.

There was also the matter of potential blackmail. If he spread the rumor around London that Amanda was the kind of woman who hired male prostitutes, her reputation and career would be in tatters. She would somehow have to secure Devlin's promise that he would never breathe a word about that dreadful birthday night to anyone.

And much as she hated to admit it, she was curious. No matter how much she berated herself for letting her dratted curiosity get the better of her, she wanted to see Devlin's establishment, his books, his bindery and offices and everything else inside that massive building on the corner of Holborn and Shoe Lane.

With Sukey's assistance, Amanda pinned her hair into a tightly braided coronet atop her head, and dressed in the most severe gown she owned, a snugly fitted, high-buttoned gray velvet with regally swishing skirts. The gown's only ornamentations consisted of a narrow belt that looked like interwoven silk cords fastened with a silver buckle, and a full white lace ruff that nestled high beneath her chin.

"Ye look like Queen Elizabeth must have, just before she had them cut off the Earl of Essex's head," Sukey commented.

Amanda laughed suddenly, in spite of her inner nervousness. "I'd like to cut off a certain gentleman's head," she said. "Instead, I'll have to settle for giving him a harsh rebuff."

"Are ye going to see yer publisher, then?" Sukey's narrow face resembled that of an inquisitive woodland creature.

Amanda shook her head at once. "He's not my publisher, nor will he ever be. I intend to make that clear to him this morning."

"Ah." The maid's expression brightened with interest. "Some gentleman ye met at the supper-party last eve? Do tell, Miss Amanda . . . is he handsome?"

"I hadn't noticed," Amanda said crisply.

Sukey appeared to suppress a delighted smile as she hurried to fetch Amanda's black wool cloak.

As they fastened the cloak around Amanda's shoulders, the footman, Charles, came inside from the front doorstep. "Miss Amanda, the carriage has arrived." The footman's middle-aged face was reddened from the bitter November breeze. A fresh, icy scent clung to his livery, mingled with the dry smell of his white-powdered hair. He retrieved a lap shawl from the entrance-hall chair, draped it neatly over his arm, then made to escort Amanda outside. "Step carefully, Miss Amanda," he warned. "There's a patch of ice on the top step—'tis a damp winter's day."

"Thank you, Charles." Amanda appreciated the footman's solicitude. Although he lacked the usual height required of a footman—most fine families preferring to hire only those who were at least six feet tall—Charles made up for his lack of physical stature with sheer efficiency. He had given the Briars family—and now Amanda herself—the benefit of loyal and uncomplaining service for nearly two decades.

Weak morning sunlight did its best to illuminate the narrow terraced houses of Bradley Square. A little iron-fenced garden was set between the two rows of homes that faced one another, and frost clung stubbornly to the dormant plants and trees set between the graveled walkways. At the hour of ten in the morning, many of the town homes' upstairs windows were still shuttered, as occupants slumbered to atone for the previous night's amusements.

Aside from a rag-seller walking along the pavement leading to the main road, and a long-legged constable with his baton tucked smartly beneath his arm, the street was quiet and still. A chilly but clean-smelling breeze rattled along the housefronts. Despite Amanda's aversion to the winter cold, she appreciated that the odors of refuse and sewage were far less acute than in the warm summer months.

Amanda stopped midway down the flight of six steps that led to the street level when she saw the carriage that Devlin had sent. "Miss Amanda?" the footman murmured, stopping with her as she stared at the vehicle.

Amanda had expected a carriage as well used and serviceable as her own. She had never thought that Devlin would send such an elegant conveyance. This was a glass-quartered coach, plated in lacquer and bronze, with steps fashioned to open and close automatically with the door. Every inch of the vehicle was polished and perfect. The beveled windows were framed with silk curtains, while the interior was upholstered in cream-colored leather.

A team of four perfectly matched chestnuts stamped and blew impatiently, their breaths puffing white in the frosty air. It was the kind of equipage that well-heeled aristocrats owned. How was it that a half-Irish publisher could afford such a carriage? Devlin must be even more successful than the rumors had led her to believe.

Marshaling her composure, Amanda approached the vehicle. A footman jumped from his carved standard and quickly opened the door, while Charles assisted Amanda up the carriage steps. The well-sprung vehicle barely jostled as she settled into the leather-upholstered seat. There was no need for the lap shawl Charles had brought, as a fur-lined carriage blanket had been provided for her. A foot warmer stocked with coals caused Amanda to shiver pleasantly as waves of heat rose beneath her skirts to her knees. It seemed that Devlin had remembered her dislike of the cold.

Almost dazedly, Amanda settled back against the soft leather upholstery and stared through the steam-fogged window at the blurry outlines of her terraced house. The door closed smartly, and the carriage rolled gently away. "Well, Mr. Devlin," she said aloud, "if you think that a mere foot warmer and a blanket will cause me to soften toward you, then you are sadly mistaken."

The carriage stopped at Shoe Lane and Holborn, where the massive white five-story building awaited her. Devlin's was swarming with customers, the jaunty glass doors swinging in constant motion as a steady stream of people entered and exited. Although she knew Devlin's was a successful establishment, nothing had prepared her for this. It was clear that Devlin's was far more than a store . . . it was an empire. And she had no doubt that its owner's keen mind was constantly devising ways to extend his reach.

The footman assisted her from the carriage and rushed to hold open the glass door with the deference one might have accorded to visiting royalty. As soon as her foot touched the threshold, Amanda was instantly met by a blond gentleman in his late twenties or early thirties. Although his height was average, his slim, well-exercised physique made him appear taller. His smile was warm and genuine, and his sea-green eyes sparkled beneath a pair of steel-framed spectacles.

"Miss Briars," he said quietly, giving her a welcoming bow, "what an honor it is to make your acquaintance. I am Mr. Oscar Fretwell. And this"—he gestured to their bustling surroundings with unmistakable pride—"is Devlin's. A store, circulating library, bindery, stationer, printer, and publisher, all under one roof."

Amanda curtsied and allowed him to guide her to a relatively sheltered corner, where bundles of books had been placed on a mahogany counter. "Mr. Fretwell, in what capacity do you work for Mr. Devlin?"

"I am his chief manager. Occasionally I serve as a reader and editor, and I bring unpublished novels to his attention if I discover they have merit." He smiled once again. "And it is my good fortune to be of service to any of Mr. Devlin's writers, whenever they require it."

"I am *not* one of Mr. Devlin's writers," Amanda said firmly.

"Yes, of course," Fretwell said, clearly anxious not to offend. "I did not intend to imply that you were. May I express what great pleasure your work has brought to myself and our subscribers? Your books are constantly on loan, and the sales are quite brisk. For the last one, *Shades of the Past*, we could not get by with an order of less than five hundred."

"*Five hundred?*" Amanda was too startled by the figure to conceal her amazement. Books were luxury items, too dear for most people to afford, and therefore, her sales of nearly three thousand volumes had been considered exceptional. However, she had not realized until this moment that a large percentage of her sales could be attributed to Devlin's support.

"Oh, yes," Fretwell began earnestly, but paused as he became aware of a minor disturbance at one of the counters. It appeared that a clerk was perturbed by the return of a book in poor condition. The subscriber, a lady covered in heavily applied face paint and perfume, was vigorously protesting the charge that the book had been damaged. "Ah, it's Mrs. Sandby," Fretwell said with a sigh. "One of our frequent subscribers. Unfortunately, she likes to borrow a book and read it at the hairdresser's. When she returns a volume, it is usually caked with powder and the pages sealed together with pomade."

Amanda laughed suddenly, glancing at the woman's old-fashioned pile of powdered hair. No doubt she—and the novel—had spent a great deal of time at the hairdresser's. "It appears that your attention is required, Mr. Fretwell. Perhaps you should settle the dispute while I wait here."

"I shouldn't like to leave you unattended," he said with a slight frown. "However . . ."

"I'll stay in this exact spot," Amanda said, her smile lingering. "I don't mind waiting."

While Oscar Fretwell hurried to smooth over the situation, Amanda gazed at her surroundings. Books were everywhere, lined neatly on shelves that went from floor to ceiling. The ceiling was two stories high, with an upper balcony that provided access to a second-floor gallery. The dazzling array of red, gold, green, and brown bindings was a feast for the eyes, while the wonderful smells of vellum, parchment, and pungent leather almost caused Amanda to salivate. An exquisite waft of tea leaves lingered in the air. For anyone who enjoyed the pursuit of reading, this place was surely paradise.

Subscribers and purchasers waited in lines at counters laden with catalogs and volumes. Wheels of cord and spools of brown paper turned constantly as clerks wrapped orders. Amanda appreciated the clerks' expertise as they quickly bound smaller stacks of volumes in paper and string. The larger orders appeared to be packed in fragrant old tea chests—ah, the source of the tea smell—and then carried out to carriages and carts by attendants.

Oscar Fretwell wore an expression of rueful amusement when he rejoined her. "I believe the matter is settled," he told Amanda in a conspiratorial whisper. "I bade the clerk to accept the book in its current condition—we'll do our best to restore it. However, I did tell Mrs. Sandby that she must try to take better care of our books in the future."

"You should have suggested that she simply leave off the hair powder," Amanda whispered back, and they shared a quick laugh.

Fretwell crooked his arm invitingly. "May I escort you to Mr. Devlin's office, Miss Briars?"

The thought of seeing Jack Devlin once more gave Amanda a strange rustling of pleasure mixed with anxiety. The prospect of being in his presence made her feel curiously alive and agitated.

She straightened her shoulders and took Fretwell's arm. "Yes, by all means. The sooner I deal with Mr. Devlin, the better."

Fretwell glanced at her with a puzzled smile. "It sounds as if you don't like Mr. Devlin."

"I do not. I find him to be arrogant and manipulative."

"Well." Fretwell appeared to ponder her words carefully. "Mr. Devlin can be a bit aggressive when he sets his mind on a particular goal. However, I can assure you there is no better employer in London. He is kind to his friends and generous to all those who work for him. Recently he helped one of his novelists to purchase a house, and he is always willing to arrange for theater tickets, or locate a specialist when one of his friends is ill, or help them in any way to resolve their personal difficulties . . ."

While Fretwell continued to offer praises of his employer, Amanda mentally added the word "controlling" to the list of adjectives she had applied to Devlin. Of course the man did his best to make his friends and employees feel indebted to him . . . then he could use their own feelings of obligation against them.

"Why and how did Mr. Devlin become a publisher?" she asked. "He's not at all like the other publishers I am acquainted with. That is to say, he doesn't seem like a bookish sort."

A strange hesitation followed, and Amanda saw from Fretwell's expression that there was some interesting and private story to tell, related to Devlin's mysterious past. "Perhaps you should ask Mr. Devlin the 'why and how' of it," Fretwell finally said. "But I can tell you this: he has a deep love of reading, and the greatest respect for the written word. And he possesses a great ability to discern a writer's particular strengths and encourage his or her highest potential for success."

"In other words, he pushes them to make a profit," Amanda said dryly.

Fretwell's smile contained a hint of teasing. "Surely you have no objections to making a profit, Miss Briars."

"Only when art is sacrificed for the sake of commerce, Mr. Fretwell."

"Oh, I think you will find that Mr. Devlin has the greatest respect for liberty of expression," he said hastily.

They proceeded to the back of the building and ascended a set of stairs illuminated by a succession of skylights. The interior of Devlin's seemed to resemble the exterior in that it was serviceable but attractive, with good-quality fittings. The various rooms they passed were heated with either fireplaces or flues, the chimneypieces all made from veined marble, the floors covered with thick carpets. Being sensitive to atmosphere, Amanda noticed that there was a general air of cheerful industry among the employees in the bindery and printing room.

Fretwell paused before a particularly fine paneled door and arched his brows inquiringly. "Miss Briars, would you like to view our rare-book collection?"

Amanda nodded and accompanied him inside. The door opened to reveal a room with walls consisting mostly of inset mahogany bookcases covered by leaded glass doors. Intricate plasterwork adorned the ceiling in a flowered medallion style that matched the thick Aubusson carpet on the floor.

"Are all of these books for sale?" Amanda asked in a hushed voice, feeling as if she had entered a king's treasure room.

Fretwell nodded. "You'll find everything from antiques to zoology. We have a wide selection of antique maps and celestial charts, original folios and manuscripts . . ." He gestured around them, as if the extensive rows of books were self-explanatory.

"I would love to lock myself in here for a week," she said impulsively.

Fretwell laughed and guided her from the room. They ascended one more floor to reach a suite of office rooms. Before Amanda had the opportunity to dwell on the sudden flurry of her nerves, Fretwell opened a mahogany door and gently urged her past the threshold. Impressions rushed at her . . . the massive desk, the large marble fireplace and leather chairs beside it, the elegant masculine ambiance and rich brown-striped paper on the walls. Sunlight streamed through a row of narrow, tall windows. It smelled like leather and vellum in this room, tinged with the faint earthy perfume of tobacco.

"At last," came a familiar deep voice, subtly shaded with laughter, and Amanda realized that Devlin was amused by the fact that she had come to see him after all. But she'd had no choice, had she?

Devlin bowed with a mocking, ceremonial flourish, and he flashed a grin as his blue gaze raked over her. "My dear Miss Briars," he said in a way that somehow robbed his words of all sincerity, "never have I passed such a long morning, anticipating your arrival. I could barely restrain myself from waiting out on the street for you."

She scowled at him. "I wish to conduct our business with all possible haste so that I may be on my way."

Devlin grinned as if she had said something clever rather than cutting. "Come sit near the fire," he coaxed.

The generous blaze behind the gilded iron screen did look inviting. After removing her hat and cloak and placing them in Oscar Fretwell's waiting arms, Amanda seated herself in a leather chair.

"Would you take some refreshments with me?" Devlin asked, all solicitous charm. "I usually have coffee at this hour."

"I prefer tea," she said shortly.

Devlin glanced at Fretwell with dancing blue

eyes. "Tea and a plate of sugar-biscuits," he informed the manager, who promptly disappeared and left them alone.

Amanda glanced discreetly at her companion, and felt her palms grow damp inside her leather gloves. It was indecent for a man to be so strikingly handsome, his blue eyes even more exotic than she had remembered, his black hair cut so that only a hint of a wave showed in the thick locks. It seemed odd that such a large, obviously robust man should be so fond of books. He did not look like the scholarly kind, nor did he seem to belong in the confines of an office room, even one as large as this.

"You have an impressive establishment, Mr. Devlin," she said. "No doubt everyone tells you so."

"Thank you. But the place is nothing close to what it is going to be. I've only just begun." Devlin sat beside her and stretched his long legs before him, studying the tips of his polished black shoes. He was as well tailored as on the previous evening, wearing a simple but fashionable coat with straight-cut front edges, and trousers in matching gray wool.

"And where will all of this lead?" she asked, wondering what more he could want.

"This year I'm going to open a half-dozen stores across the country. In two years I'll triple that number. I'm going to acquire every newspaper worth owning, and several more magazines while I'm at it."

It was hardly lost on Amanda that such a position would be accompanied by considerable social and political power. She stared at the hard-faced young man before her with a touch of wonder. "You are quite ambitious," she commented.

He smiled slightly. "Aren't you?"

"No, not at all." She paused to consider the issue carefully. "I have no aspirations for great wealth or influence. I wish merely to be secure and comfortable, and perhaps someday to achieve a certain level of proficiency in my work."

His black brows rose a fraction. "You don't believe that you're proficient now?"

"Not yet. I find many faults in my own work."

"I find none," he said softly.

Amanda couldn't prevent the wash of color that spread upward from her throat as she was captured by his steady regard. Taking a deep breath, she struggled to keep her wits from dissolving. "Flatter me all you like, Mr. Devlin," she said. "It will not soften me in the least. I have but one purpose for visiting you today—and that is to inform you that I will never accede to your plan of publishing *An Unfinished Lady*."

"Before you refuse me absolutely," he suggested gently, "why don't you hear me out? I have an offer that you might find interesting."

"Very well."

"I want to publish *An Unfinished Lady* first as a serial novel."

"A *serial novel*," Amanda repeated in disbelief.

She felt insulted by the idea, as serial novels were universally considered of far less quality and importance than the standard three-volume novel. "You can't possibly mean to bring it out in paper-jacket monthly installments like one of your magazines!"

"And then after the last installment has been published," Devlin continued evenly, "I'll bring it out again, this time as a three-decker, with cloth binding, full-page illustrations, woodcuts, and gilt edging."

"Why not simply publish it that way in the beginning? I am not a serial-novel writer, Mr. Devlin, nor have I ever aspired to be."

"Yes, I know." Although Devlin appeared relaxed, he leaned forward in his chair and stared at her with blue eyes that gleamed with heat and energy. "One can hardly fault you for that attitude. Very few of the serial novels I've ever read have been of high enough quality to capture the public's interest. And there's a particular style that's required . . . each installment has to be self-contained, with a suspenseful conclusion that makes the readers look forward to the next month's issue. Not an easy task for a writer."

"I cannot see that *An Unfinished Lady* fits that description in any way," Amanda said, frowning.

"But it does. It could easily be divided into thirty-page installments, with sufficient dramatic high points to make each issue entertaining. With relatively little work, you and I could tailor it to suit the structure of a serial novel."

"Mr. Devlin," Amanda said briskly, "in addition to my *complete* lack of interest in being known as the author of a serial book, I am hardly enthralled by the prospect of taking you on as my editor. I am also unwilling to waste my time revising a novel for which I have been paid a paltry ten pounds."

"Of course." Before Devlin could continue, Mr. Fretwell entered the room bearing a silver tea tray.

After setting the tray on a small table beside Amanda's chair, Fretwell poured tea in a Sevres china cup, and indicated a plate laden with six perfect little biscuits. Flakes of crushed sugar glittered invitingly on the surface of each biscuit. "Do try one, Miss Briars," he urged.

"Thank you, but no," Amanda said regretfully, smiling after him as he bowed and left the room once more. She removed her gloves deftly and set them on the edge of her chair. She stirred milk and sugar into her tea and sipped it carefully. The tea was a smooth, rich blend, and she thought of how nicely a biscuit would accompany it. However, with a sluggish constitution like hers, one extra bonbon or tart seemed to make all her clothes fit more tightly the next day. The only way to keep her waist relatively trim was to avoid sweets and take frequent brisk walks.

Maddeningly, the man beside her seemed to read her thoughts. "Have a biscuit," he said lazily. "If you're worried about your figure, let me assure you it is splendid in every regard. I, of all people, should know."

Amanda was flooded with embarrassment and annoyance. "I wondered how long it would be before you introduced the distasteful subject of that night!" Reaching for a biscuit, she crunched into the sweet confection and glared at him.

Devlin grinned and braced his elbows on his knees, staring at her intently. "Surely not distasteful."

She chewed the biscuit vigorously and nearly choked on a swallow of hot tea. "Yes, it was! I was deceived and molested, and I would love nothing better than to forget the whole thing."

"Oh, I won't let you forget it," he assured her. "But as to your being molested . . . it's not as if I jumped at you from the shadows. You encouraged me nearly every step of the way."

"You were not the man I thought you were! And I intend to find out exactly why that scheming Mrs. Bradshaw sent *you* instead of the man she should have sent. Right after I leave this establishment, I am going straight to Mrs. Bradshaw to demand an explanation."

"Let me do it." Although his tone was casual, it was clear that he was leaving no room for debate. "I've planned to visit her today as well. There's no reason for you to risk your reputation by being seen at her establishment. In any event, she'll explain more to me than she ever would to you."

"I already know what she will say." Amanda kept her fingers wrapped around the hot china bowl of the teacup. "Mrs. Bradshaw was clearly amusing herself at our expense."

"We'll see." Devlin stood and tended the fire, moving the gilded screen back in order to rearrange the logs with a few industrious jabs of an iron poker. The fire reawakened to new life, sending a pleasant infusion of heat into the air.

Amanda was mesmerized by the sight of him. It seemed, in the intense glow of firelight, that his easy confidence was balanced by something she had not seen in him before, a tenacity that knew no limits. She realized he was the kind of man who would woo, cajole, argue, perhaps bully and threaten anyone who got in the way of what he wanted. Half Irish, not wellborn despite his looks and bearing . . . it had to have been a hard-won victory for him to have climbed to this level of success. Devlin must have worked and sacrificed a great deal. If only he weren't such a cocky, infuriating rogue, she would have found much in him to admire.

"A paltry ten pounds," he said, recalling her to their earlier discussion about her pay for the unpublished novel. "And a royalty agreement if the book was ever published?"

Amanda smiled wryly and shrugged. "Well, I knew there was little chance of receiving anything. Authors have no way of making a publisher accountable for his expenses. I fully expected Mr. Steadman to claim there were no profits, no matter what the sales might have been."

Devlin's face was suddenly expressionless. "Ten pounds wasn't a bad sum for a first novel.

However, your work is worth much more than that now. Obviously I can't expect your cooperation unless I offer you suitable payment for *Unfinished Lady*."

Amanda poured fresh tea into her cup, doing her best to appear supremely uninterested in the conversation. "What sum would you consider 'suitable,' I wonder?"

"In the interest of fairness and an amiable working relationship, I'm prepared to pay you five thousand pounds for the rights to publish *An Unfinished Lady* as I described, first as a serial novel and then in a three-volume edition. I'll also pay you the entire sum in advance, rather than divide it into monthly publication payments." He arched one dark brow questioningly. "What do you think of that?"

Amanda nearly dropped her spoon. She fumbled to stir a little more sugar into her tea with a few unsteady swirls while her brain buzzed. Five thousand . . . it was nearly twice what she had been paid for her last novel. And this was for work that was already mostly done.

She felt her heart thump against the cage of her ribs in impatient blows. The offer seemed too good to be true . . . except that she might lose a great deal of prestige if the novel were brought out as a serial. "I suppose your offer is worth consideration," she said carefully, "although I don't care for the idea of being known as a magazine novelist."

"Then allow me to give you some numbers to

mull over, Miss Briars. I would estimate that you've sold three thousand copies of your last novel—"

"Thirty-five hundred," Amanda said a touch defensively.

Devlin nodded, a smile catching at the corners of his mouth. "Impressive numbers for a three-decker. However, if you allow me to publish you in a shilling serial edition, we'll start the printing at ten thousand, and I fully expect it to double the following month. By the last installment, I'll be printing about sixty thousand copies. No, Miss Briars, I'm not joking—I'm always sober when I discuss business. Surely you've heard of young Dickens, the reporter from the *Evening Chronicle*? He and his publisher, Bentley, are selling at least a hundred thousand each month of *The Pickwick Papers*."

"A hundred thousand," Amanda repeated, not bothering to hide her astonishment. Of course, she and every literate person in London had become familiar with Mr. Charles Dickens, as his serial novel *Pickwick* had charmed the public with its liveliness and humor. Each installment was frantically sought by booksellers' representatives on Magazine Day, while quips and phrases from each edition were exchanged in taverns and coffeehouses. Shopkeepers kept copies of *Pickwick* behind the counters to read between customers. Schoolboys tucked editions between the pages of their grammar books, despite the severe knuckle-rappings they would earn should their transgression be discovered. Despite the public excitement over *Pickwick*, however, Amanda had not expected Dickens's sales to be quite so high.

"Mr. Devlin," she said thoughtfully, "I am never accused of modesty, false or otherwise. I know that as a novelist, I possess a certain ability. But my work is not comparable to that of Mr. Dickens. My writing is not humorous, nor am I capable of imitating him—"

"I don't want you to imitate anyone. I want to publish a serial novel written in *your* style, Miss Briars . . . something resonant and romantic. I promise you, the public will follow *An Unfinished Lady* every bit as faithfully as they read the more humorous serials."

"You can't guarantee such a thing," Amanda said.

Devlin's white teeth flashed in a sudden grin. "No. But I'm willing to take the risk if you are. Whether or not the thing succeeds, Miss Briars, you'll have the money in your pocket . . . and you'll be free to spend the rest of your life writing three-volume novels, if that is your desire."

He startled Amanda by leaning over her chair, bracing his hands on the mahogany arms. She could not rise, had she wished to, without bringing her body directly against his. She felt his legs brush against the front of her skirts. "Say yes, Amanda," he coaxed. "You'll never regret it."

Amanda leaned hard against the back of her chair. Devlin's disarming blue eyes were set in a face of such perfect masculine beauty that it should have come from a painting or a sculpture. Yet there was nothing aristocratic about his looks. He possessed an earthiness, a sensuality, that was impossible to ignore. If he resembled an angel, it was a fallen one.

Her entire body seemed to pulse in response to him. She caught the intoxicating scent of his skin, the male spice that would forever saturate her memory. He made it difficult for her to think clearly, when all she wanted was to push herself up at him and slide her hands beneath his clothes. Somewhere in the back of her mind, she realized with ironic despair that her encounter with him had done absolutely nothing to silence her own unwanted physical urges.

If she accepted his offer, she would have to see him, talk to him, and somehow conceal her own treacherous response to him. Nothing was more pitiable, more laughable, than a sexually frustrated spinster pursuing a handsome man—the archetype was a standard one in comedic plays and books. She must not place herself in such a position.

"I'm afraid I cannot," Amanda said, intending to use a firm tone of dismissal. Instead, her voice was infuriatingly breathless. She tried to look away from him, but standing over her as he was, his face and body seemed to fill her vision. "I . . . I feel a certain loyalty for my current publisher, Mr. Sheffield."

His soft laugh was not at all complimentary. "Believe me," he scoffed, "Sheffield knows better than to rely on an author's loyalty. He won't be surprised by your defection."

Amanda scowled at him. "Are you suggesting that I can be bought, Mr. Devlin?"

"Why, yes, Miss Briars, I believe I am."

She would have loved to show him that he was wrong. But the thought of five thousand pounds was too tantalizing to resist. A frown tugged at the inner corners of her eyebrows. "What will you do if I turn down your offer?" she asked.

"I'll publish your book anyway, and honor the original royalty agreement you had with Steadman. You'll still make money, peaches. But not nearly as much."

"What about your threat of telling everyone about that night we . . ." The words tangled and gathered into a choking knot in Amanda's throat. She swallowed hard and continued. "Do you still intend to blackmail me with the fact that you and I—"

"Nearly made love?" he suggested helpfully, staring at her in a way that made her face prickle with heat.

"Love had nothing to do with it," she shot back.

"Perhaps not," he acknowledged, laughing softly. "But let us not bring the negotiations down to that level, Miss Briars. Why don't you simply agree to my offer so that I don't have to resort to desperate measures?"

Amanda opened her mouth to ask another question when suddenly the door vibrated from the thud of a fist, or perhaps a boot.

"Mr. Devlin," came Oscar Fretwell's muffled voice. "Mr. Devlin, I can't seem to—*oof!*"

Sounds of scuffling and physical struggle came through the door. Devlin's smile faded, and he turned away from Amanda with a sudden scowl. "What the hell . . . ?" he muttered, striding toward the door. He stopped short as the mahogany portal burst open, revealing a large, furious-faced gentleman with his fine clothes in disarray and his brown wig askew. A sour waft of spirits accompanied him, strongly evident even from where Amanda sat. She wrinkled her nose in distaste, wondering how a man could have drunk so much at this early hour of the day.

"*Devlin,*" the man roared, his corpulent jowls jiggling from the force of his wrath, "I have cornered you like a fox, and there will be no escape from me! You will pay for what you have done!"

Just behind him, Fretwell tried to pry himself free of the man's beefy comrade, who appeared to be some kind of hired thug. "Mr. Devlin," Fretwell gasped, "take care. This is Lord Tirwitt . . . the one who . . . well, he seems to believe that he was slandered in Mrs. Bradshaw's book—"

Tirwitt slammed the door in Fretwell's face and turned toward Devlin, brandishing a heavy silver cane. Fumbling a bit, he pressed a hidden catch on the handle, and a double-sided blade sprang from the end, converting the cane to a deadly weapon. "You demon from hell," he said viciously, his small, dark eyes burning in his red face as he stared at Devlin. "I will have my revenge on you and that malicious bitch Mrs. Bradshaw. For every word you published about me, I will cut a slice from you, and feed it to—"

"Lord Tirwitt, is it?" Devlin's keen gaze locked on the man's puffy face. "If you'll put that damn thing away, we'll discuss your problem like rational beings. If you hadn't noticed, there is a lady present. We'll allow her to leave, and then—"

"Any woman found in your company is no lady," Tirwitt sneered, gesturing wildly with the knife-tipped cane. "I wouldn't put her on a level above that whore Gemma Bradshaw."

A murderous coldness settled on Devlin's face, and he stepped forward, seeming unconcerned by the threat of the cane.

Amanda intervened hastily. "Mr. Devlin," she said briskly, "I find this performance remarkable. Is this some sort of farce you've arranged in an effort to frighten me into signing a contract? Or are you in the habit of receiving deranged callers in your office?"

As she had intended, Tirwitt's attention was drawn to her. "If I am deranged," he snarled, "it is because my life has been blown to bits. I have been made a laughingstock by the evil brew of lies and fantasy that this bastard has published. Ruining peoples' lives for profit . . . well, the time of his comeuppance has arrived!"

"Your name was never mentioned in Mrs. Bradshaw's book," Devlin said calmly. "All the characters were disguised."

"Certain details of my personal life were shamelessly revealed . . . enough to make my identity abundantly clear. My wife has left me, my friends have abandoned me . . . I have been stripped of everything that matters." Tirwitt breathed heavily, his rampaging fury gaining momentum. "I have nothing to lose now," he muttered. "And I will take you down with me, Devlin."

"This is nonsense," Amanda interrupted curtly. "Charging about in this manner . . . it is ridiculous, my lord. I've never witnessed such outrageous behavior—why, I'm tempted to put you in a book myself."

"Miss Briars," Devlin said carefully, "this would be a good time for you to keep your mouth shut. Let me handle the matter."

"There is nothing to handle!" Tirwitt shouted, charging forward like a wounded bull and swiping the double-sided blade in a swift arc. Devlin leapt to the side, but not before the knife caught him, cutting through the fabric of his vest and shirt.

"Get behind the desk," Devlin snapped at Amanda.

Amanda retreated to the wall instead, watching in amazement. The knife must be remarkably sharp, she thought, to have cut so easily through two layers of cloth. A crimson stain soaked rapidly through the fabric. Devlin seemed not to notice the wound on his midriff as he circled warily around the room.

"You've made your point," Devlin said in a low voice, his gaze locked with the other man's. "Now set that thing down, or you'll soon find yourself in a Bow Street gaol."

The sight of blood seemed to whet Lord Tirwitt's desire to draw more. "I've only just started," he said thickly. "I'm going to carve you like a Christmas goose before you ruin any more lives. The public will thank me."

Devlin leapt back with impressive agility as the deadly cane whistled through the air once more, narrowly missing him. "The public will also appreciate the sight of you swinging in the wind . . . they always like a good hanging, don't they?"

Amanda was impressed by Devlin's presence of mind at such a moment. However, Lord Tirwitt was clearly too maddened to care about the consequences of his actions. He continued to press his advantage, the cane whistling and jabbing as he endeavored to divest Devlin of one part of his anatomy or another. Devlin retreated to the desk, felt its edge against the back of his hips, and snatched up a leather-bound dictionary, using it as a shield. The blade slashed neatly through the cover, and Devlin hurled the heavy volume at his opponent. Turning aside, Lord Tirwitt deflected the solid blow with his shoulder, made an enraged sound as he absorbed the pain, then rushed at Devlin with the cane yet again.

While the two men struggled, Amanda glanced wildly around the room, her gaze settling on the set of iron fireplace tools by the hearth. "Excellent," she muttered, hurrying to snatch up the long, brass-handled poker.

Lord Tirwitt was too busy with attempted murder to notice her approach from behind him. Clutching the poker with both hands, Amanda raised the makeshift cudgel. She brought it down with as much force as she thought necessary, aiming for the back of his head. Her intent was to knock him unconscious without killing him. However, being unskilled in the art of combat, she did not hit him hard enough at first. It was a curious sensation, hitting the skull of a man with a poker. Her hands reverberated with the strange, rather sickening thud that the implement made. To her dismay, Lord Tirwitt spun to face her, a bemused expression twisting his face. The spear-tipped cane quivered in his meaty hands. Amanda hit him again, this time in the forehead, wincing as her blow connected.

Lord Tirwitt crumpled slowly to the floor, his eyes closing. Dropping the poker at once, Amanda stood there, feeling slightly dazed. She watched Devlin crouch over the fallen man.

"Did I kill him?" she asked unsteadily.

Chapter 5

"No, you didn't kill him," Devlin said in response to Amanda's anxious query. "A pity, but he'll live." He stepped over the unconscious man, strode swiftly to the door, and opened it to reveal the hired thug's expectant face. Before the man had a moment to react, Devlin sank a hard fist into the man's belly, causing him to double over with a groan and collapse to the floor. "Fretwell," Devlin called, barely raising his voice. One might think he were calling to request another tea tray. "Fretwell, where are you?"

The manager appeared in less than a minute, panting slightly from exertion. He was clearly relieved to see that his employer was all right. A pair of stout, muscular young men were right behind him.

"I've just sent for a Bow Street runner," Fretwell said breathlessly, "and brought a couple of the stockroom boys to help me dispatch with this . . ." He glanced distastefully at the thug. "This vermin," he finished with a grimace.

"Thank you," came Devlin's sardonic reply. "Good work, Fretwell. However, it appears that Miss Briars has the situation well in hand."

"Miss Briars?" The manager threw a bewildered glance at Amanda, who was standing over Tirwitt's crumpled body. "You don't mean to say that she . . . ?"

"Bashed his brains out," Devlin said, and suddenly the corners of his mouth twitched with irrepressible amusement.

"Before you continue to entertain yourself at my expense," Amanda said, "you might take care of that wound, Mr. Devlin, before you bleed to death in front of us."

"Good God!" Fretwell exclaimed, realizing that a patch of blood was spreading across Devlin's gray-striped vest. "I'll send for a doctor. I didn't realize that this madman had wounded you, sir."

"It's just a scratch," Devlin said matter-of-factly. "I don't need a doctor."

"I think you do." Fretwell's face turned a ghastly shade of gray as he stared at Devlin's crimson-soaked garments.

"I'll have a look at the injury," Amanda said firmly. After all her years in the sickroom, she was unfazed by the sight of blood. "Mr. Fretwell, you shall supervise the removal of Lord Tirwitt from the office, while I will tend to the wound." She looked into Devlin's indigo eyes. "Remove your coat, please, and sit down."

Devlin complied, wincing as he eased his arms from the sleeves of his coat. Amanda moved to help him, guessing that by now the slash on his side was beginning to burn like fire. Even if it were merely a scratch, it would have to be cleaned. Heaven knew what other uses the spear-tipped cane had been put to before today.

Amanda received the coat from him and draped it neatly over the back of a nearby chair. The wool still carried the heat and scent of his body. The fragrance was inexplicably alluring, almost narcotic in its effect, and for one irrational moment Amanda was tempted to bury her face in the intoxicating folds of fabric.

Devlin's attention was focused on the stockroom boys as they labored to carry Lord Tirwitt's inert body from the office. The man groaned in protest, and Devlin's face wore a look of evil satisfaction. "I hope that bastard awakens with a headache from hell," he muttered. "I hope he—"

"Mr. Devlin," Amanda interrupted, pushing him backward until he sat on the edge of the mahogany desk, "control yourself. No doubt you possess an impressive array of foul words, but I have no wish to hear them."

Devlin's white teeth gleamed in a quick grin. He sat very still as she moved to untie his gray silk cravat, her small fingers tugging at the simple knot. As she drew the length of warm silk away from his throat and began on the buttons of his shirt, Amanda was uncomfortably aware of the way he stared at her. His blue eyes were filled with warmth and mockery, leaving no question that he was enjoying the situation immensely.

He waited until Fretwell and the stockroom boys were out of the room before he spoke. "You seem to have a penchant for undressing me, Amanda."

Amanda paused on the third button of his shirt. Her cheeks flamed as she forced herself to meet his gaze directly. "Do not mistake my compassion for injured creatures as any kind of personal interest, Mr. Devlin. I once bandaged the paw of a stray dog I found in the village. I would place you in the same category as he."

"My angel of mercy," Devlin murmured, amusement dancing in his eyes, and he fell obligingly silent as she continued to unfasten his shirt.

Amanda had helped her ailing father to dress and undress many times, and she was hardly missish about such matters. However, it was one thing to help an invalid relative. It was an entirely different matter to remove the clothing of a young, healthy male.

She helped him off with his bloodstained vest, and finished the row of buttons on his shirt until the garment gaped wide open. With each inch of skin revealed, Amanda felt her face burning hotter.

"I'll do it," Devlin said, turning unexpectedly gruff when she reached for the cuffs of his shirt. He unfastened them deftly, but it was clear that the wound was making him uncomfortable. "Damn Tirwitt," he growled. "If this thing festers, I'm going to find him and—"

"It will not fester," Amanda said. "I shall clean

it thoroughly and bandage it, and in a day or two you'll be back to your usual pursuits." Gently she tugged the shirt from his broad shoulders, the golden skin gleaming in the firelight. She wadded up the stained garment, using it to blot the wound. It was a slash perhaps six inches long, located just beneath the left side of his rib cage. As Devlin had said, it was indeed only a scratch, though a rather nasty one. Amanda pressed the soft mass of the shirt firmly against the slash and held it there.

"Careful," Devlin said softly. "You'll ruin your gown."

"It will wash," she said in a matter-of-fact tone. "Mr. Devlin, do you keep some kind of spirits about the place? Brandy, perhaps?"

"Whiskey. In the small cabinet by the bookshelf. Why, Miss Briars? Are you feeling the need to fortify yourself at the sight of my naked body?"

"Insufferable coxcomb," Amanda said, although she couldn't repress a sudden smile as she stared into his teasing eyes. "No, I intend to use it to clean the wound."

She continued to hold the wadded-up shirt against his midriff, standing so close that his left knee was lost somewhere amid the rustling mass of her skirts. Devlin was motionless, making no effort to touch her, merely remaining in his half-seated posture. The gray wool trousers stretched snugly over his thighs, following the hard outlines of muscle. As if to demonstrate that he was no threat to her, he leaned back slightly, his large hands lightly gripping the edge of the desk, his body relaxed and still.

Amanda tried not to stare openly at him, but her dratted curiosity knew no limits. Devlin was as sleek and muscular as the black-and-gold tiger she had seen on exhibition at the park menagerie. Divested of his clothes, he seemed even larger, his broad shoulders and long torso looming before her. The texture of his flesh was heavy and tough, covered with skin that seemed hard but silken at the same time. His midriff was scored with rows of muscle. She had seen statues and illustrations of the male body, but nothing had ever conveyed this sense of warm, living strength, this potent virility.

And for some reason, artistic renderings had omitted a few fascinating details, such as the tufts of black hair beneath his arms, the small, dark points of his nipples, and the sprinkling of wiry hair that began just below his navel and disappeared behind the top of his trousers.

Amanda remembered the remarkable heat of his flesh, the feeling of pressing her breasts against that smooth male skin. Before Devlin could detect the sudden trembling of her hands, she moved away from him and went to the cabinet behind his desk. She found a crystal decanter filled with amber liquid and lifted it up.

"Is this the whiskey?" she asked, showing him, and he nodded. Amanda regarded the decanter curiously. The gentlemen of her experience drank port, sherry, Madeira, and brandy, but this particular form of liquor was unknown to her. "What exactly is whiskey?"

"Spirits made from barley malt," came the quiet rumble of Devlin's voice. "You might bring me a glass."

"Isn't it rather early for that?" Amanda asked skeptically, extracting a handkerchief from her sleeve.

"I'm Irish," he reminded her. "Besides, it's been a difficult morning."

Amanda carefully poured a finger of the liquor into a glass and moistened the handkerchief with a generous splash from the bottle. "Yes, I gather—" she began, then fell silent as she turned toward him. Standing behind the desk, she had an unhindered view of his bare back, and the sight was unexpectedly startling. The broad surface, narrowing to a lean waist, was developed and muscular, rippling with strength. However, the skin was crossed with faint stripes from some long-ago trauma . . . scars left from brutal thrashings and beatings. There were even a few raised ridges that showed white against the darker skin around them.

Devlin glanced over his shoulder, alerted by her sudden silence. At first his blue eyes were questioning, but almost immediately he seemed to realize what she had seen. His face turned cold and secretive, and the muscles of his shoulders bunched in visible tension. One of his brows arched slightly, and Amanda was startled by the proud, almost aristocratic cast of his features. He silently dared her to comment on a subject that was clearly forbidden. Wearing that particular expression, he could have easily been mistaken for a member of the aristocracy.

Amanda forced her own face to remain blank, and she tried to remember what his last words had been . . . something about a difficult morning. "Yes," she said evenly, coming around the desk with the glass of whiskey, "I gather that you are not accustomed to having someone attempt to murder you in your office."

"Not in the literal sense," he said wryly. Devlin seemed to relax as he realized that she was not going to ask about the scars. He accepted the whiskey glass and drank the spirits in one swallow.

Amanda was mesmerized by the movement of his long throat. She wanted to touch that warm column, and to press her mouth into the triangular indentation at the base of it. Her free hand balled into a hard fist. Good Lord, she must gain control over these urges!

Setting aside the glass, Devlin fastened his bright gaze on her. "Actually," he murmured, "the difficult part wasn't Lord Tirwitt's interruption. What I am having trouble with this morning is keeping my hands off you."

The statement was hardly courtly, but it had a certain blunt effectiveness. Amanda blinked in surprise. Carefully she reached out and took the bloodstained shirt away from his side, and dabbed at the bloody cut with the whiskey-moistened handkerchief.

Devlin jumped a little at the first stinging touch, his breath hissing. Gently Amanda dabbed at the slash again. He uttered a foul curse, shrinking back from the spirit-soaked cloth.

Amanda continued to clean the cut. "In my books," she said conversationally, "the hero would make light of the pain, no matter how great."

"Well, I'm not a hero," he growled, "and this hurts like bloody hell! Dammit, woman, could you be a bit more gentle?"

"Physically you are of heroic proportions," she observed. "However, it appears that the stature of your character is less impressive."

"Well, we can't all possess your sterling character, Miss Briars." His tone was threaded with sarcasm.

Annoyed, Amanda slapped the entire whiskey-dampened handkerchief on the wound, causing a sharp grunt to escape his lips as he struggled to master the sudden blaze of pain. His narrow blue eyes promised her a world of retribution.

They were both distracted by a sudden choking noise from nearby, and glanced in unison to discover that Oscar Fretwell had entered the room. At first Amanda thought that he was distressed by the sight of Devlin's blood. However, from the stiff quiver of his mouth and the slight watering of his sea-green eyes, it appeared that he was . . . laughing? What the devil did he find so amusing?

Masterfully the manager struggled to control himself. "I . . . ah . . . brought bandages and a fresh shirt for you, Mr. Devlin."

"Do you always keep a change of clothes at your place of business, Mr. Devlin?" Amanda asked.

"Oh, yes," Fretwell said cheerfully before Devlin could reply. "Ink stains, spills, marauding aristocrats . . . one never knows what to expect. It is best to be prepared."

"*Out*, Fretwell," Devlin said meaningfully, and the manager continued to grin as he complied.

"I like that Mr. Fretwell," Amanda said, reaching for a rolled bandage when the cut was cleaned.

"Everyone does," rejoined Devlin dryly.

"How did he come to work for you?" Carefully she wrapped the bandage around his lean midriff.

"I've known him since boyhood," he said, holding the end of the linen strip in place. "We went to school together. When I decided to enter the publishing business, he and a few of our classmates elected to follow me. One of them, Mr. Guy Stubbins, manages my accounts and bookkeeping, and another, Mr. Basil Fry, supervises my business abroad. And Will Orpin manages my bindery."

"What school did you attend?"

For a long moment there was no reply. His face was completely blank. In fact, Amanda thought he might not have heard her, and she began to repeat the question. "Mr. Devlin—"

"A little place in the middle of the moors," he said curtly. "You wouldn't know of it."

"Then why not tell me—" She tucked the loose end of the bandage neatly in place.

"Hand me my shirt," he interrupted.

The air nearly vibrated from the force of his annoyance. Shrugging slightly, Amanda abandoned the subject and reached for the neatly folded shirt. She shook it out with a deft snap and unfastened the top button. By sheer habit, she held it up for him as expertly as a seasoned valet, the way she had done so often for her father.

"You seem to be remarkably facile with men's clothing, Miss Briars," Devlin commented, buttoning the shirt unaided, concealing the wealth of muscle behind fresh white linen.

Amanda turned away, averting her gaze as he tucked the hem of the shirt into the waist of his trousers. For the first time, she enjoyed the freedom of being a thirty-year-old spinster. This was a distinctly compromising situation that no schoolroom virgin would ever have been allowed to witness. However, she could do as she liked by sheer virtue of her age.

"I took care of my father during the last two year of his life," she said in response to Devlin's comment. "He was an invalid, and required assistance with his clothes. I served as valet, cook, and nurse for him, especially toward the end."

Devlin's face seemed to change, his annoyance vanishing. "What a capable woman you are," he said softly, with no trace of irony.

She was suddenly caught by his warm gaze, and she realized somehow that he understood a great deal about her. About how the last precious years of her youth had been sacrificed for duty and love. About the inexorable pull of responsibility . . . and the fact that she had so rarely gotten to flirt and laugh and be carefree.

His mouth tilted upward at the corners in the promise of a smile, and her response to it was alarming. There was a spark of mischief in him, a sense of irreverent playfulness, that confounded her. All of the men she was acquainted with, especially the successful ones, were so utterly serious. She hardly knew what to make of Jack Devlin.

She floundered for something, anything, to break the intimate silence between them. "What did Mrs. Bradshaw write about Lord Tirwitt that would provoke him so?"

"Knowing the turn of your mind, peaches, I'm not surprised that you asked." Heading to a nearby bookcase, Devlin scanned the rows of volumes. He extracted a cloth-bound book and gave it to her.

The Sins of Madam B," Amanda said, frowning.

"My gift to you," he said. "You'll find the misadventures of Lord T in Chapter Six or Seven. You'll soon discover why he was sufficiently pro-voked to attempt murder."

"I can't take this filthy thing home with me," Amanda protested, staring down at the elaborate gilded adornment on the cover. All too soon, she made the discovery that when one looked long enough at the arrangement of curlicues, they be-gan to resemble some rather obscene shapes. She scowled up at him. "Why in heaven's name do you think I would read this?"

"For your research, of course," he said inno-cently. "You're a woman of the world, aren't you? Besides, this book isn't filthy by half." He leaned closer to her, and his velvety murmur caused the back of her neck to tingle excitingly. "Now, if you want to read something *really* decadent, I could show you some books that would make you blush for a month."

"No doubt you could," she returned coolly, while her palms turned wet on the book and a hot shiver went up her spine. She cursed silently. Now she couldn't return the damned book, or Devlin would see the moist imprint her hands had made on the leather. "I'm certain that Mrs. Bradshaw has done an excellent job of describing her profession. Thank you for the research mate-rial."

Laughter sparkled in the blue depths of his eyes. "It's the least I can do, after you dispatched Lord Tirwitt so handily."

She shrugged, as if her actions had been of no

importance. "Had I allowed him to murder you, I would never have gotten my five thousand pounds."

"Then you've decided to accept my offer?"

Amanda hesitated, then nodded, her forehead puckering in a little frown. "It seems you were correct, Mr. Devlin. I can indeed be bought."

"Ah, well . . ." He laughed quietly. "You might console yourself with the fact that you're more expensive than most."

"Besides, I have no wish to discover if you would really sink to the level of blackmailing an unwilling author to write for you."

"Usually I wouldn't," he assured her with a rascally gleam in his eyes. "However, I've never wanted an author this much."

Amanda gripped the book a little more tightly as he approached her. Stalked her, actually, moving with a stealthy slowness that made her nerves spark in sudden alarm. "The fact that I have decided to work with you does *not* give you the right to take liberties, Mr. Devlin."

"Of course." Devlin cornered her easily, not stopping until she had wedged herself against the bookshelves, the back of her head pressing against the leather spines of a row of volumes. "I was merely hoping to crown the deal with a handshake."

"A handshake," she said unsteadily. "I suppose I could allow—" She gasped and bit her lip as she felt his huge hand close over hers. Her short fingers, always so cold, were engulfed in heat. Once he had taken hold, he did not let go. It was not a handshake, it was a possession. The difference in their height was so extreme that she was forced to incline her head at an uncomfortable angle to look up into his face. Despite her sturdy and substantial figure, he made her feel almost doll-like.

There was something wrong with her breathing, a sudden wont of her lungs to take in too much air. Her senses dilated and quickened from an overabundance of oxygen.

"Mr. Devlin," she managed, her hand still caught in his, "why do you insist on publishing my novel as a serial?"

"Because owning books shouldn't be a privilege of the rich. I want to print good books in a way that the masses can afford them. A poor man needs the escape far more than a wealthy man does."

"Escape," Amanda repeated, having never heard a book described in such a way.

"Yes, something to transport your mind from where and who and what you are. Everyone needs that. A time or two in my past, it seemed that a book was the only thing that stood between me and near insanity. I—"

He stopped suddenly, and Amanda realized that he had not meant to make such a confession. The room became uncomfortably quiet, with only the jaunty snap of the fire to intrude on the silence. Amanda felt as if the air were throbbing with some unexpressed emotion. She wanted to tell him that she understood exactly what he meant, that she, too, had experienced the utter deliverance that words on a page could provide. There had been times of desolation in her own life, and books had been her only pleasure.

They were standing so close that she could almost feel the heat of his body against hers. Amanda had to bite her lower lip to keep from asking him about his mysterious past, and what he had needed to escape from, if it had something to do with the scars on his back.

"Amanda," he whispered. Although there was nothing lurid in his gaze or voice, she couldn't help remembering her birthday evening . . . how gently he had touched her skin . . . how sweet his mouth had tasted, how smooth and thick his black hair had felt against her fingertips.

She fumbled for the right words to break the spell between them; she had to extricate herself from this situation at once. But she was afraid that if she said anything, she might stutter and stammer like a nervous girl. The effect that this man had on her was appalling.

Mercifully, they were interrupted by the entrance of Oscar Fretwell, who knocked perfunctorily and came into the room without waiting for a reply. In his cheerful vigor, he seemed not to notice the way Amanda hopped away from Devlin, a guilty flush rising to the surface of her skin.

"Pardon, sir," Fretwell said to Devlin, "but the runner, Mr. Jacob Romley, has just arrived. He has taken Lord Tirwitt into custody, and wishes to interview you as to the particulars of this morning's hullabub."

Devlin did not reply, only stared at Amanda like a hungry cat that had just been eluded by an appetizing mouse.

"I must be going," she murmured, retrieving her gloves from the fireside chair and donning them hurriedly. "I'll leave you to your business, Mr. Devlin. And I will thank you not to mention my name to Mr. Romley—I have no wish to be spoken of in *Hue and Cry*, or in any other publication. You may have the credit for felling Lord Tirwitt all on your own."

"The publicity would sell more of your books," Devlin pointed out.

"I want my books to sell because of their quality, Mr. Devlin, not because of some vulgar piece of publicity."

He turned a genuinely perplexed frown on her. "What does it matter, as long as they sell?"

She laughed suddenly and addressed the manager, who waited nearby. "Mr. Fretwell, will you see me out?"

"It would be my pleasure." Fretwell gallantly presented an arm to her, and she took it as they exited the room.

Jack had always liked Gemma Bradshaw, recognizing their likeness as two hardened souls who had made something of themselves in a world that offered little opportunity for the lowly born. Each had discovered early in life that opportunity was something one had to make for oneself. This realization, combined with a bit of luck here and there, had allowed them to achieve success in their chosen fields, his of publishing and hers of prostitution.

Although Gemma had started as a streetwalker, and doubtless had excelled at it, she had quickly come to the conclusion that the threat of disease, violence, and premature aging so common to prostitutes was not for her. She found a protector with enough money to finance the purchase of a small house, and from there she had established the most successful brothel in London.

Gemma's house was run with intelligence and high standards. She had chosen and trained her girls carefully. She had made certain that her girls were treated as luxury items, high quality offered at astronomical prices, and there was no shortage of London gentlemen willing to pay for their services.

Although Jack appreciated the beauty of the girls who worked at the handsome brick house with its six white columns in front and ten balconies in back, and luxurious salons and bedrooms within, he had not accepted Gemma's standing offer of a free night with one of her girls. He had little interest in spending the night with a woman who could be had for a price. He liked to win a woman's favor, he enjoyed the arts of flirtation and seduction, and most of all, he couldn't resist a challenge.

Nearly two years had passed since Jack had approached Mrs. Bradshaw with the offer to write a book about the escapades that had taken place inside her infamous brothel, and about her own intriguing past. Gemma had liked the idea, sensing that such a publication would increase her business and enhance her reputation as the most successful madam in London. Moreover, she was justifiably proud of her achievements and was not averse to boasting.

So with the help of one of Jack's writers, she had filled her memoirs with good humor and naughty revelations. The book had succeeded beyond both of their most ambitious hopes, bringing a flood of money and publicity that had quickly boosted Gemma's establishment to a level of international repute.

Jack and Gemma Bradshaw had become friends, each relishing the opportunity to talk with brutal honesty. In Gemma's company, Jack was able to discard all the social niceties that usually prevented people from speaking plainly to each other. The amusing thought occurred to Jack that the only other woman he could talk to with such freedom was Miss Amanda Briars. It was odd, but the spinster and the madam shared the same refreshing quality of directness.

Although Gemma's schedule was always heavily laden with appointments, and Jack had called unexpectedly, he was shown to her private receiving room without delay. As he had suspected, Gemma had anticipated his visit. He was torn between amusement and irritation as he saw her lounging gracefully in the sumptuous parlor.

Like the rest of her home, the parlor had been designed specifically to flatter her coloring. The walls were covered in green brocade, the gilded furniture upholstered in soft shades of gold and emerald velvet, against which her piled-up red hair gleamed like a flame.

Gemma was a tall, elegantly voluptuous woman with an angular face and a large nose, but she possessed such remarkable style and self-confidence that she was often called a beauty. Her most attractive quality was her sincere appreciation of men.

Although most women claimed to like and respect men, there were only a few who actually did. Gemma was definitely one of them. She had a way of making a man feel comfortable, of making his faults out to be amusing rather than annoying ... of assuring him that she had absolutely no wish to change anything about him.

"My darling, I've been waiting for you," she purred, coming forward with outstretched arms. Jack took her hands and stared into her upturned face with a sardonic smile. As always, her hands were so heavily bejeweled that he could barely feel her fingers through the clattering rings and stones.

"I'm sure you have," he muttered. "We have a few things to discuss, Gemma."

She laughed in pleasure, clearly delighted by

her own clever prank. "Now, Jack, you aren't put out with me, are you? Truly, I felt that I was giving you a gift. How often would you have a chance to play stud to such a delightful creature?"

"You found Miss Briars delightful?" Jack asked skeptically.

"Naturally I did," Gemma replied, with no hint of sarcasm. Her dark eyes crinkled with amusement. "Miss Briars came to me as boldly as you please, requesting a man for her birthday the way one would order a cut of beef from the butcher. I thought it wonderfully brave of her. And she spoke to me in such a pleasant manner, just as I've always imagined respectable women talk with each other. I liked her exceedingly."

She sat gracefully on the chaise longue and motioned for him to take a nearby chair. In a habit that was second nature to her, she arranged her long legs so that their elegant shape was outlined by the skirts of her wine velvet gown. "Tolly," she commanded, and a maid seemed to appear from nowhere. "Tolly, bring Mr. Devlin a glass of brandy."

"I'd like coffee," Jack said.

"Coffee, then, with sugar and a pot of cream." Gemma's red lips—their lush color skillfully enhanced by rouge—curved in a sweetly appealing smile. She waited until the maid had left before speaking.

"I suppose you want an explanation of how the whole thing came about. Well, it was strictly by chance that you came to see me just a few hours after Miss Briars's visit. You happened to mention the book that you had acquired, and your desire to meet Miss Briars, and then the most delicious idea occurred to me. Miss Briars wanted a man, and I had none who would suit her. I could have sent Ned or Jude, but neither of those pretty-faced, empty-headed boys would do for her."

"Why not?" Jack asked darkly.

"Oh, come, now. I was not about to insult Miss Briars by sending over some lack-brains to divest her of her virginity. So as I was pondering the situation, and wondering how to locate the appropriate man for her, you arrived." She shrugged gracefully, more than pleased with herself. "It was no trouble at all to arrange things. I decided to send *you*, and since I've received no complaint from Miss Briars, I assume that you performed to her satisfaction."

Perhaps it had been the novelty of the situation, or his compulsive fascination with Amanda Briars, but for some reason, Jack had not considered until now that he owed Gemma Bradshaw his gratitude. She could easily have sent some arrogant pup who would not have appreciated Amanda's quality and beauty, and would have taken her innocence with no more thought than he would have picked an apple from a tree. The idea of that, and his reaction to it, were no less than alarming.

"You might have told me of your plans," he

growled, both furious and relieved. Good God, what if some other man had unexpectedly arrived at Amanda's house that evening, instead of himself?

"I couldn't take the chance that you might refuse. And I knew that once you met Miss Briars, you would not be able to resist."

Jack was not about to give her the satisfaction of admitting that she had been absolutely correct. "Gemma, what gave you the idea that thirty-year-old spinsters are to my taste?"

"Why, the two of you are exactly alike," she exclaimed. "Anyone could see it."

Mildly startled, he felt his brows tugging upward toward his hairline. "Alike in what way?"

"To begin with, the way you both seem to regard your hearts as if they are clock mechanisms that need repair." She snorted in amusement, and continued in a softer vein. "Amanda Briars needs someone to love her, and yet she thinks her problem is easily solved by paying for a single night with a male prostitute. And you, dear Jack, have always done your utmost to avoid getting the thing you need most—a companion. Instead, you are wedded to your business, which must be cold comfort when you're in your empty bed at night."

"I have all the damned companionship I need, Gemma. I'm hardly a monk."

"I'm not referring to mere sexual intercourse, you obtuse man. Don't you ever wish for a partner, someone you could trust and confide in . . . even love?"

Jack was annoyed to realize that he had no answer. Acquaintances, friends, even lovers, he had seemingly unlimited supplies of these. But he had never found a woman who was capable of satisfying his physical and emotional needs—and the blame rested on himself rather than on any lady in particular. There was something lacking in him, an inability to give of himself in anything but the most superficial ways.

"Miss Amanda Briars is hardly the ideal partner for a selfish bastard like me," he said.

"Oh?" She smiled provocatively. "Why don't you give it a try? You may be surprised by the results."

"I never thought you would try to play matchmaker, Gemma."

"Every now and again I like to experiment," she replied lightly. "I shall view this one with great interest to see if it takes."

"It won't," he assured her. "And if it did, I'd go hang before I let you know about it."

"Darling," she purred, "would you be so cruel as to deprive me of a little enjoyment when my intentions are so good? Now, do tell me what happened between the two of you that evening. I've nearly expired of curiosity."

He kept his face completely expressionless. "Nothing happened."

She let out a peal of delicious laughter. "You

should be more clever, Jack. I might have believed you, had you claimed there had merely been a bit of flirtation or even an argument . . . but it is clearly impossible that *nothing* happened."

Jack was not in the habit of confiding his true feelings to anyone. Long ago, he had learned the art of chatting easily without revealing anything. It had always seemed to him that there was no point in sharing secrets when most people were so damned unable to keep them.

Amanda Briars was a beautiful woman masquerading as a plain one . . . she was funny, intelligent, brave, practical, and, most of all, *interesting*. What troubled him was that he didn't know what he wanted from her. In his world women had clear uses. Some were intellectual companions, some were entertaining lovers, some were business associates, and most were either so dull or so clearly meant for matrimony as to be avoided altogether. Amanda fit into no precise category.

"I kissed her," Jack said abruptly. "Her hands smelled like lemons. I felt . . ." Finding no words to explain what had suddenly become inexplicable, he fell silent. To his dawning surprise, that quiet evening at Amanda Briars's home had assumed the form of an upheaval in his mind.

"That's all you're going to say?" Gemma complained, clearly annoyed by his silence. "Well, if that is the extent of your descriptive powers, it's no wonder that you've never written a novel."

"I want her, Gemma," he said softly. "But that's

not a good thing, for her or for me." He paused with a grim smile. "If we had an affair, it would end badly on both sides. She would come to want things I can't give her."

"And how do you know that?" Gemma mocked gently.

"Because I'm not a fool, Gemma. Amanda Briars is the kind of woman who needs—and deserves—more than half a man."

"Half a man," she repeated, laughing at the phrase. "Why do you say that? From all the reports I've heard of your anatomy, dear, you're extremely well accounted for."

Jack abandoned the subject then, understanding that Gemma had no wish or ability to discuss problems that had no concrete solution. In fact, neither did he. He turned to smile at Gemma's maid, who had entered the room with a cup of heavily creamed and sugared coffee. "Ah, well," he murmured, "there are other women in the world besides Amanda Briars, thank God."

Following his lead, Gemma mercifully let the subject drop. "Anytime you desire the company of one of my girls, just say the word. It's the least I can do for my dear publisher."

"That reminds me . . ." Jack paused to drink the hot coffee, then continued with a deliberately bland expression. "I received a visit from Lord Tirwitt at my offices this morning. He was displeased by his portrayal in your book."

"Really," Gemma said without much interest. "What did the old wind-guts have to say?"

"He tried to skewer me with a spear-point cane."

The comment sent the madam into a torrent of laughter. "Oh, dear," she gasped, "and I did try to be kind. Why, you wouldn't believe the things I omitted, things that were simply too distasteful to print."

"No one is accusing you of an excess of good taste, Gemma. Including Lord Tirwitt. If I were you, I would advise your staff to be vigilant, in case he should call on you after his stay at the Bow Street holding room."

"He wouldn't come here," Gemma said, wiping a stray tear of mirth from her kohl-smudged eyes. "It would only serve to confirm the nasty rumors. But thank you for the warning, darling."

They talked comfortably for a little while, about business and investments and politics, the kind of conversation that Jack could have had with any seasoned businessman. He enjoyed Gemma's tart humor and utter pragmatism, for they shared the same unscrupulous view that allegiance to any particular person or party or ideal was to be avoided. They would support either liberal or conservative causes according to what would best serve their own selfish purposes. Had they found themselves on a sinking ship, they would have been the first pair of rats to abandon it, and stolen the best lifeboat in the bargain.

Finally the pot of coffee had turned lukewarm, and Jack recalled other appointments he had scheduled for the day. "I've taken enough of your time," he murmured, standing and smiling as Gemma remained on the chaise. He bent and kissed her outstretched hand, his lips connecting not with skin, but with a mass of jewels that flashed and clicked beneath his mouth.

They exchanged friendly grins, and Gemma asked with seeming idleness, "Shall Miss Briars be writing for you, then?"

"Yes, but I've taken a vow of chastity where she is concerned."

"Very wise of you, darling." Her voice carried a note of warm approval, but there was a glitter of merriment in her eyes. As if she were laughing at him inwardly. Jack was perturbed to recall that his manager, Oscar Fretwell, had looked at him with the same secretive amusement this very morning. What the devil did people find so damned funny about his dealings with Amanda Briars?

Chapter 6

To Amanda's surprise, the contract from Jack Devlin was not brought to her house by an errand boy, but by Oscar Fretwell. The manager was as engaging as she had remembered, his turquoise eyes warm and friendly, his smile sincere. His polished good looks seemed to impress Sukey to no end, and Amanda had to suppress a grin as the little maid inspected him with brazen thoroughness. Amanda was certain that Sukey did not miss a detail, from the well-cut blond hair that shone like a new-minted gold coin, to the tips of his gleaming black shoes.

Sukey made a great show of bringing Fretwell to the parlor with the deference she might have accorded to visiting royalty.

At Amanda's invitation, Fretwell sat in a nearby chair and reached into the brown leather satchel at his side. "Your contract," he said, extracting a heavy sheaf of paper and giving it a triumphant rustle. "All it requires is your inspection and signature." He smiled somewhat apologetically as Amanda received the thick stack with raised brows.

"I've never seen such a long contract," she said wryly. "My lawyer's doing, no doubt."

"After your friend Mr. Talbot was finished with all the details and stipulations, it turned out to be an unusually thorough document."

"I shall read it without delay. If all is well, I will sign and return it on the morrow." She set it aside. She was surprised by her own feeling of anticipation, something she would not have expected to feel at the prospect of writing for a scoundrel like Jack Devlin.

"I am to give you a personal message from Mr. Devlin," Fretwell said, his blue-green eyes glinting behind his highly polished spectacles. "He said for me to tell you that he is wounded by your lack of trust in him."

Amanda laughed. "He is as trustworthy as a snake. In the matter of contracts, I would not leave a single detail open to question, or he would take certain advantage."

"Oh, Miss Briars!" Fretwell seemed genuinely shocked. "If that is truly your impression of Mr. Devlin, I can assure you that you are mistaken! He is a very fine man . . . why, if you only knew . . ."

"If I knew what?" she asked. She raised an eyebrow. "Come, Mr. Fretwell, tell me what you find so admirable about Devlin. I assure you, his reputation does him no credit, and while he possesses a certain slippery charm, I have so far detected no signs of character or conscience. I would be intrigued to hear just why you call him a fine man."

"Well, I will concede that Mr. Devlin is demanding, and he sets a pace that is difficult to follow, but he is always fair, and he gives generous rewards for a job well done. He has a temper, I'll admit, but he is also quite reasonable. In fact, he is more softhearted than he would want anyone to know. For example, if one of his employees is ill for a prolonged period of time, Mr. Devlin will guarantee that his job is waiting for him when he returns. That is more than most employers will do."

"You've known him for quite some time," Amanda said with a questioning lilt in her tone.

"Yes, since we were boys at school. At graduation, I and a few of the other fellows followed him to London when he told us that he intended to become a publisher."

"You all shared the same interest in publishing?" she asked skeptically.

Fretwell shrugged. "It didn't matter what the profession was. Had Devlin told us he wanted to become a dockmaster, butcher, or fishmonger, we still would have wanted to work for him. If it weren't for Mr. Devlin, we'd all be leading very different lives. In fact, few of us would be alive today if not for him."

Amanda tried to conceal her astonishment at these words, but she felt her jaw go slack. "Why do you say that, Mr. Fretwell?" To her fascination, she saw that Fretwell was suddenly uncomfortable, as if he had revealed far more than he should have.

He smiled ruefully. "Mr. Devlin places a great value on his privacy. I should not have said so much. On the other hand . . . perhaps there are a few things you should understand about Devlin. It is plain that he has taken a great liking to you."

"It seems to me that he likes everyone," Amanda said flatly, recalling Devlin's ease with others at Mr. Talbot's party, the great number of friends that had eagerly sought his attention. And he certainly got along well enough with the opposite sex. She had not missed the way the female guests at the party had fluttered and giggled in his presence, excited by the smallest attentions from him.

"That's a facade," Fretwell assured her. "It suits his purposes to maintain a wide circle of social acquaintances, but he likes very few people, and trusts even fewer. If you knew about his past, you would not be surprised."

Amanda did not usually attempt to employ charm to obtain information. She had always preferred a more straightforward approach. However, she found herself giving Fretwell the most sweetly appealing smile she was capable of. For some reason, she was very eager to learn whatever he had to tell about Devlin's past. "Mr. Fretwell," she said, "won't you trust me a little? I do know how to keep my mouth closed."

"Yes, I believe you do. However, it is hardly a subject for parlor conversation."

"I'm not an impressionable girl, Mr. Fretwell, nor am I some delicate creature given to vapors. I promise that I will not swoon."

Fretwell smiled slightly, but his tone was grave. "Has Devlin told you anything about the school that he—we—attended?"

"Only that it was a small place in the middle of the moors. He would not divulge the name."

"It was Knatchford Heath," he said, pronouncing the name as if it were a foul curse. He waited then, seeming to recall some long-ago nightmare, while Amanda puzzled over the words. The phrase "Knatchford Heath" was not unfamiliar to her—hadn't there been some ghastly popular rhyme that mentioned it?

"I know nothing about the school," Amanda said thoughtfully. "Except I have the vaguest impression . . . didn't a boy die there once?"

"Many boys died there." Fretwell smiled grimly. He seemed to distance himself from the subject even as he spoke, his voice compressing to a low monotone. "The place no longer exists, thank God. The scandal grew until no parents dared send their boys for fear of social censure. Had the school not been closed by now, I would personally burn it to the ground." His expression hardened. "It was a place attended by unwanted or illegitimate boys whose parents wanted to be rid of them. A convenient way to dispose of mistakes. That is what I was—the misbegotten son of a married lady who cuckolded her husband and wished to hide the evidence of her adultery. And

Devlin . . . the son of a nobleman who raped a poor Irish housemaid. When Devlin's mother died, his father wanted nothing to do with his bastard offspring, and so he sent the boy to Knatchford Heath. Or, as we fondly called the place, Knatchford Hell." He paused, appearing absorbed in some bitter recollection.

"Go on," she prodded gently. "Tell me about the school."

"One or two of the teachers were relatively kind," he said. "But most were fiendish monsters. It was easy to mistake the headmaster for the devil himself. When a student didn't learn his lessons well enough, or complained about the moldy bread or the slop they called porridge, or otherwise made some kind of mistake, he was disciplined with severe whippings, starvation, burning, or even worse methods. One of the employees at Devlin's, Mr. Orpin, is mostly deaf from having his ears boxed too hard. Another boy at Knatchford went blind from lack of nourishment. Sometimes a student would be tied to the gate outside and left all night, exposed to the winter elements. It was a miracle that any of us survived, and yet we did."

Amanda stared at him with a mixture of horror and compassion. "Were the boys' parents aware of what was happening to them?" she managed to ask.

"Of course they knew. But they didn't care if we died. I believe they rather hoped we would. There were never vacations or holidays. No parent ever came to see his boy at Christmas. No visitors came to inspect the conditions there. As I told you, we were unwanted. We were mistakes."

"A child is not a mistake," Amanda said, her voice suddenly unsteady.

Fretwell smiled slightly at the futility of the statement, then continued quietly. "When I came to Knatchford Heath, Jack Devlin had already been there for more than a year. I knew at once that he was different from the other boys. He seemed not to fear the teachers and headmaster as the rest of us did. Devlin was strong, clever, confident . . . in fact, if there was such a thing as a school favorite among students and staff alike, it was he. Not that he escaped the punishments, of course. He was beaten and starved as often as the rest of us. More often, in fact. I soon discovered that he would sometimes take the blame for other boys' misdeeds and be punished in their stead, knowing that the smaller ones would not be able to survive the severe whippings. And he encouraged the other larger, stronger students to do the same. We had to take care of each other, he said. There was a world outside the school, he reminded us, and if only we could survive long enough . . ."

Fretwell removed his glasses and used a handkerchief to polish the lenses with scrupulous care. "Sometimes the only difference between life and death is the ability to retain the smallest scrap of hope. Devlin gave us that little bit of hope. He made promises, impossible promises, that he later managed to keep."

Amanda was utterly silent, finding it impossible to reconcile her knowledge of the jaunty scoundrel Jack Devlin with the boy whom Fretwell had just described.

Evidently reading the disbelief in her face, Fretwell replaced his spectacles and smiled. "Oh, I am aware of how he must seem to you. Devlin paints himself as a reprobate. But I assure you, he is the most trustworthy and steadfast man I've ever known. He once saved my life at the risk of his own. I was caught stealing food from the school larder, and my punishment was to be tied to the gate all night. It was bitterly cold and windy, and I was terrified. But just after nightfall, Devlin sneaked outside with a blanket, untied me, and stayed until morning, both of us huddling under that blanket and talking about the day when we would be able to leave Knatchford Heath. At daybreak, when a teacher was sent out to retrieve me, Devlin had retied my ropes and vanished back into the school. If he had been caught helping me, I believe it would have resulted in his own death."

"Why?" Amanda asked softly. "Why did he put himself at risk for your sake, and for the others? I would have thought . . ."

"That he would have been concerned only for his own welfare?" Fretwell finished for her, and she nodded. "I confess, I've never really understood what motivates Jack Devlin. But I do know one thing for certain—he may not be a religious man, but he is a humanitarian."

"If you say so, then I believe you," Amanda murmured. "However . . ." She threw him a skeptical glance. "I find it difficult to accept that someone who once took painful beatings for others should have complained and carried on so about a mere scratch on his side."

"Ah, you're referring to your visit to the offices last week, when Lord Tirwitt attacked Devlin with that cane-sword."

"Yes."

For some reason, Fretwell began to smile. "I've seen Devlin tolerate a hundred times more pain that that without even blinking," he said. "But he is a man, after all, and not above trying to gain a little feminine sympathy."

"He desired *my* sympathy?" Amanda asked in astonishment.

Fretwell seemed ready to deliver much more of this highly interesting information, but he checked himself, as if suddenly doubtful of the wisdom of doing so. He smiled as he glanced into Amanda's round gray eyes. "I've said enough, I think."

"But, Mr. Fretwell," she protested, "you haven't finished the story. How did a boy with no family and no money eventually come to own a publishing business? And how—"

"I will allow Mr. Devlin himself to tell you the

rest someday, when he is ready. I have no doubt that he will."

"But you can't tell me only half a story!" Amanda complained, making him laugh.

"It's not mine to tell, Miss Briars." He set down his teacup and carefully refolded his napkin. "I beg your pardon, but I must be about my business, or I'll answer to Devlin."

Reluctantly Amanda sent for Sukey, who appeared with the manager's hat, coat, and gloves. Fretwell bundled himself in preparation for the brisk winter wind outside. "I hope that you will return soon," Amanda told him.

He nodded, as if he were fully cognizant that she wished to learn more from him about Jack Devlin. "I will certainly try to oblige you, Miss Briars. Oh, and I nearly forgot . . ." He reached into his coat pocket and unearthed a small object in a black velvet bag tied with silk cords. "My employer bade me to give this to you," he said. "He wishes to commemorate the occasion of your first contract with him."

"I cannot accept a personal gift from him," Amanda replied warily, not moving to take the velvet bag.

"It's a penholder," he said matter-of-factly. "Hardly an object that one attaches great personal meaning to."

Cautiously Amanda received the bag from him and emptied the contents into her open palm. A silver penholder, and a selection of steel nibs to be used with it, fell into her hand. Amanda blinked in uneasy surprise. No matter how Fretwell framed it, this pen *was* a personal object, as costly and fine as a piece of jewelry. Its heaviness attested to the fact that it was solid sterling, its surface engraved and set with pieces of turquoise. When was the last time she had received a present from a man, other than some Christmas token from a relative? She could not remember. She hated the feeling that had suddenly come over her, a sense of warm giddiness she had not experienced since girlhood. Although instinct prompted her to return the beautiful object, she did not heed it. Why shouldn't she keep the gift? It probably meant nothing to Devlin, and she would enjoy having it.

"It's lovely," she said stiffly, her fingers curling around the penholder. "I suppose Mr. Devlin bestows similar gifts on all his authors?"

"No, Miss Briars." Taking his leave with a cheerful smile, Oscar Fretwell ventured out into the cold, crackling hubbub of London at midday.

"This passage has to be removed." Devlin's long finger settled on one of the pages before him as he sat at his desk.

Amanda came around and peered over his shoulder, her eyes narrowing as she viewed the paragraphs he indicated. "It most certainly does not. It serves to establish the heroine's character."

"It slows the momentum of the narrative," he said flatly, picking up a pen and preparing to draw a line across the offending page. "As I reminded you earlier this morning, Miss Briars, this is a serial novel. Pacing is everything."

"You value pacing over character development?" she asked heatedly, snatching the page away before he could make a mark on it.

"Believe me, you've got a hundred other paragraphs that illustrate your heroine's character," he said, standing from his chair and following her while she retreated with the page in question. "That particular one, however, is redundant."

"It is *crucially* important to the story," Amanda insisted, clutching the page protectively.

Jack fought to suppress a grin at the sight of her, so adorably certain of herself, so pretty and lush and assertive. This was the first morning they had begun editing her book *An Unfinished Lady*, and so far, he had found it an enjoyable process. It was proving to be a fairly easy task to shape Amanda's novel into an appropriate form for serial publication. Until this moment, she had agreed with almost every change he had suggested, and she had been receptive to his ideas. Some of his authors were so mulishly stubborn about altering their own work, one would think he had suggested changing text in the Bible. Amanda was easy to work with, and she did not harbor great pretensions about herself or her writing. In fact, she was relatively modest about her talents, to the extent of appearing surprised and uncomfortable when he praised her.

The plot of *Unfinished Lady* centered on a young

woman who tried to live strictly according to society's rules, yet couldn't make herself accept the rigid confinement of what was considered proper. She made fatal errors in her private life—gambling, taking a lover outside of marriage, having a child out of wedlock—all due to her desire to obtain the elusive happiness she secretly longed for.

Eventually she came to a sordid end, dying of venereal disease, although it was clear that society's harsh judgments had caused her demise fully as much as disease. What fascinated Jack was that Amanda, as the author, had refused to take a position on the heroine's behavior, neither applauding nor condemning it. Clearly she had sympathy for the character, and Jack suspected that the heroine's inner rebelliousness reflected some of Amanda's own feelings.

Although Jack had offered to visit Amanda's home to discuss the necessary revisions, she had preferred to meet with him at the Holborn Street offices. Doubtless it was because of what had happened between them at her house, he thought with a pleasurable stirring of sensation at the memory. A faint grin tugged at his mouth as he mused that Amanda probably thought that she was safer from his advances here than in her own home.

"Give me that page," he said, amused by the way she retreated from him. "It has to go, Amanda."

"It stays," she countered, throwing a quick

glance over her shoulder to make certain that he wasn't backing her into a corner.

Today Amanda was dressed in a gown of soft pink wool trimmed in corded silk ribbon of a deeper shade. She had worn a bonnet adorned with China roses, which now reposed on the side of his desk, a pair of velvet ribbons draping gently toward the floor. The pink shade of the gown brought out the color in Amanda's cheeks, while the simple cut displayed her generous figure to its best advantage. Aside from Jack's considerable regard for her intelligence, he couldn't help thinking of her as a tidy little bonbon.

"Authors," he murmured with a grin. "You all think your work is flawless, and anyone who tries to change a single word is an idiot."

"And editors consider themselves the most intelligent people they know," Amanda shot back.

"Shall I send for someone else to have a look at that"—he gestured toward the page she held—"and give a third opinion?"

"Everyone here works for you," she pointed out. "Whoever you send for will certainly take your side."

"You're right," he allowed cheerfully. He held out his hand for the page, which she clutched all the more tightly. "Give it over, Amanda."

"Miss Briars to you," she returned smartly, and although she was not precisely smiling, he sensed that she was enjoying the exchange as much as he. "And I will not give you this page. I insist that it remain in the manuscript. What do you make of that?"

The challenge was too much for Jack to resist. They had already done a great deal of work that morning, and now he was ready to play. Something about Amanda absolutely compelled him to throw her off-balance. "If you don't give it to me," he said softly, "I'm going to kiss you."

Amanda blinked in astonishment. "What?" she asked faintly.

Jack didn't bother to repeat himself, with the words still rippling in the air between them, like the rings that spread when a stone dropped into a pond.

"Make your choice, Miss Briars." Jack discovered that he very much hoped she would push him to the limit. It would take very little provocation for him to carry out his threat. He had wanted to kiss her ever since she had set foot in his office that morning. The prim manner she had of pressing her lips together, distorting the voluptuous shape of her mouth . . . it distracted him to the point of madness. He wanted to kiss her senseless, until she was soft and receptive to whatever he wanted.

He saw Amanda struggle for composure, her body tensing. Hectic color crowded her face, and her fingers tautened until they began to crimp the page she so zealously protected. "Mr. Devlin," she said in the crisp voice that never failed to arouse him, "surely you don't play these ridiculous games with your other writers."

"No, Miss Briars," he said gravely, "I'm afraid you're the sole recipient of my romantic attentions."

The phrase "romantic attentions" seemed to rob her of speech. Her silver-gray eyes went round with astonishment. At that moment Jack was equally astonished to discover that although he had planned to leave her alone, he was powerless to control his reaction to her. His playfulness was abruptly shoved aside by deeper, more urgent instincts.

Although it was in his best interest to preserve a semblance of harmony between them, he did not want an amiable working relationship. He did not want an imitation of friendship. He wanted to bother and disconcert her, and make her aware of him in the same way that he was aware of her.

"No doubt it is some manner of compliment to be included in the great number of women who have received such attentions from you," Amanda finally said. "However, I haven't asked to be subjected to this sort of nonsense."

"Are you going to give me that page?" he asked with deceptive mildness.

Scowling, Amanda seemed to make a sudden decision, crumpling the parchment in her hands until it formed a tight, neat ball. She strode to the fireplace and tossed it into the flames, where it burned in molten radiance. Fire outlined the edges of the crumpled paper in blue-white heat, while the center of the ball rapidly charred and turned black.

"The page is gone," Amanda announced flatly. "You've gotten your way—now you should be satisfied."

Her gesture had been intended to dispel the tension between them, and it should have. However, the atmosphere remained curiously heavy and electric, like the burgeoning stillness that occurred just before a lightning-storm. Jack's usual easy smile felt tight as he spoke to her. "There have only been a few times in my life when I've been sorry to have gotten my way. This is one of them."

"I do not wish to play games with you, Mr. Devlin. I want to finish the work before us."

"Finish the work," he repeated, and saluted her like a soldier receiving orders from his commanding officer. Going back to his desk, he braced his hands on the mahogany surface and inspected his notes. "It's done, actually. These first thirty pages will make an excellent first installment. As soon as you finish the revisions we discussed, I'll have it printed."

"Ten thousand copies?" she asked tentatively, remembering the number he had promised her.

"Yes." Jack smiled at her uneasy expression, knowing exactly what she was worried about. "Miss Briars," he murmured, "it will sell. I have an instinct about these things."

"I suppose you must," she said doubtfully. "However . . . this particular story . . . many people will have objections to it. It is more sensational and . . . well, more *lurid* than I remembered.

I did not take a strong enough moral position on the heroine's behavior—"

"That's why it will sell, Miss Briars."

Amanda laughed suddenly. "Just as Madam Bradshaw's book did."

The discovery that she was willing to poke fun at herself was as pleasant to him as it was unexpected. Jack pushed back from the desk and came to stand next to her. Subjected to his sudden proximity, Amanda was unable to look directly into his face, her gaze sliding from the window to the floor, then latching onto the top button of his coat.

"Your sales will far exceed those of the celebrated Mrs. Bradshaw's," he told her, smiling. "And that's not because of any so-called lurid content. You've told a good story in a skillful manner. I like it that you haven't moralized about your heroine's mistakes. You've made it difficult for the reader not to sympathize with her."

"*I* sympathize with her," Amanda said frankly. "I've always thought it would be the worst kind of horror to be trapped in a loveless marriage. So many women are forced to marry because of pure economics. If more women were able to support themselves, there would be fewer reluctant brides and unhappy wives."

"Why, Miss Briars," he said softly. "How unconventional of you."

She countered his amusement with a perplexed frown. "It's only sensible, really."

He realized suddenly that this was the key to

understanding her. Amanda was so doggedly practical that she was willing to discard the hypocrisies and stale social attitudes that most people accepted without thinking. Why, indeed, should a woman marry just because it was the expected thing to do, if she were able to choose otherwise?

"Perhaps most women think it is easier to marry than to support themselves," he said, deliberately provoking her.

"Easier?" she snorted. "I've never seen a shred of evidence that spending the rest of one's days in domestic drudgery is any easier than working at some trade. What women need is more education, more choices, and then they will be able to consider options for themselves other than marriage."

"But a woman isn't complete without a man," Jack said provocatively, and laughed as her expression became thunderous. He held up his hands in self-defense, "Calm yourself, Miss Briars. I was only teasing. I have no wish to be bashed and battered as Lord Tirwitt was. Actually, I agree with your views. I'm no great proponent of the marital union. In fact, I intend to avoid it at all cost."

"Then you have no desire for a wife and children?"

"God, no." He grinned at her. "It would be obvious to any half-witted female that I'm a bad risk."

"*Quite* obvious," Amanda agreed, but she was smiling ruefully as she spoke.

Usually when Amanda finished writing a novel, she began on another right away. Otherwise, she felt uneasy and aimless. Without some kind of story in her head, she was positively adrift. Unlike most people, she never minded having to wait in a queue, or sitting in a carriage for a long time, or having long stretches of unfilled time. These were opportunities to reflect on her work-in-progress, to play with bits of dialogue in her head, to produce and discard ideas for her plot.

And yet, for the first time in years, she couldn't seem to produce a plot that excited her imagination enough to begin writing again. Her revisions on *An Unfinished Lady* were done, and it was time to launch into a new project, and still the prospect seemed curiously uninviting.

She wondered if Jack Devlin was the cause of this. For the past month that she had known him, her inner life did not seem nearly as interesting as the outside world. This was a problem she had never encountered before. Perhaps she should tell him to stop visiting her, she thought reluctantly. Devlin had developed the habit of calling at her home at least twice a week, without any kind of polite warning. It could be in the middle of the day, or even at suppertime, when she would be forced to invite him to share her evening meal.

"I've always been told that one should never feed strays," Amanda said darkly the third time he appeared uninvited for supper. "It encourages them to keep coming back."

Hanging his head in a useless effort to look penitent, Devlin sent her a coaxing smile. "Is it suppertime? . . . I hadn't realized it was so late. I'll go. No doubt my cook will have some sort of cold potato mash or warmed-over soup ready for me at home."

Amanda failed in her effort to look stern. "With your means, Mr. Devlin, I doubt that your cook is as wretched as you always make her out to be. In fact, I heard just the other day that you have a veritable mansion and a regiment of servants. I doubt they would allow you to starve."

Before Devlin could reply, a cold blast of winter air swept through the entranceway, and Amanda hurriedly bade Sukey to close the door. "Do come in," Amanda told Devlin tartly, "before I turn into an icicle."

Visibly radiating with satisfaction, he strolled into the warm house and sniffed the air with appreciation. "Beef stew?" he murmured, casting a questioning glance at Sukey, whose face split with a grin.

"Roast beef, Mr. Devlin, with mashed turnips and spinach, and the prettiest little apricot jam puddings ye've ever seen. Cook has outdone herself tonight, ye'll see."

Amanda's flicker of annoyance at Devlin's presumption was dispelled by amusement as she saw his obvious anticipation. "Mr. Devlin, you appear at my home so frequently that you never give me a chance to invite you." She took his arm and bade him to escort her to her small but elegant dining room. Although she often dined alone, she always ate by candlelight and used her best china and silver, reasoning that her lack of a husband did not mean she had to eat in spartan surroundings.

"Would you have invited me had I waited long enough?" Devlin asked, his blue eyes wicked.

"No, I would not have," she replied pertly. "I rarely welcome ruthless blackmailers to my table."

"You're not still holding that against me," he said. "Tell me the real reason. Are you still uncomfortable because of what happened between us on your birthday?"

Even now, after all the hours she had spent with him, the slightest reference to the sexual encounter between them still caused her face to flame. "No," she muttered, "it has nothing to do with that. I . . ." She stopped and sighed shortly, forcing herself to admit the truth to him. "I am not especially bold where gentlemen are concerned. Not to the extent of inviting a man to supper, unless there is some pretext such as business. I don't much care for the prospect of being refused."

As she had come to discover about him, Jack Devlin was fond of provoking and teasing her as long as she had all her defenses up. When she revealed the least hint of vulnerability, however, he became surprisingly kind. "You're a woman of property, fair of face, with abundant wit and a good reputation ... why in God's name would any man refuse you?"

Amanda searched his face for signs of mockery, but there was only an alert interest that disconcerted her. "I am hardly some siren who is able to lure anyone she chooses," she said with forced lightness. "I assure you, sir, there are indeed some men capable of refusing me."

"They're not worth having, then."

"Oh, naturally," Amanda replied with an awkward laugh, trying to dispel the disturbing sense of intimacy that blossomed in the air. She allowed him to seat her at the pretty mahogany table, set with green-and-gold Sevres china, and a silver cutlery with mother-of-pearl handles. A green glass butter dish adorned with elaborate pierced silverwork reposed between their plates. The cover of the butter dish was topped with a whimsical silver handle molded in the shape of a cow. Despite Amanda's preference for elegant simplicity, she had not been able to resist acquiring it when she had seen it at a London shop.

Devlin sat across from her with an air of comfortable familiarity. He seemed to relish being here, about to have supper at her table. Amanda was perplexed by his open enjoyment. A man like Jack Devlin would be welcome at many tables ... why did he prefer hers?

"I wonder if you're here because of a desire for my company or a liking for my cook's talents," she mused aloud. The cook, Violet, was only in her twenties, but she had a way of preparing hearty, ordinary food that made it exceptional. She had acquired her skills by working as an assistant to the cook in a large aristocratic household, making extensive notes on herbs and seasonings, and writing down hundreds of recipes in an ever-expanding notebook.

Devlin gave Amanda the slow smile that never failed to dazzle, a wry unfolding of humor and warmth. "Your cook's talents are considerable," he acknowledged. "But your company would season a crust of bread to make it fit for a king."

"I can't fathom that you find me so enjoyable," she said tartly, trying to stem the rush of pleasure that his words brought. "I do nothing to flatter or please you. In fact, I can't think of a single conversation we've ever had that hasn't resulted in some dispute."

"I like to argue," he said easily. "My Irish heritage."

Amanda was instantly fascinated by the rare reference to his past. "Did your mother have a temper?"

"Volcanic," he murmured, then appeared to laugh at some long-held memory. "She was a woman of passionate beliefs and emotions . . . for her, nothing was half measure."

"She would have been pleased by your success."

"I doubt it," Devlin said, the amusement dispersing to a quiet flicker in his eyes. "Ma didn't know how to read. She wouldn't have known what to make of a son who turned out to be a publisher. Being a God-fearing Catholic, she disapproved of entertainment other than Bible stories or hymns. The materials I publish would probably have inspired her to come after me with an iron fry pan."

"And your father?" she couldn't help asking. "Is he pleased that you've become a publisher?"

Devlin gave her a long, measuring stare before answering in a cool, rather contemplative tone. "We don't speak. I never knew my father, except as some distant figure who sent me to school after my mother died, and paid the tuition."

Amanda was aware that they were treading on the edge of a past filled with pain and bitter memories. She wondered how much he would trust her, and if she should persist in questioning him. It was a fascinating thought, that she might have the power to entice confidences from this self-possessed man that other people could not. Why should she even dare to think that she could? Well, his presence here tonight was proof of something. He did like her company—he wanted something from her—though she couldn't decide precisely what that might be.

Surely he wasn't here merely because of sexual interest, unless he was so desperate for a challenge that he had suddenly found sharp-tongued old maids to his taste.

Her footman, Charles, came to serve them, deftly setting covered glass and silver dishes before them. He assisted them in filling their plates with succulent beef and buttered vegetables, and poured wine and water into their glasses.

Amanda waited until the servant had left before she spoke. "Mr. Devlin, you have repeatedly avoided my questions about your meeting with Madam Bradshaw, and put me off with mockery and evasion. However, it is only fair, in light of my hospitality, that you finally explain what was said between you and her, and why she engineered that ridiculous meeting on the evening of my birthday. I warn you, not one morsel of apricot jam pudding will be set on your plate until you do."

His eyes gleamed with sudden enjoyment. "You're a cruel woman, to use my sweet tooth against me."

"Tell me," she said inexorably.

He took his time, leisurely sampling a bite of the roast beef and downing it with a swallow of red wine. "Mrs. Bradshaw did not believe you would be satisfied with a man of lesser intelligence than your own. She claimed that her only available men were too callow and dull-witted to suit you."

"Why should that have mattered?" Amanda asked. "I've never heard that the sexual act requires any particular intelligence. From what I've observed, many stupid people are easily able to produce children."

For some reason, that remark caused Devlin to laugh until he nearly choked. Amanda waited impatiently for him to regain his self-possession, but every time he glanced at her inquiring expression, it set off another spasm of laughter. Finally he downed half a glass of wine and stared at her with slightly watering eyes, a flush of color edging his cheekbones and the strong bridge of his nose.

"True," he said, his deep voice enriched with lingering amusement. "But the question betrays your lack of experience, peaches. The fact is, sexual satisfaction is often more difficult for women to achieve than it is for men. It requires a certain amount of skill, care, and yes, even intelligence."

As the subject for suppertime conversation, it was so far outside the bounds of propriety that Amanda turned red to her hairline. She glanced at the doorway, making certain that they were completely alone before she spoke again. "And it was Mrs. Bradshaw's opinion that you possessed the necessary qualities to, er, please me . . . whereas her employees did not?"

"Apparently." He had set his silverware down, watching the progression of emotions on her face with keen interest.

The knowledge that she should end this scandalous conversation at once, clashed violently with her curiosity to know more. Amanda had never been able to ask anyone about the forbidden subject of sexual intercourse, certainly not her parents, nor her sisters, who despite their married status seemed only a little less uninformed than she.

But here was a man who was not only able but willing to enlighten her on any question she cared to ask. Abruptly she gave up the struggle with propriety—after all, she was a spinster, and what good had her propriety ever done her? "What about men?" she asked. "Do they ever have difficulty in finding satisfaction with a woman?"

To her delight, Devlin answered the question without mockery. "To a young or inexperienced man, it's generally sufficient to have a warm female body in his vicinity. But as a man matures, he wants something more. The sexual act is more exciting with a woman who offers a bit of a challenge, who interests him . . . even a woman who makes him laugh."

"A man wants a woman to make him laugh?" Amanda asked with uncut skepticism.

"Of course. Intimacy is the most pleasurable with a partner who is willing to be playful in bed . . . someone who is amusing and uninhibited."

"Playful," Amanda repeated, shaking her head. The idea contradicted all her long-held ideas of romance and sex. One did not "play" in bed. What did he mean? Was he implying that sexual partners enjoyed jumping on the mattress and throwing pillows, as children did?

As she stared at him in bewilderment, Devlin appeared suddenly uncomfortable, his gaze alive and hot, as if blue flame had been captured in his eyes. A slight flush had risen on his face, and he seemed unable to loosen his tight clutch on his silverware. When he spoke, his voice had taken on a gravelly softness. "I'm afraid, Miss Briars, that we're going to have to change the subject. Because there's nothing I'd like better than to demonstrate what I mean."

Chapter 7

Devlin meant, Amanda realized, that he was becoming aroused by the conversation. She was stunned and embarrassed to discover that her own body had also been awakened by the intimate exchange. She felt sensation brushing along her nerves, centers of heat collecting in her breasts and stomach and between her thighs. How odd that the sight of a man, the sound of his voice, could produce such feelings—even in her practical, functional knees.

"Have I earned my apricot-jam pudding?" Devlin asked, reaching for a covered dish. "Because I'm going to have some. I warn you, only physical force will prevent it."

A smile came to her face, as he had intended. "By all means," Amanda said, pleased by the steadiness of her voice. "Do help yourself."

He expertly ladled two plump little puddings onto his plate and dug into them with boyish enthusiasm. Amanda searched for some new avenue of conversation. "Mr. Devlin . . . I would like to know how you became a publisher."

"It seemed a hell of a lot more interesting than scratching out numbers at some bank or insurance company. And I knew I wasn't going to make any money by becoming an apprentice. I wanted to start with my own shop, complete with inventory and employees, and the means to begin publishing right away. So the day after I graduated, I headed for London with a few of my schoolmates in tow and . . ." He paused, and a strange shadow crossed his face. "I arranged for a loan," he said finally.

"You must have been quite persuasive for the bank to advance you a loan sufficient to cover your expenses. Especially at such a young age."

Amanda's remark was complimentary, but for some reason, Devlin's eyes became dark and his mouth took on a moody curve. "Yes," he said softly, his voice laden with self-mockery. "I was quite persuasive." He drank deeply of his wine, then glanced at Amanda's expectant face. He resumed the story as if picking up an unwieldy burden. "I decided to begin with an illustrated magazine, and edit and publish a half-dozen three-volume novels within six months after starting the firm. There weren't enough hours in the day to get it all done. Fretwell, Stubbins, Orpin, and I all worked until we dropped—I doubt any of us slept more than four hours a night. I made decisions quickly, not all of them good, but somehow I managed to avoid making a mistake large enough to sink us. To start with, I purchased five thousand surplus books and sold them at cut-rate prices, which did not endear me to my fellow booksellers. On the other hand, I made money quickly. We couldn't have survived any other way. My peers called me an unscrupulous traitor—and they were right. But in the first year of business, I sold a hundred thousand volumes off my shelves, and paid back my loan in full."

"I'm surprised that your competitors did not conspire to put you out of business," Amanda said matter-of-factly. Everyone in the literary world knew that the Booksellers' Association and the Publishers Committee would unify to destroy anyone who didn't abide by the unwritten rule: never sell an underpriced book.

"Oh, they tried," he said with a grim smile. "But by the time they organized a campaign against me, I had acquired enough money and influence to defend myself against all comers."

"You must be quite satisfied with what you've achieved."

He gave a short laugh. "In my life so far, I've never been satisfied with anything. I doubt I ever will be."

"What more could you want?" she asked, fascinated and puzzled.

"Everything I don't have," he said, making her laugh.

The conversation became more relaxed then, and they talked of novels and writers, and the years Amanda had spent with her family in Windsor. She described her sisters and their husbands and children, and Devlin listened with an interest that surprised her. He was unusually perceptive for a man, she thought. He had a knack for hearing what she *didn't* say, as clearly as he heard her spoken words.

"Do you envy your sisters for having husbands and children?" He leaned back in his chair, a lock of black hair falling onto his forehead. Amanda was momentarily distracted by the thick, springy forelock, her fingers twitching with the desire to brush it back. She had not forgotten the texture of that dark hair, as smooth and resilient as a seal's pelt.

She pondered the question, wondering why it was that he dared to ask questions that no one else would . . . and why she responded to them. She liked to analyze other people's actions and feelings, not her own. But something compelled her to answer him truthfully.

"I suppose," Amanda said hesitantly, "that I might occasionally envy my sisters for having children. But I don't wish for a husband like either of theirs. I've always wanted someone . . . something . . . very different." As she paused reflectively, Devlin remained silent. The unhurried quietness of the room beckoned her to continue. "I've never been able to accept that married life is not what I imagined it could be. I always thought love should be irresistible and wild. That it should take complete possession of one. As the books and poems and ballads describe. But it was not that way for my parents, or my sisters, or indeed any of my acquaintances in Windsor. And yet . . . I've always known that their sort of marriage was the right kind, and my ideas of it were wrong."

"Why?" His blue eyes were bright with interest.

"Because it's not practical. And that kind of love always fades."

The corners of his mouth lifted in a beguiling smile. "How do you know that?"

"Because that is what everyone says. And it makes sense."

"And you like for things to be sensible," he mocked gently.

She shot him a challenging glance. "What, may I ask, is wrong with that?"

"Nothing." A taunting smile touched his lips. "But someday, peaches, your romantic side will triumph over your practical nature. And I hope that I'm there when it happens."

Amanda steeled herself not to bridle at his teasing. The sight of him in the candlelight, flame and shadow playing over his striking features, golden highlights touching the generous shape of his lips and the crests of his cheekbones, made Amanda feel hollow and hot, like a bottle that had been held over fire, the pressure of heat pulling sensation inward.

She longed to touch the rough, silken filaments of his hair, the velvety-hard skin, the pulse at the base of his throat. She wanted to make his breath catch in his throat, and hear him whisper Gaelic words to her again. How many women must have yearned to possess him, she thought in a sudden wash of melancholy. She wondered if anyone would ever truly come to know him, if he would ever allow any woman to share the secrets of his heart.

"What about you?" she asked. "Marriage would be a practical arrangement for a man like you."

Devlin settled back in his chair and regarded her with a smile lurking at one corner of his mouth. "How so?" he asked in a tone that was soft but crackling with challenge.

"Why, you have need of a wife to arrange things and act as hostess, and to provide companionship. And you must certainly desire children, or whom would you leave your business and property to?"

"I don't have to marry to get companionship," he pointed out. "And I don't give a damn what happens to my property once I'm gone. Besides, the world has enough children—I'll do the population a favor by declining to add to it."

"You don't seem to like children," she observed, expecting him to deny the statement.

"Not especially."

Amanda was briefly startled by his honesty. People who did not like children usually tried to pretend otherwise. It was a virtue to make a fuss over children, even the bratty ones who whined and misbehaved and generally made themselves objectionable.

"Perhaps you might feel differently about your

own," she suggested, falling back on a piece of conventional wisdom that had often been recited to her.

Devlin shrugged and replied easily, "I doubt it."

The subject of children seemed to have dispelled the feeling of unfolding intimacy between them. Devlin set his linen napkin on the table with great care and smiled slightly. "I should go now," he murmured.

Her unblinking stare had made him uncomfortable, Amanda thought with a flicker of remorse. She had a way of doing that sometimes, staring at people as if she were stripping away layers to reach the inside. She never meant to do it—it was simply a writer's habit.

"You won't take coffee?" Amanda asked. "Or a glass of port?" When he shook his head, Amanda stood, and made to ring for Sukey. "I'll have your hat and coat brought to the entrance hall, then—"

"Wait." Devlin stood also, and came around the table to her. He wore a curious expression, both absorbed and wary, like a wild animal that was being lured to take food from the hand of a stranger it did not trust. Amanda returned his intent stare with a politely inquiring smile, trying to appear composed when her heart had begun to thump in a mad rhythm.

"Yes, Mr. Devlin?"

"You have the strangest effect on me," he murmured. "You make me want to tell the truth— which is damned unusual, not to mention inconvenient."

She wasn't aware of backing away from him until she felt the brocaded wall panel press against her shoulder blades. Devlin followed her, bracing one hand near her shoulder, the other hanging loosely at his side. His pose was casual, but she felt surrounded, embraced by his nearness.

Amanda moistened her damp lips with the tip of her tongue. "What do you wish to tell me the truth about, Mr. Devlin?" she managed to ask.

The bristly fans of his lashes shrouded his expression, and he paused for a very long time, until she thought that he might not answer. Then he stared into her eyes. As they stood this close, the concentrated depths of blue were shockingly intense. "The loan," he muttered. The velvety timbre of his voice had become spare and flat, as if it were difficult for him to force the words out. "The loan I got to start my business. It wasn't from a bank or any other institution. It was from my father."

"I see," she said quietly, although they both knew that she didn't understand at all.

The large hand against the wall compacted into a fist, the knuckles pressed hard into the brocaded surface. "I'd never met him before, but I hated him. He's a peer, a wealthy man, and my mother was one of the housemaids. He either raped or seduced her, and when I was born, he tossed her out with a pittance. I wasn't the first bastard he'd sired out of wedlock, and God knows I wasn't the last. An illegitimate child has no meaning or interest for him. He has seven legal children by his wife." Devlin's upper lip curled with disgust. "From what I've seen, they're a litter of pampered, lazy good-for-nothings."

"You've met them?" Amanda asked carefully. "Your half brothers and sisters?"

"I've seen them, yes," he said in a bitter voice. "But they have no desire to become acquainted with one of their father's many bastard offspring."

Amanda nodded, staring at his proud, hard face as he continued.

"When my mother died and no one volunteered to take me in, my father had me sent to Knatchford Heath. It was . . . not a good place. A boy who had been sent there could hardly be blamed for thinking that his father wished him dead. And I was well aware that it would have been no great loss to the world if I died. It was that thought that kept me alive." He gave a short, grating laugh. "I survived on pure stubbornness. I lived purely to spite my father. I—" He broke off as he gazed into her calm face, and shook his head as if to clear it. "I shouldn't be telling you this," he muttered.

Amanda touched the front of his coat lightly, holding the edge between her fingers. "Go on," she murmured. She was very still, her body alive with the electric awareness that for some reason, he was opening to her, trusting her, in a way that he did with no one. She wanted his confidences . . . she wanted to understand him.

Devlin stayed with her, his gaze locked on her face. "When I graduated," he said gruffly, "I had nothing to borrow on, no name, no collateral, no family. And I knew I could never make something of myself without money to start with. So I went to my father, the man I hated most in the world, and I asked him to loan it to me, at any rate of interest he chose. I didn't know what else to do."

"That must have been difficult," Amanda whispered.

"The moment I saw him, I felt like I had been dipped in a vat of poison. I suppose until then I had a vague idea that he owed me something. But I knew from the way he looked at me, that I was not a son to him, or anything close to it. I was only a mistake."

A mistake. Amanda recalled that Oscar Fretwell had used the same word to describe himself and the other boys who had attended the school. "You were his son," she said. "He did owe you something."

Devlin seemed not to hear her. "The ironic thing is," he went on softly, "I look exactly like him. I resemble him more than any of his legitimate sons do ... all of them are blond and fair, like their mother. I think it amused him that I bore his stamp so obviously. And it seemed to please him that I would admit nothing about the school I had attended. He gave me every opportunity to complain about what a hell it had been, but I didn't say a word. I told him of my plans to become a publisher, and he asked how much money

I wanted from him. I knew it would be a devil's bargain. Taking money from him would be a betrayal of my mother. But I needed it too damned badly to care. And I took it."

"No one could blame you," Amanda said earnestly, but she knew that it didn't matter. Devlin was not inclined to forgive himself for his actions, no matter what anyone else said. "And you paid the loan back, didn't you? The matter is resolved now."

He smiled bitterly, as if the statement were impossibly innocent. "Yes, I paid him back in full, with interest. But it's not resolved. My father likes to boast to his friends that he gave me my start. He plays the part of benefactor, and I can't contradict him."

"The people who know you are aware of the truth," Amanda murmured. "That is all that matters."

"Yes." His expression became distracted, and Amanda sensed that he regretted having told her so much about himself. More than anything, she did not want him to be sorry for trusting her. But why had he? Why would he tell her what he clearly thought was the worst thing about himself? Had he intended to bring her closer or drive her away? His gaze dropped, and he seemed to be waiting for her censure, almost to want it.

"Jack," she said, his name tumbling from her lips before she realized it. He moved a little, as if intending to push away from her, and she reached out impulsively, her short arms catching his broad shoulders. She embraced him protectively, although it might seem ridiculous to shelter such a physically powerful creature. Devlin stiffened. To her surprise, and perhaps his, he gradually accepted her hold, hunching over to accommodate her short stature. His black head lowered almost to her shoulder. Amanda put her hand on the nape of his neck, where the warm edge of skin met the crisp edge of his collar.

"Jack . . ." She meant to sound sympathetic, but somehow her voice came out as briskly pragmatic as ever. "What you did was neither illegal nor immoral, and there is certainly no point in wasting your time with regrets. You needn't berate yourself for something you can't change. And as you say, you had no choice. If you wish for revenge against your father and siblings for their treatment of you, I suggest that you apply yourself to being happy."

He gave a brief huff of laughter against her ear. "My practical princess," he muttered, his arms tightening around her. "I wish it were that easy. But some people are not made to be happy—has that ever occurred to you?"

To a man who spent every minute of his life managing, controlling, struggling, and conquering, this moment of surrender was a damned odd experience. Jack felt dazed, as if a warm fog had suddenly descended on him and blurred the edges of the ruthless world he occupied. He wasn't certain what had caused his impetuous confession, but somehow one word had led to another, until he was blurting out secrets he had never told anyone. Not even Fretwell and Stubbins, his closest confidants. He would have preferred Amanda to mock him, or become coldly distant . . . that he could have handled with humor and sarcasm, his favorite defenses. But her support and understanding were unnerving. He couldn't seem to move away from her, no matter that the moment was spinning out far too long.

He loved her strength, her straightforward approach to life, her lack of maudlin sentimentality. It occurred to him that a woman like Amanda was what he had always needed, someone who would not be intimidated by the massive welter of ambition and turmoil that had troubled him all his life. She had an endearing confidence in her own ability to cut any problem down to size.

"Jack," she said softly. "Stay a bit longer. We'll have a drink in the parlor."

He turned his face into her hair, where the smoothly pinned-back wing at the side had ruffled into a mass of rebellious curls. "You're not afraid to be alone with me in the parlor?" he asked. "Remember what happened the last time."

He could feel her bristle. "I can manage you quite well, I believe."

Her self-assurance delighted Jack. He drew back and took her round face in his palms, and used his own weight to press her back against the wall. His spread legs contained hers within the rustling weight of her amber velvet skirts. Surprise glinted in her clear gray eyes, and a flush came over her face. She had beautiful fair skin, and the most tempting mouth he had ever seen, soft and rose-tinted, and nicely curved when she wasn't clamping her lips together in her usual habit.

"You should never say that to a man," he said. "It makes me want to prove you wrong."

He liked being able to fluster her, something he guessed that few men were able to do. She laughed unsteadily, still blushing, and she didn't seem able to think of a reply. Jack drew the pads of his thumbs lightly over the sides of her cheeks, the skin cool and silken. He wanted to warm her, to fill her with fire. He lowered his head and nuzzled the side of her face, letting his lips graze the soft skin.

"Amanda . . . what I just told you . . . it wasn't to gain your sympathy. I want you to understand what kind of man I am. Not noble. Not principled."

"I never thought you were," she said tartly, and he laughed against her cheek, and felt her shiver. "Jack . . ." She kept her cheek pressed against his, as if she enjoyed the sensation of his shaven skin. "You seem to be warning me about yourself, although I can't fathom why."

"You can't?" Jack drew back and looked down at her gravely, while his desire burned steadily through all rational considerations. Her silvery eyes were wide, as cool and refreshing as spring rain. He could stare into them forever. "Because I want you." He forced himself to speak through the sudden hoarseness of his voice. "Because you should not welcome me in for supper anymore. And when you see me walking toward you, you should run as fast as possible in the opposite direction. You're like one of the characters in your novels, Amanda . . . a good, moral woman who is getting mixed up in bad company."

"I find bad company quite interesting." She didn't look afraid of him at all, nor did she seem to understand what he was trying to tell her. "And perhaps I'm merely studying you for research purposes." She startled him by throwing her arms around his neck and touching her lips to the corner of his. "There—you see? I'm not afraid of you."

Her soft mouth burned him. Jack could no more control his response than he could stop the earth from turning. His head dove down, and he caught her mouth with his, kissing her with undiluted passion. She was luscious and sweet, her small but bountiful figure caught firmly in his arms, the abundant shapes of her breasts impelled against his chest. He explored her with deep strokes of his tongue, trying to be gentle, while a great bonfire blazed inside him. He wanted to tear the velvet dress off her and taste her skin, the tips of her breasts, the curve of her stomach, the fiery curls between her thighs. He wanted to debauch her a thousand different ways, shock her, exhaust her until she slept for hours in his arms.

Blindly he found the curves of her buttocks and

clamped his hands over them, bringing her loins against the prodding stiffness of his sex. Her skirts muffled the sensation, folds of heavy material preventing the intimate contact he longed for. They kissed even harder, straining together, until Amanda whimpered in growing agitation. Somehow Jack managed to tear his mouth away, his breath coming in steamy gusts, and he crushed her against his aroused body. "Enough," he whispered harshly. "Enough . . . or I'll take you right now."

Her face was hidden from him, but he heard the jerking rhythm of her breathing, and he felt her efforts to hold still despite the tremors that coursed through her body. Clumsily he petted her hair. The gleaming auburn curls were like coils of fire beneath his palm.

It was a long time before Jack could bring himself to speak. "Now you see why it is a bad idea to invite me into the parlor."

"Perhaps you're right," she said unsteadily.

Jack eased her away from his body, although every nerve screeched in rebellious protest. "I shouldn't have come here tonight," he muttered. "I made a promise to myself, but I can't seem to—" A soft growl rose in his throat as he realized that he was about to make yet another confession. What had happened to him, a man so scrupulously closemouthed about himself, that he couldn't seem to stop talking when he was around her? "Good-bye," he said abruptly, staring at Amanda's flushed face. He gave a brief shake of his head, wondering where the hell his self-possession had gone.

"Wait." Her fingers caught at his jacket sleeve. He looked at her small hand and struggled with the insane urge to snatch it and drag her fingers down the front of his aroused body and clamp them around his aching sex. "When will I see you again?" she asked.

A long time passed before he responded. "What are your plans for the holiday?" he asked gruffly.

Christmas was less than two weeks away. Amanda's gaze dropped, and she industriously settled the waistband of her gown to its proper place. "I intend to go to Windsor, as usual, and spend the holiday with my sisters and their families. I'm the only one who remembers the recipe for my mother's flaming brandy punch, and my sister Helen always asks me to prepare it. Not to mention the plum cake—"

"Spend Christmas with me."

"With you?" she murmured, clearly startled. "Where?"

Jack continued slowly. "I host a party at my home every year on Christmas Day, for friends and colleagues. It's . . ." He paused, unable to read her blank face. "It's a madhouse, really. Drinking, carousing, and the noise will deafen you. And by the time you manage to find your supper plate, the food is always cold. Moreover, you'd hardly know a soul there—"

"Yes, I'll come."

"You will?" He stared at her, astonished. "What

about your nieces and nephews, and the flaming brandy punch?"

She became more certain with each second that passed. "I'll write out the recipe for the punch and post it to my sister. And as for the children, I doubt they'll even notice my absence."

Jack nodded dumbly. "If you wish to reconsider," he began, but Amanda shook her head instantly.

"No, no, this will suit me very well. I welcome a change from all the screaming children and my sisters' badgering, and I deplore that bone-rattling carriage ride to Windsor and back. It will be refreshing to spend Christmas at a party filled with new faces." She began to usher him from the dining room, as if she half suspected that he would have the bad manners to rescind the invitation. "I won't keep you, Mr. Devlin, as you indicated that you wish to leave. Good night." She rang for the maid to bring his coat, and before Jack could fully grasp what was happening, he had been bundled out of the house.

Standing on the icy front doorstep, his shoes grinding into the sand that had been sprinkled to prevent them from slipping, Jack shoved his hands into the pockets of his coat. He walked slowly to his own waiting carriage while the driver prepared the horses for departure. "Why the hell did I do that?" Jack muttered to himself, stunned by the unexpected outcome of the evening. He had simply wished for an hour or two of Amanda Briars's company, and somehow he had ended up inviting her to his home for Christmas.

Jack climbed into the carriage and sat tensely, his back not quite touching the fine leather upholstery, his hands gripping his knees. He felt threatened, off-balance, as if the world he had comfortably inhabited had suddenly changed beyond his ability to adapt. Something was happening to him, and he didn't like it.

Apparently a small spinster had broken through his well-constructed defenses. He wanted to pursue her, equally as much as he wished to abandon her, and neither seemed possible. Worst of all, Amanda was a respectable lady, one who would not be content with a mere affair or a light dalliance. She would want to own the heart of any man she became involved with— she was too proud and strong-willed to desire anything less. And his calcified heart was not available to her, or to anyone.

Chapter 8

> *"Here we come a-caroling*
> *Among the leaves so green;*
> *Here we come a-wand'ring,*
> *So fair to be seen,*
> *Love and joy come to you,*
> *And to you glad Christmas too . . ."*

Amanda smiled and shivered in the open doorway as she, Sukey, and Charles listened to the children caroling on her front doorstep. The small group of boys and girls, a half-dozen in number, warbled the tune amid the folds of knitted scarves and caps that nearly concealed their faces. Only the tips of their reddened noses and the white puffs of their breath were visible as they sang.

Finally they finished the song, holding the last note as long as possible, while Amanda and the servants clapped in appreciation. "Here you are," Amanda said, giving a coin to the tallest child. "How many more houses did you plan to visit today?"

The boy answered in a thick Cockney accent. "We thought to find one more, miss, an' then it's 'ome to eat our Christmas supper."

Amanda smiled at the children, a couple of whom were stamping their feet to relieve the numbness of their toes. Many such children were sent out to carol on Christmas morning to earn some extra holiday money for the family. "Here, then," Amanda said, digging into the pocket at her waistband to find another coin. "Take this and go home at once. It's too cold for you to be outside any longer."

"Thank you, miss," the boy said in delight, and a chorus of echoes followed from his comrades. "Happy Christmas, miss!" The group hurried down the front steps and away from the house, as if they feared she would change her mind.

"Miss Amanda, ye oughtn't to give yer money away so freely," Sukey chided, following her into the house and closing the door against a rush of bitter wind. " 'Twouldn't harm those children to stay out a bit longer."

Amanda laughed and wrapped her knitted shawl more tightly around herself. "Don't scold, Sukey. It's Christmas Day. Now, let us hurry . . . Mr. Devlin's carriage will be arriving for me soon."

While Amanda attended the Christmas party at Jack Devlin's home, Sukey, Charles, and the cook, Violet, would be celebrating elsewhere with their own friends. Tomorrow, known as Boxing Day because coins and boxes of cast-off clothing and utensils were donated to the poor, Amanda and her servants would travel to Windsor for a week-long holiday at her sister Sophia's home.

Amanda would be glad to see her relatives on the morrow, but she was very pleased that she would spend today in London. How nice it was to do something different this year. She felt positively gleeful that from now on, her relatives would not always be certain of what to expect from her. "Amanda not coming?" she could almost hear her crotchety great-aunt exclaim. "But she always comes for Christmas Day—she has no family of her own. And who will make the brandy punch? . . ."

Instead, she would dance and dine with Jack Devlin. Perhaps she might even allow him to catch her under a sprig of mistletoe.

"Well, Mr. Devlin," she murmured, filled with anticipation, "we'll see what this Christmas Day will bring the both of us."

After taking a luxuriously hot bath, Amanda donned a robe and sat before the fire in her bedroom grate. She combed her hair until it dried in an explosion of reddish-brown curls. Deftly she twisted it into a coil atop her head, and allowed a few tendrils to dangle around her forehead and face.

With Sukey's assistance, she dressed in an emerald-green, corded-silk gown with two rows of fluted green velvet banding at the hem. The long velvet sleeves were confined at the wrist with jade bead bracelets, and the square neckline was cut low enough to reveal an enticing hint of cleavage. As a concession to the cold climate, she draped a burgundy silk-fringed shawl over her shoulders. A pair of Flemish-style earrings dangled from her ears like golden teardrops, gently swinging against the sides of her neck. Studying the overall effect in the mirror, Amanda smiled with pleasure, knowing that she had never looked better. There was no need to pinch her cheeks, as they were already pink with excitement. A fluff of powder on her nose, a dab of perfume behind her ears, and she was ready.

Wandering over to the window, Amanda sipped her cooling tea, and tried to still the leap of her heart when she saw that the carriage Devlin had sent for her had arrived. "How silly, at my age, to feel like Cinderella," she told herself dryly, but the ebullient feeling remained as she hurried downstairs in search of her cloak.

After the footman had handed her into the carriage, complete with foot warmers and fur-lined lap blanket, Amanda saw a wrapped present on the seat. Tentatively she touched the jaunty red bow atop the small square package, and extracted the folded notecard that had been tucked beneath the ribbon. A smile tugged at her lips as she read the brief note.

Although this is not quite as stimulating as Madam B's memoirs, you may find it of interest. Merry Christmas—

J. Devlin

While the carriage rolled along the icy street, Amanda unwrapped the present and stared at it with a quizzical smile. A book . . . a small and very old one, the leather cover ancient, the pages fragile and brown. Handling the volume with extreme gentleness, Amanda turned to the title page. "Travels into several Remote Nations of the World," she read aloud. "In Four Parts. By Lemuel Gulliver . . ."

She paused and then laughed in delight. *"Gulliver's Travels!"* She had once confided to Devlin that this "anonymous" work by Jonathan Swift, the Irish clergyman and satirist, had been one of her favorite childhood stories. This particular edition was the 1726 Motte original printing, impossibly rare.

Smiling, Amanda reflected that this small volume pleased her more than a king's ransom in jewels. No doubt she should refuse a gift that was so obviously valuable, but she couldn't make herself part with it.

She held the book in her lap as the carriage continued toward the fashionable area of St. James's. Although Amanda had never visited Jack Devlin's home before, she had heard about the place from Oscar Fretwell. Devlin had purchased the mansion from a former ambassador to France, who had decided in his declining years to establish residence on the Continent and relinquish his English holdings.

The house was located in a distinctly masculine preserve filled with handsome estates, bachelor lodgings, and exclusive shops. It was unusual for a businessman to own a mansion in St. James's, as most wealthy professionals built homes south of the river or in Bloomsbury. However, Devlin did have some aristocratic blood in his veins, and perhaps this, combined with his considerable wealth, made his presence more palatable to the neighbors.

The carriage slowed to join a queue of vehicles that had lined along the street, depositing their passengers in turn at the pavement leading to a magnificent house. Amanda could not prevent her jaw from hanging slack in astonishment as she stared through the frosted window.

The house was a splendid, towering, Georgian-style residence, red brick fronted with massive white columns and pediments, and rows of over-sized Palladian windows. The sides of the building were framed by immaculately trimmed yew and beech hedges that led to groves of coppiced trees underplanted with carpets of fresh white cyclamen.

It was a home that any person of consequence would be proud to claim. Amanda's imagination sparked to life while she waited for the carriage to reach the front walk. She pictured Jack Devlin as a boy at school, daydreaming about the life outside the grim walls of Knatchford Heath. Had he known somehow that he would someday live in such a place as this? What emotions had motivated him on the long, difficult climb from there to here? More important, would he ever find a respite from his own endless ambition, or would it keep driving him ruthlessly until the day he died?

Devlin didn't have the necessary limits that ordinary men possessed . . . he lacked the ability to relax, to feel contentment, to enjoy his own accomplishments. Despite that, or perhaps because of it, Amanda thought that Devlin was possibly the most fascinating person she had ever encountered. And she knew without a doubt that he was dangerous.

"But I am not some dreamy-headed schoolgirl," Amanda told herself, finding comfort in the knowledge of her own good sense. "I am a woman who can see Jack Devlin for what he is . . . and there is no danger as long as I don't allow myself to do something ridiculous." Such as fall in love with him. No; her heart contracted anxiously at the very thought. She did not love him, nor did she wish to. Finding amusement in his company was enough. She would keep reminding herself that Devlin was not a man whom a woman could have for a lifetime.

The carriage stopped, and a footman hastened to help Amanda to the pavement. She took his arm as he guided her up the icy, sanded steps that led to the double entrance doors. Conversation, music, and heat billowed from the brilliantly lit interior. Boughs of holly and mistletoe were strung along the banisters and cornices with scarlet velvet ribbons. The smell of spicy greenery and flowers mingled with the promising scents of an elaborate dinner being set out in the dining room.

There were many more guests than Amanda had expected, at least two hundred. While the children played in a separate parlor that had been designated for their use, the adults moved about in a large circuit of visiting rooms. Cheerful music that originated in the drawing room filtered throughout the house.

Amanda felt a pleasurable quake of her nerves as Devlin found her. He was elegant in a black coat and trousers, with a charcoal waistcoat tailored neatly to his lean torso. However, the gentlemanly attire did nothing to conceal his piratical nature. He was too irreverent and too obviously calculating to fool anyone into thinking he was a gentleman.

"Miss Briars," he said in a low voice, taking both her gloved hands in his. He raked her with a frankly approving glance. "You look like a Christmas angel."

Amanda laughed at his flattery. "Thank you for the lovely book, Mr. Devlin. I will treasure it. But I'm afraid I have nothing for you."

"The sight of you in that low-cut dress is the only gift I want."

She frowned at him, casting a quick glance around them to see if anyone was close by. "Hush . . . what if someone were to overhear you?"

"They would think that I have an itch for you," he murmured *sotto voce*. "And they would be correct."

"An itch," she repeated coolly, inwardly delighting in the exchange. "Dear me, how poetic."

He grinned at her. "I haven't your talent for writing rapturous descriptions of carnal lust, I'll freely admit—"

"I'll thank you not to mention such filthy subjects on a sacred holiday," she whispered sharply, her cheeks flaming.

Devlin grinned and placed one of her hands on his arm. "Very well," he said, relenting, "I'll behave like a choirboy for the rest of the day, if that will please you."

"It would be a pleasant change," she said primly, making him chuckle.

"Come with me—I want to introduce you to some friends."

It was not lost on Amanda that Devlin wore a distinctly proprietary air as he walked her into the large drawing room. Moving from one group of smiling guests to another, he deftly made introductions, exchanged good wishes, and offered a few small jokes with a natural ease that amazed her.

Although he had not staked a claim in any overt manner, there was something in his tone or expression that implied that he and Amanda were linked in a way that went beyond business. She was disconcerted by her own reaction to it.

She had never been half of a couple before, had never received envious glances from other women, or admiring stares from men. In fact, no man had ever made the effort of publicly establishing his claim on her, and yet in a subtle way, she sensed this was what Devlin was doing.

They progressed through the circle of large visiting rooms. For those guests who did not wish to dance or sing, there was a mahogany-paneled parlor in which a crowd was busily engaged in a game of charades, and another in which people sat at card tables to enjoy games of whist. Amanda recognized many of the guests—writers, publishers, and journalists whom she had encountered at various social events in the past few months. It was a lively crowd, the infectious holiday spirit seeming to spread from the youngest face to the oldest.

Devlin brought Amanda to a halt by a refreshment table, where a few children were engaged in a game of snapdragon. They stood on chairs around a bowl of steaming-hot punch, snatching up burning raisins in their small fingers and popping them quickly into their mouths. Devlin laughed at the sight of the sticky faces that turned toward him.

"Who is winning?" he asked, and they all pointed to a pudgy, mop-haired boy.

"Georgie is! He's gotten the most raisins so far."

"I have the quickest fingers, sir," the boy admitted with a sugar-smeared grin.

Devlin smiled and urged Amanda toward the huge bowl. "Have a try," he coaxed, and the children all began to giggle.

Amanda sent him a discreet frown. "I am afraid it would take too long to remove my gloves," she said demurely.

Devlin's blue eyes sparkled with wicked amusement. "I'll do it for you, then."

He stripped off his own glove, and before Amanda could utter a word of protest, he reached into the bowl. Snatching up a hot raisin, he popped it into her mouth. Amanda took it automatically, the morsel seeming to burn a hole in her tongue. The children erupted into gales of approving laughter. Amanda ducked her face to hide an irrepressible smile, while the rich-brandied raisin spread its sweet flavor through the interior of her mouth. After swallowing the little tidbit, she raised her head and regarded him reprovingly.

"Another?" Devlin asked with studied innocence, his fingers poised over the bowl once more.

"Thank you, no. I don't wish to spoil my appetite."

Devlin smiled and sucked the sticky spot the raisin had left on his finger, then replaced his glove. The children congregated around the bowl once more, resuming their game. They gave little pretend shrieks of pain as their fingers hovered over the scalding liquid. "What next?" he asked, leading Amanda away from the punch table. "Would you like some wine?"

"I shouldn't like to monopolize your time—surely you should be receiving your guests."

Devlin took her to a corner of the drawing room, taking a glass of wine from the tray of a passing servant. He gave the glass to Amanda and lowered his head to murmur in her ear. "There's only one guest who matters to me."

Amanda felt a prickling blush rise in her cheeks. She felt as if she were in a dream. This couldn't be happening to Amanda Briars, the spinster from Windsor . . . the sweet music, the lovely surroundings, the handsome man whispering seductive nonsense in her ear. "You have a beautiful home," she said unsteadily, in an effort to break the spell he seemed to have cast on her.

"I take no credit for it. I bought the place as I found it, furnishings and all."

"It's a very large house for just one person."

"I entertain a great deal."

"Have you ever kept a mistress here?" Amanda had no idea why she had dared to voice the shocking question that had popped into her mind.

He smiled, his voice gently mocking. "Why, Miss Briars . . . asking such a question on a sacred holiday . . ."

"Well, have you?" she persisted, having ventured too far to retreat now.

"No," he admitted. "I've had an affair or two,

but no mistresses. From what I've observed, it's too damned inconvenient—not to mention expensive—to get rid of a mistress once a man tires of her."

"When did your last affair end?"

Devlin laughed quietly. "I'm not answering any more questions until you tell me why you've taken such an interest in my bedroom activities."

"I may decide to base a character on you someday."

The remnants of a delicious grin lingered on his lips. "Then you may as well learn something else about me, my inquisitive little friend—I like to dance. And I'm rather good at it. So if you'll allow me to demonstrate . . ."

He removed the wineglass from her hand and set it on a small table, then led her toward the drawing room.

For the next few hours, the dreamlike feeling remained as Amanda danced, drank, laughed, and participated in holiday games. Devlin's duties as host occasionally took him away from her side, but even when he was standing on the other side of the room, Amanda was aware of his gaze on her. To her amusement, he sent her frankly brooding stares when she talked too long with any particular gentleman, for all the world as if he were jealous. In fact, Devlin actually dispatched Oscar Fretwell to intervene after she had danced twice with a charming banker named "King" Mitchell.

"Miss Briars," Fretwell exclaimed pleasantly,

his blond hair gleaming beneath the light of the chandeliers, "I don't believe you've danced with me yet . . . and Mr. Mitchell cannot be allowed to keep such a charming lady all to himself."

Regretfully Mitchell handed her over to the manager, and Amanda smiled at Fretwell as they began a quadrille. "Devlin sent you, didn't he?" she asked dryly.

Fretwell grinned sheepishly and didn't bother to deny it. "I was told to inform you that King Mitchell is a divorced man and a gambler, and is very bad company."

"I thought him quite entertaining," Amanda replied archly, and moved through the next figures of the quadrille. She caught sight of Devlin, standing in the wide arch between the drawing room and the parlor. Returning his frowning gaze with a cheerful little wave, Amanda continued the quadrille with Fretwell.

When the dance concluded, Fretwell escorted her to the refreshment table for a cup of punch. As a servant ladled the raspberry-colored liquid into a crystal cup, Amanda became aware of a stranger standing at her elbow. She turned and smiled at the man.

"Have we met, sir?"

"To my great regret, no." He was a tall, rather plain-looking man, his ordinary appearance enhanced by one of the close-trimmed beards that had recently become fashionable. His large nose was balanced by a pair of handsome brown eyes, and his mouth curved in an easy, comfortable smile. A full head of cropped russet hair was threaded with silver at the temples. Amanda judged him to be at least five or even ten years older than she . . . a mature man, established and quietly confident.

"Allow me to make the introductions," Fretwell said, adjusting his spectacles more securely on his nose. "Miss Amanda Briars, this is Mr. Charles Hartley. As it happens, the two of you write for the same publisher."

Amanda was intrigued by the fact that Hartley was also employed by Jack Devlin. "Mr. Hartley has my sympathy," she said, making both gentlemen laugh.

"With your permission, Miss Briars," Fretwell murmured with clear amusement, "I'll leave the two of you to commiserate while I go to greet some old friends who have just arrived."

"Certainly," Amanda said, sipping the tart, sweet punch. She glanced at Hartley as his name struck a chord of recognition. "Surely you're not *Uncle* Hartley?" she asked in delight. "The one who writes books of children's verse?" Receiving his nod of confirmation, she laughed and touched his arm impulsively. "Your work is wonderful. Truly wonderful. I've read your stories to my nieces and nephews. My favorite is about the elephant who complains all the time, or perhaps the king who finds the magical cat—"

"Yes, my immortal verses," he said in a dry, self-deprecating tone.

"But you're so clever," Amanda said sincerely.

"And it's so difficult to write for children. I could never come up with a thing that interests them."

He smiled with a warmth that made his ordinary face seem almost handsome. "I find it difficult to believe that any subject would be beyond your talent, Miss Briars."

"Come, let's find a private corner and talk," Amanda urged. "I have many questions I would love to ask you."

"That is a most appealing suggestion," he said, presenting his arm and leading her away.

Amanda found his company to be restful and soothing, different in every way from the dazzling stimulation that Jack Devlin's presence offered. Ironically, although Hartley made his living by writing books for children, he was a widower and had no children of his own.

"It was a good marriage," he confided to Amanda, his large hands still cradling a crystal punch cup, even though he had drained it several minutes earlier. "My wife was the kind of woman who knew how to make a man feel comfortable. She was very unaffected and agreeable, and never put on the silly airs that most females seem to have nowadays. She spoke her mind freely, and she liked to laugh." Hartley paused and considered Amanda thoughtfully. "She was rather like you, as a matter of fact."

Jack managed to extricate himself from a deadly dull conversation with a pair of classical scholars, Dr. Samuel Shoreham and his brother, Claude, both of whom were earnestly attempting to convince him that he should publish their manuscript on Greek antiquities. Striding away from the pair with poorly concealed relief, Jack found Fretwell nearby. "Where is she?" he asked the manager curtly. There was no need to explain who "she" was.

"Miss Briars is occupying the settee in the corner, with Mr. Hartley," Fretwell said. "She is perfectly safe with him, I assure you. Hartley is not one to make improper advances to a lady."

Jack glanced at the pair and then moodily surveyed the brandy in the glass he held. A strange, bitter smile pulled at his mouth, and he spoke to Fretwell without looking up.

"What *do* you know of Charles Hartley, Oscar?"

"You're referring to his situation, sir? His character? Hartley is a widower, and he is known to be an honorable man. He is of moderate wealth, born of a good family, and his reputation is completely free of scandal." Fretwell paused briefly and smiled. "And I believe he is adored by children everywhere."

"And what do you know of me?" Jack finally asked softly.

Fretwell frowned in confusion. "I'm not certain what you're asking."

"You know my business practices—I'm not honorable, nor am I scandal-free. I've made a fortune, but I'm illegitimate and I come from bad blood. On top of that, I don't like children, I abhor the idea of marriage, and I've never managed to have a relationship with a woman that lasted longer than six months. And I'm a selfish bastard . . . because I'm not going to let any of that stop me from pursuing Miss Briars, despite the fact that I am the last thing she needs."

"Miss Briars is an intelligent woman," Fretwell said quietly. "Perhaps you should allow her to decide what she needs."

Jack shook his head. "She won't realize her mistake until after she's made it," he said grimly. "Women never do in these matters."

"Sir . . ." Fretwell said uneasily, but Jack walked away, rubbing the back of his neck in the unconsciously weary gesture of a man who was driven by a ferocious will that dominated his better instincts.

Christmas dinner was superb, as course after course of remarkable dishes was served to guests, who all exclaimed in delight. The uncorking of wine bottles provided a steady rhythmic undertone to the clinking of glassware and the hum of animated conversation. Amanda lost count of the various delicacies that were offered to her. There were four kinds of soup, including turtle and lobster, and several roast turkeys dressed with sausages and herbs.

A never-ending parade of servants brought platters of veal in béchamel sauce, capons, sweetbreads, roast quail and hare, venison, swans' eggs, and a dazzling array of vegetable casseroles. Puddings made of exotic fish and game were presented in steaming silver bowls, followed by trays of luxury fruits and salads, and crystal plates laden with truffles in wine. There were even tender stalks of asparagus, well out of season and therefore highly prized at Christmastime.

As much as Amanda enjoyed the marvelous meal, she was barely aware of what she was eating, so enthralled was she by the man beside her. Devlin was extraordinarily charming, telling stories with a droll wit that certainly came from his Irish heritage.

A heavy, sweet ache formed inside Amanda, one that had nothing to do with the wine she had drunk. She wanted to be alone with Devlin, wanted to lure and possess him, if only for a little while. The sight of his hands made her mouth go dry. She remembered the incredible warmth of his body against hers . . . she wanted to feel it again. She wanted to pull him inside herself . . . she wanted the peace of physical release to encompass them both, to lie relaxed and happy in his arms. She'd had such an ordinary life, and Devlin seemed as brilliant as a comet streaking across the sky.

After what seemed an eternity, dinner was concluded and the guests separated into groups, some men remaining at the table for port, some ladies congregating in the parlor for tea, whereas many of both sexes gathered at the piano to sing carols. Amanda prepared to join the latter group, but before she could reach the piano, she felt Devlin's hand close around her elbow, and his deep voice murmured in her ear.

"Come away with me."

"Where are we going?" she asked pertly.

His polite social expression did little to mask the vibrant desire in his eyes. "To find a convenient bower of mistletoe."

"You'll cause a scandal," she warned, caught between laughter and alarm.

"Are you afraid of scandal?" He guided her through the drawing room door and down a darkened hallway. "You'd better stay with your respectable friend Hartley, then."

Amanda made a sound of amused disbelief. "You almost sound jealous of that kind, gentlemanly widower—"

"Of course I'm jealous of him," Devlin muttered. "I'm jealous of every man that looks at you." He pulled her into a large, shadowy room that smelled of leather and vellum and tobacco. It was the library, she realized dimly, while her heart thundered in excitement at the prospect of being alone with him. "I want you all to myself," Devlin continued gruffly. "I want all those damned people to leave."

"Mr. Devlin," she said shakily, her breath catching as he backed her against a bookcase and stood with his powerful body almost touching hers. "I think you've had too much to drink."

"I'm not drunk. Why is it so difficult for you to believe that I want you?" She felt his warm hands come to either side of her head, clasping her skull gently. His lips touched her forehead, cheeks, nose in soft, scorching kisses that drew fire to the surface of her skin. He spoke quietly, his rum-scented breath caressing her. "The question is, Amanda . . . do you want me?"

Words fluttered and collided inside her, while her body strained toward him so willfully that she could no longer keep from pressing forward into the large, muscular shape of him. He took her against him, urging her hips forward until their bodies were molded together as tightly as the layers of their clothing would allow.

The relief of being clasped firmly, held close by his hands, was so great that Amanda couldn't hold back a sudden gasp. He nuzzled into her bare throat, kissing, tasting, and her knees wobbled at the sensations that streaked through her. "Beautiful Amanda," he muttered, his breath rushing fast and hot against her skin. "*A chuisle mo chroi* . . . I said that to you once before, remember?"

"You didn't tell me what it meant," she managed to say, resting her soft cheek on his shaven, faintly scratchy one.

He pulled his head back and stared down at her with shadowed eyes that looked black instead of blue. His broad chest moved jerkily from the force of his breathing. "The very pulse of my heart," he whispered. "From the first moment we met, Amanda, I knew how it would be between us."

Her fingers trembled as she clutched the soft twilled wool of his lapels. This was desire, she thought dimly, and it was a hundred times more powerful than anything she had experienced before. Even on the night he had given her the shatteringly sweet climax that had kindled her senses to a brand-new awareness of pleasure, he had still been a stranger to her. And she was learning that there was a very great difference between wanting an attractive stranger and wanting a man she had come to care about. Through the shared confidences, the debates, the frequent laughter, and the simmering tension, something new had developed between them. Attraction and liking had changed into something dark and elemental.

He'll never be yours, her heart warned her swiftly. *He will never belong to you. He will never want to marry, or endure any kind of restrictions on his freedom. It will come to an end someday, and you'll be alone again.* She was too much of a realist to avoid the unsettling truth.

But all thought was chased away as his mouth closed over hers. His lips teased, settled, insisting until her own mouth relaxed and opened to him. Her response seemed to cause a small shock within him—she felt the reverberations in his throat and chest, and then the kiss turned harder, deeper, his tongue exploring her in eager surges. The invasion excited her, and she squeezed herself more tightly against him, until the abundant mounds of her breasts were compressed against his chest.

Devlin tore his mouth away from hers as if he could stand no more, his lungs dilating in swift expansions, his hands clamping tightly over her body. "God," he muttered into the pinned-up curls of her hair. "The way you fill my arms . . . it makes me insane. You're so sweet . . . so soft . . ." He kissed her again, his mouth hot and demanding, feeding on hers as if she were some choice delicacy that he craved. As if he were addicted to her, as if only the taste and texture of her could assuage his violent need. She felt delight coiling in all the tender places of her body, tightening, waiting for the trigger that would release the gathering tension in one ecstatic explosion.

His hands moved over her bodice, fumbling slightly as he searched the panels of corded green silk. The cool flesh of her breasts plumped out over the square neckline, their fullness resisting the tight containment of the gown. He bent and pressed his lips to the deep valley of her cleavage, then spread slow kisses over the revealed skin. Her nipples rose in hard points beneath the gown, and he touched them through the silk fabric, his thumbs rubbing, stroking, his fingers gently plucking. Amanda whimpered in distress, remembering their other time together on her birthday, how her body had been exposed to him in the firelight, the way his mouth had licked and tugged at her bare breast. She wanted that intimacy again, with a desperation that felt like madness.

Devlin seemed to read her mind, for his hand cupped over the rise of her breast and squeezed firmly to ease the yearning ache. "Amanda," he said hoarsely, "let me take you home tonight."

Her mind was foggy with sensuality. It took a long time for her to answer. "You've already offered the use of your carriage," she whispered.

"You know what I'm asking."

Yes, of course she understood. He wanted to go home with her, and accompany her to her bedroom, and make love in the bed that no one but she had ever slept in. Resting her forehead against his hard chest, Amanda nodded unsteadily. It was time. She understood the risks, the limits, the possible consequences, and she was willing to accept all of that in return for the sheer joy of being with him. One night with him . . . one hundred . . . whatever fate allowed her, she would take.

"Yes," she said into the soft, damp linen of his shirt, where the scent of his skin mingled deliciously with traces of starch and cologne and Christmas greenery. "Yes, come home with me tonight."

Chapter 9

Amanda had little awareness of time for the rest of the evening, only that it seemed to take an eternity for the guests to leave. Finally, weary children were bundled into the waiting carriages by parents flushed with wine and holiday cheer. Couples murmured discreetly in the entrance-way, exchanging plans and promises, as well as a few hasty kisses beneath the swag of mistletoe over the door.

Amanda saw very little of Devlin during the last hour of the party, as he was occupied with bidding the guests good-bye and accepting their good wishes. An irrepressible smile edged her lips as she realized what he was doing: subtly ushering the partygoers out the door and to their carriages with all possible speed. Clearly he was eager to be rid of them and alone with her. From the wary glance he directed her way, Amanda guessed that he suspected she might change her mind about her promise.

However, nothing would come between them

this evening. She had never felt so undefended and willing and filled with expectation. She waited with forced patience, sitting in a small blue-and-gold parlor and dreamily contemplating the yellow blaze in the marble fireplace. When all the guests were gone and the house bustled with servants cleaning and the musicians were carefully packing away their instruments, Devlin came to her.

"Jack." His name rose softly in her throat as he sank to his haunches before her and took one of her hands.

The firelight skimmed unevenly over one side of his face, highlighting half his features in brilliant yellow, leaving the rest in shadow. "It's time for you to go home now," he said, staring at her, not with his usual jaunty confidence or any hint of a smile. Instead, his gaze was intent and arrested, as if he were trying to read her private thoughts. "Do you want to leave alone," he continued gently, "or shall I accompany you?"

The tip of her gloved finger touched his cheek, where flame-glow touched the closely shaven bristles and turned them to brilliant flecks of gold. She had never seen a mouth as beautiful as his, the upper lip so perfectly shaped, the lower one softer, fuller, containing the promise of carnal delight. "Come with me," she said.

The interior of the carriage was cold and dark. Amanda placed her slippered feet directly on the foot warmer. Devlin's large body settled beside hers, his long legs taking up most of the available space below the seats. He laughed as he saw her greedily absorbing the heat of the coal-filled porcelain box after the footman closed the carriage door with a quiet click.

Devlin slid an arm around Amanda's shoulders, lowering his head to whisper in her ear. "I can make you warm." The carriage rolled away, jostling slightly as the springs over the wheels absorbed the uneven bumps of the road.

Amanda found herself being lifted effortlessly into her companion's lap. *"Jack!"* she exclaimed breathlessly while he pulled away her burgundy shawl and drew one hand over the back of her gown. He seemed not to hear her, his gaze fastened on the pale gleam of her half-exposed breasts as his other hand expertly found one ankle beneath her skirts.

"Jack!" she gasped again, pushing at his chest, but he exerted enough pressure on her back to cause her to collapse against him.

"Yes?" he murmured, his mouth brushing the soft skin of her throat.

"Not in a *carriage*, for heaven's sake."

"Why not?"

"Because it's . . ." The tip of his tongue touched her skin, tickling a sensitive nerve at the side of her throat, and she paused to suppress a little moan of excitement. "Vulgar. Common."

"Exciting," he whispered back. "Have you ever thought of making love in a carriage, Amanda?"

She jerked her head back to stare at him in

amazement, barely able to see his shadowed face in the dark interior of the vehicle. "Of course not! I can't even imagine how such a thing would be accomplished." When she saw the white gleam of his teeth, she immediately regretted her words. "No, no, don't tell me!"

"Instead, I'll show you," he said, murmuring intimate, mortifying things while his fingers worked stealthily at the back of her gown. She felt, from the series of little tugs and the loosening of her bodice, that he was making rapid headway with the garment.

When she had agreed to let him make love to her this evening, she had envisioned a romantic scenario in her own bedroom, *not* in his carriage. He stole kisses from her half-open lips and dragged his mouth along her throat. "Don't," she moaned. "We're almost there . . . the footman will know . . . oh, do stop!"

Jack cuddled her on his lap, staring into her shadowed gray eyes, always so alive with intelligence and challenge. Now the silvery depths were vulnerable, molten, utterly alluring. Excitement caused his heart to pound riotously, the mad pulse concentrating in his loins, bringing his cock to leaping arousal. He wanted to plunge into her, squeeze and bite and lick every tender inch of her.

He took her mouth in an ardent kiss, searching for her tongue, greedily absorbing the delicious taste of her. She responded willingly, letting him kiss her exactly as he wanted, her body arching as he spread the back of her gown open. His hand searched the length of her spine until he encountered the edge of her corset. Impatiently he tugged at the laces until they loosened and the stiff-boned garment relinquished its tight containment of her body. Amanda began to breathe in deep surges as her lungs were liberated from the prison of starch and stays.

Jack peeled the silk dress away from her front, and unhooked the front of the corset. The round shapes of her breasts spilled forth, covered only in the crumpled tissue of her chemise. Blindly he lifted Amanda higher on his lap and searched for the shadow of a nipple, found it, captured and licked and softly bit it through the linen. The sweet crest hardened in his mouth, and each scalding touch of his tongue drew a gasp from Amanda's throat. He pulled at the chemise, felt the delicate fabric tear beneath his fingers, then kept pulling until both her breasts were naked. Groaning, he buried his mouth in the valley between them, cupped his hands beneath the plump weights.

"Jack . . ." She could barely speak through her shallow, unfinished breaths. "Oh, Jack."

His avid mouth found her nipple again, his tongue circling the silken tip and lingering at the edge where the crest met the pale skin of her breast. The fragrance of her animated a response so primal that he lost all awareness of the world outside the dark, swaying carriage. Greedily intent on claiming his prey, he slid his hands beneath her skirts and settled her swaying body over his, spreading her thighs so that she straddled him fully.

As he might have expected, Amanda was no passive partner, her mouth entreating his with eager kisses, her hands wandering busily over his chest and midriff. The tightly fitted layers of his clothes and cravat defeated her, and she tugged at them with a moan. "Help me," she said shakily, fumbling at the waist of his trousers. "I want to touch you."

"Not yet." His palms slid over her drawers, finding the curve of her buttocks. "If you touch me now, I won't be able to control myself."

"I don't care." She tugged harder and managed to unfasten the top button. "I want to know how you feel . . . to hold you in my hands . . ." Her fingers moved over the hard shape that reared beneath the front of his trousers. The slight pressure caused him to jerk and groan. "Besides," she reminded him breathlessly, "you are the one who started this."

She was so adorably imperious, so passionate, that Jack felt his heart contract with a feeling he had never known before . . . a feeling that was too dangerous to examine. "All right, then," he said, his voice filled with lust and amusement. "Far be it from me to deny you anything you want."

He brushed aside her exploring hand and deftly unfastened the remaining six buttons. His erection sprang free of the thick, twilled fabric, twitching at the proximity of Amanda's soft female flesh. Jack's hands shook as he fought to control the urge to bring her fully over him and thrust inside her virginal body. Instead, he waited with forced patience, his teeth gritting as her cool fingers settled cautiously on the taut length of him, brushing the silken skin that stretched so tightly over the stiff upthrust of his sex.

"Oh," she said, her eyes half closing, her hand moving in gentle exploration. "I didn't expect . . . it's so hot . . . and the skin is so . . ."

Jack turned his face to the side, breath hissing through his clenched teeth as he struggled to endure the sensation. He felt Amanda's soft cheek press against his. "Does it hurt when I touch you?" she whispered, her fingers hesitating near the pulsing head of his erection.

"No, God, no . . ." He let out a shaken laugh that ended in a groan. "It feels good. *Mhuirnin* . . . you're killing me . . . you must stop now." Taking hold of her wrist, he eased her hand away, and reached for the long slit of her drawers. He pulled at the opening until he felt stitches pop, then reached inside with his thumb and grazed the patch of damp red curls.

"My turn," he murmured, kissing her hot face as he drew his thumb gently into the crevice hidden beneath the curls, repeating the action until the feminine lips were swollen and separated. He felt her thighs tighten around his, and he used his legs to keep hers spread wide, her body rendered open and helpless to his touch.

Locating the entrance to her body, he stroked,

teased, until he felt the gathering moisture against his fingertip. Amanda groaned and pressed against his hand, seeking more stimulation. He kept his touch maddeningly light, resting his thumb just above the delicate rise of female flesh that had become swollen and unbearably sensitive. She trembled and writhed as he circled his thumb in tickling swirls.

Carefully he brought their loins together, not penetrating her, just allowing the sensitive underside of his sex to rub into the wet notch between her legs. Each jolt of the well-sprung carriage urged their bodies closer. Jack closed his eyes as the sensation climbed to an excruciating height. He froze with pleasure as his self-control began to shatter. He was going to climax soon . . . no, he couldn't allow that, not here, not yet. Cursing in his throat, he clutched her round hips in his hands and pushed her back from his straining erection.

"Jack," she gasped, "I need you . . . need you . . . oh, Lord, please—"

"Yes," he muttered, his entire body stiff and sweating. "I'll give you ease, darling. Soon. But we can wait a little longer, *mhuirnin* . . . we'll do this properly, in a comfortable bed. I never meant to go this far in the carriage . . . it's just . . . I couldn't help myself. Turn around now, and let me fasten your dress—"

"Don't wait," she said thickly. "I want you now." She kissed his mouth, using her tongue to taste him, incite him, and his thighs turned to iron beneath her.

"No." He laughed unsteadily and cupped her face in his hands, brushing kisses against her mouth. "You'll regret it if we don't wait . . . oh, sweet . . . let me stop while I'm still able."

"I've waited thirty years," she whispered, lurching awkwardly to bring herself over him. "Let me decide when and where. Please. You decide the next time."

The mention of "the next time," and the thought of all he was going to do to her, with her, for her, became too much for him to resist. "We shouldn't," he heard himself saying raspily, even as he reached beneath her skirts and positioned her over his hips.

"I don't care. Do it now . . . now . . ." Her words dissolved in a low moan as she felt his thumb teasing her once more, while his middle finger slid inside her.

Jack stared into the drowsy gray softness of her eyes, watched her lashes lower as the color of passion ascended her cheeks. Her hands clutched at his shoulders, his chest, and she pushed closer to him, gasping, and he felt the hot interior of her body tightening around the gentle invasion of his finger. Her mouth sought his, and he kissed her as deeply as she wanted, slowly plunging his tongue in rhythm with the thrust of his finger, using all his skill to bring her closer, closer.

A shaken sound escaped her, and then a moan, and she clutched him tightly as an intense climax streaked through her. She shivered, arched, crushed herself against him, while her sheath contracted in sinuous ripples. Murmuring low in his throat, Jack withdrew his finger and positioned her over his aching sex. He teased the wet opening to her body with the head of his shaft, circling, nudging, and Amanda pressed down on him eagerly. She caught her breath at the first pain of his entry, but her body continued to push downward until he finally penetrated her with one sure thrust.

Jack tilted his head backward, eyes closed, his forehead drawn in a fierce frown. The feminine weight of her pressed on his thighs, while her body held his in a snug clasp. The pleasure of it was too great to bear. He couldn't think or speak, couldn't form her name. He could only sit there while sensation glided over him in relentless waves. He felt Amanda lean forward, her parted lips touching his exposed throat where the pulse throbbed beneath his jaw. Her tongue brushed his skin in dainty exploration, and he breathed harshly. His hips lifted against hers, his cock nudging deeper inside her, and her sheath squeezed tightly in response. He heard his own full-throated cry as he drove in the final thrust of release, straining and shuddering in ecstasy. Finally able to move, he clutched her head in his hands, devouring her, aware that his kisses were probably bruising her tender mouth, but she didn't seem to mind.

The sound of their labored breathing was slow to diminish. Jack held Amanda against his chest, resting his large hand over her rumpled hair while the other moved in circles over her naked back. She shivered at the contrast between the cool air and his warm hand. He muttered a curse and fumbled with the back of her corset, realizing that the carriage was slowing.

"Dammit. Dammit. We're there now."

Amanda remained relaxed and pliant against him, not seeming to share his sudden urgency. Languidly she reached over and latched the door. When she spoke, her voice was thick and husky. "It's all right, Jack."

Scowling, he jerked the edges of her dress together and fastened it deftly. "I should have kept my head . . . should have made us both wait. That was no way to take a virgin. I intended to be gentle with you, I was going to—"

"It was exactly what I wanted." She regarded him with a slight smile, her face still flushed, her gray eyes brilliant. "And I wasn't your usual sort of virgin, so I fail to see why we should have done it the conventional way."

Still frowning, Jack took hold of her waist and lifted her, and she gasped as he withdrew from her body. Understanding her intimate needs, Jack somehow managed to find the handkerchief in his coat pocket, and he gave it to Amanda silently. Clearly embarrassed, she used it to blot the abundant wetness between her thighs. "I hurt you," Jack said in gruff remorse, and she shook her head immediately.

"The discomfort wasn't as great as I had been led to expect," she said. "One hears tales of agonizing wedding nights, but it wasn't nearly as terrible as I thought it might be."

"Amanda," he muttered, amused despite himself by her chatter, and he hugged her tightly. He kissed her hair and the side of her face and the corner of her mouth.

The carriage came to an abrupt stop. They were at Amanda's house. Muttering beneath his breath, Jack tugged and jerked at his clothes, settling them into place, while Amanda tried to restore her coiffure. She refastened a few hairpins, then found her burgundy shawl and draped it over her shoulders. "How do I look?" she asked.

Jack shook his head ruefully as he glanced at her. No one could mistake the remaining flush on her cheeks, or the soft sparkle of her eyes, or her lusciously swollen mouth, for anything other than the results of physical passion. "Like you've been ravished," he said flatly.

She astonished him by smiling. "Hurry, please. I want to go inside my house and consult a looking glass. I've always wanted to know what a ravished woman looks like."

"And then what?"

Her gray eyes regarded him steadily. "And then I want to remove all your clothes. I've never seen a completely naked man before."

A reluctant smile hovered at the corners of his lips. "I'm at your disposal." He reached out to play with a tendril of fiery hair that curled near her ear.

She was silent for a moment, staring at him

without blinking, and he wondered what thoughts occupied her mind. "That is something we should discuss," she finally murmured. "I suppose we had better set terms."

"Set terms?" His hand stilled in her hair.

"For our affair." An uncertain frown marred the smoothness of her brow. "You do want an affair with me, don't you?"

Chapter 10

"Hell, yes, I want an affair." Jack stared at her with amused resignation as he added, "But I should have known you'd want to plan the damned thing out."

"Is that wrong of me?" Amanda asked. "Why shouldn't I try to arrange an affair in a sensible manner?"

"All right," he murmured, his voice vibrant with laughter. "Let's go inside and negotiate. I can hardly wait to hear your plans."

The footman opened the carriage door, and Amanda allowed Jack to escort her inside the empty house. Her legs were shaky and the place between her thighs was wet and sore and stinging. Wryly she reflected that this was certainly a Christmas that she would never forget. A straggling curl of reddish-brown hair fell from her disheveled coiffure, dangling over her right eye. She pushed back the springy lock, tucking it behind her ear, and thought of Jack's urgent fingers clasping her head, his mouth fitted securely to hers.

Surely she hadn't just surrendered her virginity in such a manner . . . and yet the insistent soreness between her thighs, and the invisible but tangible imprints of his hands on her body, were proof that she had. She searched her soul for regrets, but she had none.

No man had ever made her feel so desirable and fulfilled, and so unlike a spinster. She only hoped that she could keep from revealing her love to him.

For she did love him.

The realization had come over her, not with the immediacy of a summer thunderstorm, but with the slow persistence of April rain. She thought it unlikely that any woman could keep from falling in love with Jack Devlin, as handsome and wily and damaged as he was. She entertained no illusions about his loving her in return, or about the potential of his interest in her withstanding the test of time. If he were capable of loving a woman, he would have done so long before now, with one of the many women he had known in the past.

And even if a woman did manage to entrap him into marriage, it would doubtless be a miserable, unfulfilling experience. He was a handsome man with wealth and position; women would forever be throwing themselves at him. And he'd never be able to return a wife's love.

She would simply take what she could have of him, and do her best to ensure that the affair would not end in bitterness on either side.

They went into the parlor, where Jack extracted matches from a silver match safe and struck a fire in the grate. Amanda sank to the flowered carpet before the leaping blaze, stretching her hands toward the warmth. Lowering himself to the space beside her, Jack slid an arm behind her back. She felt him kiss the top of her head, his mouth moving gently amid the disheveled curls.

"Now tell me your terms, before I ravish you again," he said, his voice husky.

She struggled to remember exactly which points she had wished to make. It was difficult to think clearly with his body so close to hers. "First, I insist on our mutual discretion," she said. "I have a great deal to lose, should our intimate relationship become public knowledge. There will be rumors, of course, but as long as we do not flaunt our activities, there will be no great scandal. And also . . ." She paused as she felt his hand coast along her spine. Her eyes closed, the firelight flickering in scarlet patterns across her eyelids.

"Also?" he prompted, his breath hot against her ear.

"Also, I wish for our affair to be of a limited duration. Three months, perhaps. At the end of that time, we shall conclude the liaison as friends, and go our separate ways."

Although she could not see Jack's face, she sensed from the sudden tension in his body that the request had startled him. "I suppose you have a list of reasons for that. God knows I'd like to hear them."

Amanda nodded decisively. "From what I have observed, it always seems that affairs end in boredom, or arguments, or jealousy. But if we decide in advance exactly when and how the affair should be over, we may still be able to part amicably. I should hate to lose your friendship when the passion ends."

"Why are you so certain that it will end?"

"Well, no affair can last forever . . . can it?"

Instead of answering, he countered with another question. "What if neither one of us wants to break things off in three months?"

"So much the better. I would rather end it still wanting more, than to drag it out until we are both sick of each other. Besides, our chances of getting caught increase with time . . . and I have no wish to become a social pariah."

He urged her to face him, and it seemed that he was somehow torn between amusement and annoyance. "I will still want you in three months," he told her. "And when that time comes, I reserve the right to try and change your mind."

"You may do your worst," she informed him with a gathering smile. "But you will not change my mind. I have a very strong will."

"So do I."

They shared gazes filled with pleasurable challenge. Jack's hands curved around Amanda's shoulders, and he nudged her forward, his mouth lowering to hers. They were interrupted, however, by the sounds of someone entering the house, and Jack paused in mid-motion.

"My servants," Amanda said ruefully. She struggled upward from the floor. Jack rose in a fluid movement, pulling her with him to a standing position.

Despite having known Sukey for most of her life, and enduring the woman's constant needling concerning the lack of a male companion in her life, Amanda was embarrassed by the compromising situation. She felt her face turn hot, even as she assumed a perfectly bland expression. Sukey came to the parlor door and her face went blank with astonishment when she saw that Amanda was alone in the house with Jack Devlin. The disarray of Amanda's clothes and hair, and the intimate atmosphere of the parlor, left little doubt as to what had occurred between them.

"Pardon, Miss Amanda."

Amanda went to her immediately. "Good evening, Sukey. I trust you and Charles enjoyed your Christmas revels?"

"Very well, miss. A fine night indeed. Is there aught I can do before I settle in for the evening?"

Amanda nodded. "Please bring a ewer of hot water to my bedroom."

"Yes, miss." Scrupulously avoiding the sight of Amanda's guest, the housemaid hurried away and headed down to the kitchen.

Before Amanda could move, she felt Jack's hands catch her waist from behind. Gently he pulled her back against his chest, and lowered his head to nuzzle the side of her throat. The pressure of his mouth was hot and light, sending a thrum of delight down to her toes. "I have a condition of my own to add to our agreement," he said against her skin.

"What is it?" The sound of her own voice, thick and pleasure-fogged, was unfamiliar to her.

"If we are to be lovers for such a short time, then I am going to make the most of it. I want you to promise that you'll withhold nothing from me." His hand moved down her side in a long caress as he whispered, "I want to do everything with you, Amanda."

"How would you define 'everything'?" she parried.

He laughed softly instead of replying, the sound reverberating along every nerve.

Amanda turned to him with a defensive frown. "I can hardly be expected to agree to something if I don't know what it is!"

Jack's mouth twitched with suppressed amusement. "I gave you a copy of Gemma Bradshaw's memoirs," he said, straight-faced. "That would have provided a considerable amount of enlightenment."

"I didn't read all of it," Amanda replied pertly. "Only certain parts . . . and then I found it much too lurid to continue."

"I wouldn't have thought a lady who was willing to lose her virginity in a carriage would turn out to be so prudish." He grinned at her reproving scowl. "Here's our bargain, then. We'll end our affair in three months, per your request, as long as you are willing to do everything described in Gemma's book with me."

"You're not being serious," Amanda said, utterly appalled.

"Within reason, of course. One can't be certain that everything in that book is anatomically possible. But it would be interesting to find out, wouldn't it?"

"You are depraved," she informed him. "You are corrupt and degenerate."

"Yes, and for the next three months, I'm all yours." He surveyed her with a wickedly speculative gaze. "Now, exactly how did Chapter One begin?"

Amanda was torn between laughter and horror as she wondered just how much of his outrageous proposal was in earnest. "I believe it started with a particular gentleman being shown the door."

Jack covered her mouth with his in a deep, sweetly invasive intrusion. "I seem to recall that it started this way," he murmured. "Let me take you upstairs and demonstrate further."

Amanda led him to the staircase, but paused before ascending the first step, feeling a surge of bashfulness. In the dark confines of his carriage, it had been easy for her to surrender her hold on reality. However, here in the familiar surroundings of her home, she was all too awkwardly aware of what she was doing.

Seeming to understand her twinge of uncertainty, Jack stopped and pinned her against the banister, his fingers curving around the polished wood on either side of her. His lips held the hint of a smile. "Shall I carry you?"

She stood a step higher than he, so that their faces were level. "No, I am too heavy. You'll drop me, or tumble and break both our necks."

His blue eyes sparkled with devilish amusement. "I'll have to teach you not to underestimate me."

"It's not that, I'm just—" She squeaked in surprise as he bent and lifted her easily in his arms. "Oh, don't! No, Jack, you'll drop me."

But his grip on her was solid, and he appeared not to feel her weight as he carried her up the stairs. "You're not even half my size," he said. "I could carry you for miles and never miss a breath. Now stop squirming."

Amanda threw her arms around his shoulders. "You've made your point," she gasped. "Set me down, please."

"Oh, I will set you down," he assured her. "Right onto your bed, as soon as we reach it. Which room is yours?"

"The second door down the hall," she said, her voice muffled against his chest. She had never been carried anywhere like this, and while she felt slightly ridiculous, there was a certain primitive appeal about it. She rested her cheek on his shoulder and allowed herself to enjoy the sensation of being swept up in the arms of a powerful man.

They reached her bedroom, and Jack closed the door with his heel. He set her carefully onto the large bed with its barley-sugar twist posts and yellow-gold damask hangings. Curls of steam rose from the ewer of hot water that had been placed on the corner washstand. Tendrils of flame danced in the fireplace as kindling ignited into a sputtering blaze.

Amanda watched Jack with wide eyes, wondering if he intended to undress right there in front of her. He tossed his coat onto the nearby dressing table and removed his waistcoat and cravat.

Amanda cleared her throat, while her heart picked up an agitated pace and her blood stirred with restless heat. "Jack," she murmured, "we aren't really going to do Chapter One, are we?"

He grinned as he realized she was referring to *The Sins of Madam B.* "I confess, peaches, that my memory needs refreshing. I can't recall how the damn thing begins . . . unless you would care to enlighten me?"

"No," she said abruptly, making him laugh.

Jack approached her with his shirt half unbuttoned, the lamplight gleaming over the muscular surface of his chest. He reached for the teardrop earrings that dangled against her jawline. He removed them gently, and rubbed her sore earlobes with his thumbs and forefingers. Setting the jewelry aside on the night table, he unpinned her hair. Amanda closed her eyes, her breath coming in unsteady swishes. His every motion was slow and careful, as if she were some fragile creature that required extremely gentle handling.

"There must have been some part of Gemma's

book that you liked." Removing her shoes, he dropped them to the carpeted floor. "Something that intrigued you ... that excited you."

She jumped a little as she felt his hands clasp her ankles and slide up to her garters. The bands were untied with a few deft twists. Jack rolled down her silk stockings one at a time, pausing to stroke the firm curves of her calves. His fingertips tickled the susceptive places behind her knees, causing her legs to twitch in pleasured reaction.

"I would hardly tell you such things," she protested with a choked laugh. "Besides, I didn't like any part of that dreadful book."

"Oh, yes, you did," he said softly. "And you are going to tell me, peaches. After all we've shared so far, a fantasy or two won't be that difficult."

She hedged. "You tell me yours first."

He closed his hands around her ankles, pulling her toward him. "I have fantasies that involve every part of you. Your hair, your mouth and breasts ... even your feet."

"My *feet?*" She jolted in reaction as she felt his thumbs stroke over her arches, soothing away little knots of tension. He placed her foot on the front of his trousers, right where a thick, heavy ridge strained against the blend of wool and broadcloth. The heat of his body saturated the fabric and seemed to scorch the sole of her foot, and her toes curled in automatic reaction.

Feeling embarrassed and aroused, Amanda peeked at him through her lashes, and saw the hint of playfulness in his devil-blue eyes. She snatched her foot away and heard him laugh. Then he removed the rest of his clothes and let them rustle to the floor. The room became quiet, except for the crackle of the little fire in the hearth. Amanda risked a shy glance at the bare male form in front of her, and her gaze was riveted by the sight. The interplay of darkness and firelight threw every detail of him into stark relief, all muscle and golden skin and intimate shadows, and long, sinewy lines that conveyed both elegance and power. She had not imagined that someone could be so comfortable with his own nakedness, and yet he stood before her as easily as if he were fully dressed. His body was aroused, a gloriously masculine flaunting of desire that he made no effort to conceal. As Amanda stared at him, a low, coursing pleasure filled her limbs. She had never wanted anything in her life as she did in this moment . . . to feel the heavy naked weight of his body over hers, to feel his breath pelt her skin and his hands grasp and guide her.

"Now you've seen a completely naked man," Jack said. "What do you think?"

She moistened her dry lips with her tongue. "I think that thirty years is too long to have waited for this."

He reached around her and unfastened the back of her gown. The smell of his skin, warm and slightly salty, gave her the same slightly dizzy feeling she sometimes had when she had drunk her wine too quickly. She put her hands on his shoulders to steady herself, her fingertips tingling from the hard, satiny texture of him.

Gently he eased her to the floor and pushed the loosened dress downward until she stepped out of it. Left in her light corset and chemise and drawers, Amanda edged away from him with an abashed murmur.

"Jack..." She went to the washstand and poured some steaming water into a painted earthenware bowl. "If you wouldn't mind waiting behind the dressing screen," she said without looking at him, "I need a moment of privacy."

He came up behind her, his hands settling at her waist. "Let me help you."

"No, no," she said in a sudden paroxysm of embarrassment. "If you'll just go over there... I'll manage by myself."

But he hushed her with a kiss and ignored her protests while unfastening her corset and stripping away her undergarments. Flushing deeply, Amanda forced herself to hold still as he gazed at her body. She was well aware of her defects: legs that should have been longer, hips that were too wide, a stomach that was not quite flat. But as Jack stared at her, a visible pulse appeared in his throat, and his hand shook slightly when he touched the undercurve of her breast. One might have thought he were beholding a goddess instead of a thirty-year-old spinster. "Damn, how I want you," he said, his voice rasping in his throat. "I could eat you alive."

She puzzled over the baffling and somewhat

alarming statement. "Please don't try to claim that I am beautiful. We both know that is not the case."

Jack soaked a linen cloth in the hot water and wrung it out, then gently cleansed her inner thighs. To her mortification, he bade her place a foot on a nearby chair, thereby exposing herself more fully to his ministrations. "Every man has his own preferences," he said. The cloth was rinsed and soaked again, and he placed it directly between her thighs, so that the heat eased the soreness caused by their encounter in the carriage. "You happen to fulfill all of mine."

Amanda leaned forward until her cheek rested against his bare shoulder, relaxing against his invitingly warm body. "You prefer short women with large hips?" she asked skeptically.

His free hand coasted over the generous shape of her buttocks, and she felt him smile against her cheek. "I prefer everything about you. The way you feel beneath my hands, the way you taste . . . every curve and valley. But as much as I desire your body, your most attractive feature is here." He tapped her temple with his fingertip. "You fascinate me," he murmured. "You always have. You are the most original, challenging woman I have ever encountered. I've wanted to take you to bed from the first moment I saw you on your front doorstep."

She stood quietly, allowing him to cleanse and soothe her, and apply more hot compresses between her legs. When he was finished, he pulled her with him to the bed, and lifted her to the linen-covered mattress. Her heart knocked violently against her ribs, and the walls of the room seemed to disintegrate, leaving only darkness and firelight and the warm tangle of their limbs.

"Jack," she whispered as he stretched her out beneath him, the stiffly bobbing weight of his arousal brushing against the inside of her knee. Her hands found his buttocks, squeezing the densely textured flesh like a cat kneading with its paws, and Jack gasped against her hair. Emboldened, she slid one hand to his sex and touched him, her fingers closing tightly around the pulsing shape. He moved to his side to give her more access to his body, letting her touch him in any manner she wished.

Gently she cupped the fuzz-covered pouch at the base of his sex, which felt cool and soft in comparison to the turgid shaft. Her fingertips traced over the ridges of veins that led all the way up to a broad tip. Experimentally she drew the pad of her thumb over the satiny bulb, and he clenched his hands in her hair and groaned.

"Does that please you?" she whispered.

It appeared that he found it difficult to speak. "Yes," he finally managed with a smothered laugh. "God, yes . . . if you please me any more, I will probably explode." He tilted her head back and brought their faces together, his features shimmering with a mist of sweat, his eyes ablaze with blue light. His large hand covered hers, helping to guide the head of his shaft to the thatch of soft, wiry curls between her legs. His palm moved to her thigh, hitching it over his hip so that she was spread open for him. "Rub it against yourself," he murmured.

Amanda's entire body turned crimson. Slowly she took the head of his shaft in her fingers and brought it to the damp furrow between her thighs. Her breath rushed in harsh surges as she rubbed the tip of his organ over her intimate flesh, until the moisture from her own body made him slippery.

"Jack," she moaned, pushing his sex against the wet cove of her body, "take me now. Please. I want you inside me. I want—"

He interrupted her with a deep kiss, his tongue playing with hers, his hands folding over her breasts. "Turn around," he whispered. "Lie on your side, and hold your bottom against me."

Amanda groaned as his fingers gently pinched her nipples. "No, I want—"

"I know what you want." His mouth slid over her hot face. "And you shall have it, my love. Just do as I tell you."

Amanda obeyed him with a sob, settling so that her back was pressed against his chest, and his body was wedged behind hers spoon-fashion.

She felt the rise of his erection against her buttocks, and she writhed against him, her need so acute that all shame had vanished. He kissed and bit the nape of her neck, and murmured instructions, urging her to part her legs and arch her back. To her surprise, she felt him enter her from behind. She gave a guttural moan as he drove deeper, filling her until she was stretched tightly around him. Although he was gentle, she felt a pinch of discomfort, her body still unaccustomed to this intimate invasion.

"Does it hurt?" he whispered against her earlobe.

"Yes, a little," she gasped.

His big hands coasted over the front of her body, stroking her breasts, her quivering stomach, then moving to the aching peak of her sex. His clever fingertip rested close to the tingling flesh without quite touching it, teasingly elusive, sliding away each time Amanda strained to push herself against it.

He tormented her until she began to writhe, desperately working for the stimulation he held just out of reach. Each time her hips surged forward, he followed the movement, thrusting deeper into the grasping depths of her body. The soreness disappeared as each liquid glide sent a rush of delight through her, and the exquisite tension climbed higher, higher, until she bit her lips to hold back a scream.

"Jack, please, please," she moaned, her every limb stiff, her skin sweating until even the roots of her hair were wet. She clawed at the gentle hand between her legs, straining to reach the climax he withheld.

"All right, my love," came his dark voice in her ear. "You've earned your pleasure." She felt him pinch the throbbing little nub between his thumb and forefinger, and he gently stroked the silken flesh even as he thrust hard and straight inside her. It seemed that the world exploded in sensation and fire as her body clamped on his invading hardness with spasms of ecstasy. The rippling of her inner muscles brought him to the same rocketing climax, and he withdrew from her with a groan, spilling his seed on the sheets.

Exhausted, satiated, Amanda rolled to face him, her arms sliding around his back. She felt the slight ridges of scars from long-ago beatings, and her hands lingered on the marks, fingertips softly stroking. Jack went very still, the cadence of his breath changing. His lashes lowered, concealing his thoughts from her.

She stroked the small of his back and then moved her hands up the powerful length of his spine. Finding the scars once more, she touched them lightly, as if she could soothe them away. "Mr. Fretwell once told me that you took many beatings meant for other children at the Knatchford Heath school," she said. "You tried to protect the smaller boys from harm."

His mouth tightened with annoyance. "Fretwell talks too damned much."

"I was glad that he told me . . . I would never have guessed you were capable of such sacrifice."

His shoulders moved in a careless shrug. "It was nothing. I have a tough Irish hide—I never felt the thrashings as much as the younger boys would have."

Amanda snuggled closer to him, careful to keep

her voice sympathetic rather than pitying. "Don't make light of what you did."

"Hush." Jack placed gentle fingers over her lips. Dark color touched the crests of his cheeks. "Next you'll make me out to be a damned saint," he said gruffly, "and believe me, that is not the case. I was a hellion, and I grew up to be a reprobate."

Amanda applied her tongue to one of his fingers, tickling the inside crease.

Surprised by the playful swipe of her tongue, Jack jerked back his hand and grinned down at her, the shades of bitter regret vanishing from his eyes. "Little witch." He pulled back the covers and shifted Amanda's body onto the expanse of smooth linen sheets. "I think we can put your tongue to better use than that," he murmured, and covered her mouth with his own.

Chapter 11

Amanda's relatives were not pleased by the news that she would not be coming to Windsor for the remainder of the holidays. They made their disgruntlement known through a cache of rapidly posted letters that Amanda declined to answer. Usually she would have taken the time to soothe their ruffled feathers, but as the days slipped by, she couldn't bring herself to care. Her entire existence had become centered on Jack Devlin. The hours when they were apart passed with unbearable slowness, whereas the evenings sped by in a sweetly frantic rush. He always came to her after dark fell, and left just before dawn, and with each hour she spent in his arms, she only craved him more.

Jack treated her as no man ever had, regarding her not as a sedate spinster but as a woman of warmth and passion. On the occasions when Amanda's inhibitions got the better of her, he teased her ruthlessly, provoking a temper she had never suspected herself of having. There were times, however, when Jack's mood changed and he was no longer a mocking rogue but a tender lover. He would spend hours cuddling and stroking her, making love with exquisite gentleness. During those times, he seemed to understand her with a thoroughness that frightened her, as if he could see into her very soul.

Just as they had agreed, Jack made her read certain chapters of *The Sins of Madam B*, and he openly enjoyed her squirming discomfort at having to enact particular scenes in bed with him.

"I can't," she said in a muffled voice one evening, pulling the bed linens over her scarlet face. "I just can't. Choose something else—I'll do anything but that with you."

"You promised you would try," Jack said, his eyes gleaming with amusement as he jerked the sheets away from her.

"I don't recall anything of the kind."

"Coward." He kissed the top of her spine and worked his way down her back, and she felt him smile against her skin. "Be brave, Amanda," he whispered. "What do you have to lose?"

"My self-respect!" She tried to wriggle free, but he pinned her down and gently nipped the sensitive spot between her shoulder blades.

"Just give it a try," he coaxed. "I'll do it to you first—wouldn't you like that?" He flipped her over and kissed her quivering stomach. "I want to taste you," he murmured. "I want to put my tongue in you."

If it were possible to die of mortification, she

would have expired right then and there. "Perhaps later," she said. "I need some time to accustom myself to the idea."

A flare of laughter mingled with the heat in his eyes. "You decided to limit our affair to three months. That doesn't leave much time." His mouth played around the small circle of her navel, his warm breath wafting inside the hollow. "One kiss," he urged, and his fingertip parted the curls between her thighs to alight on a place of startling sensation. "Right here. Will that be too much for you to bear?"

She made a helpless noise at the touch of his fingertip. "Just one," she said unsteadily.

His mouth descended, and she felt his fingers sifting through the springy hair, spreading her gently. His lips parted, his tongue investigating her with a circling stroke. She felt the pull of ecstasy in every limb, her nerves screaming for more, all coherent thought shattering at the sight of his head between her thighs.

"One more?" he asked huskily, and he bent his head again before she could deny him. His mouth touched her again, wetting the aching rise of flesh, his tongue stroking and prodding with delicate skill. He did not ask for further consent but simply did as he wanted, settling between her legs with a sigh of pleasure while she cried out and strained and trembled. Sensation unfurled inside her and raced through every vein. She lay spread-eagled beneath him while her body acceded eagerly to the sweet torment of his mouth.

Momentum gathered, hurtling her ever higher, until she had lost all hope of controlling the wild groans that emanated from her chest.

She felt his tongue slip inside her, a sleek, repeated plunging that caused her hips to rise in helpless surges. He returned to the tender nub of her sex, drawing it inside the suction of his mouth, while his finger penetrated the wet channel between her thighs. He teased the slick inner surface in a way that made her beg for release, until they both knew that she would allow anything, everything, that he might want.

He slipped a second finger inside her body, thrusting deeply to find an unbearably sensitive place. Gently he teased and rubbed while his mouth drew harder, his caresses steady, rhythmic, until she sobbed and cried out as the world exploded in bliss.

Several minutes later Amanda let him pull her atop his body so that she rested on a long plane of muscle and sinew. "You must have had many affairs, to be so skilled," she murmured, feeling a sharp twinge of jealousy at the thought.

His brows quirked as he clearly wondered whether she was being critical or complimentary. "I haven't, actually," he said, playing with her long hair, spreading it over his chest. "I happen to be fairly discerning when it comes to this sort of thing. Besides, I've always been so damned involved in my work that I've never had a great deal of time for affairs."

"What about love?" Amanda levered herself up

on his chest, staring into his dark face. "Haven't you ever fallen madly in love with someone?"

"Not to the extent that I let it interfere with my business."

Amanda laughed suddenly, reaching to smooth a lock of black hair back from his forehead. He had beautiful hair, thick and shiny, slightly coarse beneath her fingers. "It wasn't love, then. Not if you could dismiss it so easily when it became inconvenient."

"And you?" Jack countered, running his warm hands along her arms until gooseflesh raised on the backs of them. "Obviously you've never fallen in love."

"Why are you so certain?"

"Because you wouldn't have remained a virgin if you had."

"Cynic," she accused with a smile. "Can't one love genuinely but chastely?"

"No," he returned flatly. "If it's real love, it has to include physical passion. A man and a woman can never really know each other otherwise."

"I disagree. I believe that emotional passion is far more intense than the physical kind."

"For a woman, perhaps."

Reaching for a pillow, she swatted it over his grinning face. "You primitive lout."

Jack chuckled, easily divested her of the pillow, and grasped her wrists in his large hands. "All men are primitive louts," he informed her. "Some just happen to conceal it better than others."

"Which explains why I have never married."

Amanda wrestled with him briefly, enjoying the sensation of rubbing along his brawny naked body until his erection rose hot and hard between them. "*Very* primitive," she said throatily, continuing to squirm until he gave a groaning laugh.

"*Mhuirnin,*" he muttered, "I feel compelled to remind you that I've done my best to satisfy you so far this evening . . . and you haven't yet returned the favor."

Amanda lowered her mouth to his, kissing him ardently and winning his eager response. She felt oddly unlike herself, wicked and remarkably free of inhibition. "I had better remedy that," she remarked, her voice humming low in her throat. "I should hate not to be fair."

Their gazes met, hers adventurous, his bright and passion-filled. Then Jack's eyes closed as Amanda slid lower on his body, her mouth trailing a slow path along his taut skin.

For a woman who had always believed in the credo "Moderation in all things," an affair with Jack Devlin was disastrous to her equilibrium. Her emotions careened from one extreme to another, from the all-consuming pleasure of being with him to the obsession and despondency that filled her when they were apart. There were private moments when melancholy rolled over her like a blanketing fog. It had something to do with a bittersweet understanding that this was all temporary, that soon their season of passion would be over. Jack was not really hers, nor would he ever be. The more Amanda came to understand him, the more she recognized his elemental unwillingness to give himself completely to a woman. She found it ironic that a man who was willing to take risks in every other area of his life should find it impossible to take the one chance that mattered most.

Amanda often felt deeply frustrated, wanting for the first time in her life to have all of a man, his heart as well as his body. It was her particular misfortune to desire this of Jack Devlin. But, she reminded herself, that did not mean that she had to remain alone for the rest of her years. Jack had taught her that she was a desirable woman, one with qualities that many men might appreciate. If she wanted, she could find a partner for herself after the affair was over. But in the meantime . . . in the meantime . . .

Mindful of the scrutiny of others, Amanda took care to arrive separately at parties, and to treat Jack with the same polite friendliness that she accorded the other men present. She did not betray their relationship with a single look or word. Jack was similarly careful to observe the proprieties, treating her with an exaggerated respect that both annoyed and amused her. As the weeks passed, however, Jack no longer seemed to regard their affair, and the need for secrecy, as lightly as he once had. It appeared to bother him that he could not claim her publicly. The fact that he had to share her company with others was a source of increasing frustration, one that he finally admitted to Amanda when they both attended a musical evening. He had managed to pull her away from the general assemblage during intermission, and steered her to a small parlor that was clearly not intended for the guests' use.

"Have you gone mad?" Amanda gasped as he closed them both inside the unlit room. "Someone may have seen you pull me out of the main rooms. There will be gossip if it is noticed that we have both disappeared at the same time—"

"I don't care." His arms closed around her, jerking her against the solid weight of his body. "For the past hour and a half, I've had to sit apart from you and pretend not to notice other men leering at you. I want to go home with you now, dammit."

"Don't be ridiculous," she said shortly. "No one is leering at me. I don't know what you are trying to accomplish with this pretend fit of jealousy, but I assure you that it is unnecessary."

"I know a leer when I see one." He drew his hands along the silk-and-velvet bodice of her russet-colored gown, letting his palm cover the exposed valley of her cleavage. "Why did you wear this dress tonight?"

"I've worn it before, and you seemed to like it." She shivered as the warmth of his hand passed over her tender skin.

"I liked it in *private*," he muttered. "I never wanted you to wear it in public."

"Jack," she began, her stifled laugh cut short when he bent and dragged his mouth over the exposed skin of her chest. "Stop," she whispered, quivering at the greedy stroke of his tongue in the vale between her breasts. "We'll be found out . . . oh, let me go back before the music begins."

"I can't help it." His voice was soft and gruff, his breath striking her skin in hot exhalations. He gathered her body against his and kissed her, his mouth tasting of brandy as he searched her avidly.

Amanda's rising panic was swamped in a surge of desire so overwhelming that she couldn't breathe, couldn't think, her body helpless in his demanding hands. He pulled at her skirts, thrusting his hands inside her drawers so roughly that she feared they might tear. She gasped when his fingers slid between her thighs, searching and fondling the soft flesh until she writhed desperately. "Not now," she said with a faint sob. "We'll be together in a few hours. You can wait until then."

"No, I can't." His breath quickened as he felt the moisture from her aroused body. Pulling at the tapes of her drawers, he loosened the undergarment and dropped it to her ankles, then fumbled with the fastenings of his trousers. He urged her back against the closed door and kissed her neck, the bristle from his shaven jaw abrading her and making her skin tingle.

"Jack," she whimpered, tilting her head back even while the fear of being discovered made her heartbeat escalate to a violent clatter.

His mouth muffled her protests in a crush of heat and sensation, and to her despair, she could not resist the wicked pleasure of it. She kissed him back, opening to him eagerly, letting her thighs part as his leg intruded between hers. His erection nudged against her, a thrust of hardness and silk, and her hips jerked in an involuntary movement to accommodate him. He pushed more strongly, entering her in a deep, sure glide. Amanda groaned as she was filled completely, her body clamping tightly around the delicious invasion. One of his hands caught her knee from beneath, urging her leg higher against his, and he pushed strongly within her.

She shuddered, her body locked to him, and then a languorous warmth suffused her as she relaxed to his rhythm. Their clothes rustled together, crushed masses of silk and broadcloth and velvet separating them everywhere except in the wet, naked heat of their loins. She leaned against the door, her body rising with each upward drive. She was utterly possessed by him, no longer caring about the risk they were taking, conscious only of the ecstasy of his flesh joined to hers. Muttering fiercely into the curve of her neck, he thrust faster, creating silken friction that finally drove her into a scalding orgasm. He smothered her guttural cries with his mouth, and began to slide out of her in the way he always did just before climax. But it seemed that suddenly he was possessed by some irresistible primal urge, and instead of withdrawing, he buried himself inside her. His large body shook with the power of his release, and his quiet groan vibrated against her damp skin.

They remained together in the pulsing aftermath, breathing harshly, while his mouth moved gently over hers. Finally breaking the kiss, Jack spoke in a rasping whisper. "Dammit . . . I shouldn't have done that."

Feeling dazed, Amanda could barely manage a reply. Since their affair had begun, they had taken measures to prevent pregnancy, and this was the first time that Jack had left the outcome to chance. She tried to calculate the most likely days for conception. "It's all right, I think," she murmured, placing her hand on the side of his face. Although she could not see his expression, she felt the tautness of his jaw, and a terrible sense of unease came over her.

"Sophia!" Amanda exclaimed in disbelief. She hurried across the little entrance hall of her home to where her oldest sister was waiting. "You might have let me know you were planning a visit—I would have made preparations."

"I merely want to see if you're alive or dead," came Sophia's acerbic reply, making Amanda laugh.

Although Sophia was meddling and bossy by nature, she was also a loving sister with strong maternal instincts. She had often given voice to the family's sentiments concerning Amanda's untoward behavior. It was Sophia who had protested the loudest when Amanda had become a novelist and moved to London. Letters would arrive from Sophia, filled with advice that greatly amused Amanda, for they counseled her to beware of the temptations of town life. Perhaps Sophia would not have been surprised had she learned that Amanda had actually dared to hire a male prostitute for her own birthday. It seemed that her eldest sister recognized, as few others did, the streak of recklessness that occasionally surfaced in Amanda's character.

"I am very much alive," Amanda said brightly. "Only quite busy." She glanced at her sister's familiar figure with a fond smile. "You look well, Sophia." For years, Sophia had possessed the same soft, slightly round-shouldered figure. Her hair was worn in the same neatly pinned chignon and she wore the same sweet vanilla scent that their mother had favored. Sophia was exactly as she appeared—an attractive country matron who competently managed a dull but respectable husband and five boisterous children.

Sophia held her at arm's length and gave her a head-to-toe inspection. "I had feared to find you ill. That was the only reason I could fathom for your insistence on staying away from Windsor."

"You could think of only one reason?" Amanda countered, laughing as she ushered her sister inside the house.

Sophia's mouth quirked wryly. "Explain to me why I have been forced to come see you here, rather than receive you at my home. After avoiding the family at Christmas, you had promised to visit in January. It is now mid-February, and I have not heard a word from you. And don't hand me nonsense about how overworked you are. You are always busy, and you've never let it keep you away from Windsor before."

She removed her traveling-bonnet, a pretty but practical design of blue wool with a slanting crown and a brim that was shallow at the back and wider at the front.

"I am sorry that you have gone to such trouble," Amanda replied contritely, taking her sister's hat and matching cloak with its overlapping square collar. "However, I am delighted to have you here." She took her time about setting the articles of apparel on the bentwood hanging rack in the entrance hall, making certain they were firmly placed on the porcelain-tipped hooks.

"Come with me to the parlor," she urged. "Your timing could not be better, as I have just prepared a pot of tea. How were the roads from Windsor? Did you have difficulty—"

"Where are the servants?" Sophia interrupted suspiciously, following her into the cream-and-blue parlor.

"Sukey is at market with the cook, Violet, and Charles has gone to the wineshop."

"Excellent. Now we may enjoy some privacy while you explain what has been going on."

"Why do you think something has been going

on?" Amanda parried. "I assure you, life is plodding along much the same as it always has."

"You are a poor liar," Sophia informed her serenely, seating herself on the settee. "Amanda, I must remind you that Windsor is hardly isolated from town. We do hear of goings-on in London, and there have been rumors concerning you and a certain gentleman."

"Rumors?" Amanda regarded her with surprised dismay.

"And you look different."

"Different?" In her sudden consternation, Amanda could only flush guiltily and repeat her sister's words like some addled parrot.

"There is a look about you that makes me suspect that the rumors are true. You are indeed carrying on some kind of liaison with someone, aren't you?" Sophia pursed her lips as she regarded her younger sister. "Obviously it is entirely within your rights to arrange your life as you choose . . . and I have accepted that you are not one to bow to the dictates of convention. If you were, you could have married a man from Windsor and settled near your family. Instead, you sold Briars House, took up residence in London, and dedicated yourself to pursuing a career. I have often told myself, if all this makes you happy, then you are welcome to it—"

"Thank you," Amanda interrupted with a touch of gentle sarcasm.

"However," Sophia continued gravely, "your actions are now placing your entire future at risk.

I wish you would confide in me, and allow me to help you sort things out."

Amanda was tempted to counter Sophia's words with as many bold-faced lies as were required to calm her suspicions. However, as she shared a long gaze with her sister, her eyes burned, and she felt a tear drop down her cheek.

"Sophia . . . what I need at the moment is an understanding listener. Someone who will not pass judgment on my actions. Could you possibly do that for me?"

"Of course not," came Sophia's crisp reply. "Of what use would I be to you if I did not give you the benefit of my good judgment? Otherwise, you might as well confide in the nearest tree stump."

Laughing unsteadily, Amanda blotted her wet eyes with her sleeve. "Oh, Sophia, I am afraid you will be quite shocked by my confession."

While their tea cooled in their cups, Amanda blurted out the story of her relationship with Jack Devlin, prudently editing a few details such as the circumstances of their first meeting. Sophia was expressionless as she listened, reserving comment until Amanda finished with a watery sigh.

"Well," Sophia said thoughtfully, "I do not find myself as shocked as I perhaps should be. I know you quite well, Amanda, and I have never thought you would be happy living alone forever. While I do not approve of your actions, I understand your need for companionship. I must point out that had you taken my advice and married a nice man from Windsor, you would not be in your current predicament."

"Unfortunately, one cannot simply go out and make oneself fall in love with an appropriate man."

Sophia made an impatient gesture. "Love is not the issue, dear. Why do you think I settled for marrying Henry?"

The question stunned Amanda. "Why, I . . . I never realized you considered it 'settling.' You've always seemed so happy with Henry."

"And so I have been," Sophia replied pertly. "That is my point. When my marriage began, I did not love Henry, but I recognized that he possessed an admirable character. I understood that if I wanted a family and a solid place in society, I needed a respectable partner. And love, or something very much like it, does come in time. I enjoy and value the life I have with Henry. It is something you could have, too, if you are willing to set aside your stubborn independence and your romantic illusions."

"And if I don't?" Amanda murmured.

Sophia met her gaze directly. "Then you will be the worse off for it. It is always more difficult for those who swim against the current. I am only stating the facts, Amanda, and you know that I am right. And I tell you most emphatically, you must shape your life to fit the conventions. My advice is to end the affair at once, and apply yourself toward finding a gentleman who will be disposed to marry you."

Amanda rubbed her aching temples. "But I love Jack," she whispered. "I don't want anyone else."

Sophia regarded her sympathetically. "Believe it or not, I do understand, dear. However, you might bear in mind that men such as your Mr. Devlin are like rich desserts—enjoyable for the moment, but generally bad for the constitution. Moreover, it is no crime to marry a man whom one likes. In fact, in my opinion, it is a great deal better than marrying a man whom one loves. Friendship always lasts longer than passion."

"What is the matter?" Jack asked quietly, stroking the curve of Amanda's naked back. They lay together amid a tangle of sheets, the air humid and scented like sea salt in the aftermath of their lovemaking. Jack leaned over to kiss the back of her pale shoulder. "You've been distracted tonight. It has something to do with your sister's visit today. Did the two of you quarrel?"

"No, not at all. In fact, we had a nice long talk, and she dispensed a great deal of sensible advice before she departed back to Windsor." Amanda frowned as she heard him mutter some foul words regarding her sister's "sensible advice," and she propped herself up on one elbow. "I could not help agreeing with many of her opinions," she murmured, "even though I did not want to."

His hand stilled on her back, his thumb resting lightly on the indentation of her spine. "What opinions?"

"Sophia has heard rumors about our relationship. She said that a scandal is brewing, and that I must end the affair at once or risk having my reputation destroyed." A wan smile touched her lips. "I have a great deal to lose, Jack. If I become a ruined woman, my entire life will change. I will no longer be invited to social gatherings, and many of my friends will no longer speak to me. Most likely I will have to move to a remote place in the country, or go to live abroad."

"I am taking the same risk," he pointed out.

"No," she replied with a wry smile, "you know quite well that men are never judged the same as women in these matters. I would become a pariah, whereas you would receive a mere slap on the wrist."

"What are you saying?" Suddenly his tone was laced with baffled anger. "I'll be damned if you're going to end the affair a month and a half early!"

"I should never have agreed to such an arrangement." She turned away from him with a miserable groan. "It was madness. I wasn't thinking clearly."

Jack pulled her back against him, his hands moving possessively over her body. "If you're worried about scandal, I'll find ways for us to be more discreet. I'll buy a house in the country where we can meet without anyone's notice—"

"It's no use, Jack. This . . . this thing that has happened between us . . ." Amanda paused in sudden consternation, searching helplessly for the appropriate word. Finding none, she sighed impatiently at her own lack of nerve. "It cannot continue."

"A few words from your straitlaced older sister, and you're ready to end our relationship?" he asked incredulously.

"Sophia confirmed my own feelings. I've known since the beginning that this was wrong, and yet I haven't been able to face that fact until now. Please don't make things difficult."

He swore savagely and pressed her onto her back, his powerful body looming over hers. His face was set, but Amanda could practically see the rapid calculation of his thoughts. When he spoke, his voice was carefully controlled. "Amanda, I'm not going to lose you. You and I both know that our three-month agreement was just a game. The affair was never going to be limited to such a short time. From the beginning, I understood the risk of scandal, and I decided that I would protect you from any and all consequences of our relationship. You have my word on that. Now, let's be done with this nonsense and continue as we have been."

"How could you possibly protect me from scandal?" Amanda asked, bewildered. "Are you saying that you would marry me to save my ruined reputation?"

He met her gaze without blinking. "If necessary."

But the unwillingness in his eyes was easy to read, and Amanda understood how unpleasant a duty it would be for him to marry anyone. "No," she murmured. "You have no desire to be a husband or father. I would not ask that of you . . . or of myself. I deserve better than to be regarded as a millstone around your neck."

The words seemed to hang suspended in the air. Amanda felt both resigned and wretched as she watched Jack's set face. He had never pretended to want more of her than a mere affair. She could hardly blame him for his feelings. "Jack," she said unsteadily. "I will always think of you with . . . with fondness. I hope that we may even continue to work together. I very much want the relationship between us to remain friendly."

He looked at her in a way he never had before, his mouth twisting at one corner, his eyes gleaming with something akin to outrage. "So friendship is what you want," he said softly. "And fondness is all you feel for me."

Amanda forced herself to hold his gaze. "Yes."

She did not entirely understand the cast of bitterness on his face. A man did not look like that unless he had been deeply hurt, and yet she did not believe that he cared enough about her to feel that way. Perhaps his pride was wounded.

"It is time to say good-bye," she whispered. "You know it is."

His face was blank as he continued to stare at her. "When will I see you again?" he asked gruffly.

"In a few weeks, perhaps," she said hesitantly. "And then we will be able to meet as friends, I hope."

The air was charged with a peculiar, pained silence until Jack spoke again. "Then let's say goodbye in the same way we began," he muttered, and reached for her with rough hands. In all the times Amanda had imagined or written about lovers parting, it had never been with this harsh urgency, as if he wanted to hurt her.

"Jack," she protested. The grip of his hands eased, secure but no longer punishing.

"One more display of fondness isn't too much to ask, is it?" He spread her legs with his knee and thrust inside her with no preliminaries. Amanda caught her breath at the feel of him driving deep inside her, establishing a demanding, pounding rhythm that resonated throughout her being. The pleasure kindled and rose, her hips arching with each stroke. Her eyes closed, and she felt his mouth on her breasts, catching at her nipples, gently biting and stroking with his teeth and tongue. She struggled to press closer to him, urging her entire body up into his, craving the heat and weight of him. He kissed her, his mouth opening hungrily over hers, and she moaned as a rippling climax overtook her, washing through her in searing waves. He withdrew from her in an abrupt jerking motion, his breath rattling in his throat, his body trembling and taut in the throes of his own release.

Usually when they made love, Jack held and caressed her afterward. This time, however, he rolled away and left the bed with a harsh exhalation.

Amanda bit her lip and held still as Jack searched for his clothes and dressed silently. Perhaps if she had managed to explain things in a different way, a better way, Jack would not have reacted with this baffling anger. She tried to speak, but her throat was clenched too tightly to allow words, and all she could manage was a strange, broken sound.

Hearing the faint noise, Jack shot her a searching glance. Reading the pain that must have been obvious on her face did not seem to mollify him. In fact, it only seemed to frustrate him further.

He finally spoke in a cold, stiff manner, forcing the words out between clenched teeth. "I'm not finished with you yet, Amanda. I'll be waiting."

Amanda had never known a silence as absolute as the one that occupied the bedroom after he left. Gathering the sheet around her in great bunches of linen that still retained the warmth and scent of his body, she tried to calm herself enough to think. They had exchanged no promises or commitments ... neither of them had ever dared to believe in any kind of permanence.

She had expected to feel pain at their final parting, but she had not expected a sense of loss so profound that it seemed as if part of her had been amputated. In the weeks and months to come, she would discover all the ways that the affair had changed her, all the ways in which she would never be the same. For now, however, she would try to rid herself of the unwanted details that crowded her mind ... thoughts of Jack's dark blue eyes, the taste of Jack's mouth, the misty heat of his skin as he moved over her in passion ... the wonderful low timbre of his voice as he murmured in her ear.

"Jack," she whispered, and rolled over to bury her face in the pillow as she cried.

The biting February breeze was a welcome shock as Jack walked out into the night. He shoved his hands deep into his coat pockets and strode without his usual purpose or sense of direction. It did not matter where he went, or how far; all that mattered was that he did not stop. He felt as if he had been drinking badly distilled whiskey, the kind that made his mouth dry and his head feel as if it had been stuffed with wool. It seemed impossible that a woman he wanted so badly did not want him. While he understood Amanda's fear of scandal and its consequences, he could not seem to make himself accept that he could no longer see her, talk to her, possess her ... that their affair had so abruptly become a thing of the past.

It was not that he blamed Amanda for her decision. In fact, had he been a woman in her circumstances, he probably would have done the same thing. But he could not drive away a sense of anger and loss. He felt more intimacy with Amanda than he had with any other person in his life. He had told her things he had found it difficult to admit even to himself. It was not merely the delight of her body that he would miss. He loved her prickly intelligence, her easy laughter ... he loved simply to be in the same room with her, though he could not explain fully why her companionship was so thoroughly satisfying.

Opposing urges battled inside him. He could return to her this minute, argue and coax until she allowed him back into her bed. But that was not what she wanted ... it was not what was best for her. Swearing quietly, Jack increased his pace, walking faster and farther away from her home. He would do as she asked. He would give her the friendship she wanted, and somehow he would find a way to remove her from his heart and mind.

Chapter 12

The London Season, with its rituals of suppers, balls, parties, and teas, began in March. There were events for every strata of society, most notably the insufferably dull gatherings of blue bloods to match suitable husbands with appropriate wives to ensure the continuation of their lineage. However, anyone of good sense took care to avoid these gatherings of the aristocracy, as the conversation was slow and self-congratulatory, and one was likely to find oneself trapped in the company of pompous half-wits.

More sought after were the invitations to events attended by what could be considered the upper middle class . . . people of undistinguished bloodlines but considerable wealth or celebrity. This group included a number of politicians, rich landowning barons, businessmen, physicians, newspapermen, artists, and even a few well-heeled merchants.

Since her move to London, Amanda had been readily welcomed to suppers and dances, private concerts, and theater evenings, but lately she had refused all invitations.

Although she had enjoyed herself at these affairs in the past, she could not seem to take an interest in going anywhere. She had never truly understood the phrase "heavy heart" until now. More than four weeks had passed since she had seen Jack, and her heart felt like a lead weight that imposed painful pressure on her lungs and ribs. There had even been times when breathing had been a laborious effort. She despised herself for pining after a man, hated the useless melodrama of it, and yet she couldn't seem to stop. Surely time would ease her longing, but the prospect of months, years, without him filled her with gloom.

On the occasion when Oscar Fretwell had come to collect the latest revisions for Amanda's serial novel, he had been a source of plentiful information concerning his employer. Jack had become insatiable in his efforts to achieve ever-greater heights of success. He had acquired a notable newspaper called the *London Daily Review*, boasting a dizzying circulation of one hundred fifty thousand. He had also opened two new stores, and had just bought a new magazine. It was rumored that Jack had more ready money to lay his hands on than almost any other man in England, and that the annual cash flow at Devlin's was approaching the one-million-pound mark.

"He's like a comet," Fretwell had confided, adjusting his glasses in his habitual gesture, "hurtling along faster than anyone or anything around him. I can't recall the last time I saw him partake of a full meal. And I am certain that he never sleeps. He stays long after everyone else leaves for the day, and returns in the morning before anyone else arrives."

"Why should he be so driven?" Amanda had asked. "I should think that Devlin would want to relax and enjoy what he has accomplished."

"One would think so," Fretwell had replied darkly. "More likely he'll push himself into an early grave."

Amanda couldn't help wondering if Jack was missing her. Perhaps he was endeavoring to keep himself so busy that he had little time to dwell on the end of their affair. "Mr. Fretwell," she said with an awkward smile, "has he mentioned my name of late? ... that is ... was there any message he wished you to impart to me?"

The manager's face was carefully blank. It was impossible to discern whether Jack had confided anything about their affair to him, or revealed any clue as to his feelings. "He seems quite pleased by the sales of the first installment of *Unfinished Lady*," Fretwell said a bit too brightly.

"Yes. Thank you." Amanda had masked her disappointment and longing with a strained smile.

Realizing that Jack was doing his best to put their relationship squarely in the past, Amanda knew that she had to do the same. She began to accept invitations again, and forced herself to laugh and make small talk with her friends. However, the truth was that nothing could dispel her loneliness, and she found herself waiting and listening constantly for the smallest mention of Jack Devlin. It was inevitable that one day they would attend the same event, and that thought filled her with dread and anticipation.

To Amanda's surprise, she was invited to a ball given in late March by the Stephensons, with whom she was not at all well acquainted. She vaguely recalled having met the elderly Mr. and Mrs. Stephenson the previous year, having been introduced at a party by her lawyer, Thaddeus Talbot. The family owned a string of South African diamond mines, which had added the allure of great wealth to the luster of a solid and well-respected name.

Prompted by curiosity, Amanda decided to attend. She wore her finest gown for the occasion, a confection of pale pink satin with an enormous collar of white ruffled gauze that exposed the tops of her shoulders. The full skirts rustled and swished crisply as she moved, occasionally revealing a glimpse of her lace slippers with pink ribbon ties. She had dressed her hair in a loose-curling topknot, with a few tendrils dangling against her cheeks and neck.

Stephenson Hall was a classically English house, a dignified design of red brick and giant white Corinthian columns that rose over a wide stone-paved forecourt. The ceiling of the ballroom was painted with trompe l'oeil emblems of the seasons, matching the elaborate leaf-and-flower motif of the shining parquet floor below. Hundreds of guests milled beneath the shimmering light shed by two of the largest chandeliers that Amanda had ever seen.

Immediately upon arriving, Amanda was greeted by the Stephensons' eldest son, Kerwin, a corpulent man in his early thirties, who had arrayed himself in an astonishing manner. There were glittering diamond pins affixed in his hair, diamond buckles on his shoes, diamond buttons on his coat, and diamond rings on every finger. Amanda could not help but stare at the extraordinary sight of a man who had managed to decorate every part of his body with jewels. Proudly, Stephenson swept a hand along the front of his glittering coat and smiled at her. "Remarkable, is it not?" he asked. "I can see that you are dazzled by my brilliance."

"It almost hurts to look at you," Amanda replied dryly.

Mistaking the remark for a compliment, Stephenson leaned closer to murmur conspiratorially, "And just think, my dear . . . the fortunate woman who eventually weds me will be similarly adorned."

Amanda smiled wanly, aware that she was the target of a host of jealous stares from matrimonially minded dowagers and their charges. She wished she could reassure them *en masse* that she had no interest in the ridiculous fop.

Unfortunately, Stephenson could not be per-

suaded to leave her side for the rest of the
evening. It seemed he had decided that Amanda
should be given the honor of writing his life's
story. " 'Twould be a sacrifice of my valuable privacy," he reflected, his multitude of rings
sparkling as he clamped a pudgy hand firmly on
Amanda's arm, "but I can no longer deny the
public the story they desire so greatly. And only
you, Miss Briars, have the ability to capture the
essence of its subject. Me. You will enjoy writing
about me, I vow. 'Twill hardly seem like work."

It finally dawned on Amanda that this was the
reason she had been invited to the ball—the family must have agreed that she was to be given the
honor of writing their pompous heir's biography.

"You're very kind," she murmured, caught between outrage and laughter as she glanced
around at her surroundings for any avenue of escape. "However, I must tell you that biographies
are not my forte—"

"We will find a private corner," he interrupted
her, "and we will sit together for the rest of the
evening while I tell you the story of my life."

Amanda's blood curdled at the prospect. "Mr.
Stephenson, I could not deny the other women at
the ball the chance to enjoy your company—"

"They will have to console themselves," he said
with a regretful sigh. "After all, there is only one
of me—and for this evening, Miss Briars, I am
yours. Come now."

As Amanda was practically dragged to a small
velvet settee in the corner, she saw Jack Devlin's

dark face. The sight of him caused her heart to lurch. She had not known that he would be attending the ball . . . it was all she could do not to stare openly. Jack was handsome, princely even, in his black formal wear, his black hair brushed back from his face. He was standing in a group of men, watching her over the rim of his brandy glass with an expression of mocking satisfaction. His white teeth gleamed in a quick grin as he witnessed her predicament.

Abruptly Amanda's longing changed to burning annoyance. The evil wretch, she thought, glaring at him as she was tugged along behind Stephenson's corpulent form. She should not be surprised that Jack would take pleasure in seeing her discomfort.

Silently Amanda fumed as Stephenson monopolized her for the next two hours, orating grandly about his beginnings, his accomplishments, his opinions, until she longed to scream. Sipping from a glass of punch, she watched as everyone else at the party was happily dancing, laughing, and talking, while she was trapped on a settee with a self-important windbag.

Worse, every time someone approached them, and it looked as if rescue might be likely, Stephenson waved the person away and continued his incessant chatter to Amanda. Just when she was considering a feigned illness or a pretend swoon in order to be rid of him, help came from the quarter she desired the least.

Jack stood before them with an expressionless

face, ignoring Stephenson's attempts to shoo him away. "Miss Briars," he murmured, "are you enjoying the evening?"

Stephenson responded before Amanda could speak. "Devlin, you have the honor of being the first to hear the good news," he crowed.

Devlin arched his brow as he glanced at Amanda. "Good news?"

"I have convinced Miss Briars to write my biography."

"Have you?" Devlin sent Amanda a mildly chiding gaze. "Perhaps you've forgotten, Miss Briars, that you have contractual obligations to me. Despite your enthusiasm for the project, you may have to delay it for a while."

"If you say so," she murmured, nearly choking with a galling mixture of annoyance and gratitude. Silently she flashed him a message, her gaze promising vengeance if he did not rescue her immediately.

Devlin bowed and extended a gloved hand. "Shall we discuss the matter further? During a waltz, perhaps?"

Amanda needed no further urging. She practically leapt from the settee, which had developed all the appeal of a torture chamber, and seized Devlin's hand. "Very well, if you insist."

"Oh, I do," he assured her.

"But my life's story . . ." Stephenson protested. "I haven't yet finished with my years at Oxford . . ." He spluttered indignantly as Jack ushered Amanda toward the whirl of dancing couples in the drawing room. An effervescent waltz floated through the air, but its cheerful melody did little to soothe Amanda's irritation.

"Aren't you going to thank me?" Jack asked. He took her gloved hand and slid his arm around her.

"Thank you for what?" she responded sourly. Her cramped leg muscles objected to the prospect of a dance after the prolonged stay on the settee, but she was so relieved to be away from her tormentor that she ignored the pain.

"For rescuing you from Stephenson."

"You waited two hours to do so," she said tersely. "You'll get no thanks from me."

"How was I to know that you wouldn't find Stephenson attractive?" he asked, all innocence. "Many women do."

"Well, they are welcome to him. You have allowed me to be tormented by the most pretentious ass of a man that I've ever encountered."

"He is respectable, educated, unmarried, and wealthy—what more could you want?"

"He is *not* educated," Amanda countered with barely suppressed vehemence. "Or at least, if he is, his knowledge is limited to one subject. Himself."

"He knows a great deal about gemstones," Jack remarked blandly.

Amanda was tempted to hit him, right there before the mass of dancing couples. Reading her expression, Devlin laughed and tried to appear contrite. "I'm sorry. Truly. Here, I'll make it up to you. Tell me whom you most want to meet tonight, and I'll see to it at once. Anyone at all."

"Don't bother," she said grudgingly. "Being subjected to Mr. Stephenson for so long has put me in a foul temper. I'm only fit company for you."

His eyes gleamed with heathen laughter. "Dance with me, then."

He pulled her into the waltz with splendid economy of movement, somehow compensating for the radical difference in their heights. Amanda was struck anew how tall he was, the strength and sleek power of his body concealed in civilized evening attire.

As she might have expected, he was an excellent dancer, not merely proficient but graceful. He led her firmly, allowing no opportunity for a misstep. His hand was strong on her back, providing just the right amount of support and pressure to guide her.

The smell of starched linen mixed with the scent of his skin, salty and clean and spiced with a hint of cologne. Amanda hated it that Jack smelled so much better than any other man she knew. If only she could bottle the essence and pour it on some other man.

The ebullient music flowed around them, and Amanda felt herself relaxing in Devlin's firm hold. She had seldom danced in her youth, since most men of her acquaintance had seemed to think she was too dignified to enjoy such an activity. Although she had not been precisely a wallflower, she had certainly not been in high demand as a dance partner.

As they turned and circled amidst the other couples, Amanda noticed the subtle changes in Devlin's face. In the weeks since their separation, it seemed that he had lost some of his jauntiness and swagger. He appeared older, with new brackets forming on either side of his mouth, and a pair of creases that frequently appeared between his heavy brows. He had lost weight, which threw his cheekbones into new prominence and emphasized the hard angle of his jaw. And there were shadows beneath his eyes that attested to a regular lack of sleep.

"You look very tired," she said bluntly. "You should sleep more."

"I've been languishing for want of you," he said in a voice so light and mocking that it implied just the opposite. "Is that the reply you were hoping for?"

She stiffened at the soft jeer. "Let me go. The strap on my slipper has come loose."

"Not yet." His hand remained at the center of her back. "I have some good news to share with you. The first issue of *Unfinished Lady* has sold out completely. Installment number two is in such high demand that I'm doubling the print order this month."

"Oh. That is indeed good news." But the pleasure she ordinarily would have felt was undercut by the terrible tension that stretched between them. "Jack, my slipper—"

"Dammit," he muttered, stopping the swirling waltz and leading her away from the dancing.

Amanda held onto his arm as he guided her to a gilded chair set at the side of the drawing room. Silently she cursed the slipper and the delicate ribbon that tied it to her ankle, feeling it loosen until she could hardly keep the thing on.

"Sit," came Jack's curt order, and he knelt beside her, reaching for her foot.

"Stop that," Amanda snapped, aware that they were attracting many amused and curious glances.

A few guests were even tittering behind fans or gloved hands at the spectacle of proper Miss Amanda Briars being attended to by a notorious rake like Jack Devlin. "People are staring," she said in a softer tone as he drew the slipper from her foot.

"Settle your feathers. I've seen slipper-ribbons come loose before. In fact, some women even arrange it on purpose as an excuse to show off their ankles to their partners."

"If you are implying that I would use such a stupid pretext to—to—well, you are even more insufferably conceited than I thought!" Amanda flushed with embarrassment and glared at him as he glanced down at the flimsy slipper with a sudden smile.

"Why, Miss Briars," he murmured. "How frivolous of you."

She had purchased the dancing slippers on impulse. Unlike her other shoes, they had been designed with no thought to functionality or quality. They were hardly anything more than a thin sole and a one-inch heel held together with bits of lace and ribbon, and tiny embroidered flowers at the toe. One of the frail silk ribbons that affixed the shoe to her ankle had snapped in two, and Jack knotted the two frayed ends with a few deft twists of his fingers.

He assumed a properly impassive expression as he replaced the slipper on her foot and wrapped the ribbon around her ankle. However, there was a betraying remnant of laughter in his eyes, making it clear that he was enjoying her helplessness, and the attention they were attracting. Amanda kept her face averted, focusing fiercely on her hands as they twisted together in her lap.

Devlin took care to keep from exposing an untoward glimpse of Amanda's ankle as he replaced the shoe, his fingers cupped briefly around the back of her foot to hold it steady. She had never liked her legs, for they were sturdy and too short. Odes were never written to a woman with practical ankles, only to those who had slender, dainty ones. Yet her unromantic ankles were exquisitely sensitive, and she couldn't keep from quivering as she felt the clasp of Devlin's fingers, the heat of his hands penetrating the silk barrier of her stocking and burning the skin beneath.

The touch was fleeting, but Amanda felt it down to the marrow of her bones. She was confounded by the immediacy of her desire, the way her mouth turned dry, the nerve-rattling thrill of pleasure that went through her entire body. Abruptly she did not care that they were in a crowded drawing room. She wanted to sink to the polished floor with him, crush her mouth to his skin, tug his weight over her until she felt the intimate heat of him thrusting inside her. The primitive thoughts that raced through her head while she sat in these civilized surroundings made her horrified and dizzy.

Jack released her shod foot and rose before her. "Amanda," he said quietly. She felt his gaze on her downbent head.

She could not look up at him, could barely speak. "Please leave me alone," she finally managed to whisper. "Please."

Strangely, he seemed to understand her dilemma, for, after giving her a polite bow, he complied.

Amanda took several long breaths to settle her thoughts. The time she had spent apart from Jack had not eased her desire for him . . . she was filled with a longing and loneliness that drove her close to despair. How was she to bear these infrequent encounters with him? Was she to suffer like this for the rest of her life? And if so, what was to be done about it?

"Miss Briars?"

A low-pitched voice fell pleasantly on Amanda's ears. Raising her troubled gaze, she beheld a familiar face. A tall, brown-and-silver-haired man had approached her, his plain bearded face enhanced by a smile. His chocolate-colored eyes twinkled as he saw her hesitation. "I don't expect you to remember me," he said in a self-effacing way, "but we met at Mr. Devlin's Christmas party. I'm—"

"Of course I remember," Amanda said with a slight smile, relieved that his name had come to her mind. He was the popular author of children's verse, with whom she'd shared an enjoyable conversation at Christmas. "How nice to see you again, Uncle Hartley. I had no idea you would be attending the party this evening."

Hartley laughed at her use of his pen name. "I can't comprehend why the most charming woman present would not be dancing. Perhaps you would favor me with a quadrille?"

She gave a regretful shake of her head. "The straps on my right slipper won't tolerate it, I'm afraid. I will be fortunate if I can manage to keep the dratted thing on my foot for the rest of the evening."

Hartley regarded her in the manner of a man who was uncertain if he was being rebuffed or not. Amanda alleviated his discomfort by giving him another smile. "However," she added, "I do believe I could manage a trip to the refreshment table, if you would be kind enough to escort me?"

"I would be delighted," came his sincere reply, and he proffered his arm in a show of courtesy. "I had hoped very much to see you again after our conversation at Mr. Devlin's Christmas party," he said as they proceeded slowly to the refreshment room. "Unfortunately, it seems that you have not moved in society very often of late."

Amanda threw him a sharp glance, wondering if he had heard the rumors about her affair with Jack. But Hartley's expression was kind and polite, with no trace of accusation or insinuation.

"I have been occupied with work," she said abruptly, trying to dismiss a sudden pang of shame . . . the first time she had ever experienced such an emotion.

"Of course, a woman of your great talent . . . it takes time to create such memorable work." Hartley brought her to the refreshment table and gestured for a servant to fill a plate for her.

"And you?" Amanda asked. "Have you been writing more children's verse?"

"I'm afraid not," Hartley said cheerfully. "I have been spending most of my time with my sister and her brood. She has five daughters and two sons, all of them as bright-eyed and mischievous as a pack of fox cubs."

"You enjoy children," Amanda remarked with a questioning lilt.

"Oh, completely. Children have a way of reminding one of the true purpose of life."

"Which is?"

"Why, to love and be loved, of course."

Amanda was startled by his simple sincerity. She felt a wondering smile touch her lips. How remarkable it was to find a man who was so unafraid of sentiment.

Hartley's brown eyes were steady and warm, but his mouth softened with regret amid the neatly trimmed shape of his beard as he continued. "My late wife and I were never able to have children, to both our disappointment A house without children can be very quiet indeed."

While they moved along the refreshment line, Amanda's smile remained. Hartley was an impressive gentleman, kind and intelligent, and attractive despite his lack of true handsomeness. There was something about his broad, symmetrical face, with its large nose and rich brown eyes, that struck her as infinitely appealing. It was the kind of face that one could view every day and never tire of. She had been far too dazzled by Jack Devlin to notice Hartley before. Well, she vowed silently, she would not make that mistake again.

"Perhaps you will allow me to call on you sometime," Hartley suggested. "I would enjoy taking you for an airing in my carriage when the weather turns."

Mr. Charles Hartley was no fairy-tale hero, no dashing figure from a book, but a quiet, steady fellow who shared her interests. Hartley would never sweep her off her feet, but help her to keep them planted firmly on the ground. Although he was not what anyone would call exciting, Amanda had experienced enough excitement in her brief affair with Jack Devlin to last a lifetime. Now she wanted something—someone—who was solid and real, whose main ambition apparently was to lead a pleasant and ordinary life.

"I would like that very much," Amanda said, and to her relief, she soon made the discovery that while she was in Charles Hartley's solicitous company, she was able to put all thoughts of Jack Devlin from her mind.

Chapter 13

Making his last rounds of the day, Oscar Fretwell visited each floor of the building to check equipment and lock doors. He paused before Devlin's office. A light was burning inside, and a peculiar scent emanated from behind the closed door . . . the pungent tang of smoke. Mildly alarmed, Fretwell knocked on the portal and shouldered his way inside. "Mr. Devlin—"

Fretwell stopped and regarded the man who was both employer and friend with barely concealed amazement. Devlin was seated at his desk, surrounded by the ever-present piles of documents and books, puffing methodically on a long cigar. A crystal plate loaded with burned-out stubs, and a handsome cedar box that was half filled with more cigars, attested to the fact that Devlin's smoking had been going on for some time.

In an effort to compose his thoughts before speaking, Fretwell took the opportunity to remove his glasses and polish them with scrupulous care. When he replaced them, he gave Devlin a measuring stare. Although he rarely used Devlin's first name, feeling it necessary to demonstrate his absolute respect for the man before his employees, he used it deliberately now. For one thing, everyone had gone home for the day. For another, Fretwell felt the need to reestablish the connection that had existed between them since boyhood.

"Jack," he said quietly, "I didn't know you had a taste for tobacco."

"Today I do." Devlin drew again on the cigar, his narrowed blue gaze fastening onto Fretwell's face. "Go home, Fretwell. I don't want to talk."

Ignoring the muttered command, Fretwell wandered over to a window, unlocked the frame, and opened the panel to admit a cleansing breeze into the stuffy room. The dense blue haze that hung in the air began to disperse slowly. While Devlin's sardonic gaze remained on him, Fretwell approached the desk, inspected the box of cigars, and drew one out. "May I?"

Devlin grunted his assent, picking up a glass of whiskey and downing it in two gulps. Extracting a tiny scissor-case from his own pocket, Fretwell tried to snip the capped end off the cigar, but the tough wrapping of leaves resisted his efforts. Diligently he continued to saw away at the cigar until Devlin snorted and reached for it. "Give me the damned thing."

Producing a wickedly sharp knife from his desk drawer, Devlin made a deep circular cut around the cap, removing the ragged edge left by the scissors. He handed Fretwell the cigar and a matchbox, and watched as he lit and drew on it until the tobacco produced an acrid, aromatic smoke that flowed smoothly.

Sitting in a nearby chair, Fretwell puffed in companionable silence while he contemplated what he could say to his friend. The truth was, Devlin looked like the very devil. The past few weeks of ruthless work and drinking and lack of sleep had finally taken their toll. Fretwell had never seen him in such a state before.

Devlin had never struck him as a particularly happy sort of man, seeming to view life as a battle to be won rather than something he should find a measure of enjoyment in, and given his past, no one could blame him. But Devlin had always seemed invincible. As long as his business concerns were succeeding, he was charmingly arrogant, nonchalant, reacting to good news and bad with sardonic humor and a steady head.

Now, however, it was clear that something was bothering Devlin, something that mattered to him very much. The mantle of invincibility had been stripped away, leaving behind a man who was so bedeviled that he could not seem to find refuge.

Fretwell had no difficulty in discerning when the trouble had begun—at the first meeting between Jack Devlin and Miss Amanda Briars. "Jack," he said cautiously, "it is obvious that you have been somewhat preoccupied of late. I don't suppose there is anything—or anyone—that you would care to discuss—"

"No." Devlin dragged a hand through his black hair, disheveling the thick locks, tugging absently at the front forelock

"Well, there is something I would like to bring to your attention." Fretwell puffed thoughtfully on his cigar before continuing. "It seems that two of our writers have begun . . . I'm not certain what to call it . . . an involvement of some kind."

"Really." Devlin arched a black brow.

"And since you always like to be informed of any significant personal developments concerning your authors, I think you should be made aware of the rumors. It seems that Miss Briars and Mr. Charles Hartley have been seen together quite often of late. Once at the theater, a few times driving in the park, and at various social events—"

"I know," Devlin interrupted sourly.

"Forgive me, but I thought that at one time you and Miss Briars—"

"You're turning into an interfering old biddy, Oscar. You need to find a woman for yourself and stop worrying about other people's private affairs."

"I have a woman," Fretwell replied with extreme dignity. "And I don't choose to interfere in your private life, or even comment about it, unless it begins to affect your work. Since I own a share of this business, albeit a small one, I have a right to be concerned. If you drive yourself into a decline, every employee at Devlin's will suffer. Including myself."

Jack scowled and sighed, crushing out the stub of his cigar on the crystal plate. "Dammit, Oscar," he said wearily. Only his manager and longtime friend would dare to press him this way. "Since it's clear that you won't leave me the hell alone until I answer . . . yes, I'll admit that at one time I had an interest in Miss Briars."

"Quite a strong interest," Fretwell murmured.

"Well, that's all over now."

"Is it?"

Devlin gave a low, humorless laugh. "Miss Briars has too much sense to desire any entanglement with me." He rubbed the bridge of his nose and said flatly, "Hartley's a good choice for her, don't you think?"

Fretwell was compelled to answer honestly. "If I were Miss Briars, I would marry Hartley without hesitation. He's one of the most decent fellows I've ever met."

"It's all settled, then," Devlin said brusquely. "I wish the two of them well. It's only a matter of time before they wed."

"But . . . but what about you? Will you stand by and allow Miss Briars to go to another man?"

"Not only will I stand by, I'll escort her to the chapel myself, if she requires it. Her marriage to Hartley will be best for all concerned."

Fretwell shook his head, understanding the private fear that moved Devlin to cast away the woman who clearly meant so much to him. It was a strange, self-imposed isolation that all the survivors of Knatchford Heath seemed to share. None of them seemed able to forge lasting ties with anyone.

Of the few who had dared to marry, such as Guy Stubbins, Devlin's bookkeeping manager, had these unions that were sorely troubled. Trust and fidelity were damnably elusive for those who had endured the hell of Knatchford Heath. Fretwell himself had scrupulously avoided marriage, managing to love and lose a very good woman rather than take the risk of attaching himself to her permanently.

Yet he hated to see Jack Devlin suffer the same fate, especially as the man's feelings appeared to run far deeper than he had first suspected. After Amanda Briars married another man, it was likely that Devlin would never be the same.

"What will you do, Jack?" he wondered aloud.

Devlin pretended to misunderstand the question. "Tonight? . . . I'll leave off work and go to Gemma Bradshaw's place. Perhaps I'll purchase some ready female companionship."

"But you don't sleep with whores," Fretwell said, startled.

Devlin smiled darkly, gesturing to the plate of ashes. "I don't smoke, either."

"I've never had a picnic indoors before," Amanda remarked with a laugh, viewing her surrounding with glowing eyes. Charles Hartley had invited her to his small estate, built on the outskirts of London, where his younger sister, Eugenie, was hosting a luncheon. Amanda liked her immediately upon meeting her. Eugenie's dark eyes were filled with a lively youthfulness that belied her matronly status as a mother of seven, and she possessed the same aura of serenity that made Charles so appealing.

The Hartleys were a family of good blood, not aristocrats but respectable and well heeled. It made Amanda admire Charles all the more. He had the means to live an indolent life if he so desired, and yet he had chosen to occupy himself with writing for children.

"It's not an authentic picnic," Charles admitted. "However, it is the best we could do, considering the fact that it is too cold to enjoy oneself outdoors just yet."

"I do wish your children were here," Amanda said impulsively to Eugenie. "Mr. Hartley speaks of them so often that I feel as if I know them."

"Heavens," Eugenie exclaimed, laughing, "not for our first meeting. My children are a lot of perfect little hellions. They would frighten you away, and we would never see you again."

"I doubt that very much," Amanda replied, taking the seat that Charles held for her. The indoor picnic had been laid out in an octagonal-shaped sunroom featuring an atrium set in the center of the stone floor. Here a "white garden" planted with white roses, snowy lilies, and silver magnolias gave off a delicious scent that drifted across the table laden with linen, crystal, and silver. The white linen cloth had been scattered with pink rose petals that matched the flowered Sevres china.

Eugenie picked up a glass of sparkling champagne and regarded Charles with a smiling gaze. "Shall you make a toast, dear brother?"

He gazed at Amanda as he complied. "To friendship," he said simply, but the warmth in his eyes seemed to convey a deeper feeling than mere friendship.

Amanda sipped the beverage, finding it to be refreshingly tart and cold. She felt festive and yet completely comfortable in Charles Hartley's company. Lately they had spent a great deal of time together, riding in his carriage or attending parties and lectures. Charles was a complete gentleman, making her wonder if there were ever any improper thoughts or ideas in his head. He seemed incapable of rudeness or vulgarity. *All men are primitive louts*, Jack had once told her . . . well, he had been wrong. Charles Hartley was living proof of that.

The reckless passion that had tormented Amanda faded like the glowing embers of a once-roaring fire. She still thought of Jack far more often than she would have wished, and during the rare occasions when they met, she experienced the same hot and cold chills, the same excruciating awareness, the same intense yearning for things she could not have. Fortunately, it didn't happen often. And when it did, Jack was unfailingly polite, his blue eyes friendly but cool, and he spoke only of business matters that concerned them both.

Charles Hartley, on the other hand, made no secret of his feelings. It was easy to like this kind, uncomplicated widower, who clearly needed and wanted a wife. He was everything Amanda admired in a man; cerebral, moral, his character sensible and yet seasoned with dry wit.

How odd it seemed that after so many years, her life had finally come to this . . . being courted by a good man, knowing with near certainty that it would lead to marriage if she chose. There was something different about Charles Hartley from any other man she had ever known—it was astonishingly easy to trust him. She knew in her soul that he would always treat her respectfully. Moreover, they shared the same values, the same interests. In a short time, he had become a remarkably dear friend.

She wished that she could bring herself to feel more of a physical attraction to Charles. Whenever she tried to imagine being in bed with him, the thought was not in the least exciting. Perhaps that feeling would develop over time . . . or perhaps she would be able to find contentment in the kind of pleasant but passionless marriage that her sisters seemed to have.

This was the right path for her to take, Amanda reassured herself silently. Sophia had been correct—it was time for her to have her own family. If Charles Hartley eventually proposed to her, she would marry him. She would slow the pace of her career, perhaps even give it up entirely, and lose herself in the everyday concerns that ordinary women faced. *It is always more difficult for the people who swim against the current*, Sophia had counseled her, and the truth of those words had sunk in more deeply every day. How nice it would be, how pleasant, to surrender her fruitless desires, and finally be like everyone else.

As Amanda dressed for a carriage drive with Charles, she noticed that her best carriage gown, made of heavy apple-green corded silk, with a flattering V-shaped stomacher, was almost too snug to fasten.

"Sukey," she said with a sigh of displeasure as the maid strained to close the buttons at her back, "perhaps you might pull my corset laces a bit more tightly. I suppose I'll have to begin some kind of slimming regimen. Heaven knows what I've done to gain so much weight in the past few weeks."

To her surprise, Sukey did not laugh or commiserate or dispense advice, only stood behind her without moving.

"Sukey?" Amanda questioned, turning around. She was perplexed by the odd expression on the maid's face.

"P'raps I'd better not lace you tighter, Miss Amanda," Sukey said carefully. "It might do ye harm if ye are . . ." Her voice faded off.

"If I am what?" Amanda was bewildered by the

maid's silence. "Sukey, tell me your thoughts at once. Why, you almost look as though you think I'm—"

Abruptly she broke off as she understood the woman's unspoken question. She felt the blood ebbing from her face, and she put a hand to her midriff.

"Miss Amanda," the maid asked cautiously, "how long has it been since yer monthly courses have come?"

"A long time," Amanda said, her voice sounding distant and strangely detached. "Two months, at least. I've been too busy and distracted to give it a thought until now."

Sukey nodded, seemingly robbed of the ability to speak.

Amanda turned and went to a nearby chair. She sat with the unfastened dress sagging in shimmering folds around her. An odd feeling had come over her, as if she had been suspended in midair, with no way to gain purchase on the ground far below. It was not a pleasurable sensation, this terrible lightness. She wished desperately for a way to anchor herself, to catch hold of something reassuringly solid.

"Miss Amanda," Sukey said a long moment later, "Mr. Hartley will arrive soon."

"When he does, send him away," Amanda replied numbly. "Tell him . . . tell him that I am not feeling well today. And then send for a doctor."

"Yes, Miss Amanda."

She knew the doctor would only confirm what

she suddenly felt quite certain of. The recent changes in her body, and her feminine instincts, pointed to the same conclusion. She was pregnant with Jack Devlin's child . . . and she could not imagine a worse dilemma.

Unmarried women who found themselves pregnant were often described as being "in a predicament." The shortcomings of that phrase nearly made Amanda laugh hysterically. Predicament? No, it was a disaster, one that would change her life in every way.

"I'll stay with ye, Miss Amanda," Sukey murmured. "No matter what."

Even in the chaos of her thoughts, Amanda was moved by the woman's instant loyalty. Blindly she caught at the maidservant's rough, work-worn hand and clutched it. "Thank you, Sukey," she said hoarsely. "I don't know what I shall do if . . . if there is a baby . . . I would have to go somewhere. Abroad, I suppose. I would have to live away from England for quite a long while."

"I wearied of England years ago," Sukey said stoutly. "All this rain an' gray gloom, an' the cold that settles in yer bones . . . nay, it's not fer a woman of my warm nature. Now, France or Italy . . . those are the places I allus dreamed of."

A mirthless laugh stuck in Amanda's throat, and she could only whisper in reply, "We'll see, Sukey. We'll see what is to be done."

Amanda refused to see Charles Hartley, or anyone else, for a week after the doctor verified that she was pregnant. She sent Hartley a note explaining that she was suffering with a touch of *la grippe*, and required several days to rest and recover. He responded with a sympathetic message and a delivery of beautifully arranged hothouse flowers.

There was much to consider, and important decisions to make. Try as she might, Amanda could not blame Jack Devlin for her condition. She was a mature woman who had understood the risks and consequences of an affair. The responsibility rested squarely on her shoulders. Although Sukey had tentatively suggested that Amanda go to Jack with the news, the very idea had made her recoil in horror. Absolutely not! If there was one thing Amanda knew for certain, it was that Jack Devlin did not want to be a father or a husband. She would not burden him with this problem—she was capable of providing for herself and the baby.

There was only one course of action. She would pack up her household and go to France as soon as possible. Perhaps she would invent a fictional husband who had died, leaving her a widow . . . some kind of ruse that would allow her to take part in local French society. She would still be able to earn a handsome living by publishing from abroad. There was no reason for Jack ever to find out about a child whom he surely did not want and whose existence he would most likely resent. No one would know the truth except her sister Sophia, and, of course, Sukey.

Channeling all her energies into planning and

list-making, Amanda made preparations for the drastic upheaval her life would soon undergo. Toward that end, she allowed Charles Hartley to call on her one morning so that she could tell him good-bye.

Charles arrived at her home with a bouquet of flowers. He was dressed in his elegant, solidly traditional brown coat and fawn trousers, with a dark silk cravat tied neatly beneath his beard. Amanda felt a sharp pang of regret that she would never be able to see him after this day. She would miss his kind, open face and the comfortable, uncomplicated companionship he offered. It was a pleasure to be with a man who did not excite her or challenge her, a man who led a life as calm and quiet as Jack Devlin's was fast and turbulent.

"Lovely as ever, though a bit pale," Charles pronounced, smiling at Amanda as he gave his overcoat and tall hat to Sukey. "I have worried about you, Miss Briars."

"I am much better now, thank you," Amanda replied, forcing an answering smile to her lips. She bade Sukey to take the flowers and put them in water, and invited Charles to sit beside her on the settee. For a few minutes they engaged in light conversation, talking about nothing in particular while Amanda's mind busily winnowed out various ways to tell him that she was going to leave England for good. Finally she could think of no delicate way to put it, and she spoke with her natural brisk bluntness. "Charles, I am glad we have this opportunity to talk, as it will be our last. You see, I've recently decided that England is no longer the best place for me to live. I plan to establish a home elsewhere—in France, actually, where I believe the mild climate and the slower pace of life will suit me much better than here. I will miss you dearly, and I do hope we may correspond now and then."

Charles's face was wiped clean of expression, and he absorbed the news silently. "Why?" he murmured at last, and reached for one of her hands, holding it in both his large ones. "Are you ill, Amanda? Is that why you require a warmer climate? Or are there circumstances of a different nature that compel you to move? I do not wish to pry, but I have a good reason for asking, as I will explain shortly."

"I am not ill," Amanda said with a faint smile. "You are very kind, Charles, to show such concern for my welfare—"

"It is not kindness that inspires my questions," he said quietly. For once, his usually untroubled brow was puckered, and his mouth had tightened until it was nearly concealed in the trim mass of his beard. "I do not wish you to go anywhere, Amanda. There is something I must tell you. I had not wanted to reveal it so soon, but it seems that circumstances are forcing me to be a bit precipitate. Amanda, you must know how I care—"

"Please," she interrupted, her heart contracting with anxious alarm. She did not want him to make any confessions to her . . . God forbid that he might say he loved her, when she was pregnant with another man's child! "Charles, you are a dear friend, and I have been fortunate to have known you these past several weeks. But let us leave it at that, please. I am departing for the Continent in a matter of days, and anything you say cannot change that fact."

"I'm afraid I can't be silent." He held her hands more tightly, although his voice was still calm and warm. "I will not let you go without telling you how very much I value you. You are very special to me, Amanda. You are one of the finest women I have ever known, and I want—"

"No," she said, her throat suddenly aching. "I am not a fine woman, or a good one in any regard. I have made terrible mistakes, Charles, ones that I have no wish to explain to you. Please, let us say no more, and part as friends."

He considered her for a long time. "You are in some kind of trouble," he said quietly. "Let me help you. Is it financial? Legal?"

"It is a kind of trouble that no one can solve." She could not look at him. "Please go," she said, rising from her chair. "Good-bye, Charles."

He tugged her back to the settee. "Amanda," he murmured, "in light of my feelings for you, I believe you owe me something . . . the chance to be of service to someone I care for deeply. Tell me what is the matter."

Half touched and half annoyed by his persistence, Amanda forced herself to look directly into his gentle brown eyes. "I am pregnant," she blurted out. "You see? There is nothing that you or anyone can do. Now please leave, so that I may sort through the utter mess I've made of my life."

Charles's brown eyes widened, and his lips parted. Of all the things he might have suspected, it was clear that this was the last. How many people would be similarly shocked, Amanda thought, by the fact that the sensible spinster novelist would have carried on an affair and become pregnant as a result? In spite of her dilemma, she almost took a grim satisfaction in having done something so utterly unpredictable.

Charles continued to hold her hands in a secure clasp. "The father . . . I assume it is Jack Devlin," he said rather than asked, with no trace of censure in his tone.

Amanda colored as she stared at him. "You'd heard the rumors, then."

"Yes. But I could see that whatever had occurred between you in the past was definitely over."

Amanda let out a small, dry laugh. "Apparently it is not quite over," she managed to reply.

"Devlin is not willing to do his duty by you?"

Charles's reaction was not at all what she might have expected. Instead of withdrawing from her in distaste, he seemed as calm and friendly as ever, genuinely interested in her welfare. Amanda knew that he was too much of a gentleman to betray her confidence. Anything she told him would not be turned into gossip-fodder. It was a tremendous relief to confide in someone, and she found herself returning the pressure of his grip as she spoke.

"He does not know, nor will he ever. Jack has made it quite clear in the past that he does not want to marry. And he would certainly not be the kind of husband I would wish for. That is why I am going away . . . I cannot stay in England as an unwed mother."

"Of course. Of course. But you must tell him. I do not know Devlin well, but he must be given the opportunity to take responsibility for you and the child. It is not fair to him, or the child, to keep such a secret."

"There is no point in telling him. I know what his response will be."

"You cannot bear this burden alone, Amanda."

"Yes, I can." Suddenly she felt very calm, and she even smiled slightly as she looked into his broad, concerned face. "Truly, I can. The child will not suffer at all, and neither will I."

"Every child needs a father. And you will need a husband to help and sustain you."

Amanda shook her head decisively. "Jack would never propose to me, and if he did, I would never accept."

The words seemed to unlock some secret daredevil in Charles, some extraordinary impulse that exhorted him to blurt out a question that amazed her. "What if *I* proposed to you?"

She stared at him without blinking, wondering

if he had taken leave of his senses. "Charles," she said patiently, as if half suspecting that he had not understood her before, "I am expecting another man's child."

"I would like to have children. I would regard this one as my own. And I would very much like to have you as my wife."

"But why?" she asked with a bewildered laugh. "I've just told you that I'm going to have a child out of wedlock. You know what that indicates about my character. I am not at all the kind of wife you require."

"Let me be the judge of your character, which I find as estimable as ever." He smiled into her pale face. "Do me the honor of becoming my wife, Amanda. There is no need for you to move far away from family and friends. We would have a very good life together. You know we suit each other. I want you . . . and I want this child as well."

"But how can you accept someone else's bastard as your own?"

"Perhaps many years ago I would not have. But now I am entering the autumn of my life, and one's perspective changes greatly with maturity. I am being offered a chance at fatherhood, and, by God, I will take it."

Amanda regarded him with astonished silence, and then an unwilling laugh escaped her. "You surprise me, Charles."

"*You* have surprised *me*," he returned, his beard parting with a smile. "Come, do not take a long time to consider my proposal—it is hardly flattering."

"If I did accept," she said uncertainly, "you would claim this baby as your own?"

"Yes—on one condition. You must first tell Devlin the truth. I could not in good conscience rob another man of the chance to know his own child. If what you say about him is true, he will certainly not cause any trouble for us. He will even be glad to be absolved of the responsibility for you and the child. But we must not begin a marriage with lies."

"I can't tell him." Amanda shook her head decisively. She could not conceive what his response might be. Anger? Accusation? Sullen resentment or mockery? Oh, she would rather burn at the stake than have to present him with news of his unborn bastard!

"Amanda," Charles said softly, "it is likely that someday he will find out. You cannot spend years with that possibility hanging over your head. You must trust me in this . . . telling him about the child is the right thing to do. After that, you have nothing to fear from Devlin."

She shook her head unhappily. "I don't know if it would be fair to any of us if I agreed to marry you, and I can't be certain that telling Jack about the baby is the right thing. Oh, I wish I knew what to do! I used to be so certain about the correct choices . . . I used to think I was so wise and practical, and now the sterling character I thought I possessed is in shambles, and—"

Charles interrupted with a quiet chuckle. "What do you *wish* to do, Amanda? The choice is simple. You may go abroad and live among strangers, and raise your child without a father. Or you may stay in England and marry a man who respects and cares for you."

Amanda regarded him uncertainly. Put that way, the choice given to her made everything clear. A curious sense of relief mingled with resignation caused her eyes to sting. Charles Hartley was so quietly strong, with a flawless moral compass that amazed her. "I had no idea you could be so persuasive, Charles," she said with a sniffle, and he began to smile.

In the four months since Jack had begun publishing regular installments of *An Unfinished Lady*, it had become a sensation. The clamoring on the "Row," that section of Paternoster Row north of St. Paul's, was deafening each month on Magazine Day, and the booksellers' representatives all wanted one thing—the latest issue of *Unfinished Lady*.

Demand was climbing higher than Jack's most optimistic estimations. The success of Amanda's serial publication could be attributed to the excellent quality of the novel, the intriguing moral ambiguity of the book's heroine, and the fact that Jack had paid for extensive publicity, including advertisements in all the notable London newspapers.

Now vendors were selling *Unfinished Lady* merchandise: a specially created cologne inspired by the novel, ruby-colored gloves similar to the ones the heroine wore, gauzy red "Lady" scarves to be worn around the throat or tied around the brim of a hat. The most requested music at any fashionable ball was "The Unfinished Lady" waltz, composed by an admirer of Amanda's work.

He should be pleased, Jack told himself. After all, he and Amanda were both making a fortune from her novel and would continue to do so. There was no doubt that he would sell many editions of the final book when he finally brought it out in a handsome three-volume format. And Amanda seemed agreeable to the prospect of writing a brand-new serial novel for his publishing division.

However, it had become impossible for Jack to take pleasure in any of the things he used to. Money no longer excited him. He did not need further wealth—he had made far more than he could spend in a lifetime. As London's most powerful bookseller as well as publisher, he had acquired so much influence over the distribution of *other* publishers' novels that he could exact huge discounts from them for any book they wished him to carry. And he did not hesitate to make use of his advantage, which had made him even richer, if not exactly admired.

Jack knew that he was being called a giant in the publishing world—a recognition he had long worked for and craved. But his work had lost its power to absorb him. Even the ghosts of his past had ceased to haunt him as they once had. Now the days passed in a dull gray haze. He had never felt like this before, impervious to all emotion, even pain. If only someone could tell him how to break free of the suffocating gloom that enshrouded him.

"Merely a case of *ennui*, my boy," an aristocratic friend had informed him sardonically, using the upper-class term for a case of terminal boredom. "Good for you—a solid case of *ennui* is quite the fashion nowadays. You would hardly be a man of significance if you didn't have it. If you wish for relief, you need to go to a club, drink, play cards, diddle a pretty light-skirts. Or travel to the Continent for a change of scene."

However, Jack knew that none of these suggestions would help worth a damn. He merely sat in his prison of an office and dutifully negotiated business agreements, or stared blankly at piles of work that seemed exactly like the work he had finished last month, and the month before. And waited intently for news of Amanda Briars.

Like a faithful hunting hound, Fretwell brought him tidbits whenever he came across them . . . that Amanda had been seen at the opera with Charles Hartley one evening, or that Amanda had visited the tea gardens and had looked quite well. Jack mulled over each piece of information incessantly, damning himself for caring so deeply about the minutiae of her life. Yet Amanda was the only thing that seemed to reawaken his pulse. He who had always been known for his insatiable drive could now only seem to work up an interest in the sedate social activities of a spinster novelist.

When he found himself too frustrated and restless to attend to his work one morning, Jack decided that physical exertion might do him some good. He was accomplishing nothing in his office, and there was work to be done elsewhere in the building. He left a pile of unread manuscripts and contracts on his desk and occupied himself instead with carrying chests of freshly bound books to a wagon at street level, where they would be carted off to a ship moored at the wharf.

Removing his coat, he worked in his shirtsleeves, lifting the chests and crates to his shoulder and carrying them down long flights of stairs to the ground floor. Although the stock lads were a bit unnerved at first to see the owner of Devlin's performing such menial work, the hard labor soon caused them to lose all trace of self-consciousness.

After Jack had made at least a half-dozen trips from the fifth floor to the street, lugging book-filled crates to the wagon behind the building, Oscar Fretwell managed to find him. "Devlin," he called, sounding perturbed. "Mr. Devlin, I—" He stopped in amazement as he saw Jack loading a crate onto the wagon. "Devlin, may I ask what you are about? There's no need for you to do that—God knows we hire enough men to carry and load crates—"

"I'm tired of sitting at my damn desk," Jack said curtly. "I wanted to stretch my legs."

"A walk in the park would have accomplished the same thing," Fretwell muttered. "A man in your position does not have to resort to stock-room labor."

Jack smiled slightly, dragging his sleeve across his damp forehead. It felt good to sweat and exercise his muscles, to do something that did not require any thought, but merely physical effort.

"Spare me the lecture, Fretwell. I was of no use to anyone in my office, and I'd rather do something more productive than stroll through the park. Now, is there something you wished to tell me? Otherwise, I have more crates to load."

"There is something." The manager hesitated and gave him a searching stare. "You have a visitor—Miss Briars is waiting in your office. If you wish, I will tell her that you are not available . . ." His voice trailed away as Jack strode to the stairs before he had even finished the sentence.

Amanda was here, wanting to see him, when she had taken care to avoid him for so long. Jack felt a peculiar tightness in his chest that gave a strained quality to his heartbeat. He struggled not to take the stairs two at a time, but proceeded up the five flights to his office at a measured pace. Even so, his breathing was not quite normal when he reached the top. To his chagrin, he knew the overexertion of his lungs had nothing to do with physical labor. He was so damned eager to be in the same room with Amanda Briars that he was panting like an amorous lad. He debated whether he should change his shirt, wash his face, find his coat, all in the effort to appear collected. He decided against it. He did not want to keep her waiting any longer than necessary.

Struggling to maintain an impassive facade, he entered his office and left the door slightly ajar. His gaze immediately shot to Amanda, who was standing by his desk with a neat paper-wrapped package held at her side. A strange expression crossed her face as she saw him . . . he read anxiety and pleasure there before she sought to cover her discomposure with a bright, false smile.

"Mr. Devlin," she said briskly, coming toward him. "I've brought you the revisions for the last installment of *Unfinished Lady* . . . and a proposal for another serial novel, if you are interested."

"Of course I'm interested," he said thickly. "Hello, Amanda. You're looking well."

The commonplace remark did not begin to describe his reaction to her appearance. Amanda looked fresh and ladylike, dressed in a crisp blue-and-white gown with a pristine white bow tied at the throat and a row of pearl buttons that extended down the front of the bodice. As she stood before him, he thought he detected the scent of lemons and the whisper of perfume, and all his senses kindled in response.

He wanted to crush her against his hot, sweating body, kiss and maul and devour her, tangle his big hands in her neat braided coiffure, rip the row of pearl buttons until her sumptuous breasts spilled into his waiting hands. He was ravaged by an all-consuming hunger, as if he hadn't eaten for days and suddenly realized that he was starving. The violent rush of awareness and sensation, when he had felt nothing for weeks, made him nearly dizzy.

"I am quite well, thank you." Her forced smile disappeared as she stared at him, and there was a flash in her silver-gray eyes. "There is a streak of dirt on your cheek," she murmured. She tugged a clean, pressed handkerchief from her sleeve and reached toward his face. Hesitating almost imperceptibly, she dabbed at the right side of his face. Jack stood still, his muscles turning rigid until his body seemed to have been carved in marble. After the smudge was removed, Amanda used the other side of the handkerchief to blot the streaks of sweat on his face. "What in heaven's name have you been doing?" she murmured.

"Work," he muttered, using all the force of his will to keep from seizing her.

A faint smile touched her soft lips. "As always, you cannot seem to conduct your life at a normal pace."

The remark did not sound admiring. In fact, it almost sounded a touch pitying, as if she had come to some new understanding that eluded him. Jack scowled and leaned over her to place the paper-wrapped package on his desk, deliberately forcing her to retreat backward a step or else have her body come into full contact with his. He was pleased to see that she flushed, some of her composure eroding. "May I ask why you brought this to me in person?" he asked, referring to the revisions.

"I'm sorry if you would have preferred—"

"No, it's not that," he said gruffly. "I just wanted to know if you had a particular reason for seeing me today."

"Actually, there is something." Amanda cleared her throat uncomfortably. "I will be attending a party tonight given by my lawyer, Mr. Talbot. I believe you have received an invitation—he indicated that you were on his guest list."

Jack shrugged. "Mostly likely I did receive one. I doubt that I'll attend."

For some reason, the information seemed to relax her. "I see. Well, perhaps it is best that you receive the news from me this morning. In light of our . . . considering that you and I . . . I did not want you to be caught off guard when you heard . . ."

"Heard what, Amanda?"

The color in her face climbed higher. "Tonight, Mr. Hartley and I will be announcing our betrothal at Mr. Talbot's party."

It was news that he had been expecting, and yet Jack was stunned by his own reaction. Some great yawning gap opened inside, admitting a spill of pain and ferocity. The rational part of his mind pointed out that he had no right to be angry, but he was. The blistering anger was directed toward

Amanda, and Hartley, but most of all to himself. Grimly he controlled his expression and forced himself to remain still, though his hands actually trembled with the urge to shake her.

"He is a good man." Defensiveness was strung tightly through her tone. "We have everything in common. I expect to be very happy with him."

"I'm sure you will," he muttered.

She gathered her composure like an invisible mantle and straightened her shoulders. "And you and I will continue on as we have been, I hope."

Jack knew exactly what she meant. They would maintain the facade of distant friendship, work together occasionally, their relationship kept carefully impersonal. As if he had never taken her innocence. As if he had never touched and kissed her intimately, and known the sweetness of her body.

His chin jerked downward in an abbreviated nod. "Have you told Hartley about the affair?" he couldn't help asking.

She surprised him by nodding. "He knows," she murmured, her mouth twisting wryly. "He is a very forgiving man. A true gentleman."

Bitterness spread through him. Would he himself have accepted the information like a gentleman? He doubted it. Charles Hartley was indeed the better man.

"Good," he said brusquely, feeling the need to annoy her. "I would hate for him to stand in the way of our professional relationship—I foresee making a pile of money off you and your books."

A scowl worked between her brows, and the corners of her mouth tightened. "Yes. Heaven forbid that anything should stand in the way between you and your profits. Good day, Mr. Devlin. I have much to accomplish today . . . Wedding arrangements to make." She turned to leave, the white plumes on her little blue bonnet agitating with each step as she headed for the door.

Jack forbore to ask sarcastically if he would be invited to the blessed event. He watched stonily, not offering to escort her out as a gentleman should have.

Amanda paused at the doorway, looking back at him over her shoulder. For some reason, it seemed that she wanted to tell him something else. "Jack . . ." Her forehead was scored with a perturbed frown, and she appeared to struggle with words. Their gazes locked, troubled gray eyes staring into hard, opaque blue. Then, with a frustrated shake of her head, Amanda turned and left the office.

With his head, heart, and groin all burning, Jack made his way to his desk and sat down heavily. He fumbled in a drawer for a glass and his ever-present decanter of whiskey, and poured himself a drink.

The sweetly smoky flavor filled his mouth, soothing his throat with a hot glow as he swallowed. He finished the drink and poured another. Perhaps Fretwell was right, Jack mused sourly—a man of his position had better things to do than carry crates of books. He would forgo any kind of work today, as a matter of fact. He would simply sit here and drink, until all feeling and thought were extinguished, and the images of Amanda naked in bed with mannerly Charles Hartley would drown in a sea of spirits.

"Mr. Devlin." Oscar Fretwell hovered in the doorway, his bespectacled face showing concern. "I did not wish to bother you, but—"

"I'm busy," Jack growled.

"Yes, sir. However, you have another visitor, a Mr. Francis Tode. It seems that he is a solicitor in charge of dispensing your father's estate."

Jack was very still, staring at the manager without blinking. Dispensing his father's estate. There could be no reason for that unless . . . "Send him in," he heard himself say in a flat tone.

The unfortunately named Mr. Tode actually did resemble an amphibian, diminutive of stature, bald, and big-jowled, with moist black eyes that were disproportionately large for his face. However, his gaze was keenly intelligent, and he wore a demeanor of gravity and responsibility that Jack immediately liked.

"Mr. Devlin." He came forward to shake hands. "Thank you for agreeing to see me. I regret that we have not met under happier circumstances. I have come to deliver a piece of very sad news."

"The earl is dead," Jack said, gesturing for the solicitor to have a seat. It was the only explanation that made sense.

Tode nodded, his liquid black eyes filled with polite sympathy. "Yes, Mr. Devlin. Your father passed away in his sleep last evening." He glanced at the whiskey bottle on Jack's desk and added, "It seems that you have already heard."

Jack laughed shortly at the man's assumption that he was drinking out of grief over the passing of his father. "No, I hadn't heard."

There was a moment of awkward silence. "Good God, how closely you resemble your father," the solicitor remarked, staring as if mesmerized by Jack's hard face. "There is certainly no doubt as to who sired you."

Moodily Jack swirled some whiskey in his glass. "Unfortunately so."

The solicitor did not appear to be surprised by the negative comment. No doubt the earl had acquired a good many enemies during his long, pernicious lifetime, including a few bitterly discontent bastard children. "I am aware of the fact that you and the earl were . . . not close."

Jack smiled slightly at the understatement and made no reply.

"However," Tode continued, "the earl did see fit before he died to include you in his will. A token, of course, to a man of your obvious means . . . yet it is something of a family prize. The earl left you a country property with a small estate manor in Hertfordshire. Well situated and maintained. A jewel, really. It was built by your great-great-grandfather."

"What an honor," Jack murmured.

Tode ignored the sarcasm. "Your brothers and sisters certainly think so," he replied. "Many of them had an eye on it before your father's passing. Needless to say, they were universally surprised that he left it to you."

Good, Jack thought with a sting of mean satisfaction. He took pleasure in having displeased the privileged group of snobs who had chosen to take so little notice of him. No doubt there was a great deal of whining and grousing about the fact that an ancient family property had been left to an illegitimate half brother.

"Your father had the codicil written not long ago," Tode remarked. "Perhaps it will interest you to know that he followed your achievements with a great deal of interest. He seemed to believe that you were like him in many ways."

"He was probably right," Jack said, self-disgust slithering through him.

Tilting his head a bit, the solicitor regarded him thoughtfully. "The earl was a very complicated man. Apparently he had everything in the world that one could wish for, and yet the poor fellow seemed to lack the talent for happiness."

The turn of phrase interested Jack, temporarily pulling him from the well of bitterness. "Does it require a particular talent to be happy?" he asked, still staring at his whiskey glass.

"I've always believed so. I am acquainted with a tenant farmer on your father's lands who lives in a crude stone cottage with a dirt floor, yet he has always struck me as finding far more pleasure in life than your father. I've come to think that the condition of happiness is something a man chooses, rather than something that merely befalls one."

Jack shrugged at the observation. "I wouldn't know."

They sat together in silence, until Mr. Tode cleared his throat and stood. "I wish you well, Mr. Devlin. I will take my leave for now, and in short time I will send the materials relevant to your inheritance." He paused in a moment of patent embarrassment before adding, "I'm afraid there is no diplomatic way to say this . . . however, the earl's legitimate children have asked me to tell you that they wish to have no communication with you of any kind. In other words, the funeral . . ."

"Have no fear, I won't be attending," Jack said with a brief, ugly laugh. "You may inform my half brothers and sisters that I have as little interest in them as they have in me."

"Yes, Mr. Devlin. If I may be of assistance to you, please do not hesitate to inform me."

After the solicitor had left, Jack stood and paced around the room. The whiskey had gone to his head—it seemed his usual tolerance for the stuff had disappeared. His head ached, and he felt empty, hungry, weary. A mirthless smile tugged at his mouth. It had been a hell of a day so far, and the morning wasn't even over.

He felt curiously removed from his past and his future, as if he were somehow standing outside his own life. Mentally Jack cataloged all the reasons he should be content. He had money, property, land, and now he had inherited a family estate, a birthright that should have been given to a legitimate heir rather than a bastard. He should have been very pleased.

But he did not care about any of it. He wanted only one thing—to have Amanda Briars in his bed. Tonight and every night. To own her, and to be owned by her.

Somehow Amanda was the only thing that would prevent him from ending like his father, rich and callous and mean-spirited. If he could not have her . . . if he had to spend the rest of his life watching her grow old with Charles Hartley . . .

Jack swore, his pacing becoming more agitated until he circled the room like a caged tiger. Amanda had made what was clearly a good choice for herself. Hartley would never encourage her to do something unladylike or unconventional. He would shroud her in comfortable propriety, and before long the impulsive woman who had once tried to hire a prostitute for her birthday would be buried beneath layers of respectability.

Jack stopped by the window, flattening his hands on the cool pane. Grimly he acknowledged that it was far better for Amanda to marry a man like Hartley. No matter what it took, Jack would quell his own selfish desires and think more of her needs than his own. If it killed him, he would accept the match and wish them both well, so that Amanda would never realize how he felt about her.

Amanda smiled up at her soon-to-be-betrothed. "At what time will you make the announcement, Charles?"

"Talbot has given me leave to do so whenever I wish. I thought we would wait until the dancing begins, and you and I would start the first waltz as a betrothed couple."

"A perfect plan." Amanda tried to ignore the unsettled feeling in her stomach.

They stood together on one of the outside balconies that extended from the drawing room of Mr. Thaddeus Talbot's home. The party was well attended, with over a hundred and fifty guests having gathered to enjoy the fine music and bountiful delicacies that were standard at any of Talbot's events. Tonight Amanda and Charles would announce their pending nuptuals to their friends and acquaintances. Afterward the banns would be read in church for three weeks, and they would have a small wedding in Windsor.

Amanda's sisters, Sophia and Helen, had been delighted by the news that their younger sibling was to wed. *I fully approve of your choice, and cannot conceal my great pleasure that you paid heed to my counsel*, Sophia had written. *From all reports, Mr.*

Hartley is a decent and quiet-living gentleman, his pedigree estimable, and his fortune well founded. I have no doubt that this marriage will be of great benefit to all parties concerned. We look forward to welcoming Mr. Hartley into our family, dear Amanda, and I do congratulate you on your most judicious selection of a partner . . .

Judicious, Amanda thought with silent amusement. It was hardly the way she might have once wished to describe her choice of a fiancé, but it would certainly do.

Hartley glanced around to make certain they were not being observed, then bent to kiss her forehead. It felt odd to Amanda to be kissed by a man with a beard, the softness of his lips surrounded by the wiry brush of hair.

"How happy you've made me, Amanda. We are perfectly matched, are we not?"

"We are," she said with a little laugh.

He took her gloved hands and squeezed them. "Allow me to fetch you some punch. We'll share a few moments of privacy out here—it's so much more peaceful than the crush inside. Will you wait for me?"

"Of course I will, dear." Amanda returned the squeeze of his hands, sighing as the disquieting feeling left. "Hurry, Charles—I shall miss you if you are gone for long."

"I will indeed hurry," he replied with an affectionate laugh. "I would not be fool enough to leave the most attractive woman at the party unaccompanied for more than a few minutes." He opened the glass-paned doors that led to the drawing room. A burst of music and conversation accompanied his exit, the sounds quickly muffled as the doors were closed once more.

Moodily Jack surveyed the elegant throng of guests in the drawing room of Thaddeus Talbot's red brick home, hunting for a glimpse of Amanda. Music drifted from the paneled copse at one end of the room, an exuberant rendition of a Croatian folk tune that lent a vivacious mood to the gathering.

A fine night for a betrothal announcement, he thought bleakly. Amanda was nowhere to be seen, but Charles Hartley's tall form was visible at the refreshment table.

Every particle of his being rebelled at the idea of talking civilly with the man. Yet somehow it seemed necessary. He would make himself accept the situation like a gentleman, no matter how foreign that behavior was to his nature.

Forcing his face into an expressionless mask, Jack approached Hartley, who was directing a servant to fill two cups with fruit-colored punch.

"Good evening, Hartley," he murmured. The man turned toward him, his wide, square features seeming untroubled, his smile gentle amid the trim thatch of his beard. "It seems that congratulations are in order."

"Thank you," Hartley said carefully. In tacit agreement, they both withdrew from the refreshment table and found an unoccupied corner of the room where they would not be overheard. "Amanda told me that she visited you this morning," Hartley commented. "I had thought that after she broke the news you might have . . ." He paused, giving Jack an assessing glance. "But it seems that you have no objections to the marriage."

"Why would I? Naturally I want the best for Miss Briars."

"And the circumstances do not trouble you?"

Thinking that Hartley was referring to the affair with Amanda, Jack shook his head. "No," he said with a hard smile. "If you can overlook the circumstances, then so can I."

Looking perplexed, Hartley spoke in a guarded murmur. "I would like you to know something, Devlin. I will do my best to make Amanda happy, and I will be an excellent father to her child. Perhaps it is easier this way, with your lack of involvement—"

"Child," Jack said softly, his gaze arrowing to the other man's face. "What the hell are you talking about?"

Hartley was very still, appearing to devote unusual concentration to a distant point on the floor. When he glanced upward, his brown eyes were crinkled with dismay. "You don't know, do you? Amanda assured me that she had told you this morning."

"Told me what? That she—" Jack broke off in

utter confusion, wondering what in God's name Hartley had meant. Then he understood. A child, a child . . .

Dear God.

The news was like an explosion in his brain, setting every cell and nerve afire. "My God," he whispered. "She's pregnant, isn't she? With my child. And she would have married you without telling me."

Hartley's silence was reply enough.

At first Jack was too stunned to feel anything. Then fury kindled, and dark color washed over his face.

"It seems that Amanda could not bring herself to discuss it with you after all." Hartley's quiet murmur filtered through the angry buzzing in his brain.

"She will damn well have to," Jack muttered. "You had better delay your betrothal announcement, Hartley."

"Perhaps that is best," he heard Hartley say.

"Tell me where she is."

Hartley complied, and Jack went in search of Amanda, his mind seething with unwelcome recollections. He had too many memories of helpless little boys struggling to survive in a merciless world. He had tried to protect them—he even bore the marks of that effort on his own body. But ever since then, he had wanted to be responsible only for himself. His life had been his own, to be dealt with on his own terms. For a man who did not want to have a family, avoiding such a fate had been a simple enough matter.

Until now.

That Amanda had tried to cut him so neatly out of the situation was maddening. She knew full well that he had not wanted to take the risk of marriage and all that went with it. Perhaps he should even be grateful that she had completely absolved him of responsibility. But gratitude was the last thing he felt. He was filled with outrage and possessiveness, and a primitive need to claim her once and for all.

Chapter 14

A gentle breeze rustled through the leaves, bringing with it the scent of fresh-turned earth and lavender blossoms. Amanda drew to the side of the balcony, where she was completely concealed from view. As she leaned against the wall of the house, the rough texture of the red brick gently abraded her bare shoulders.

She had worn a pale blue, corded-silk gown with a low-cut back, and draperies of gauze that crossed over the bodice in an X pattern. The long sleeves of the gown were made of more transparent gauze, while her hands were encased in white gloves. The flash of her bare arms beneath the filmy blue silk made Amanda feel sophisticated and daring.

The French doors opened and closed. Amanda glanced sideways, her eyes so accustomed to the darkness that they were temporarily dazzled by the light from inside. "Back so soon, Charles? The line at the punch bowl must have shortened considerably since we arrived."

There was no reply. Quickly Amanda realized that the dark silhouette before her was not that of Charles Hartley. The man approaching her was tall, broad-shouldered, and moved with a stealthy grace that could have belonged to no one other than Jack Devlin.

The night seemed to whirl around her. She swayed a little in her heeled slippers, her balance precarious. There was something alarmingly deliberate about Jack's movements, as if he were bent on cornering and devouring her like a tiger with its prey. "What do you want?" she asked warily. "I warn you, Mr. Hartley will be returning to me soon, and—"

"Hello, Amanda." His voice was silken and menacing. "Is there something you'd like to tell me?"

"What?" Amanda shook her head in bewilderment. "You're not supposed to be here tonight. You said you wouldn't come. Why—"

"I wanted to wish you and Hartley well."

"Oh. That is very kind of you."

"Hartley seemed to think so. I spoke with him not a minute ago."

A thrill of unease ran through her as his towering form leaned over hers. Unaccountably, her teeth began to chatter, as if her body were becoming aware of an unpleasant knowledge that her mind had not yet accepted. "What was said between you?"

"Take a guess." When Amanda remained obstinately silent, shivering in her fine gown, he reached for her with a quiet snarl. "You little coward."

Too stunned to react, Amanda went rigid as his punishing arms closed around her. His hand caught the back of her head, heedless of ruining her tidy coiffure, and he forced her face upward. She gasped, made a move to free herself, but his mouth dove and captured hers, blazing, insistent, feeding hungrily off the warmth and taste of her. Amanda quivered and pushed at him, struggling to ignore the wild pleasure that flared inside her, the eager response that was immune to shame or reason.

The heat and pressure of his lips was delicious, and her craving for him was so great that she actually panted when she tore herself away from him. She tottered backward a step, fighting for balance in a night that had suddenly been thrown wildly off-kilter. The brick wall came hard against her back, preventing further retreat.

"You're mad," she whispered, her heart pounding with a violence that hurt.

"Tell me, Amanda," he said roughly. His hands slid over her, making her body quiver inside the blue silk gown. "Tell me what you should have said this morning at my offices."

"Go away. Someone will see us out here. Charles will come back, and he—"

"He has agreed to postpone the betrothal announcement until you and I have had an opportunity to talk."

"About what?" she cried, pushing his hands

away. Desperately she tried to feign ignorance. "I have no interest in discussing anything with you, certainly not about some past dalliance that means nothing now!"

"It means something to me." His large hand clamped over her belly in a blatantly possessive clasp. "Especially in light of the child you're carrying."

Amanda went weak with guilt and fear. Had she not been so alarmed by Jack's contained fury, she would have sagged against him in search of physical support. "Charles should not have told you." She shoved at his chest, which felt as unyielding as the mortar and brick behind her. "I did not want you to know."

"It is my right to know, damn you."

"It changes nothing. I am still going to marry him."

"Like hell you are," he said harshly. "If you were making the decision for yourself alone, I wouldn't say a word about it. But there is someone else involved now—my child. I have a say in his future."

"No," she whispered frantically. "Not when I've come to a decision that is right for me and the baby. Y-you can't give me what Charles can. My God, you don't even like children!"

"I'm not going to walk away from my own child."

"You have no choice!"

"Don't I?" He caught her in a light but tenacious hold. "Listen carefully," he said in a quiet tone that caused the hairs on her nape to prickle and rise. "Until this is settled, there will be no betrothal between you and Hartley. I will wait for you at the front of the house in my carriage. If you don't come in exactly fifteen minutes, I will find you and carry you out bodily. We can leave discreetly, or we can cause a scene that will be gossiped about in every parlor in London on the morrow. You decide."

He had never talked to her this way before, his soft voice underlaid with steel. Amanda had no choice but to believe him. She wanted to rail and scream, her frustration escalating to an unbearable pitch. To her utter self-disgust, she found herself near tears, like the witless heroines of the sensation novels she had always enjoyed making jest of. Her mouth trembled as she struggled to control her explosive emotions.

Jack saw that sign of weakness, and something in his face relaxed. "Don't cry. There is no need for tears, *mhuirnin*," he said in a gentler voice.

She could hardly speak; her throat was clotted with misery. "Where are you taking me?"

"To my home."

"I—I need to speak with Charles first."

"Amanda," he said softly, "do you think he can save you from me?"

Yes, yes, her mind cried silently. But as she stared up into the dark face of the man who had once been her lover and was now her adversary, all hope was burned to ashes. There were two sides to Jack Devlin, the charming rogue and the ruthless manipulator. He would do whatever was necessary to have his way. "No," she whispered bitterly.

Despite the excruciating tension between them, Jack smiled slightly. "Fifteen minutes," he warned, and left her shivering in the darkness.

It was testament to Jack's skill as a negotiator that he was quiet during the carriage ride to his house. While he maintained a strategic silence, Amanda stewed in a mixture of confusion and outrage. Her stays and laces seemed to compress her upper body until she could barely breathe. The pale blue silk gown that had felt so light and elegant earlier this evening was now tight and uncomfortable, and her jewelry was too heavy. The pins in her hair scratched her scalp. She felt trapped, bound, and utterly miserable. By the time they reached their destination, her internal debate had left her exhausted.

The marble entrance hall was dimly lit, with only one lamp to relieve the shadows upon the pristine facades of marble statues. Most of the servants had retired for bed, except a butler and two footmen. Starlight streamed through a stained-glass window above, sending rays of lavender, blue, and green across the central staircase.

Keeping one hand at the small of Amanda's back, Jack guided her up two flights of stairs. They entered into a suite of rooms she had never seen before, a private receiving room that connected to a bedroom beyond. Their affair had been conducted at her home, not his, and Amanda stared curiously at the unfamiliar surroundings. It was a dark, luxuriously masculine retreat, the walls covered in stamped leather, the floors thickly carpeted in an Aubusson pattern of crimson and gold.

Deftly Jack lit a lamp, then came to her. He removed her gloves, gently tugging at the tip of each finger to loosen them. She stiffened as her bare hands were enclosed in the warm strength of his.

"This is my fault, not yours," he said quietly. His thumbs stroked over the blunt points of her knuckles. "I was the experienced partner in our affair. I should have taken more care to prevent this from happening."

"Yes, you should have."

Jack clasped her against his body, ignoring the way she flinched when his arms closed around her back. His nearness caused gooseflesh to rise all over her body, and a nerveless, excited quiver ran through her. Gently he pulled her closer and spoke into the curling mass of her pinned-up hair.

"Do you love Hartley?"

Dear Lord, how she wanted to lie. Her mouth spasmed as she tried to form the word "yes," but she couldn't seem to make a sound. Finally her shoulders slumped in defeat, and she felt weak all over from the silent struggle. "No," she said hoarsely. "I like and esteem him, but it is not love."

He let out a sigh, his hands moving from her arms to her back. "I've wanted you, Amanda. Every damn day since I left you. I thought about going to another woman, but I couldn't."

"If you are asking me to continue our affair, I can't." Hot tears tipped over her lashes. "I will not become your mistress and condemn my child to a life of secrecy and shame."

Jack's hand slid beneath her chin, and he forced her to look at him. There was a strange mixture of tenderness and ruthless purpose in his expression. "When I was a boy, I used to wonder why I had been born a bastard, why I didn't have a family like other children did. Instead, I watched my mother take a string of lovers, hoping to God each time that she could get one of them to marry her. With every new man who appeared, she told me to call him Papa . . . until the word lost all meaning for me. Understand this, Amanda. My child will not grow up without his real father. I want to give him my name. I want to marry you."

The moment spun out with a queer, dizzying flourish, and she swayed against him. "You don't really want to marry me. You want to ease your conscience by telling yourself that you've done the honorable thing. But soon you will tire of me, and before long I will find myself stashed away in the country so that you may conveniently forget about me and our child—"

Jack interrupted the slew of bitter, fearful words by shaking her briefly, his face turning hard. "You don't really believe that, dammit. Do you have so little trust in me?" As he read the answer in her eyes, he swore beneath his breath. "Amanda . . . you know that I never break my promises. I promise that I will be a good husband. A good father."

"You don't know how to be those things!"

"I can learn."

"One does not 'learn' to want a family," she said scornfully.

"But I do want you." Jack kissed her, his mouth pressing and demanding until she opened to welcome him inside. His hands moved over her back and buttocks, molding and squeezing as if he were trying to pull her inside himself. Even through the layers of her skirts, she could feel the hard, arching shape of his arousal. "Amanda," he said raggedly, rubbing his lips over her face and hair, imprinting kisses on every part of her he could reach. "I can't stop wanting you . . . needing you. I've got to have you. And you need me, too, even if you are too stubborn to admit it."

"I need someone who will be solid and steady and faithful," she gasped. "This will burn out someday and then—"

"Never," he rasped. His mouth closed over hers once more, in a ravaging kiss that sent a jolt of need through her. He picked her up and set her on the massive four-poster bed, his lungs working like bellows as he fought for self-control.

Standing over her, he stripped off his waistcoat and silk necktie, and began to unfasten his shirt.

Amanda's mind was foggy with confusion and desire. He could not simply carry her off to his bedroom in this primitive manner . . . and yet she could not ignore the insistent clamoring of her own body. The past weeks of deprivation had suddenly become too much, and she wanted him with an urgency that was almost painful.

Red-faced and shaking, she watched as Jack shrugged out of his shirt and dropped it to the floor, revealing the gleaming muscled expanse of his chest and the brawny width of his shoulders. He leaned over her and reached for her legs. As he unfastened and removed each shoe, his warm hand clasped over her cold toes and chafed them gently. He raised her skirts to her knees, and his gentle fingers slid to her garters. "Did you do this with Hartley?" he asked, staring at her knees while he removed the garters and unrolled her stockings.

"Did I do what?" Amanda asked unsteadily.

Jealousy lent an abraded edge to his tone. "Don't play games with me, Amanda. Not about this."

"I have not been intimate with Charles," she muttered, biting her lip as he stripped the layer of silk from her legs and stroked her calves.

Amanda could not see his face, but she sensed that her answer had relieved him. Carefully he tugged at her drawers, removing them from beneath her skirts, and reached for the back of her gown. She held still, her body filled with an ache of anticipation as he unfastened her gown and drew it over her head. A small murmur of relief escaped her when her corset was undone, and she was finally free of the biting pressure of her stays. She felt his hands on her body, gently searching through the paper-thin cotton of her chemise. He cupped her breasts, the heat of his hands causing her nipples to rise eagerly into his palms and harden with a stinging sensation. She moaned as he bent and opened his mouth over a ripe peak, licking and soothing. The delicate fabric became wet from his ministrations, and she lifted herself upward with an incoherent sound.

His fingers grasped the edge of the chemise and he tore it neatly, easily, exposing the abundant curves of her breasts. Gathering the pale, cool flesh into his hands, Jack kissed and suckled until Amanda was tense and gasping beneath him. "Will you be my wife?" he murmured, his hot breath puffing against her moist pink nipples. When she remained silent, his fingers squeezed the curves of her breasts, urging her to answer. "Will you?"

"No," she said, and he laughed suddenly, his eyes bright with passion.

"Then I'll keep you in this bed until you change your mind." He reached down to the front of his trousers, freed himself, and climbed over her. "You will, eventually. Do you doubt my stamina?"

Her legs spread, and her entire body jumped in reaction as she felt the stiff, blunt-tipped heat of his sex brush against the nest of dark curls between her thighs. She strained upward, wanting him so badly that she had to grit her teeth to keep from crying out. "You are mine," he whispered, entering her slowly, the head of his shaft nudging inside. "Your heart, your body, your mind, the seed growing in your belly . . . all of you." He filled her, impelling himself deeper until she had to lift her legs around his back to accommodate him.

"Tell me who you belong to," he whispered, pushing rhythmically, stretching her swollen flesh until she groaned at the weight of him inside her, over her, around her.

"You," she gasped. "You. Oh, Jack—"

He thrust again and again, his body tireless, his hand slipping between her thighs to touch and stroke the vulnerable peak hidden in the thicket of curls. She climaxed at once, overcome with the searing delight of his possession.

Keeping their bodies joined, Jack rolled onto his back so that she straddled his long, muscular body, and he clasped her hips to guide her in a new rhythm. "I can't," she moaned, her breasts swaying before his face, but his hands gripped and moved her insistently, and she felt the urgent need building again. This time when she convulsed, he joined her with a deep groan, driving the pounding climax into the center of her body.

They remained fused together for long, throbbing minutes, their skin warm and salty with mingled perspiration.

Clasping his hands around her curly head, Jack brought Amanda's mouth to his. He kissed her lightly, his lips warm and teasing. "Sweet Amanda," he whispered, and she felt him smile against her mouth. "I swear I'll have a 'yes' out of you by morning."

Amanda's small, expedient wedding to Jack Devlin caused an uproar among family and friends. Sophia could not have been more disapproving, predicting that the union would someday result in separation. "I hardly need point out that the two of you have nothing in common," her sister had said acidly, "except for certain physical appetites that are too indecent to mention."

Had Amanda not been in the midst of emotional upheaval, she would have replied that there was one more thing that she and Jack had in common. However, she was not yet ready to impart the news of her pregnancy, and she managed to remain silent.

It had not been so easy, though, to face Charles Hartley. She would have preferred condemnation to the gentle kindness he showed her. He was so forgiving, so damnably understanding, that she felt utterly wretched as she tried to explain that she would not be marrying him, but Jack Devlin.

"Is this what you want, Amanda?" was his only question, and she responded with a shame-faced nod.

"Charles," she managed to say, nearly choking on her guilt, "you have been dreadfully ill-used by me—"

"No, never say that," he interrupted, beginning to reach for her, then checking himself. He held back and gave her a faint smile. "I have been the better for knowing you, Amanda. All I desire is your well-being. And if marriage to Devlin will secure your happiness, I will accept it without complaint."

To Amanda's annoyance, when she repeated the conversation to Jack later, he did not seem to feel a shred of remorse. He only shrugged nonchalantly. "Hartley could have fought for you," he pointed out. "He chose not to. Why should you or I take the blame for that?"

"Charles was being a gentleman," she retorted. "Something you obviously have little experience with."

Jack grinned and pulled her onto his lap, his hands cupping insolently over her bodice. "Gentlemen don't always get what they want."

"And scoundrels do?" she asked, making him laugh.

"This scoundrel has." He kissed her soundly, until all thoughts of Charles Hartley were banished from her mind.

* * *

To Amanda's dismay, the news of her hasty marriage had filled the gossip pages of London papers with lurid speculation. The publications that Jack owned were, of course, moderately respectful, but the ones he did not own were merciless. The public seemed titillated by the marriage between London's most successful publisher and a celebrated novelist. During the fortnight after their wedding, new details of their relationship—many of them fabricated—surfaced every day in publications such as *The Mercury*, *The Post*, *The Public Ledger*, *The Journal*, and *The Standard*. Understanding the voracious appetite of the news industry, Amanda told herself that soon the gossips would lose interest in her marriage to Jack and find some new subject to exploit. However, there was one story that managed to distress her, and despite its obvious untruth, she was disturbed enough to approach her new husband with it.

"Jack," she said warily, approaching him in their massive green-and-burgundy bedroom.

"Mmm?" Jack shrugged into a neat charcoal-colored waistcoat that matched his trousers exactly. The sleek, powerful lines of his body were followed faithfully by the clothes, which had been tailored in the new fashion, a fit that was easy and comfortable rather than snug. Picking up a patterned silk stock that had been selected by his valet, Jack examined it critically.

Amanda extended the paper to him. "Have you

seen this item in the *London Report*'s gossip section?"

Jack set aside the stock and took the paper. His gaze scanned the rustling page with practiced speed. "You know I don't read gossip."

Amanda frowned and folded her arms across her chest. "It is about you and me."

He smiled lazily, still scanning the printed lines. "I especially don't read gossip about myself. It annoys the hell out of me when it's false, and even more so when it's true."

"Well, perhaps you can explain to me which category this bit of news falls into . . . truth or untruth."

Hearing the rising tension in her voice, Jack glanced at her face and then dropped the paper onto a nearby table. "You tell me what it says," he suggested, becoming serious as he realized that she was genuinely upset. His hands came to her shoulders, stroking her upper arms. "Relax," he urged gently. "Whatever it is, I have no doubt that it's of little consequence."

She remained stiff against him. "It's a nasty little piece that speculates on the unions of older women and younger men. There is a mocking paragraph on how wise a man like you must be to reap the benefits of an older woman's 'grateful enthusiasm.' It's a completely dreadful article, and it makes me sound like a lust-crazed old crone who has managed to ensnare a young man for stud service. Now, tell me at once if there is any truth in it!"

One would have wished for immediate denial.

Instead, Jack's expression became guarded, and Amanda realized with a sinking heart that he was not going to refute the newspaper's claim. "There is no solid proof of my age," he said carefully. "I was born a bastard, and my mother never registered the event in any parish records. Any speculation that I am younger than you is merely that—a bit of guesswork that no one can confirm."

Amanda jerked back and stared at him incredulously. "You told me the first time we met that you were thirty-one years of age. Was that true or not?"

Jack sighed and rubbed the back of his neck. Amanda could practically see the series of rapid calculations in his mind as he devised a strategy to handle the situation. She did not want to be handled, damn him! She merely wanted to know if he had lied to her about something as fundamental as his age. Finally he seemed to acknowledge that there was no way to avoid admitting the truth.

"It was not true," he said gruffly. "But if you recall, you were damned sensitive about your thirtieth birthday at the time. And I knew that if you became aware that I might be a year or two younger than you, I'd probably be set out on my ear at once."

"A year or two?" Amanda repeated, her voice taut with suspicion. "That's all?"

The wide line of his mouth tightened impatiently. "Five years, dammit."

She felt suddenly as if she could not breathe properly, her lungs deflating inside her chest. "You're only five-and-twenty?" she managed in an airless whisper.

"It makes no difference." His sudden reasonable manner sparked fury amid her distress.

"It makes every difference in the world," she cried. "For one thing, you lied to me!"

"I didn't want you to think of me as a younger man."

"You *are* a younger man!" She glared at him vehemently. "Five years . . . oh, God, I can scarcely believe I've married someone who is practically a . . . a boy!"

The word seemed to catch him off guard, and his entire face hardened. "Stop it," he said quietly. He caught her as she backed away from him, his big hands closing around her.

"I'm no damned boy, Amanda. I take care of my responsibilities, and as you know, I have a hell of a lot of them. I'm not a coward, a gambler, or a cheat. I'm loyal to the people I care about. I know of no other requirements for being a man."

"Perhaps honesty?" she suggested acidly.

"I shouldn't have lied to you," he admitted. "I swear I will never do so again. Please forgive me."

"This cannot be resolved that easily." She rubbed her brimming eyes with miserable wrath. "I don't *want* to be married to a younger man."

"Well, you've got one," he said flatly. "And he's not going anywhere."

"I could seek an annulment!"

Jack's sudden chuckle infuriated her. "If you do that, peaches, I'll be forced to publish exactly how many times and ways I've already had you. No magistrate in England would grant you an annulment after that."

"You wouldn't dare!"

He smiled and pulled her resisting body against his. "No," he murmured. "Because you are not going to leave me. You're going to forgive me, and we'll put this behind us for good."

Amanda strove to retain the remnants of her anger. "I don't want to forgive you," she said, her voice muffled against his shoulder. She stopped struggling, however, and let herself rest against his chest, sniffling back her remaining tears.

He held her for a long time, cuddling her in the shelter of his body, murmuring apologies and endearments into the curve of her neck and the soft indentation beneath her ear. She began to relax against him, unable to maintain the mortified resentment of discovering that she was the older partner in their marriage. Indeed, there was nothing she could do about it now. They were locked together legally and every other way.

His hands moved to the backs of her hips, pressing her lower body against the tremendous, arching shape of his erection.

"If you think I will go to bed with you after

this," she said against his shirtfront, "you are absolutely mad."

Jack rubbed her slowly against the bulge of his sex. "Yes. I'm mad over you. I adore you. I lust after you constantly. I love your sharp tongue and your big gray eyes and your voluptuous body. Now come to bed and let me demonstrate what a younger man can do for you."

Startled to hear the word "love" escape his lips, Amanda inhaled sharply at the feel of him through the veil of her white, ruffled dressing gown. He tugged the shoulders of the garment until her upper half was exposed. "Later," she said, but the glide of his fingertips over her back left trails of fire in their wake, and the downy hairs on her body prickled in sudden excitement.

"It has to be now," he insisted, a flick of amusement in his voice. He nudged his burgeoning loins against her. "After all, you can't allow me to go around like this all day."

"From what I've learned so far, this is your natural condition," came her pert reply. She felt his mouth touch her neck and wander to the pulse at the base of her throat.

"And I depend exclusively on you to relieve it," he murmured, tugging at the ribbon tie that closed the front of her gown. The covering of fine white muslin dropped from her body, and he clasped her naked limbs against his clothed ones.

"You'll be late for work," she said.

His bold hand traveled over the full shapes of

her buttocks, squeezing and kneading the pliant flesh. "I am helping you with *your* work," he informed her. "I am giving you new material to use for your next novel."

A gurgle of reluctant amusement rose in her throat. "I would never put such a vulgar scene in my book."

"*The Sins of Mrs. D,*" he mused, lifting her in his arms and carrying her to the unmade bed. "We'll give Gemma Bradshaw some competition." He released her to the bed, gazing appreciatively at her abundant pink-and-white flesh, and the cascade of her auburn curls.

"Jack," she said faintly, torn between excitement and mortification. She reached for a sheet to cover her naked body.

He joined her among the heap of snowy bed linens, still fully clothed. Snatching the sheet from her grasp, he pulled it far away from her and spread her limbs wide beneath his.

"You can't solve anything by taking me to bed," she told him, gasping a little as the silken fabric of his waistcoat brushed over her breasts.

"No. But I can make both of us feel a hell of a lot better."

Her hands came up to his arms, gliding over the muscular shapes covered in thin shirtsleeves. "Is there anything else that you have lied to me about?"

His blue eyes stared directly into hers. "Nothing," he said without hesitation. "Just that minor, inconsequential difference in age."

"Five years," she moaned in renewed discomfort. "Good God, every birthday will be an agonizing reminder. I can't bear it."

Rather than look remorseful, the scoundrel actually had the temerity to smile. "Let me ease your pain, darling. Just lie still for a little while."

Amanda would have liked to prolong her disgruntlement for at least a few more minutes, but his mouth covered hers gently and the clean, salty spice of his skin teased her nostrils. Her body arched upward as a current of pleasure hummed through her. It felt strange to be held bare against his clothed body . . . she was more exposed, far more vulnerable, than if he had been naked, too. A small sound rose in her throat, and she plucked at the layers of fabric that concealed him from her.

"No," Jack whispered, moving downward to kiss the firm angle of her collarbone. "Put your hands down."

"I want to undress you," she protested, but he caught her wrists and pressed them firmly at her sides.

Amanda closed her eyes, the rhythm of her lungs quickening. His breath touched her nipple like a waft of steam, and she pushed upward with a muted groan when she felt the exquisite flick of his tongue. "Jack," she panted, reaching for his dark head, but once again he took her hands and brought them to her sides.

"I told you to lie still," he murmured, his voice caressing. "Be a good girl, Amanda, and you'll get what you want."

Perplexed, aroused, she tried to relax beneath him, though her hands clenched in an effort to keep from reaching for him again.

Murmuring his approval, he bent over her breasts, softly kissing the space between them, the tender undercurves, the resilient plumpness at the sides. Her nipples tightened into aching peaks, and she felt a mist of sweat break out on her skin as she waited, waited, until finally he covered one tip with his mouth and tugged. Searing delight coursed from that one point of contact to the rest of her body, and her loins swelled in eager preparation for him.

One large hand came to rest lightly on her belly, just above the triangle of auburn curls. She could not prevent the pleading undulation of her hips, and Jack pressed firmly on her stomach, keeping her flat against the mattress. "I told you not to move," he said, sounding amused rather than threatening.

"I can't help it," Amanda gasped.

He laughed softly. His thumb circled her navel, exciting the responsive skin. "You *will* help it, if you want me to continue."

"Yes," she said, beyond pride or dignity. "I'll be still. But *hurry*, Jack."

Her shameless pleas seemed to delight him. Perversely, he became even slower, if possible, covering every inch of her skin with lazy kisses and nibbles. She felt him touch the curls between her legs, his palm brushing as gently as a breeze, and she wanted his fingers against her, inside her, so badly that she could not prevent a pleading moan.

His lips searched through the curls, found her, and the strong, immediate suction of his mouth caused her breath to catch sharply. Delight shot through her, scalding and relentless, and she felt his fingers stroking into the crease between her thighs. His wet finger traveled lower, too low, softly delving between her buttocks in a way that made her start uneasily. "No," she whispered. "No, wait . . ."

But his finger slid inside her, in a place so strange and impermissible that her mind went blank from the shock of it. The gentle glide continued, and she tried to push him away, but somehow her body trembled and yielded, and the pleasure enveloped her in a hot, saturating cloud. She cried out again and again, thrashing, arching, until finally the sensation eased and she breathed in frantic bursts.

While her limbs still twitched in delicious aftermath, she felt Jack unfastening his trousers. He came into her deep and hard, and she wrapped herself around him, moaning, while he plundered and possessed her. Amanda kissed his taut face, his mouth, his shaven cheeks, loving the heat of him inside her, the way he groaned in the manner of a man who had been thoroughly sated.

They lay wrapped together for several minutes, her naked thigh hooked over his trouser-clad one. Amanda felt so exhausted and replete that she doubted she would ever move again. She rested a hand on her husband's taut belly.

"Now you may go to work," she finally said.

He laughed low in his throat and kissed her thoroughly before he left the bed.

Although Jack Devlin was not a scholarly man, he possessed a combination of intelligence and instinct that amazed Amanda. The sheer weight of his business concerns would have crushed a lesser man, yet he handled them with cool competence. It seemed that his range of interests knew no bounds, and he shared his many enthusiasms with her, opening her mind to ideas that had never occurred to her before.

To Amanda's surprise, Jack discussed business matters with her, treating her as if she were an equal partner rather than a mere wife. No man had ever accorded her such a mixture of indulgence and respect. He encouraged her to speak freely, challenging her opinions when he did not agree with them and acknowledging openly when he was wrong. He urged her to be bold and adventuresome, and in this pursuit he took her everywhere with him, to sporting events, taverns, scientific exhibitions, even to business meetings at which her presence was received with frank astonishment by the other men attending. Although Jack must have been aware that such behavior was not condoned by society, he did not seem to care.

Most mornings Amanda reserved time to write

in a spacious room that had been redecorated for her use. The soothing sage-green walls were lined with towering mahogany bookcases, while framed engravings occupied the spaces between. Instead of the usual ponderous furnishings that one would find in a library or reading room, the desk and chairs and settee were light and feminine. As Jack added constantly to Amanda's collection of pen holders, many of them jeweled and engraved, she kept them in a leather-and-ivory case on her desk.

In the evenings Jack often liked to entertain, for there was a never-ending horde who wished to court his favor . . . politicians, artists, merchantmen, and even aristocrats. It surprised Amanda to realize how much influence her husband possessed. People treated him with wary friendliness, knowing that he could sway the public view on any issue he took an interest in. They were invited everywhere, from balls and yacht-parties to simple picnics, and they were seldom seen out of each other's company.

It was clear to Amanda that for all her apparent compatibility with Charles Hartley, he would never have penetrated her soul the way Jack did. Jack understood her with a thoroughness that almost frightened her. He was infinitely flexible, unpredictable, sometimes treating her like the fully mature woman she was, other times holding her on his lap as if she were a little girl, coaxing and teasing until she dissolved into helpless laughter. One evening he ordered a bath to be prepared before the fireplace in their room, and a supper tray sent up. He dismissed the maids and bathed her himself, his strong hands caressing her beneath the hot, soapy water. Afterward he combed her long hair and fed her bites from the supper plate while she relaxed against his chest and stared dreamily at the blaze in the hearth.

Jack's strong appetites certainly extended to the bedroom, where the intimacy they shared was so raw and relentless that Amanda sometimes feared she would not be able to face him in the bright light of day. Jack let her hide nothing from him, either physically or emotionally, and she was never quite comfortable with being so ruthlessly exposed. He took, and he gave, and he demanded, until it seemed that she no longer belonged to herself. He taught her things that no lady should know. He was the kind of husband she had never known she needed: a man who shook her from her complacency and inhibitions, a man who made her cavort and play until she had lost all bitterness over the responsibility-laden years of her youth.

With the publication of the last installment of *An Unfinished Lady*, Amanda's position as England's premier female novelist was unchallenged. Jack laid out plans to publish the entire novel in a three-volume format, with one edition bound in expensive calfskin leather and another, more affordable version bound in a "false-silk" cloth.

Demand for the forthcoming three-decker edition of *Unfinished Lady* was so high that Jack estimated it would set sales records. He celebrated by purchasing a diamond-and-opal necklace with matching earrings for Amanda, a set so ridiculously opulent that she laughingly protested when she saw it. The necklace had originally been made for Catherine the Great, empress of Russia, three-quarters of a century earlier. The design was called "moon and stars," with fiery opal moons set in gold filigree, and large clusters of diamond stars set between them.

"I can't possibly wear such a thing," Amanda told him as she sat naked in bed, clutching the sheets around herself.

Jack approached her with the necklace in hand, the morning sun causing the jewels to sparkle with unearthly brilliance. "Oh, yes, you can." He sat behind her on the mattress and pushed the curling mass of her auburn hair to one shoulder. As he fastened the heavy piece around her throat, she gasped at the coldness of the stones against her sleep-warmed skin. He dropped a kiss onto one bare shoulder and gave her a hand mirror. "Do you like it?" he asked softly. "We'll exchange it for some other design, if you prefer."

"The necklace is magnificent," she said dryly. "But it is not appropriate for a woman like me."

"Why not?"

"Because I know quite well what my limitations are. You may as well tie a peacock feather to a pigeon's tail!" Reluctantly she reached behind her neck and tried to unclasp the piece. "You are very generous, but this is not—"

"Limitations," Jack repeated with a snort. He took hold of her hands and gently pushed her down to the mattress. His hot blue gaze roved over her naked body, lingering on the pale, pure expanse of her chest as the opals scattered miniature rainbows on her skin. His expression was infused with lust and adoration as he lowered his head to kiss her throat, his tongue venturing into the little spaces between the diamonds and round opals. "Why can't you see yourself as I see you?"

"Stop it," she said, squirming as she felt the protrusion of his aroused sex through the fabric of his robe. "Jack, don't be silly."

"You are beautiful," he insisted, moving over her, his muscled thighs straddling hers. "And I am not going to let you leave this bed until you admit it."

"Jack," she groaned, rolling her eyes.

"Repeat after me . . . 'I am beautiful.' "

She pushed at his chest, and he caught her wrists and stretched them over her head. The movement caused her breasts to rise, while the heavy web of diamonds warmed to the temperature of her skin. Amanda felt herself turning crimson, but she forced herself to stare into his intent eyes. "I am beautiful," she said, in the tone one might use to humor a madman. "Now may I be released?"

His teeth flashed in a wicked grin. "I'll give you

release, madam." He bent lower, his mouth nearly touching hers. "Say it again," he whispered close to her lips.

She tugged at her imprisoned hands, and struggled playfully to free herself. Jack allowed her to writhe beneath him until his robe had parted, the sheet had been kicked away, and their naked loins were enjoined. The blazing heat of his sex pulsed against her, and her body throbbed in response. Breathing heavily, she opened her knees, widening herself for him. He kissed her breasts, the wet heat of his mouth surrounded by the scratchiness of an early-morning beard.

"Tell me," he muttered. "Tell me."

She surrendered with a moan, too inflamed to care how foolish she might sound. "I am beautiful," she said through gritted teeth. "Oh, Jack—"

"Beautiful enough to wear a necklace made for an empress."

"Yes. Yes. Oh, God—"

He slid inside her, making her whimper, making her body flex in wrenching pleasure. She clutched him with her arms and legs, her hips tilting urgently to match each downward plunge. She stared at the face above hers. Jack's eyes narrowed to intense blue slits. His hands covered the sides of her head in a gentle clasp, and he made love to her until she groaned in release. He shuddered and spent his own passion, pulsing violently inside her warm body. When he finally caught his breath, he smiled and nudged his now-softened sex deeper inside her. "That will teach you not to refuse my gifts." He rolled onto his side, bringing her with him.

"Yes, sir," she murmured with pretend meekness, and he grinned as he gave her buttocks a pat of approval.

As Amanda became acquainted with her husband's many projects, she took a particular interest in an ailing journal called the *Coventry Quarterly Review*. It had been suffering for some time from Jack's benign neglect, and consisted of review essays that examined recent developments in literature and history. It was clear to Amanda that the *Review* would do splendidly if only it had an editor who was strong enough to shape it, and give the publication some intellectual weight.

Filled with ideas on what should be done with the journal, Amanda wrote a prospectus that included suggestions of possible topics, contributors, and books to review, as well as an outline of the general direction it should follow. *The* Review *should be remade into a progressive and unsentimental publication*, she proposed, *favorable to reform and social change. On the other hand, it should retain a tolerance for existing systems and structures, and seek to refine them rather than tear them down, so as to preserve the best features of society while weeding out the worst . . .*

"It's good," Jack pronounced after reading the prospectus, his gaze distant as his mind clicked with a multitude of thoughts. "Very good." They sat together in the outdoor conservatory of their home. Jack sat in one chair and propped his feet up, while Amanda curled up on the cushions of a small settee with a cup of hot tea cradled in her hands. A cool afternoon breeze wafted in through the open archways.

Seeming to come to a decision, Jack regarded Amanda with keen blue eyes. "You've set out the perfect course for the *Review*. Now I need an editor available who would be willing or able to handle such a project."

"Perhaps Mr. Fretwell?" she suggested.

Jack shook his head immediately. "No, Fretwell is too damned busy, and I doubt he would take an interest in this. It's a touch more intellectual than he would prefer."

"Well, you've got to find someone," Amanda insisted, regarding him over the rim of her cup. "You can't simply let the *Review* wither on the vine!"

"I have found someone. *You*. If you're willing to take it on."

Amanda laughed ruefully, certain that he was teasing her. "You know that is impossible."

"Why?"

She pulled distractedly at a stray curl that dangled over her forehead. "No one would read such a publication if it were known that a woman was in charge. No respected writers would even want to contribute to it. Oh, it would be a different case if it were a fashion publication or a light journal for ladies' entertainment, but something as weighty as the *Review* . . ." She shook her head at the thought.

A look came over his face, the one she had come to recognize as his enjoyment of a seemingly impossible challenge. "What if we set up Fretwell as a mere figurehead?" he suggested. "We'll appoint you as his 'assistant editor,' when in reality you'll be in charge of everything."

"Sooner or later the truth will come out."

"Yes, but by then you'll have established such credibility and done such a damned fine job that no one would dare suggest replacing you." He stood and paced around the conservatory, his enthusiasm gaining momentum. He shot her a glance filled with challenge and pride. "You, the first woman editor of a major magazine . . . by God, I'd like to see that."

Amanda regarded him with alarm. "You're being ridiculous. I've done nothing to merit such responsibility. And even if I did well, no one would ever approve."

Jack smiled at that. "If you gave a damn about others' approval, you would never have married me instead of Charles Hartley."

"Yes, but this . . . it is outrageous." She could not seem to wrap her mind around the idea of herself as a magazine editor. "Besides," she added with a frown, "I barely have enough time to work as it is."

"Are you saying that you don't want to do it?"

"Of course I want to do it! But what about my

condition? I'll be in confinement soon, and then I'll have a newborn baby to care for."

"That could be managed. Hire as many people as you like to help. There is no reason you couldn't do most of the work at home."

Amanda devoted herself to finishing her tea. "I would be in complete charge of the journal?" she asked. "Commissioning all articles . . . hiring a new staff . . . selecting the books for review? Answerable to no one?"

"Not even to me," he said flatly.

"And when it is eventually discovered that a woman has been the active editor rather than Mr. Fretwell, and I become a notorious figure and all the critics have their say . . . you will stand by me?"

Jack's smile faded slightly, and he came to stand over her, bracing his hands on the arms of her chair. "Of course I'll stand by you," he said. "Dammit, woman, that you should even ask such a thing—"

"I will make the *Review* shockingly liberal," she warned, tilting her head back to look at him. Her hands touched the backs of his, fingertips venturing beneath the edge of his sleeves, brushing the coarse hair of his arms. Her brilliant smile coaxed forth an answering grin from him.

"Good," he said softly. "Set the world afire. Just let me hand you the matches."

Filled with a mixture of excitement and wonder, Amanda lifted her mouth to receive his kiss.

Chapter 15

As Amanda laid out her plans for the *Coventry Quarterly Review*, she made an ironic and surprising discovery—her marriage to Jack had given her far more freedom than she had enjoyed as a single woman. Because of him, she now had the money and influence to do as she wished . . . and most important, she had a husband who encouraged her to do exactly as she pleased.

He was not cowed by her intelligence. He took pride in her accomplishments and showed no hesitation in praising her to others. He prompted her to be bold, to speak her mind, to behave in ways that "proper" wives would never dare. In their private hours, Jack seduced and teased and tormented her nightly, and Amanda loved every moment of it. She had never dreamed that a man would feel this way about her, that a husband could regard her as a temptress, that he would take such pleasure in her less-than-perfect body.

A greater surprise still was Jack's apparent enjoyment of their home life. For a man who had led an existence of relentless socializing, he seemed content to slow the busy, almost frantic pace of his days. He was reluctant to accept more than a handful of the slew of invitations that arrived each week, preferring to spend his evenings in privacy with her.

"We could go out a bit more often if you like," Amanda had suggested to him one night as they prepared to have supper by themselves. "We've been asked to at least three parties this week, not to mention a soiree on Saturday and a yachting party on Sunday. I do not want you to forgo the pleasure of other people's company out of some mistaken notion that I wish to keep you all to my-self—"

"Amanda," he had interrupted, taking her into his arms, "I've spent the past few years going out nearly every evening and feeling alone in the midst of a crowd. Now I finally have a home and a wife and I want to enjoy them. If you wish to go out, I'll escort you anywhere you want. But I would rather stay here."

She reached up to stroke his cheek. "You're not bored, then?"

"No," he replied, suddenly introspective. His brows quirked as he looked at her. "I'm changing," he said gravely. "You're turning me into a tame husband."

Amanda rolled her eyes at his teasing. " 'Tame' is the last word I would use to describe you," she said. "You are the most unconventional husband I could imagine. One wonders what kind of father you will make."

"Oh, I'll give our son the best of everything. I'm going to spoil the hell out of him, and send him to the best schools, and when he comes back from his grand tour, he's going to run Devlin's for me."

"What if we have a girl?"

"Then she'll run it for me," came his prompt reply.

"Silly man . . . a woman could never do such a thing."

"*My* daughter could," he informed her.

Rather than argue, Amanda smiled at him. "And then what will you do while your son or daughter is in charge of your store and your companies?"

"I'll spend my days and nights pleasing you," he said. "It's a challenging occupation, after all." He laughed and dodged as she went to swat his attractive backside.

The worst day of Jack's life began innocuously, with all the pleasant rituals of breakfast and good-bye kisses, and a promise to return home for lunch after the morning's work at his offices. A light but saturating rain fell outside, the gray sky burgeoning with clouds that promised worse storms to come. As Jack stepped into the warm and inviting atmosphere of his store, where customers were already crowding to seek refuge from the rain, a tingle of enjoyment ran down his spine.

His business was flourishing, a loving wife awaited him at home, and the future looked infinitely promising. It seemed too good to be true, that his life should have started out so badly and have come to this turn. Somehow he had ended up with more than he deserved, Jack thought, and grinned as he bounded up the flights of stairs to his private office.

He worked briskly until noon, then began to stack papers and manuscripts in preparation of his departure for lunch. A light tap came at the door, and Oscar Fretwell's face appeared. "Devlin," he said quietly, looking troubled, "this message has arrived for you. The man who brought it said it was quite urgent."

Frowning, Jack took the note from him and scanned it rapidly. The words scrawled in black seemed to leap off the paper. It was Amanda's handwriting, but in her haste she had not bothered to sign it.

Jack, I am ill. Have sent for the doctor. Come home at once.

His hand squeezed around the paper, crushing it into a compact ball. "It's Amanda," he muttered.

"What shall I do?" Fretwell asked immediately.

"Take care of things here," Jack said over his shoulder, already striding from the office. "I'm going home."

During the short, frantic ride to his house, Jack's thoughts rocketed from one possibility to another. What in God's name could have happened to Amanda? She had been blooming with health this very morning, but perhaps some accident had befallen her. Increasing panic caused his insides to twist, and by the time he reached his destination, he was white-faced and grim.

"Oh, sir," Sukey cried as he rushed into the entrance hall, "the doctor is with her right now—it came on so sudden—my poor Miss Amanda."

"Where is she?" he demanded.

"I-in the bedroom, sir," Sukey stammered.

His gaze dropped to the bundle of bed linens in her arms, which she promptly gave over to a housemaid and bade her take them to be washed. Jack saw with alarm that crimson blotches marred the snowy fabric.

Striding rapidly to the stairs, he took them three at a time. Just as he made it to his room, an elderly man wearing a doctor's black coat crossed the threshold. The man was short and narrow-shouldered, but he possessed an air of authority that far exceeded his physical stature. Closing the door behind him, he lifted his head and regarded Jack with a steady gaze. "Mr. Devlin? I am Dr. Leighton."

Recognizing the name, Jack reached out to shake his hand. "My wife has mentioned you before," he said tersely. "You were the one who confirmed her pregnancy."

"Yes. Unfortunately, these matters do not always achieve the conclusion we hope for."

Jack stared at the doctor without blinking, while his blood seemed to run cold in his veins. A sense of disbelief, of unreality, descended on him. "She's lost the baby," he said softly. "How? Why?"

"Sometimes there are no explanations for miscarriage," came Leighton's grave reply. "It happens to perfectly healthy women. I have learned in my practice that at times nature takes its own course, regardless of our wishes. But let me assure you, as I have told Mrs. Devlin, that this need not prevent her from conceiving and delivering a healthy baby the next time."

Jack looked down at the carpet with fierce concentration. Strangely, he couldn't help thinking of his father, now cold in his grave, unfeeling in death as he had been in life. What kind of man could produce so many children, legitimate and illegitimate, and care so little about any of them? Each small life seemed infinitely valuable to Jack, now that he had lost one.

"I might have caused it," he muttered. "We share a bedroom. I . . . I should have left her alone—"

"No, no, Mr. Devlin." In spite of the seriousness of the situation, a faint, compassionate smile appeared on the doctor's face. "There are cases in which I've prescribed that a patient abstain from marital intercourse during pregnancy, but this was not one of them. You did not cause the miscarriage, sir, any more than your wife did. I promise you, it was no one's fault. Now, I have told Mrs. Devlin that she must rest for the next few days until the bleeding stops. I will return before the end of the week to see how she is healing. Naturally her spirits will be somewhat low for a while, but your wife seems to be a strong-minded woman. I see no reason why she should not recover quickly."

After the doctor took his leave, Jack entered the bedroom. His heart was riven with sorrow as he saw how small Amanda looked in the bed, all her usual fire and high spirits extinguished. He went to her and smoothed her hair back, and kissed her hot forehead.

"I'm sorry," he whispered, gazing into her empty eyes. He waited for any kind of response, despair or anger or hope, but his wife's normally expressive face remained blank. She knotted a loose fold of her dressing gown in one fist, twisting the delicate fabric and balling it in her palm.

"Amanda," he said, taking her hard fist into his hand, "please talk to me."

"I can't," she managed in a constricted voice, as if some outward force were clutching at her throat.

Jack continued to hold her ice-cold fist in his warm fingers. "Amanda," he whispered. "I understand what you're feeling."

"How could you possibly understand?" she asked woodenly. She pulled at her fist until he released it, and she focused on some distant point on the wall. "I'm tired," she murmured, though her eyes were round and unblinking. "I want to sleep."

Baffled, hurt, Jack eased away from her. Amanda had never been like this with him before. It was the first time she had ever shut him out of her feelings, and it was as if she had taken an ax and neatly severed all connection between them. Perhaps if she rested, as the doctor had advised, she would wake up and that terrible blankness would have left her eyes. "All right," he murmured. "I'll stay close by, Amanda. I'll be here if you should need anything."

"No," she whispered without any trace of emotion. "I don't need anything."

For the next three weeks, Jack was forced to grieve alone while Amanda remained in some inner retreat that no one was allowed to share. She seemed determined to isolate herself from everyone, including him. Jack was at his wit's end to know how to reach her. Somehow the real Amanda had vanished, leaving only a vacuous shell. According to the doctor, Amanda only required more rest. However, Jack was not so certain. He feared that losing the baby was a blow from which she would never recover, that the vibrant woman he had married might never return.

In desperation, he summoned Sophia from Windsor for the weekend, despite his dislike of the disapproving shrew. Sophia did her best to console Amanda, but her presence had little effect.

"My advice is to be patient," she told Jack upon her departure. "Amanda will recover herself eventually. I do hope that you will not exert pressure on her, or make demands that she is not ready to accommodate."

"What is that supposed to mean?" Jack muttered. In the past, Sophia had made no secret of her opinion that he was a lowbred scoundrel with all the self-control of a rutting boar. "No doubt you think I'm planning to waylay her and demand my husbandly rights as soon as you depart for Windsor."

"No, that is not what I think." Sophia's lips curved into an unexpected smile. "I was referring to demands of an *emotional* nature, Devlin. I do not believe that even you would be so brutish as to force yourself on a woman in Amanda's condition."

"Thank you," he said sardonically.

They studied each other for a moment, the smile remaining on Sophia's face. "Perhaps I have been wrong in making such a harsh judgment of you," she announced. "One thing has become clear to me of late . . . no matter what your faults, you do seem to love my sister."

Jack met her gaze squarely. "Yes, I do."

"Well, perhaps in time I may give my approval to the match. Certainly you are no Charles Hartley, but I suppose my sister could have married someone worse than you."

He smiled wryly. "You're too kind, Sophia."

"Bring Amanda to Windsor for a visit when she is ready," Sophia commanded, and he bowed as if in obedience to a royal edict. They shared strangely companionable smiles before a footman escorted Sophia to her waiting carriage.

Wandering upstairs, Jack found his wife at the bedroom window, watching as Sophia's carriage rolled along the front drive. Amanda was staring at the scene outside as if transfixed, a visible pulse beating in her throat. There was an untouched supper tray on a nearby table.

"Amanda," he murmured, willing her to look at him. For a moment her spiritless gaze held his, then dropped when he came to stand behind her. She stood and suffered his brief hug without responding. "How long will you go on like this?" he couldn't help asking. When she did not respond, he swore softly. "If you would just talk to me, dammit—"

"What is there to say?" she replied tonelessly.

Jack turned her to face him. "If you have nothing to say, then, by God, I do! You're not the only one who has lost something. It was my child, too."

"I don't want to talk," she said, wrenching herself away from him. "Not now."

"No more silence between us," he insisted, following as she retreated. "We must deal with what happened, and find a way to put it behind us."

"I don't want to," she choked. "I . . . I want to end our marriage."

The words shocked him down to his marrow. "What?" he asked, stunned. "Why in God's name would you say that?"

Amanda struggled to answer, but no more words were possible. Suddenly all the emotion she had battened down for the past three weeks surged upward with desperate force. Although she tried to stem the painful eruption, she could not suppress the sobs that seemed to rip the inner cavities of her chest. She crossed and uncrossed her arms around her body, over her head, trying to contain the violent spasms. She was frightened by her own lack of self-control ... feeling as though her very soul would crumble to ruins. She needed something, someone, to restore her disintegrating sanity.

"Leave me alone," she whimpered, covering her streaming eyes with her hands. She felt her husband's gaze rake over her and she stiffened. She could not ever remember falling to pieces like this in front of anyone, having always believed that such ugly emotions should be managed in private.

Jack's arms closed around her, cuddling her against his broad chest. "Amanda ... darling ... put your arms around me. There." He was so solid, steady, his body supporting hers, the scent and feel of him as familiar as if she had known him for her entire life.

She clutched at him while words tumbled forth in wild abandon. "The only reason we married was because of the baby. Now he is gone. Nothing will ever be the same between us."

"You're not making sense."

"You didn't want the baby," she wept. "But I did. I wanted him so much, and now I've lost him, and I can't bear it."

"I wanted him, too," Jack said in a shaken voice. "Amanda, we'll get through this, and someday we'll have another."

"No, I'm too old," she said, and a fresh deluge of painful tears welled from inside her. "That's why I miscarried. I waited too long. I'll never be able to have children now—"

"Hush. That's ridiculous. The doctor said he's delivered babies from women much older than you. You're not thinking clearly."

Jack picked her up easily and carried her to a small velvet-upholstered armchair, then sat with her in his lap. He picked up the folded linen napkin from the dinner tray and blotted her eyes and cheeks. He was so capable and steady that Amanda felt some of her panic evaporate. Obediently she blew her nose into the napkin and let out a quivering sigh, resting her head on his shoulder. She felt the warmth of his hand on her back, moving in a slow stroke that calmed her shattered nerves.

He held her for a long time, until her breathing eventually matched the even rhythm of his, and the tears dried to salt trails on her cheeks.

"I didn't marry you just because of the baby,"

Jack said quietly. "I married you because I love you. And if you ever mention the idea of leaving me again, I'll . . ." He paused, clearly trying to think of a punishment dire enough. "Well, just don't," he finished.

"I've never felt as terrible as I do now. Not even when my parents died."

His deep chest reverberated beneath her ear as he spoke. "Neither have I. Except . . . I'm so damned glad to hold you. It's been hell the past few weeks, not being able to talk to you, touch you."

"Do you really think we could have a baby someday?" she asked in a raw whisper.

"If that's what you want."

"Is it what *you* want?"

"At first it was difficult for me to accept the idea of being a father," Jack admitted. He kissed the edge of her jawline, and the side of her throat. "But then we started to make plans, and the baby became real to me. And I thought of all the small boys at Knatchford Heath whom I was never able to help or protect, and instead of the old despair, I felt . . . hope. I realized that at last there was going to be one child in this world I *could* take care of. It was a new beginning for me. I . . . I wanted to make his life wonderful."

Amanda raised her head and stared at him with swimming eyes. "You would have," she whispered.

"Then let's not give up hope just yet, peaches. When you're ready, I'll devote myself day and night to the task of getting you with child. And if it doesn't take, we'll find some other way. God knows there are plenty of children in the world who need a family."

"You would do that for me?" she asked tremulously, unable to believe that the man who had once been so opposed to the idea of having a family was now prepared to make such a commitment.

"Not only for you." He kissed the tip of her nose and the soft curve of her cheek. "For myself as well."

Amanda put her arms around his neck and hugged him tightly. Finally the crushing grief began to ease its iron grip around her heart. She felt a sense of relief that was so acute, it made her light-headed. "I don't know what to do now," she murmured.

Jack kissed her again, his mouth hot and tender against her flushed skin. "Tonight you're going to stop thinking for a few hours, and eat, and rest."

The thought of food made her wince and grimace. "I couldn't."

"You haven't eaten in days." He reached for the tray, uncovered the plate of food, and picked up a spoon. "Try a little," he said firmly. "I'm a great believer in the restorative powers of . . ." He glanced at the contents of the bowl that had been hidden by the silver-domed cover. "Potato soup."

Amanda regarded the spoon and his purposeful face, and for the first time in three weeks, a wobbly smile touched her lips. "You're a bully."

"And I'm bigger than you," he reminded her.

She took the spoon from him and leaned over to glance at the velvety-white soup, scattered with chopped watercress leaves. A griddle-cooked muffin reposed on a small plate beside it, as well as a dish of berry pudding heaped with fresh raspberries. Pudding *à la framboise*, the cook called it, having recently taken a fancy to renaming many of her recipes in French.

Jack surrendered the chair and watched her dip the spoon into the soup. She ate slowly, the warmth of the soup filling her stomach, while Jack sat beside her and frequently held a goblet of wine to her lips. As Amanda drank and ate, the color came back to her face, and she relaxed heavily into the chair. She glanced at the handsome man beside her, and a rush of love nearly overwhelmed her. He made her feel as if anything were possible. Impulsively she caught at his large hand, bringing it to her face. "I love you," she said.

He stroked her cheek and caressed the line of her jaw with the backs of his knuckles. "I love you more than life, Amanda." He leaned close and brushed his mouth over hers, gently, as if he understood how bruised and vulnerable she felt . . . as if he could heal her with a kiss. She lifted her hand to the back of his neck and let her fingertips drift into the thick locks of hair at his nape. She accepted the subtle intrusion of his tongue in her mouth, let him search for the taste of wine, until the kiss seemed to burn with volcanic heat.

She turned her head to the side with a little murmur, feeling drowsy and enervated, her eyes closing as she felt his fingers at the bodice of her gown. One button was released, two, three, in a series of light tugs that caused the concealing fabric to fall away from her skin. His lips drifted to her throat, finding the sensitive place at the side, and he nibbled softly until she gave a faint moan.

"Jack . . . I'm so tired . . . I don't think . . ."

"You don't have to do anything," he whispered against her throat. "Just let me touch you. It's been so long, sweetheart."

Breathing deeply, Amanda did not try to summon any more words, only leaned her head back against the chair. Feeling dreamlike, she did not open her eyes when she felt him move away, but waited passively while he dimmed the lamps and then returned to her. The subdued light was almost ghostly, barely penetrating the darkness of her closed eyelids. Jack had removed his shirt . . . her hands encountered the bareness of his shoulders, brawny and warm and burgeoning with muscle. He knelt before her chair, between her parted knees, and reached inside the open front of her dressing gown to cup her breasts in his gentle hands. His thumbs smoothed over the nipples, stroking, teasing, until they contracted into firm nubs. He leaned forward to take one in his mouth.

Amanda arched away from the chair, her head tilted back, and she gasped at the sweet tug of his mouth. He pinched her other nipple between his thumb and forefinger, in a light but persistent stroke that made her fingertips dig into the resilient surface of his shoulders. She felt imprisoned by his mouth and hands, every part of her focused on his slow and deliberate seduction. He lifted the lacy hem of her dressing gown, pushed it to her waist, and drew his thumbs from her dimpled knees to the voluptuous inner curves of her thighs. Her legs parted for him, muscles trembling in response to the heat of his hands. Although he knew how badly she wanted him to touch her, he kept his hands on the tops of her thighs.

Jack possessed her mouth with kisses so light and lazy that she clenched her fists in frustration, wanting more. Smiling against her beseeching mouth, he ran his hands down her taut legs to her knees. His fingers tucked behind them, finding the softly creased hollows in back. Gently he bent her knees, lifting first one, then the other, until her legs were hooked over the padded arms of the chair. She had never been so brazenly displayed, held open and stretched before him.

"Jack," she protested, her breasts lifting as she struggled for breath, "what are you doing?"

He took his time about answering. His agile mouth wandered from her throat to the hard peaks of her breasts, while his hands smoothed over the little hill of her stomach, the fleshy curves of her hips, the soft upturned shapes of her buttocks. It was hardly a flattering position, but a flicker of embarrassed vanity was immediately extinguished in a torrent of desire. Her toes curled as pleasure surged through her, and she began to lift her legs free of the chair.

"No," came his silken whisper, and he pressed her back down, keeping her legs spread wide apart. "I'm having my dessert. Amanda *à la framboise.*"

He reached for the table, plucked something from a china plate, and brought it to her lips. "Open your mouth," he said, and she obeyed in confusion. Her tongue curled around the small shape of a ripe raspberry. The sweet, tangy flavor burst in her mouth as she chewed and swallowed. Jack's lips urged hers to open, and he shared the taste with her, his tongue hunting for every trace of fruity sweetness that lingered inside. Another raspberry was placed in the little indentation of her navel, and she gasped as he bent to lap it up with his tongue, tickling and swirling inside the sensitive hollow.

"That's enough," she said shakily. "Enough, Jack."

But he seemed not to hear, his hands wicked and gentle as he reached between her thighs . . . and suddenly she jolted from the peculiar sensation of his fingers nudging something inside her . . . raspberries, she thought, her muscles tightening as she felt the trickle of fruit juice in the intimate recess of her body. Her mouth trembled, barely able to form words. "Jack, no. Take them out. Please—"

His head lowered obligingly, and her limbs went taut with shame and pleasure as his mouth covered her. Guttural moans slipped from her throat as he gently licked and ate, devouring raspberry sweetness along with the moisture of her body. Her eyes closed tightly, and she panted for breath, holding still as his tongue reached inside her with silken strokes.

"How delicious you are," he whispered against her sensitive flesh. "The raspberries are gone, Amanda. Shall I stop now?"

Desperately she reached for his dark head, pulled him harder against her, and his tongue slipped over the aching bud of her sex. The silence of the room was punctured by her gasping breaths, the suckling sounds he made, and the creak of the chair as she rocked forward, upward, straining to capture his tantalizing mouth. Just as she thought she could no longer bear the intimate torture, the tension exploded in a rapturous burst of fire. She cried out and shuddered, her legs jerking against the upholstered chair arms, and the spasms went on and on until she finally begged him to stop.

When the racing of her heart slowed and she could summon the strength to move, she unhooked her legs from the chair and reached for

Jack. She clung to him as he picked her up and carried her to the bed. As he settled her onto the mattress, she refused to release her hold around his neck. "Come to bed with me," she said.

"You need to rest," he replied, standing beside the bed.

She caught at the front of his trousers before he could move away, and pried the top button loose. "Take these off," she commanded, working at the second button, and the third.

Jack's grin gleamed in the semidarkness, and he obeyed, stripping away the rest of his clothes. The sleek, powerful heaviness of his naked body joined hers on the bed, making her shiver pleasantly at the feel of his warm skin. "Now what?" he asked. His breath caught as she moved over him, her round breasts brushing his chest and then his stomach, while her long locks dragged gently against his skin.

"Now I shall have *my* dessert," she said, and for a long time there were no words, no thoughts, only the two of them joined in passion.

Afterward, he cuddled her at his side and a sigh of contentment escaped him. Then his chest moved with a rumbling laugh, and Amanda stirred against him. "What is it?" she asked curiously.

"I was thinking of that first night we met . . . that you were willing to pay me for doing this. And I was trying to calculate how much you owe me after all the times we've slept together."

As weary as she was, Amanda couldn't prevent a sudden laugh. "Jack Devlin . . . how can you think of money at a time like this?"

"I want you to be so deeply in my debt that you'll never be free of me."

She smiled and pulled his head to hers. "I'm yours," she whispered against his lips. "Now and forever, Jack. Does that satisfy you?"

"Oh, yes." And he spent the rest of the night showing her how much it did.

Epilogue

"Papa, you're supposed to catch me!" the small boy exclaimed, toddling toward his father's long form stretched on the grass.

Jack smiled lazily at the dark-haired child who stood above him. Named for Amanda's father, Edward, their son possessed an unending supply of energy and a vocabulary that far outstripped the average three-year-old. Young Edward loved to talk, which was hardly a surprise when one considered his parentage. "Son, I've spent the better part of an hour playing chase with you," Jack said. "Let an old man have a few minutes of rest."

"But I'm not finished yet!"

With a sudden laugh, Jack seized the boy and pulled him down for a game of roll-and-tickle.

Lifting her gaze from the papers in her lap, Amanda watched the pair play. They were spending the hottest part of the summer at Jack's inherited estate, a place so exquisitely landscaped that it could have been the subject of a painting by

371

Rubens. All it required were a few angels and billowing clouds overhead, and the illusion would have been complete.

The estate garden led from a semi-circular brick pattern at the back of the seventeenth-century house to a manicured upper garden, a white stone arch, and a vividly hued wilderness garden and oval pond below. The family often had picnics beneath the shade of a majestic old sycamore tree, its trunk clothed in thick swaths of hydrangea. The nearby pond, edged with feathery grass fronds and yellow irises, provided a welcome place to dangle their feet.

Replete from a lavish picnic that had been packed by the cook, Amanda tried to turn her attention back to the work she had brought. After four years under her management, the *Coventry Quarterly Review* had become the most widely read review magazine in England. Amanda was proud of her accomplishments, particularly in proving that a female editor could be as bold, intellectual, and freethinking as any man. When the public had eventually discovered that a woman was the driving force behind a national magazine, the controversy had only helped to increase sales. As he had promised Jack had been a stalwart defender, sharply denying all suggestions that it must be he, and not his wife, who had done the work on the paper.

"My wife needs no assistance from me in forming her opinions," he had told critics sardonically. "She is more capable and professional than most men of my acquaintance." He encouraged Amanda to enjoy her newfound notoriety, which had made her the most sought-after guest at every fashionable London supper-party. Her "clever mind" and "original wit" were universally praised in the highest literary and political circles.

"I am being trotted out like a trick pony," Amanda had once complained to Jack after a gathering, during which her every utterance had been given scrupulous attention. "Why is it so difficult for people to believe that someone who wears a dress could also have a brain?"

"No one likes a woman to be too clever," Jack had replied, smiling at her annoyance. "We men like to maintain our appearance of superiority."

"Then why aren't *you* threatened by a woman's intelligence?" she asked with a little scowl.

"Because I know how to keep you in your place," he replied with a maddening grin, and reared back, laughing, as she leaped on him to exact revenge.

Smiling at the memory, Amanda listened while Jack spun a tale of dragons and rainbows and magic spells, until Edward finally went to sleep in his lap. Carefully, Jack laid the boy's slumbering form on the linens that covered the grass.

Amanda pretended not to notice as her husband settled by her side.

"Put that away," he commanded, nuzzling his face into her loose hair.

"I can't."

"Why not?"

"I have a demanding employer who complains when the *Review* is past its deadline."

"You know how to make him stop complaining."

"I don't have time for that now," Amanda said primly. "Let me work, if you please." But she did not protest when she felt his arms slide around her. His mouth pressed against the side of her neck, sending a shot of pleasure down to her toes.

"Do you have any idea how much I desire you?" He curved his fingers over the shape of her stomach, where their second child moved gently inside her. His hand wandered along her leg to her ankle and insinuated beneath her skirts. The sheaf of papers fell from her hands, fluttering to the grass.

"Jack," she said breathlessly, leaning back against him, "not in front of Edward."

"He's sleeping."

Amanda turned in his arms and applied her mouth to his, giving him a slow, tantalizing kiss. "You'll have to wait until tonight," she said when their lips parted. "Really, Jack, you are incorrigible. We've been married for four years. You should have tired of me by now like any normal respectable husband would have."

"Well, there is your problem," he said reasonably, his fingers playing behind her knee. "I've never been respectable. I'm a scoundrel, remember?"

Smiling, Amanda lowered herself to the warm

grass and tugged him over her, until his shoulders blocked out the dappled sunlight that pierced through the rustling screen of leaves overhead. "Fortunately I have found that it is far more entertaining to be married to a scoundrel than a gentleman."

Jack smiled, but the mischievous sparkle in his blue eyes was supplanted by a reflective glow. "If you could go back and change things . . ." he murmured, stroking the loose curls back from her face.

"Not for all the riches in the world," Amanda replied, turning her face to kiss his gentle fingertips. "I have everything that I ever dared to dream about."

"Then dream some more," he whispered, just before his mouth closed over hers.